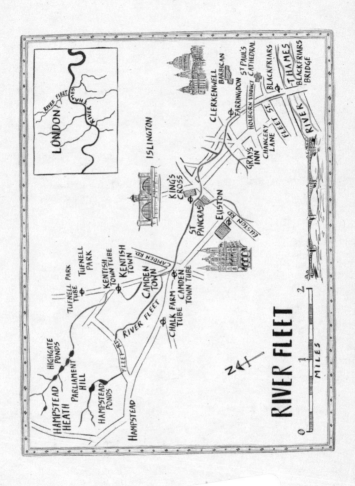

RIVER FLEET

PENGUIN BOOKS

Blue Monday

Blue Monday

NICCI FRENCH

PENGUIN BOOKS

PENGUIN BOOKS

Published by the Penguin Group

Penguin Books Ltd, 80 Strand, London WC2R ORL, England

Penguin Group (USA) Inc., 375 Hudson Street, New York, New York 10014, USA

Penguin Group (Canada), 90 Eglinton Avenue East, Suite 700, Toronto, Ontario, Canada M4P 2Y3
(a division of Pearson Penguin Canada Inc.)

Penguin Ireland, 25 St Stephen's Green, Dublin 2, Ireland (a division of Penguin Books Ltd)

Penguin Group (Australia), 707 Collins Street, Melbourne, Victoria 3008, Australia
(a division of Pearson Australia Group Pty Ltd)

Penguin Books India Pvt Ltd, 11 Community Centre,
Panchsheel Park, New Delhi – 110 017, India

Penguin Group (NZ), 67 Apollo Drive, Rosedale, Auckland 0632, New Zealand
(a division of Pearson New Zealand Ltd)

Penguin Books (South Africa) (Pty) Ltd, Block D, Rosebank Office Park,
181 Jan Smuts Avenue, Parktown North, Gauteng 2193, South Africa

Penguin Books Ltd, Registered Offices: 80 Strand, London WC2R ORL, England

www.penguin.com

First published by Michael Joseph 2011
Published in Penguin Books 2012
Reissued in this edition 2012

002

Copyright © Joined-up Writing, 2011
Map of the River Fleet © Maps Illustrated, 2011
All rights reserved

The moral right of the author has been asserted

Typeset by Jouve (UK), Milton Keynes
Printed in Great Britain by Clays Ltd, St Ives plc

ISBN: 978–1–405–92472–6

www.greenpenguin.co.uk

To Edgar, Anna, Hadley and Molly

1987

In this city there were many ghosts. She had to take care. She avoided the cracks between the paving stones, skipping and jumping, her feet in their scuffed lace-up shoes landing in the blank spaces. She was nimble at this hopscotch by now. She had done it every day on the way to school and back ever since she could remember, first holding on to her mother's hand, dragging and jerking her as she leaped from one safe place to the next; then on her own. Don't step on the cracks. Or what? She was probably too old for such a game now, already nine, and in a few weeks' time she would be ten, just before the summer holidays began. Still she played it, mostly out of habit but also nervous about what might happen if she stopped.

This bit was tricky – the paving was broken up into a jagged mosaic. She got across it, one toe pressing into the little island between the lines. Her plaits swung against her hot cheek, her school bag bumped against her hip, heavy with books and her half-eaten packed lunch. Behind her, she could hear Joanna's feet following in her steps. She didn't turn. Her little sister was always trailing after her, always getting in her way. Now she heard her whimpering: 'Rosie! Rosie, wait for me!'

'Hurry up, then,' she called over her shoulder. There were several people between them now, but she caught a glimpse of Joanna's face, hot and red under her dark fringe. She looked anxious. The tip of her tongue was on her lip in concentration. Her foot landed on a crack and she wobbled, hitting another. She always did that. She was a clumsy child who spilled food and stubbed her toes and stepped in dog poo. 'Hurry!' Rosie repeated crossly, weaving her way past people.

It was four o'clock in the afternoon and the sky was a flat blue; the light flared on the pavement, hurting her eyes. She rounded the corner towards the shop and was suddenly in the shade where she slowed to a walk, for the danger was over. The paving stones were replaced by Tarmac. She passed the man with the pockmarked face who sat in the doorway with a tin beside him. There weren't any laces in his boots. She tried not to look at him. She didn't like the way he smiled without really smiling, like her father sometimes, when he was saying goodbye on a Sunday. Today was Monday: Monday was when she missed him most, waking up to the week and knowing he wasn't there again. Where was Joanna? She waited, watching the other people flow past her – a flurry of youths, a woman with a scarf round her head and a large bag, a man with a stick – and then her sister emerged from the dazzle of light into the shadows, a skinny figure with an oversized bag, knobbly knees and grubby white ankle socks. Her hair was sticking to her forehead.

Rosie turned again and walked towards the sweetshop, considering what she would buy. Perhaps the Opal Fruits . . . or perhaps Maltesers, though it was so hot they would melt on the way home. Joanna would buy the strawberry laces and her mouth would be pink and smudged. Hayley from her class was already in there and they stood together at the counter, picking out sweets. The Opal Fruits, she decided, but she had to wait to pay until Joanna arrived. She glanced towards the door and for a moment she thought she saw something – a blur, a trick of the light, something different, like a shimmer in the hot air. But then it was gone. The doorway was empty. Nobody was there.

She tutted loudly, over a screech of brakes.

'I always have to wait for my little sister.'

'Poor you,' said Hayley.

'She's such a cry-baby. It's boring.' She said this because it was something she felt she ought to say. You had to look down on your younger siblings, roll your eyes and sneer.

'I bet,' said Hayley, companionably.

'Where is she?' With a theatrical sigh, Rosie put down her packet of sweets and went to the entrance to look outside. Cars drove by. A woman wearing a sari walked past, all gold and pink and sweet-smelling, and then three boys from the secondary school up the road, jostling against each other with their sharp elbows.

'Joanna! Joanna, where are you?'

She heard her voice, high and cross, and thought: I sound like my mum in one of her moods.

Hayley stood beside her, chewing noisily on her bubble-gum. 'Where's she gone, then?' A pink bubble appeared out of her mouth and she sucked it back in again.

'She knows she's supposed to stay with me.'

Rosie ran to the corner where she had last seen Joanna and stared around, squinting. She called again, though her voice was drowned by a lorry. Maybe she had crossed the road, had seen a friend on the other side. It wasn't likely.

She was an obedient little girl. Biddable, their mother called her.

'Can't find her?' Hayley appeared at her side.

'She's probably gone home without me,' said Rosie, aiming at nonchalance, hearing the panic in her tone.

'See you, then.'

'See you.'

She tried to walk normally, but it didn't work. Her body wouldn't let her be calm. She broke into a ragged run, her heart bumping in her chest and a nasty taste in her mouth. 'Stupid idiot,' she kept saying. And 'I'll kill her. When I see her, I'll . . .' Her legs felt unsteady. She imagined herself getting hold of Joanna by the bony shoulders and shaking her until her head wobbled.

Home. A blue front door and a hedge that hadn't been cut since her father had left. She stopped, feeling a bit sick, the nauseous sensation she had when she was going to get into trouble for something. She banged the knocker hard because the bell didn't work any more. Waited. Let her be there, let her be there, let her be there. The door opened and her mother appeared, still in her coat from work. Her eyes took in Rosie and then dropped to the space beside her.

'Where's Joanna?' The words hung in the air between them. Rosie saw her mother's face tighten. 'Rosie? Where's Joanna?'

She heard her own voice saying, 'She was there. It's not my fault. I thought she'd gone home on her own.'

She felt her hand grabbed and she and her mother were running back down the road the way she had come, along the street where they lived and up past the sweetshop where children hung around the door, past the man with the pockmarked face and the empty smile, and round the corner out of the shade and into the dazzle. Feet slamming and a stitch in her ribs, over the cracks without pausing.

All the while she could hear, above the banging of her heart and the asthmatic wheezing of her breath, her mother calling, 'Joanna? Joanna? Where are you, Joanna?'

Deborah Vine pushed a tissue against her mouth as if to stop the words streaming out of her. Outside the back window, the police officer could see a slender dark-haired girl standing in the small garden quite still, her hands by her side and a school bag still hanging off her shoulder. Deborah Vine looked at him. He was waiting for her answer.

'I'm not sure,' she said. 'About four o'clock. On her way home from school, Audley Road Primary. I would have collected her myself except it's hard to get there on time from work – and anyway she was with Rosie and there are no roads to cross and I thought it was safe. Other mothers leave their children to go home alone and they have to learn, don't they, learn to look after themselves, and Rosie promised to keep an eye on her.'

She drew a long, unsteady breath.

He made a note in his book. He rechecked Joanna's age. Five and three months. Where she was last seen. Outside the sweetshop. Deborah couldn't remember the name. She could take them there.

The officer closed his notebook. 'She's probably at a friend's house,' he said. 'But have you got a photograph? A recent one.'

'She's little for her age,' said Deborah. She could hardly get the words out. The officer had to lean forward to hear her. 'A skinny little thing. She's a good girl. Shy as anything when you first meet her. She wouldn't go off with a stranger.'

'A photo,' he said.

She went to look. The officer glanced again at the girl in the garden with her blank white face. He'd have to talk to her, or one of his colleagues perhaps. A woman would be better. But maybe Joanna would turn up before it was necessary, tumble in. She had probably wandered off with a friend and was playing with whatever five-year-old girls play with – dolls and crayons and tea-sets and tiaras. He stared at the photograph Deborah Vine passed him, of a girl with dark hair like her sister's and a thin face. One chipped tooth, a severe fringe, a smile that looked as if she had turned up her mouth when the photographer told her to say 'cheese'.

'Have you got hold of your husband?'

Her face twisted.

'Richard – my . . . I mean, their father – doesn't live with us.' Then as if she couldn't stop herself, she added: 'He left us for someone younger.'

'You should let him know.'

'Does that mean you think this is really serious?' She wanted him to say no, it didn't really matter, but she knew it was serious. She was damp with fear. He could almost feel it rising off her.

'We'll keep in touch. A female officer is on her way here.'

'What shall I do? There must be something I can do. I can't just sit here waiting. Tell me what to do. Anything.'

6

'You could phone people,' he said. 'Anywhere she might have gone.'

She clutched at his sleeve. 'Tell me she'll be all right,' she insisted. 'Tell me you'll get her back.'

The officer looked awkward. He couldn't say that and he couldn't think of what else to say.

Every time the phone rang it was a little bit worse. People knocking at the door. They'd heard. What a terrible thing, but of course it would be all right. Everything would be all right. The nightmare would end. Was there anything they could do, anything at all? Only ask. Say the word. Now the sun was low in the sky and shadows lay over streets and houses and parks. It was getting cold. All over London, people were sitting in front of TV sets or standing at stoves, stirring the pot, or gathering in smoke-fugged groups in pubs, talking about Saturday's results and holiday plans, moaning about little aches and pains.

Rosie crouched in the chair, her eyes wide. One of her plaits had come undone. The female police officer squatted beside her, large and plump and kind, patted her hand. But she couldn't remember, didn't know, mustn't speak: words were dangerous. Nobody had told her. She wanted her father to come home and make everything all right, but they didn't know where he was. They couldn't find him. Her mother said he was probably on the road. She pictured him on a road that stretched away from him and dwindled into the distance under a dark sky.

She squeezed her eyes tightly shut. When she opened them, Joanna would be there. She held her breath until her chest ached and her blood hammered in her ears. She could make things happen. But when she opened her eyes to the police officer's nice concerned face, her mother was still crying and nothing had changed.

At nine thirty the following morning, there was a meeting in what had been designated the operations room at Camford Hill police station. It was the moment when what had been a frantic search was turned into a co-ordinated operation. It was given a case number. Detective Chief Inspector Frank Tanner assumed command and made a speech. People were introduced to each other. Desks were assigned and argued over. An engineer installed phone lines. Cork boards were nailed to walls. There was a special sort of urgency in the room. But there was something else that nobody said out loud but everybody felt: a sickness somewhere in the stomach. This wasn't a teenager or a husband who had disappeared after an argument. If it had been, they wouldn't have been here. This was about a five-year-old girl. Seventeen and a half hours had passed since she had last been seen. It was too long. There had been an entire night. It had been a cool night; this was June and not November, and that was something. Still. A whole night.

DCI Tanner was just giving details of the press conference that was taking place later that morning when he was interrupted. A uniformed officer had come into the room. He pushed his way through and said something to Tanner that nobody else could hear.

'Is he downstairs?' said Tanner. The officer said that he was. 'I'll see him now.'

Tanner nodded at another detective and the two of them left the room together.

'Is it the father?' said the detective, who was called Langan.

'He's only just arrived.'

'Are they on bad terms?' Detective Langan said. 'Him and his ex.'

'I reckon,' said Tanner.

'It's usually someone they know,' said Langan.

'That's good to hear.'

'I was just saying.'

They arrived outside the door of the interview room.

'How are you going to play it?' said Langan.

'He's a worried father,' said Tanner, and pushed the door open.

Richard Vine was on his feet. He was dressed in a grey suit with no tie. 'Is there any news?' he said.

'We're doing everything we can,' said Tanner.

'No news at all?'

'It's early days,' said Tanner, knowing as he said it that it wasn't true. That it was the reverse of the truth. He gestured to Richard Vine to sit down.

Langan moved to one side so that he could observe the father as he talked. Vine was tall, with the stoop of a man who feels uncomfortable with his height, and had dark hair that was already turning grey at the temples, though he couldn't have been more than his mid-thirties. He had dark, beetling brows and was unshaven; there was a bruised look to his pale, slightly puffy face. His brown eyes were red-rimmed and looked sore. He seemed dazed.

'I was on the road,' said Vine, without being asked. 'I didn't know. I didn't hear until early this morning.'

'Can you tell me where you were, Mr Vine?'

'I was on the road,' he repeated. 'My work . . .' He stopped and pushed a flap of hair back from his face. 'I'm a salesman. I spend a lot of time on the road. What's that got to do with my daughter?'

'We just need to establish your whereabouts.'

'I was in St Albans. There's a new sports centre. Do you want to know the times? Do you need proof?' His voice sharpened. 'I wasn't anywhere near here if that's what you're thinking. What's Debbie been saying about me?'

'I'd like to know times.' Tanner kept his voice neutral. 'And anyone who can corroborate what you're telling us.'

'What do you think? That I've abducted her and hidden her away somewhere, because Debbie won't let me have the kids overnight, that she turns them against me? That I've . . .' He wasn't able to say the words.

'These are just routine questions.'

'Not to me! My little girl's gone missing, my baby.' He sagged. 'Of course I'll bloody tell you times. You can check them. But you're wasting your time on me and all the while you're not looking for her.'

'We're looking,' said Langan. He thought: seventeen and a half hours. Eighteen, now. She's five years old and she's been gone eighteen hours. He stared at the father. You could never tell.

Later, Richard Vine squatted on the floor beside the sofa where Rosie huddled, still in her pyjamas and her hair still in yesterday's plaits.

'Daddy?' she said. It was almost the first thing she'd said since her mother had called the police yesterday afternoon. 'Daddy?'

He opened his arms and gathered her in. 'Don't worry,' he said. 'She'll come home soon. You'll see.'

'Promise?' she whispered against his neck.

'Promise.'

But she could feel his tears on the top of her head, where the parting was.

They asked her what she could remember, but she couldn't remember anything. Just the cracks in the pavement, just choosing sweets, just Joanna calling her to wait. And her swell of anger against her little sister, her desire for her to be somewhere else. They said it was very important that she should tell them everyone she saw on that walk home from school. People she knew and people she didn't know. It didn't matter if she didn't think it was important: that was for them to decide. But she hadn't seen anyone, just Hayley in the sweetshop and that man with the pockmarked face. Shadows flitted through her mind. She was very cold, though it was summer outside the window. She put one end of her unravelling plait into her mouth and sucked it violently.

'Still not saying anything?'

'Not a word.'

'She thinks it was her fault.'

'Poor kid, what a thing to grow up with.'

'Sssh. Don't talk as if it's over.'

'Do you really think she's still alive?'

*

They made lines and walked across the wasteland near the house, very slowly, stooping occasionally to pick things up from the ground and put them into plastic bags. They went from door to door, holding a photograph of Joanna, the one the mother had passed over on that Monday afternoon, with a block fringe and an obedient smile on her thin face. It was a famous photo now. The papers had got hold of it. There were journalists outside the house, photographers, a television crew. Joanna became 'Jo' or, even worse, 'Little Jo', like a saintly child heroine from a Victorian novel. There were rumours. It was impossible to know where they started but they spread quickly round the neighbourhood. It was the tramp. It was a man in a blue estate car. It was her father. Her clothes had been found in a skip. She'd been seen in Scotland, in France. She was definitely dead and she was definitely alive.

Rosie's granny came to stay with them and Rosie went back to school. She didn't want to go. She dreaded the way people would look at her and whisper about it behind her back and suck up to her, trying to be her friend because this big thing had happened to her. She sat at her desk and tried to concentrate on what the teacher was saying, but she could feel them behind her. *She let her little sister get snatched.*

She didn't want to go to school but she didn't want to stay at home either. Her mother wasn't like her mother any more. She was like someone pretending to be a mother, but all the time she was somewhere else. Her eyes flickered about. She kept putting her hands over her mouth as if she was keeping something in, some truth that would otherwise burst free. Her face became thin and pinched and old. At night, when Rosie lay in bed and watched the car lights from the road outside move across her ceiling, she could hear her mother moving around downstairs. Even when it was dark and everyone else in the world was asleep, her mother was awake. And her father was different too. He lived alone again now. He hugged her too tightly. He smelt funny – sweet and sour at the same time.

Deborah and Richard Vine sat in front of the TV cameras together. They still shared a surname, but they didn't look at each other. Tanner had told them to keep it simple: tell the world how they missed Joanna and appeal to whoever it was who had taken her to let her come home. Don't worry about showing emotion. The media would like that. Just so long as it didn't stop them speaking.

'Let my daughter come home,' said Deborah Vine. Her voice broke; she covered her newly haggard face with one hand. 'Just let her come back home.'

Richard Vine added, more violently, 'Please give us our daughter back. Whoever knows anything, please help.' His face was pale and blotched with red.

'What do you think?' Langan asked Tanner.

Tanner shrugged. 'You mean, are they sincere? I've got no idea. How can a kid disappear like that, into thin air?'

There wasn't a summer holiday that year. They had been going to go to Cornwall, to stay on a farm. Rosie remembered them planning it, how there would be cows in the fields and hens in the yard and even an old fat pony the owners might let them ride. And they would go to the nearby beaches. Joanna was scared of the sea – she shrieked when waves went over her ankles – but she loved building sandcastles and looking for shells, eating ice cream cones with chocolate Flakes stuck into the top.

Instead, Rosie went to her grandmother's house for a few weeks. She didn't want to go. She needed to be at home, for when Joanna was found. She thought Joanna might be upset if she wasn't there; it would be as if she didn't care enough to wait.

There were meetings in which detectives leafed through statements by fantasists, previous offenders, eyewitnesses who had seen nothing.

'I still think it's the father.'

'He has an alibi.'

'We've been through this. He could have driven back to the area. Just.'

'No one saw him. His own daughter didn't see him.'

'Maybe she did. Maybe that's why she won't say anything.'

'Anyway, anything she saw she won't remember now. It will just be memories of memories of suggestions. Everything's covered over.'

'What are you saying?'

'I'm saying she's gone.'

'Dead?'

'Dead.'

'You're giving up on her?'

'No.' He paused. 'But I am taking some of the men off the case.'

'That's what I said. You're giving up.'

One year later, a photograph enhanced by a new computer program, which even its inventor warned was speculative and unreliable, showed how Joanna might have changed. Her face was slightly filled out, her dark hair a little bit darker. Her tooth was still chipped and her smile was still anxious. Some newspapers carried it, but only on an inside page. There had been a murder of a particularly photogenic thirteen-year-old girl and this had dominated the headlines for weeks. Joanna was an old story now, a tingle in the public memory. Rosie stared at the picture until it blurred. She was scared she wouldn't recognize her sister when she saw her, that she would be a stranger. And she was scared that Joanna wouldn't recognize her either – or would know her but turn away from her. Sometimes she went and sat in Joanna's room, a room that hadn't been altered since the day she disappeared. Her teddy was on her pillow, her toys stacked in the underbed boxes, her clothes – which would be too small for her – neatly folded in drawers or hanging in the wardrobe.

Rosie was ten now. Next year, she would go to secondary school. She had begged to go to the one a mile and a half away in the next borough, two bus journeys, because there she would no longer be the girl who had lost her little sister. She would just be Rosie Vine, year seven, shy and quite small for her age, who did all right in every subject but wasn't the best at anything except, perhaps, biology. She was old enough to know that her father drank more than he should. Sometimes her mother had to come and fetch her home because he couldn't look after her properly. She was old enough to feel that she was an older sister without a younger sister, and sometimes she felt Joanna's presence like a ghost – a ghost with a chipped tooth and a plaintive voice, asking her to wait. Sometimes she would see her on the street and her heart would miss a beat and then the face would resolve into the face of a stranger.

Three years after Joanna disappeared, they moved to a smaller house a mile or so away, nearer to Rosie's school. It had three bedrooms, but the third one was tiny, like a box room. Deborah Vine waited until Rosie had left in the morning before she packed away Joanna's things. She did it methodically, lifting soft piles of vests and shirts into boxes, folding up dresses and skirts and tying them into bin bags, trying not to look at the pink plastic dolls with their long manes of nylon hair and their fixed, staring eyes. In the new computer-enhanced image, Joanna looked quite composed, as if her childish anxiety had slipped away from her. Her chipped tooth had been replaced with an undamaged one.

Rosie started her periods. She shaved her legs. She fell in love for the first time, with a boy who barely knew she existed. She wrote her diary under her bedcovers and locked it with a silver key. She watched her mother dating a stranger with a bristly brown beard and pretended she didn't mind. She poured her father's drink down the sink, though she knew it would do no good. She went to her grandmother's funeral and read a poem by Tennyson in a quiet voice no one could really hear. She cut her hair short and started going out with the boy she had been so smitten with when she was younger, but he couldn't live up to her idea of him. She kept a small pile of printouts in her underwear drawer: Joanna at six, seven, eight, nine. Joanna at thirteen. She thought her sister looked exactly like *she* did, and for some reason this made her feel worse.

'She's dead.' Deborah's voice was flat, quite calm.

'Have you come all this way to tell me that?'

'I thought we owed each other at least that much, Richard. Let her go.'

'You don't know she's dead. You're just abandoning her.'

'No.'

'Because you've found a new husband and now . . .' His glance at her pregnant belly was full of disgust. 'Now you're going to have another happy family.'

'Richard.'

'And forget all about her.'

'That's not fair. It's been eight years. Life has to go on, for all of us.'

'*Life has to go on.* Are you going to tell me that this is what Joanna would have wanted?'

'Joanna was five when we lost her.'

'When *you* lost her.'

Deborah stood up, thin legs on high heels and a round stomach pushing at her shirt. He could see her belly button. Her mouth was a thin, trembling line. 'You bastard,' she said.

'And now you're deserting her.'

'You want me to destroy myself as well?'

'Why not? Anything rather than *life has to go on*. But don't worry. I'm still waiting.'

When Rosie went to university she called herself Rosalind Teale, taking her step-father's name. She didn't tell her father. She still loved him, though she was scared by his chaotic, unchanging grief. She didn't want anyone to say: 'Rosie Vine? Why does that ring a bell?' Even though there was less and less chance of that. Joanna had melted into the past, was a wisp of memory now, a forgotten celebrity, a one-hit wonder. Sometimes, Rosie wondered if her sister was just a dream.

Deborah Teale – Vine, as was – prayed secretly, fiercely, for a son, not a daughter. But first Abbie and then Lauren arrived. She crouched over their baskets at night to hear them breathe; she clutched at their hands. She wouldn't let them out of her sight. They reached Joanna, they overtook her and they left her behind. In the attic, the boxes of Joanna's clothes stood unopened.

The case was never actually closed. Nobody made a decision. But there was less and less to report. Officers were reassigned. Meetings became more sporadic, then merged into other meetings, and then the case wasn't mentioned at all.

Rosie, Rosie. Wait for me!

Chapter One

It was ten to three in the morning. There were four people walking across Fitzroy Square. A young couple, huddled together in the wind, had made their way up from Soho where they had been at a club. For them, Sunday night was coming gradually to an end. Though they hadn't said it to each other, they were delaying the moment when they had to decide whether they were getting into separate cabs, or into the same cab. A dark-skinned woman in a brown raincoat and a transparent polythene hat tied under her chin was shuffling north along the east side of the square. For her it was Monday morning. She was going to an office on Euston Road, to empty bins and vacuum floors in the dark early morning for people she never saw.

The fourth person was Frieda Klein and for her it was neither Sunday night nor Monday morning but something in between. As she stepped into the square, the wind hit her full on. She had to push her hair away from her face so that she could see. Over the previous week the leaves on the plane trees had turned from red to gold but now the wind and rain had shaken them free and they were rippling around her like a sea. What she really wanted was to have London to herself. This was the closest she could get to that.

She stopped for a moment, undecided. Which way should she go? North, across Euston Road to Regent's

Park? That would be deserted all right, too early even for the runners. Sometimes in summer Frieda would go there in the middle of the night, climb over the fence and head into the darkness, look at the glitter on the water of the lake, listen to the sounds from the zoo. Not tonight, though. She didn't want to pretend that she wasn't in London. Not south either. That would take her across Oxford Street into Soho. Some nights she would lose herself in the oddity of the creatures who came out or stuck around in the middle of the night, the dodgy little cab firms who'd take you home for whatever they could get you to pay, the clusters of police, delivery vans dodging the crowds and the congestion charge, and, more and more, people who were still eating, still drinking, whatever time it was.

Not tonight. Not today. Not now with a new week just about to wake itself up reluctantly and blearily get going. A week that would have to face up to November, to darkness and rain, with only more darkness and more rain to come. It was a time when you ought to sleep and wake again in March or April or May. Sleep. Frieda had the sudden suffocating sense that she was surrounded by people lying asleep, alone or in pairs, in flats and houses and hostels and hotels, dreaming, watching films inside their heads. She didn't want to be one of them. She turned east, past the closed shops and restaurants. There was a flash of activity as she crossed Tottenham Court Road, with its night buses and taxis, but then it was quiet once more, and she could hear the clatter of her footsteps as she walked along past anonymous mansion blocks, shabby hotels, university buildings, even some houses that had improbably survived. It was a place where many people lived but it didn't feel like it. Did it even have a name?

Two police officers sitting in a parked patrol car saw her as she approached Gray's Inn Road. They looked at her with a bored kind of concern. This wasn't necessarily a safe area for a woman to walk alone at night. They couldn't quite make her out. Not a prostitute. She wasn't particularly young, mid-thirties maybe. Long dark hair. Medium height. Her long coat hid her figure. She didn't look like someone on her way back from a party.

'Didn't fancy spending the whole night with him,' said one.

The other grinned. 'I wouldn't kick her out of bed on a night like this,' he said. He wound down the window as she approached. 'Everything all right, miss?' he asked, as she passed.

She just pushed her hands tightly into the pockets of her coat and walked on without giving any sign that she had heard.

'Charming,' said one of the officers, and returned to filling out the incident report on something that really hadn't been much of an incident at all.

As Frieda walked on, she heard the words of her mother in her ear. It wouldn't have hurt to say hello, would it? Well, what did she know? That was one of the reasons why she did these walks. So that she didn't have to talk, didn't have to be on show, be looked at and appraised. It was a time for thinking, or not thinking. Just walking and walking during those nights when sleep wouldn't come and when she could get the mess out of her head.

Sleep was meant to do that, but it didn't do it for her even when it came in little snatches. She crossed Gray's Inn Road – more buses and taxis – and walked down an alley, so small that it was like it had been forgotten about.

As she turned into King's Cross Road, she saw that she was approaching two teenage boys. They were dressed in hoodies and baggy jeans. One of them said something to her that she couldn't properly make out. She stared at him and he looked away.

Stupid, she said to herself. That was stupid. It was one of the main rules about walking in London: you don't make eye contact. It's a challenge. This time he had backed down, but you only needed one.

Almost without thinking, Frieda took a path that wound off the main road, then back and then off it again. For most people who worked there or drove through it, this was just an ugly and unremarkable part of London, office blocks, flats, a railway cutting. But Frieda was walking along the course of an old river. She had always been drawn to it. Once it had flowed through fields and orchards down to the Thames. It had been a place for people to sit by, to fish in. What would they have thought, men and women sitting on a summer evening, dangling their feet in the water, if they had seen its future? It had become a rubbish dump, a sewer, a ditch clogged with shit and dead animals and everything else that people couldn't be bothered to do anything with. Finally it had been built over and forgotten about. How could a river be forgotten about? When she walked this way, Frieda always stopped by a grating where you could still hear the river flowing deep below, like an echo of something. And when you had left that behind, you could still walk between the banks rising on either side. Even the occasional street name hinted at the wharves where barges had been unloaded and before that the rises, the grass slopes where people sat and just watched the crystal water flow down into the Thames. That was London. Things built on things built on things built on things, each in their turn forgotten about but each somehow leaving a trace, if only a rush of water heard through a grating.

Was it a curse that the city covered so much of its past, or was it the only way a city could survive? Once she'd had a dream of a London where buildings and bridges and roads were demolished and excavated so that the ancient rivers flowing to the Thames could be opened up to the sky once more. But what would be the point? They were probably happier the way they were, secret, unnoticed, mysterious.

When Frieda reached the Thames, she leaned over as she always did. Most times you couldn't see where the stream flowed out of its pitiful little pipe, and this morning it was far too dark. She couldn't even hear the sound of its splash. Down here on the river, the southerly wind was fierce but it was strangely warm. It felt wrong on a dark November morning. She looked at her watch. It wasn't yet four. Which way? East End or West End? She chose West, crossed the river and headed upstream. Now, finally, she was tired, and the remainder of the walk was a blur: a bridge, government buildings, parks, grand squares, across Oxford Street, and by the time she felt the familiar cobblestones under her feet of the mews where she lived it was still so dark that she had to scrape around on her front door with her key to find the lock.

Chapter Two

Carrie saw him from a distance, walking across the grass towards her in the fading light, his feet stirring the piles of damp brown leaves, his shoulders slightly hunched and his hands thrust deep into his pockets. He didn't see her. His eyes were fixed on the ground in front of him and he moved slowly and heavily, like a man just woken from sleep, still sluggish and wrapped up in his dreams. Or nightmares, she thought, as she watched her husband. He looked up and his face cleared; his steps quickened slightly.

'Thanks for coming.'

She put an arm through his. 'What's up, Alan?'

'I just had to get away from work. I couldn't stay there any longer.'

'Did something happen?'

He shrugged at her, ducked his head. He looked like a boy still, she thought, although his hair was prematurely grey. He had a child's shyness and rawness; you could see his emotions on his face. He often seemed slightly at a loss and people wanted to protect him, especially women. *She* wanted to protect him, except when she wanted protecting herself and then her tenderness was replaced by a weary kind of irritation.

'Mondays are always bad.' She made her voice light and brisk. 'Especially Mondays in November when it's starting to drizzle.'

'I had to see you.'

She pulled him along the path. They had walked this route so many times before that their feet seemed to steer them. The light was fading. They passed the playground. She averted her eyes, as she always did nowadays, but it was empty except for a few pigeons pecking around the rubberized Tarmac. On to the main path and past the bandstand. Once, years ago, they had had a picnic there. She didn't know why she remembered it so clearly. It had been spring and one of the first warm days of the year, and they had eaten pork pies and drunk warm beer from the bottle and watched children run around on the grass in front of them, tripping over their own shadows. She remembered lying on her back with her head in his lap and he'd stroked her hair from her face and told her she meant the world to him. He wasn't a man of many words, so perhaps that was why she held such things in her memory.

They went over the brow of the hill towards the ponds. Occasionally they took bread for the ducks, although that was really something for little kids to do. Anyway, the ducks were being chased away by Canada geese that puffed their chests and stretched their necks and ran at you.

'A dog,' she said. 'Perhaps we should get a dog.'

'You've never said that before.'

'A cocker spaniel. Not too big but not too small and yappy either. Do you want to talk about what you're feeling?'

'If you want a dog, let's get one. How about as a Christmas present to each other?' He was trying to work himself up into enthusiasm for it.

'Just like that?'

'A cocker spaniel, you say. Fine.'

'It was just an idea.'

'We can give him a name. Do you think it should be a him? Billy. Freddie. Joe.'

'That isn't what I meant. I shouldn't have said anything.'

'Sorry, it's my fault. I'm not . . .' He stopped. He couldn't quite think of what it was he wasn't.

'I wish you'd tell me what happened.'

'It's not like that. I can't explain.'

Now they found themselves back at the children's playground as if they were drawn to it. The swings and the seesaw were empty. Alan halted. He took his arm out of hers and gripped the railings with both hands. He stood like that for some moments, very still. He put one hand flat against his chest.

'Aren't you feeling well?' Carrie said.

'I feel odd.'

'What kind of odd?'

'I don't know. Odd. Like a storm's coming.'

'What storm?'

'Wait.'

'Take my arm. Lean on me.'

'Hold on a second, Carrie.'

'Tell me what you're feeling? Does it hurt?'

'I don't know,' he whispered. 'It's in my chest.'

'Shall I call a doctor?'

He was bowed over now. She couldn't see his face.

'No. Don't leave me,' he said.

'I've got my mobile.' She fumbled under her thick coat and brought it out from the pocket of her trousers.

'I feel like my heart's going to burst through my chest it's pounding so hard.'

26

'I'm calling an ambulance.'

'No. It'll pass. It always does.'

'I can't just stand here, watching you suffer.'

She tried to put an arm around him, but he was such an awkward shape, bunched up on himself, and she felt useless. She heard him whimper and for a moment she wanted to run away and leave him there, bulky and hopeless in the twilight. But of course she couldn't do that. And gradually she could sense that whatever it was that gripped him was loosening, until at last he straightened up again. She could make out beads of sweat on his forehead although his hand, when she took it, was cold.

'Better?'

'A bit. Sorry.'

'You've got to do something about it.'

'It'll be all right.'

'It won't. It's getting worse. Do you think I don't hear you in the night? And it's affecting your work. You've got to go to Dr Foley.'

'I've been to him. He just gives me those sleeping pills that knock me out and give me a hangover.'

'You've got to go again.'

'I've had all the tests. I saw it in his eyes. I'm no different from half the people who go to their doctor. I'm just tired.'

'This isn't normal. Promise me you'll go, Alan?'

'If you say so.'

Chapter Three

From where she sat in her red armchair in the middle of the room, Frieda could see the wrecking ball swinging into the buildings on the site across the road. Entire walls shivered and then crumbled to the ground; inside walls suddenly became outside walls and she could see patterned wallpaper, an old poster, a bit of a shelf or a mantelpiece; hidden lives suddenly exposed. All morning she had watched it. Her first patient, a woman whose husband had died suddenly two years ago and whose grief and shock had never abated, sat bowed over and sobbing before her, her pretty face pink and sore from weeping. Without her attention slackening, Frieda saw it from the corner of her eye. When her second patient, referred to her for his escalating obsessive-compulsive disorder, fidgeted in his chair, stood up and then sat down again, raised his voice in anger, Frieda saw the ball smashing into the block of apartments. How could something that had taken so long to build up collapse so quickly? Chimneys folded, windows shattered, floors disappeared, walkways were obliterated. By the end of the week, everything would be rubble and dust, and men in hard hats would walk across the razed ground, stepping over children's toys and sticks of furniture. In a year's time, new buildings would stand on the ruins of the old.

She told the men and women who made their way to

her room that she could offer them a bounded space where they could explore their darkest fears, their most inadmissible desires. Her room was cool, clean and orderly. There was a drawing on one wall, two chairs facing each other with a low table in between, a lamp casting a soft light in winter, a pot plant on the windowsill. Outside, an entire street of houses was being cleared away, but in here, they were safe from the world, just for a while.

Alan knew that Dr Foley was irritated by him. He probably talked about him to his partners at the practice: 'That bloody Alan Dekker again, moaning about not sleeping, not coping. Can't he just pull himself together?' He had tried to pull himself together. He had taken the sleeping pills, cut down on the alcohol, done more exercise. He had lain awake at night with his heart racing, so fast that it was impossible to believe it wouldn't burn itself up, and sweat pouring off him. He had sat rigid at his desk at work, his hands clenched, staring at the papers in front of him, waiting for the physical dread to pass, hoping his colleagues wouldn't notice. Because it was humiliating to lose control like this. It scared him. Carrie talked about a midlife crisis. He was forty-two, after all. This was just the age when men went off the rails, drank and bought motorbikes and had affairs, trying to be young again. But he didn't want a motorbike and he didn't want an affair. He didn't want to be young again. All that awkwardness and pain, that sense of being in the wrong life. Now he was in the right life, with Carrie, in the small house they'd saved for, and would be paying for for another thirteen years. There were things he dreamed of having, but surely everyone had dreams and hopes for themselves, and they didn't collapse in the park or wake up crying. And sometimes he had these nightmares – he didn't even want to think about them. It wasn't normal. Surely it wasn't normal. He just wanted them to go away. He didn't want to be the kind of person who had such things in his head.

'The pills you gave me aren't working,' he said to Dr Foley. He had to stop himself apologizing for being there again and for wasting the doctor's time, when the surgery was full of patients with real illnesses, real pain.

'Still having trouble sleeping?' Dr Foley wasn't looking at him. He was looking at his computer screen and tapping something into it, frowning.

'It's not just that.' He tried to keep his voice steady. His face felt rubbery, as though it belonged to someone else. 'I get these horrible feelings.'

'You mean pain?'

'My heart feels like it's being pumped up and there's a metallic taste in my mouth. I don't know.' He struggled for words but couldn't find them. All he could say was: 'I don't feel myself.' It was a phrase he kept using, and each time he did so, it felt as though he was digging a hole inside himself. Once he had cried out to Carrie, 'I can't feel myself,' and even at the time he had recognized how odd that sounded.

Dr Foley turned his chair and faced him. 'Has anything been troubling you lately?'

Alan didn't like him staring at his computer but he preferred that to being looked at like this: as if the doctor was looking inside him at things Alan didn't want to know about. What could he see?

'I had it when I was much younger, this feeling of panic. It was a feeling of loneliness, like in a nightmare, of being completely alone in the universe. Of wanting something, but I didn't know what. After a few months, it went away. Now it's back.' He waited, but Dr Foley didn't react: he didn't seem to have heard him. 'It was when I was at college. I thought it was the sort of problem people got at that age. Now I think I'm having a mid-life crisis. It's stupid, I know.'

'The drugs obviously aren't helping. I'd like you to go and see someone.'

'What do you mean?'

'Someone you can talk to. About your feelings.'

'You think it's all in my mind?' He had a vision of himself as mad, his face contorted and savage, the horrible feelings he was trying to keep tamped down inside himself suddenly liberated and possessing him entirely.

'It can be very helpful.'

'I don't need to see a psychiatrist.'

'Try it,' said Dr Foley. 'If it doesn't work, you won't have lost anything.'

'I can't afford to pay.'

Dr Foley started to tap on his keyboard. 'This is a GP referral. You won't have to pay. It'll be a bit of a journey, but these people are good. They'll contact you with a date for an assessment. And we'll take it from there.'

It sounded so grave. Alan had just wanted Dr Foley to give him different medicine, to make it all go away, like a stain that could be wiped clean, leaving no trace. He put his hand against his heart, feeling its painful bump. He just wanted to be an ordinary man with an ordinary life.

*

31

There is a place where you can see and not be seen, an eye pressed to a small hole in the fence. It's playtime and they spill out from their classrooms and run across the yard. Boys and girls, all shapes and sizes. Black and brown and pink, with blond hair and dark hair and the shades in between. Some are almost full-grown, spotty boys with clumsy feet and girls with breasts just budding under their thick winter clothes, and they won't do at all. But some are tiny; they hardly look big enough to be away from their mothers, with their stringy legs and baby voices. They're the ones to watch.

It's drizzling in the schoolyard and there are puddles on the ground. Just a few feet away, a little boy with a buzz-cut jumps into one violently, and a grin splits his face at the splashing. A girl with straw hair in high pigtails and thick glasses that are misted over stands in the corner and watches the crowd. She puts her thumb in her mouth. Two miniature Asian girls hold hands. A squat white boy kicks a skinny black boy and runs away. A group of girls whisper nasty things to each other, snigger, look sideways out of their dangerous eyes.

But they are all just a moving crowd. No one stands out. Not yet. Keep watching.

Chapter Four

At two o'clock in the afternoon, Frieda left the room that she rented on the third floor of a mansion block and walked to her house, which was only seven minutes away along back roads that hid behind the arterial routes of the city. Just a few hundred yards away was Oxford Street, with its jostle and noise, but here it was deserted. The muted November light made everything seem grey and still, like a pencil drawing. Past the electrical shop where she bought her light bulbs and fuses, past the twenty-four-hour newsagents, the dimly lit grocers, the low-rise flats.

Frieda didn't pause until she reached her house, where she felt the same sense of relief that she always had when coming home, closing the door against the world outside, breathing in the smell of cleanliness and safety. From the moment she had seen it, three years ago, she had known she had to have it, even though it had been neglected for years and had seemed shoddy and misplaced, squeezed between the ugly lock-ups on its left and the council flats on its right. Now, after the work had been done on it, everything was in its place. If she closed her eyes, she would still be able to find each object, even the sharpened pencils on her desk. Here in the hall, the large map of London and the hooks where her belted trench coat hung. Here in the living room, whose window gave out on to the street, the thick-pile rug over the bare boards, the squashy chair and deep sofa on either side of the open fire that she lit each evening, from October through until March. Near the window a chess table, the only item of furniture she had ever inherited. The house was narrow, the width of a single room. Its stairs went steeply up to the first floor, where there was a bedroom and a bathroom, and then even more steeply up to the top floor, which consisted only of her study, with a sloping roof and her desk near the skylight, on which she kept all her drawing things. Reuben called her home her den, or even her lair (with her as its dragon, keeping people out). It was true that it was dark in here. Lots of people knocked through walls, enlarged windows, let in air and light; Frieda preferred snug, enclosed spaces. She had painted the walls in deep colours, matt reds and bottle greens, so that even in summer the house felt dim, as if it was half underground.

She picked the letters up from the doormat and put them on the kitchen table without even glancing at them. She never opened her mail in the middle of the day. Sometimes she forgot about it for a week or more until people rang to complain. Nor did she check her answering-machine messages. In fact, it had only been in the last year that she had finally bought an answering machine and she steadfastly refused to have a mobile, to the incredulity of all those around her, who didn't believe that people could actually function without one. But Frieda wanted to be able to escape from incessant communications and demands. She didn't want to be at anyone's beck and call, and she liked cutting herself off from the urgent inanities of the world. When she was on her own, she liked to be truly alone. Out of contact and adrift.

She had thirty minutes before her next patient. Often she had lunch at her friends' café in Beech Street, Number 9, but not today. She made herself a quick lunch: toast and Marmite, a few small tomatoes, a cup of tea, an oat biscuit and an apple that she quartered and cored. She took the plate through to the living room and sat in the chair by the fire that she had already laid ready for later. She closed her eyes for a moment and let her tiredness settle inside her, then ate her toast slowly.

The phone rang. At first she didn't answer it, but she didn't have the answering machine turned on, and whoever was on the other end didn't give up. Finally she picked up.

'Frieda. It's Paz. Is everything all right? Were you in the bath?'

Frieda sighed. Paz was the administrator at the Warehouse, which wasn't a warehouse at all. It was a clinic that had relocated to an old warehouse and taken a name that had sounded cutting edge in the early eighties. Frieda had trained there, then worked there and now was on the board. When Paz called her at home, it wasn't to deliver good news.

'No, I wasn't in the bath. It's the middle of the day.'

'I'd have a bath in the middle of the day if I was at home. Especially on a Monday. I hate Mondays, don't you?'

'Not really.'

'Everyone hates Mondays. It's the low point of the week. When the alarm clock goes off on Monday morning and it's still dark outside, and you know you have to haul yourself out of bed and begin all over again.'

'Did you really ring me to talk about how you hate Mondays?'

35

'Of course not. I wish you'd get yourself a mobile.'

'I don't want a mobile.'

'You're a dinosaur. Are you coming in on Thursday?'

'I'm meeting Jack.' She was supervising Jack's therapy training.

'Could you come in a bit earlier?' said Paz. 'We'd like some input.'

'I can give you input over the phone. What's it about?'

'Better face to face,' said Paz.

'It's Reuben, isn't it?'

'Just a little talk. And you and Reuben . . .' Her sentence trailed away, leaving a whole history unspoken.

Frieda bit her lip, imagining what was going on. 'What time do you want me?'

'Can you come at two?'

'I've a patient until two. I can get there for two thirty. Will that do?'

'Perfect.'

She returned to her toast, which was cold now. She didn't want to think about the clinic, or about Reuben. Her job was to deal with the mess and pain inside other people's heads, but not *his* mess and not *his* pain. He was out of bounds.

Joe Franklin was her final patient of the day. For the last sixteen months, he had been coming to see her on a Tuesday afternoon, at ten minutes past five – although sometimes he didn't make it, or came just as his time was up. Frieda would wait without irritation, catching up with her notes or doodling on her pad of paper. She never left before all of his fifty minutes had gone by. She knew that she was the one reliable point of his tumbling, kaleidoscopic week. Once he had told her that it was the thought of her sitting slender and straight-backed in her large red armchair that kept him going, even if he couldn't get to her.

Today he was thirty-five minutes late. He came staggering blindly over the threshold, like a man who had just escaped from a car crash and was still in shock; his mouth was working but no words came out. Frieda saw that his shoelaces were trailing loose, and that the buttons on his shirt were done up wrongly. She could see his stomach through it, shockingly white. His fingernails were too long and a bit dirty. His thick blond hair needed a wash. He hadn't shaved recently. Frieda guessed he had been in bed for several days and had only now dragged himself out to get here.

He let himself crumple into the chair facing her, the low table between them. He still hadn't met her gaze. He stared out of the window at the line of cranes standing suspended in the thickening dusk like ghostly figures, although Frieda wondered if he was actually seeing anything out there. There was a beaten look to him. He was a lovely young man, golden and luminous, but on days like today you couldn't see that. His face was contorted; the light had gone out of it. He looked bruised and heavy.

Silence filled the room, not anxious but restful, and they sat inside it. This was a place of safety. Joe gave a long sigh and turned his head. His eyes filled with tears.

'Bad?' asked Frieda. She pushed the box of tissues towards him.

He nodded.

'You got here. That's something.'

37

He picked a single tissue out of the box and held it softly against his face, dusting it delicately as if it was sore, then dabbed his wet eyes. He screwed up the tissue and put it on the table in a tight wet ball, then took another to repeat the process. He leaned forward and put his face in his hands. He looked up as if to speak, opened his mouth, but no words came, and when Frieda asked if there was something he wanted to say, he shook his head violently, like a beast at bay. At six o'clock, when the time came for him to leave, he hadn't said a single word.

Frieda stood up and opened the door for him. She watched him blunder down the stairs, his laces flapping, and then she stood at her window and saw him come out on to the street. He walked past a woman who didn't pay him any special attention. Frieda looked at her watch. She was going out. She needed to get ready. Well, there was no hurry.

Eight hours later Frieda swung her legs out of a bed that wasn't hers. 'Is there anything to drink?' she said.

'There's some beer in the fridge,' said Sandy.

Frieda walked into the kitchen and took a bottle from the fridge door. 'Is there an opener?' she called.

'If we went to your place, you'd know where things were,' he said. 'The drawer next to the stove.'

Frieda flipped the top off the beer and walked back into the bedroom of Sandy's small Barbican flat. She looked out of the window at the lights shimmering in the dark. Her mouth felt dry. She took a sip of the beer and swallowed. 'If *I* lived on the fifteenth floor, I'd spend my life looking out of the window. It's like being on the top of a mountain.'

She walked back to the bed. Sandy was lying wrapped in the tangled sheets. She sat on the edge and gazed down at him. He didn't look like a Sandy; he had a more Mediterranean appearance, with olive skin and hair that was blue-black like a raven's wing, except for a few streaks of silver. He held her stare without smiling.

'Oh, Frieda,' he said.

Frieda felt that her heart was like some old chest that had been heaved up from the seabed, its barnacled lid prised open after all this time. Who knew what treasures she would find inside? 'Do you want some beer?'

'Give me some from your mouth.'

She tipped the bottle and took a swig, then leaned over him, their lips almost touching. She felt the cool liquid trickle into his mouth. He gulped at it, coughed and laughed.

'It's probably better from the bottle,' she said.

'No,' he said. 'It's better from your mouth.'

They smiled at each other, and then the smiles faded. Frieda put her hand on his smooth chest. They started to say something at the same time and both apologized, then tried to speak at the same time again.

'You first,' said Frieda.

He touched the side of her face. 'I wasn't ready for this,' he said. 'It's happened so quickly.'

'You make that sound like a bad thing.'

He pulled her down on to the bed beside him and leaned over her, running a hand down her body. 'Oh, no,' he said. 'But I feel I don't know where I am.' There was a pause. 'Say something.'

'I think I was going to say the same thing. This wasn't part of the plan.'

Sandy smiled. 'You have a plan?'

'Not really. I spend my time helping people sort the story of their lives. Give them a narrative. But I don't know what mine is. And now I feel I'm being carried away on something. I'm not sure what it is.'

Sandy kissed her on the neck and the cheek, and then deeply, mouth to mouth. 'Are you going to stay the night?'

'One day,' said Frieda. 'But not now.'

'And can I come to yours?'

'One day.'

Chapter Five

Detective Constable Yvette Long looked across at her boss, Detective Chief Inspector Malcolm Karlsson. 'Are you ready for this?' she said.

'Does it matter?' he said, and they stepped outside.

It was the side door of the court but there was no escaping the reporters and the cameras. He tried not to flinch at the lights. It would make him look shifty and defeated when it was shown on the news. He could make out some of the faces from the press gallery over the previous weeks. He heard a muddle of questions being shouted at him.

'One at a time,' he said. 'Mr Carpenter.' This was addressed to a bald man clutching a microphone.

'Is the acquittal a personal humiliation or a failure of the system?'

'I decided on a prosecution in conjunction with the Crown Prosecution Service. That's all I've got to say.'

A woman put up her hand. She was from one of the quality papers. He couldn't remember which.

'You've been accused of bringing the case prematurely. What's your response?'

'I was in charge of the inquiry. I take full responsibility.'

'Are you restarting your inquiry?'

'Investigating officers will consider any new evidence.'

'Do you think this operation was a waste of manpower and public money?'

'I thought we assembled a compelling case,' said Karlsson, trying to suppress a feeling of nausea. 'The jury apparently disagreed.'

'Will you resign?'

'No.'

Later that day there was, following tradition, a wake at the Duke of Westminster pub. A group of officers formed a noisy huddle in the corner, under a display of nautical knots in a glass case. DC Long sat down next to Karlsson. She was holding two glasses of whisky, then saw that he had barely touched the one he already had.

Karlsson looked across at the other officers. 'They're in quite a good mood,' he said. 'Considering.'

'Because you took all the blame,' she said. 'Which you shouldn't have done.'

'That's my job,' he said.

Yvette Long looked around and gave a start. 'I can't believe it,' she said. 'Crawford's here. The cunt that dropped you in it. He's actually here.'

Karlsson smiled. He'd never heard her swear before. She must be really angry. The commissioner hovered at the bar, then came over and sat with them. He didn't notice DC Long glaring at him. He slid a glass of whisky across to Karlsson. 'Add that to your collection,' he said. 'You deserve it.'

'Thank you, sir,' said Karlsson.

'You took one for the team today,' Crawford said. 'Don't think I didn't notice. I know I pushed you. There were political reasons. We needed to be seen to be doing something.'

Karlsson pushed his glasses together, as if he were considering which one to drink from first. 'It was my decision,' he said. 'I was in charge.'

'You're not talking to the press now, Mal,' said Crawford. 'Cheers.' He drained his glass and stood up. 'Can't stop,' he said. 'There's a dinner with the home secretary. You know the sort of thing. I'll just wander over and commiserate with the lads.' Then he leaned closer to Karlsson, as if he was confiding something personal. 'Still,' he said. 'You're due a result. Better luck next time.'

Reuben McGill still smoked like it was the 1980s. Or the 1950s. He took a Gitane from his packet, lit it and snapped his lighter shut. At first he didn't speak and Frieda didn't either. She sat opposite his desk and scrutinized him. In a way he looked better than he had when she had first met him, fifteen years earlier. His full head of hair was now grey, his face was more wrinkled, even jowly, but that just added to his vagrant charm. He still wore jeans and an open-necked shirt. This was a man who was telling you – telling his patients – that he wasn't part of the system.

'Good to see you,' he said.

'Paz rang me.'

'Did she now? It's like being surrounded by spies. Are you a spy as well? So, what do you think? Now that you've been summoned.'

'I'm on the board of the clinic,' said Frieda. 'It means that if someone expresses a concern, I need to respond.'

'So respond,' said Reuben. 'What should I do? Tidy my desk?'

The surface of the desk was hidden under piles of books and papers and files and journals. There were pens and mugs and plates.

'It's not the mess,' said Frieda. 'What I can't help noticing is that it's the same mess as when I came in here three weeks ago. I'm not clear why you haven't introduced new mess. Why it hasn't changed.'

He laughed. 'You're dangerous, Frieda. I should only agree to meet you on neutral territory. As you've probably heard, Paz and the rest of them don't think that I've ticked enough boxes, dotted enough *i*s. I'm sorry, I'm too busy caring for people.'

'Paz is looking out for you,' said Frieda. 'So am I. You talk about ticking boxes. Maybe it's a warning sign. And maybe it's better to hear from the people who love you before the people who don't love you start to notice. Allegedly there are such people.'

'Allegedly,' said Reuben. 'You know what you'd do if you really wanted to help me?'

'What?'

'You'd come and work here full-time.'

'I'm not sure that would be a good idea.'

'Why not? You could still have your own patients. And you could keep an eye on me.'

'I don't want to keep an eye on you, Reuben. I'm not responsible for you and you're not responsible for me. I like to have autonomy.'

'What did I do wrong?'

'How do you mean?'

'Almost from the moment you came here as an eager young student, I saw you as the person who'd take this over from me some day. What happened?'

Frieda gave a frown of disbelief. 'One, you were never going to hand your baby over to anyone. And two, I don't want to run anything. I don't want to spend my life checking that the phone bill's been paid and that the fire doors are kept closed.' Frieda paused. 'When I first came here, I knew that it was – just at that moment – the best place in the world for me. It's hard to keep something like that up. I couldn't.'

'You think I haven't? Is that what you're saying – that it's gone downhill?'

'It's like a restaurant,' said Frieda. 'You cook a great meal one night. But you've got to do it the next night and the next. Most people can't manage that.'

'I'm not making fucking pizza. I'm helping people cope with their lives. What am I doing wrong? Tell me.'

'I didn't say you were doing anything wrong.'

'Except you have concerns about me.'

'Perhaps,' said Frieda, carefully, 'you should delegate a bit more.'

'Is that what people think?'

'The Warehouse is your creation, Reuben. It's been an extraordinary achievement. It's helped people. But you can't be too possessive of it. If you are, it will collapse as soon as you leave. Surely you don't want that. It's not the same place as it was when you started it in your back room.'

'Of course it's not.'

'Have you ever thought that your present lack of grip on things here is a way of letting go, without having to admit that's what you're doing?'

'Lack of grip? Because my desk is in a mess?'

'And that perhaps it would be better to do it more rationally?'

'Fuck off. I'm not in the mood for therapy.'

'I was going anyway.' Frieda stood up. 'I've got a meeting.'

'So, am I on some kind of probation?' said Reuben.

'What's the problem with crossing *t*s? If you don't cross them, you can't tell that they're *t*s.'

'Who's your meeting with? Is it to do with me?'

'I'm seeing my trainee. It's our regular session and we won't be talking about you.'

Reuben stubbed his cigarette out in what was already an overflowing ashtray. 'You can't just hide away in your little room talking to people for the rest of your life,' he said. 'You've got to get out in the world and get your hands dirty.'

'I thought that talking to people in a little room was our job.'

When Frieda came out of Reuben's office she found Jack Dargan hovering in the corridor. He was a gangly young man – ardent, clever and impatient – and he was on attachment to the clinic, just as Frieda had been when she was his age. He sat in on group-therapy sessions, and he had a patient. Each week Frieda met him to discuss their progress. On the first day they had met, aware that it was a cliché, knowing that she was aware of it and despising himself, Jack had fallen head over heels in love with her.

'I need to get out of here,' she said. 'Come on.'

They passed a man coming towards them, a lost expression on his round face, his spaniel eyes baffled.

'Can I help you?' she asked.

'I'm looking for Dr McGill.'

'In there.' She nodded towards the closed door.

As she walked out of the clinic, past Paz, who was talking on the phone garrulously and throwing her ringed hands around in extravagant gestures, she felt suddenly like a mother duck with a solitary duckling walking after her. There was a bus coming up the hill as they came out on to the road and she and Jack climbed aboard. He was flustered. He didn't know whether to sit on the seat beside her or to take the one in front or behind. When he did take the one next to her, he sat on her skirt and leaped up again as if scalded.

'Where are we going?'

'There's a café some people I know run. It's their new venture and near where I live. It's open through the day.'

'Fine,' said Jack. 'Great. Yes.' And ground to a halt.

Frieda stared out of the window, saying nothing, and Jack looked surreptitiously at her. He'd never been quite this close to her. His thigh touched hers and he could smell her perfume. When the bus swung round a corner, his whole body pressed against hers. He knew nothing about her life. She had no ring on her left hand so presumably she wasn't married. But did she live with someone? Did she have a lover? Maybe she was gay – he couldn't tell. What did she do when she left the clinic? What did she wear when she wasn't wearing her mannish suits, her plain skirts? Did she ever let her hair down, dance, drink too much?

When they got off the bus, Jack had to walk swiftly to keep up with Frieda as she led him through a maze of

47

streets, into Beech Street. It was full of one-room restaurants and cluttered cafés, little art galleries, shops selling cheese, ceramic tiles, stationery. There was a one-day dry-cleaner's, a hardware shop, a twenty-four-hour supermarket with newspapers in Polish and Greek as well as English.

Number 9 was warm inside, and plainly decorated. It smelt of baking bread and coffee. There were only half a dozen wooden tables, most of them empty, and some stools at the bar.

The woman behind the counter raised her hand in greeting. 'How are you since this morning?'

'Good,' said Frieda. 'Kerry, this is my colleague, Jack. Jack, this is Kerry Headley.'

Jack, pink with gratification at being called Frieda's colleague, muttered something.

Kerry beamed at him. 'What can I get you? There aren't many cakes left – Marcus is going to make some more soon. He's collecting Katya from school at the moment. There are a few flapjacks left.'

'Just coffee,' said Frieda. 'From your shiny new machine, thanks. Jack?'

'Same,' said Jack, although he was already twitchy with caffeine and nerves.

They sat at a table by the window, facing each other. Jack took off his bulky coat and Frieda saw that he was wearing brown corduroy trousers and a vividly striped open-necked shirt with a lime green T-shirt visible underneath. His trainers were grubby and his tawny hair was wild, as if he'd spent the day pushing his fingers into it in exasperation.

'Is that what you wear when you see your patient?' said Frieda.

'It's not the exact clothes. This is just what I wear. Is that a problem?'

'I think you should wear something more neutral.'

'Like a suit and tie?'

'No, not like a suit and tie. Something boring, like a plain shirt or a jacket. Something more invisible. You don't want the patient to get too interested in you.'

'There's not much chance of that.'

'What do you mean?'

'This guy I'm meant to be giving therapy to is just completely self-absorbed. That's what his real problem is. I mean, that's bad, isn't it? If I'm starting to find my very first patient a complete pain in the arse.'

'You don't need to like him. You just need to help him.'

'This guy,' Jack continued, 'is having problems with his marriage. But it turns out that the problems have arisen because there's a woman in his office he wants to sleep with. He's basically gone into therapy because he wants me to agree with him that his wife doesn't understand him and that it's OK for him to go and explore other possibilities. It's like he's got to go through the hoops so that he can give himself permission and feel good about it.'

'And?'

'When I was at medical school I thought I was being trained to cure people. In their bodies, in their minds. I'm not very happy if my job as a therapist is just to make him feel all right about cheating on his wife.'

'Is that what you think you're doing?' Frieda looked at him attentively, noting his mixture of nervousness and impassioned eagerness. He had eczema on his wrists and his nails were bitten. He wanted to please her and he wanted to challenge her. He spoke quickly, in a rush of words, and the colour came and went on his cheeks.

'I don't know what I'm doing,' said Jack. 'That's what I'm saying. This is where I can be honest, right? I don't feel comfortable encouraging him to be unfaithful. On the other hand, I can't just say, "Thou shalt not commit adultery." That's not therapy.'

'Why shouldn't he commit adultery?' said Frieda. 'You don't know what his wife is like. She could be forcing him into it. She could be committing adultery herself.'

'All I know about her is what he tells me. You say people need to find a narrative for their lives. He seems to have found one and it's bloody convenient for him. I'm trying to have empathy for him, though he makes that difficult, but he's not trying to have empathy for his wife. Or anyone. I'm troubled by this. I don't know what to do. I don't want to just collude with him in being a sleazebag. What would you do?'

And he sat back and picked up his coffee, spilling some of it as he lifted it to his mouth. Behind him, a stocky man came through the door, towing a child, whose large school backpack made her look like a tortoise. The man nodded at Frieda and raised his hand in greeting.

'You can't give therapy to the world,' said Frieda. 'And you can't go out and change it to suit yourself. All you can do is deal with that little bit of the world that's in your patient's head. You don't want to give him permission, that's not your job. But you want him to be honest with himself. When I talk about a narrative, I didn't mean that any narrative would do. You could start by trying to get him to understand why he wants your approval for this. Why doesn't he just go and do it?'

'If I put it like that, maybe he will just go and do it.'

'At least he'll be taking responsibility for it, instead of shuffling it off on you.' Frieda paused and thought for a moment. 'Are you getting on with Dr McGill in those group-therapy sessions?'

Jack looked wary. 'I don't think he has much time for me. Or any of us, actually. I'd heard so much about him before I got a placement at the Warehouse, but he seems a bit stressed and distracted. I don't think we're his priority. You're the one who knows him, aren't you?'

'Maybe.'

Chapter Six

Lately, Reuben McGill had started to find fifty minutes a long time to go without a cigarette. He finished one in his office and put an extra-strong mint lozenge into his mouth. He knew it was useless. People could smell cigarettes on you now whatever you did. It had been different twenty years ago, when everything in the world had smelt very slightly of cigarette smoke. Still, what did it matter? Why was he even sucking a mint to cover it up? It wasn't as if it was illegal.

He stepped into the waiting room to find Alan Dekker waiting there, ready for his first session. He led him through to one of the three session rooms they had in the clinic. Alan looked around. 'I thought there'd be a couch,' he said. 'Like you see in films.'

'You don't want to believe everything you see in films. I think it's better just to face each other. Like normal people.'

He gestured Alan into a grey upright armchair, stiff at the back so that it would make him sit straight and face forward. Reuben sat opposite. They were about six feet apart. Not so close that the proximity was oppressive. Not so far that anybody needed to raise their voice.

'So what do you want me to say?' said Alan. 'I'm not used to this.'

'Just talk,' said Reuben. 'We've got plenty of time.'

It had been only three minutes, maybe four, since Reuben had finished his cigarette. He had extinguished it on the railing out on the fire escape, though it was only a little more than half smoked, and dropped it into the concrete area below. He wanted a cigarette again. Or, at least, he couldn't stop himself thinking about a cigarette. It wasn't just about smoking it. It was a way of measuring out the time, and it was something to hold. Suddenly he didn't know where to put his hands. On the arms of the chair felt too formal. On his lap felt too bunched up, as if he were trying to hide something. He moved between one and the other.

When Reuben had created the clinic in 1977, he was only thirty-one years old and one of the most famous analysts in the country. In fact, it had been more like a group or a movement than a clinic. He had developed a version of therapy that was more eclectic and less rule-bound than the traditional therapies at the time. It was going to transform the whole discipline. His picture appeared in magazines. He was interviewed in newspapers. He presented TV documentaries. He wrote books with mysterious, slightly erotic-sounding titles (*Desire and Learned Helplessness, The Playfulness of Love*). He had started out in the living room of his Victorian terraced house in Primrose Hill, and even when the clinic became an NHS-funded institution and moved up to Swiss Cottage, it had kept a Bohemian feel. The Warehouse had been designed by a modernist architect, who retained the steel girders and rough brick walls of the original building, then threw in lots of glass and stainless steel. Yet gradually something had been lost. What Reuben found hard to admit to himself was that there had never really been a new version of therapy. Reuben McGill had been a handsome and charismatic figure, and he had attracted colleagues and patients the way a religious leader attracted followers. Gradually the handsomeness and the charisma had faded. His therapeutic methods had proved hard to replicate, and the range of conditions for which they were deemed suitable had gradually narrowed and narrowed. The Warehouse was a success and well respected. It changed some people's lives, but it wasn't going to change the world.

He remained a gifted analyst, but in recent years something had happened. He had read somewhere that airline pilots, after decades of flawless service, could develop a fear of flying. He had heard of old actors who had suddenly experienced stage fright so debilitating that they could no longer perform in the theatre. He had heard of an equivalent fear of analysts, which was the dread that they weren't real doctors, that they couldn't offer the kinds of cure that other branches of the profession could, that it was all just talk, smoke and mirrors. Reuben had never experienced that. What was a cure, really, after all? He knew he was some kind of a healer. He knew he could do something for the people who came to him, wounded in ways they couldn't express.

It was simpler than that, more embarrassing. Suddenly — or was it gradually? — he had started to find his patients boring. That was the real difference between analysis and other forms of medicine. In the latter, the patient presented and you examined his arm or scanned her breast or looked under the tongue. But if you were an analyst, you had to hear the symptoms over and over again, going on and on, hour after hour. In the early years, it hadn't been like that. Sometimes Reuben had felt he was listening to a particularly pure form of literature, an oral literature, that needed interpreting, decoding. Gradually he had come to think it was a terrible kind of literature, clichéd and repetitive and predictable, and later that it was no kind of literature at all, just an outpouring of unformed, unreflective verbiage, and he had started to let it flow past him, like a river, like traffic, like when you stand on a motorway bridge and watch cars and lorries rush under you, people you know nothing about and care nothing about. They would talk and sometimes cry, and he would nod and think about other things and wait for the cigarette that was coming at exactly nine minutes before the hour.

'These thoughts were like a cancer,' said Alan. 'You know what I mean?'

There was a pause.

'I'm sorry?' said Reuben.

'I said: "Do you know what I mean?"'

'In what way?'

'Were you listening to what I was saying?'

There was another pause. Reuben sneaked a look at his watch. They were twenty-five minutes into the session. He had no memory of anything that had been said. He tried to think of something to ask. 'Do you feel you're not being listened to?' he said. 'Can we talk about that?'

'Don't give me that,' said Alan. 'You haven't been paying attention.'

'Why do you say that?'

'Tell me one thing I've said. Just one thing. Anything.'

'I'm sorry, Mr . . . erm . . .'

'Do you even remember my name? It's James.'

'I'm sorry, James . . .'

'It's not James! It's Alan. Alan Dekker. And I'm leaving and I'm going to complain about you. You're not getting away with this. You're not someone who should be seeing patients.'

'Alan, we need to –'

Both of them stood up and for a moment they confronted each other. Reuben reached forward to catch hold of Alan's sleeve, but then hesitated and raised his hands, letting him go.

'I can't believe this,' said Alan. 'I said it wouldn't do any good. They said you've got to give it a chance. It'll help. Just co-operate.'

'I'm sorry,' said Reuben, in a whisper, but Alan was no longer there to hear it.

Chapter Seven

On Friday afternoon Frieda was at the clinic again, collecting books from its little library for a talk she was going to give in a few weeks' time. Most people had already gone home, but Paz was still there and beckoned her over.

Paz had only been at the Warehouse for six months. She had been brought up in London and spoke with an estuary accent, but her mother was from Andalucía and Paz herself was dark-haired, dark-eyed. She was intense and added a certain melodrama to the clinic, even on calm days. Now there was a sense of extra urgency about her.

'I've been trying to call you,' she said. 'Did you talk to Reuben?'

'You know I did. Why? What's he done?'

'First off, he simply didn't turn up for his patients this afternoon. And I can't get hold of him.'

'That's bad.'

'There's more. This patient.' Paz looked at the paper in front of her. 'He was in distress, having panic attacks, and he was sent to Reuben by his GP. It went badly. Really badly. He's going to make an official complaint.'

'What about?'

'He says Reuben didn't listen to a word he said.'

'What does Reuben have to say about it?'

'He's said bloody nothing. He probably thinks he can

get away with it. Maybe he can. But he's messed this patient around. And he was angry. Very angry.'

'It'll probably sort itself out.'

'That's the thing, Frieda. Sorry to land this on you. But I sort of already persuaded him – Alan Dekker, I mean – not to do anything until he'd talked to you. I thought you could maybe take him on yourself.'

'As a patient?'

'Yes.'

'Oh, God,' said Frieda. 'Can't Reuben sort out his own disasters?' Paz didn't reply, just gave her a pleading look. 'Have you talked to Reuben about this? I can't just take his patient away.'

'Kind of.'

'What does that mean?'

'It means that he isn't really talking. But I gathered he wanted you to take him on. If you would.'

'All right. All right. I can do an assessment, I guess.'

'Tomorrow?'

'Tomorrow's Saturday. I can see him on Monday. Half past two at my place.'

'Thanks, Frieda.'

'In the meantime, check out Reuben's schedule and think about transferring other patients as well.'

'You think he's that bad?'

'Maybe Alan Dekker was just the first to notice.'

'Reuben won't like it.'

Every Friday, Frieda walked to Islington to visit her niece, Chloë. It wasn't a social call: Chloë had just turned sixteen and would take her GCSEs in June, and Frieda was giving her extra tuition in chemistry, a subject that Chloë (who thought she might want to be a doctor herself) regarded with a mixture of loathing and rage, almost as if it were a person who was out to get her. It had been her mother Olivia's idea, but Frieda had only agreed to it once Chloë herself had grudgingly committed herself to one hour each Friday afternoon, from four thirty to five thirty. She hadn't always stuck to it. Once she hadn't turned up at all (but only once, after Frieda's reaction); quite often she slouched in late, banging her folders down on the kitchen table, among all the unwashed dishes and the piles of unopened bills, glaring at her aunt, who would ignore her moods.

Today they would be working through covalent bonding. Chloë hated covalent bonding. She hated ionic bonding. She hated the Periodic Table. She hated balancing equations. She abhorred converting mass into moles and vice versa. She sat opposite Frieda, her dark blonde hair hanging down over her face and the sleeves of her over-sized hoodie pulled over her hands so that only her fingers, with their black-painted nails, showed. Frieda wondered if she was hiding something. Nearly a year ago now, Olivia had rung Frieda up, hysterical, to say that Chloë was cutting herself. She did it with the blade from her pencil sharpener or the needle on her compasses. Olivia had only discovered because she'd opened the door of the bathroom and seen score marks over her daughter's arms and thighs. Chloë had told her that it was nothing, she was making a stupid fuss, everyone did it, it didn't do any harm. Anyway, it was all Olivia's fault, because she didn't understand what it was like to be her, the only child with a mother who treated her like a baby and a father who had run off with a woman not much older than his daughter. *Disgusting*. If that's what it meant to be an adult, she never wanted to grow up. Then she'd locked herself into the bathroom and refused to come out – at which point Olivia called Frieda. Frieda had arrived and sat on the stairs outside the bathroom. She told Chloë that she was there if she wanted to talk, and would wait for an hour. Ten minutes before her time was up, Chloë emerged from the bathroom, her face swollen with weeping, new marks on her arms, which she'd shown to Frieda with an angry defiance: *There, look what she made me go and do . . .* They had talked – or, rather, Chloë had blurted out half-articulated sentences about the relief of running a blade over her skin and watching the bubbles of red form, her rage about her *pathetic* father and, *oh, God*, her drama queen of a mother, the revulsion she felt at her own adolescent, changing body. 'Why do I have to go through this?' she had wailed.

Frieda didn't think Chloë cut herself any more, but she never asked. Now, she turned her gaze away from the pulled-down sleeves, the sullen set of her face, and concentrated on the chemistry.

'When metals react with non-metals, what happens, Chloë?'

Chloë yawned loudly, her mouth opening wide.

'Chloë?'

'Dunno. Why do we have to do this on a Friday? I wanted to go into town with my friends.'

'We've had this discussion before. They share electrons. We'll start with single covalent bonding. Take hydrogen. Chloë?'

Chloë muttered something.

'Have you heard a word I said?'

'You said *hydrogen*.'

'Right. Do you want to get out a notebook?'

'Why?'

'It helps to write things down.'

'D'you know what Mum's gone and done?'

'No, I don't. Paper, Chloë.'

'Only joined a dating agency.'

Frieda closed the textbook and pushed it away from her. 'You object?'

'What do you think? Of course I object.'

'Why?'

'It's pathetic, like she's desperate for sex.'

'Or she's lonely.'

'Huh. It's not as if she lives all by herself.'

'You mean, she's got you?'

Chloë shrugged. 'I don't want to talk about it. You're not my therapist, you know.'

'OK,' said Frieda, mildly. 'Back to hydrogen. How many electrons does hydrogen have?'

'You don't care, do you? You don't care one bit. My dad was right about you!' Her voice wavered at the expression on Frieda's face. She had learned by now that any mention of Frieda's relationship to her family was forbidden, and for all her defiance she was in awe of her aunt and dreaded her disapproval. '*One*,' she said sulkily. 'It has one bloody electron.'

Chapter Eight

When she had been in the neurology rotation of her medical training, Frieda had treated a man who had been in a car crash that had destroyed the part of his brain that dealt with facial recognition. Suddenly he was unable to tell people apart: they had become collections of features, patterns without emotional meaning. He no longer recognized his wife or his children. It had made her think about how unique each human face is and how extraordinary our capacity to read it. At home, she had dozens of books of portraits, some of them by famous photographers, but others that she had picked up in second-hand bookshops by anonymous recorders of unknown and long-dead subjects. Sometimes, when she was unable to sleep and even walking couldn't tire her into oblivion, she would take down a book and thumb through it, peering into the faces of men and women and children, trying to see their interior lives in the expression in their eyes.

She recognized Alan Dekker at once as the man she had seen outside Reuben's office. His face – round and creased, with faint, blotchy freckles – was not exactly handsome, but it was appealing. His eyes were a sad brown, and there was something in them that reminded her of a dog expecting to be beaten but asking for affection none the less. His voice shook and he punched one fist into his open palm as he spoke. She noticed his nails were bitten down to the quick.

'You think – you think – you think . . .' he said. He was used to being interrupted. He spoke to fill in the gaps until he could get the right words out. 'You think it was easy for me to go to that man?'

'It's never easy,' said Frieda. 'It must have taken courage.'

Alan stopped for a moment, looking confused. 'I went because of Carrie, my wife. She drove me there. I think I wouldn't have done it otherwise. He made a fool out of me.'

'He let you down.'

'He wasn't paying attention. He didn't even remember my name.'

He looked at Frieda but she just nodded and waited, leaning forward slightly in her chair.

'What's more he's being paid, out of taxpayers' money. I'm going to deal with him.'

'That's up to you,' said Frieda. 'I just want to say clearly that there was no excuse for the way he treated you.' She paused, thought for a moment and silently cursed. There really didn't seem to be any other way. 'Whatever you plan to do, I was hoping that you and I could talk things over.'

'Are you trying to talk me out of it?'

'I wanted to talk about your feelings, about your suffering. Because you are suffering, aren't you?'

'That's not the point,' said Alan. His eyes had filled with tears and he blinked them away. 'That's not why I'm here.'

'How would you describe it?'

Alan looked up at her. Frieda saw something yield in his expression as if he was surrendering himself.

'I'm not good with words,' he said. 'Everything feels wrong. I've taken sick leave. My heart feels too big for

63

my chest. There's a taste in my mouth, like metal. Or blood. And I have thoughts, pictures going through my mind. I wake at night with them. I can't – It's like I'm not in my own life. I just don't feel myself and I'm scared. I can't . . .' He paused and gulped. 'I can't make love to my wife. I love her but I can't manage it.'

'It happens,' said Frieda. 'You probably don't realize how common it is.'

'I feel terrible about it,' said Alan. 'About everything.'

The two of them looked at each other.

'When you went to see Dr McGill you were taking the first step. It went wrong. I'm sorry about that. Do you think you can try again? With me?'

'That's not why I came here. I . . .' He stopped and gave up as if the effort was too great. 'Do you think you can help me?'

Frieda looked at him – his bitten nails, his anxious face splashed with pale freckles and badly shaved, his supplicating eyes. She gave him a nod. 'I'd like to see you three times a week,' she said. 'I want you to treat it as a priority. Each session will last fifty minutes, and if you arrive late, I will still end at the same time. Do you think you can manage that?'

'I think so. Yes.'

She took her diary out of the drawer.

Chapter Nine

They stood together on Waterloo Bridge. Frieda wasn't looking at the Houses of Parliament or the London Eye or St Paul's, the glittering mass of the city reflected in the brown water. She was staring down at the currents of the river, where they swirled around the foot of the bridge. She almost forgot Sandy was with her until he spoke.

'Don't you prefer Sydney?'

'Sydney?'

'Or Berlin?'

'No. I think I have to get to work now, Sandy.'

'Maybe Manhattan.'

'You can only really love one city. This one's mine.'

'Is that Essex?' said Alan, looking at the picture on the wall.

'No,' said Frieda.

'Where is it?'

'I don't know.'

'Why did you get it, then?'

'I wanted a picture that wasn't too interesting. That wouldn't distract people.'

'I like pictures that have things in them, like old-fashioned sailing ships where you can see all the details, the ropes and the sails. That's not my kind of picture. It's too fuzzy, too moody.'

Frieda was about to say that that was a good thing because they weren't here to talk about pictures when she stopped herself. 'Is moody necessarily a bad thing?'

Alan nodded. 'I get it,' he said. 'You think everything means something. What you do is read things into what I say.'

'So what would *you* like to talk about?'

Alan sat back and folded his arms, as if he was fending Frieda off. On Monday, he had been anxious and needy. Today he was assertive, defensive. At least he had turned up. 'You're the doctor. Or, at least, a sort of doctor. You tell me. Don't you get me to go on about my dreams? Or should I talk about when I was a child?'

'All right,' said Frieda. 'I'm a doctor. So tell me what's wrong with you. Explain why you're here.'

'As far as I know, I'm here so that I don't make a complaint against that other doctor. That guy is a complete disgrace. I know you all want to stick together. I still might make a complaint.'

Alan kept shifting his position. Uncrossing his arms, pushing his hands through his hair, looking at Frieda, then looking away.

'There are places for you to complain,' she said. 'If that's what you decide to do. But not here. This is a place where you come and talk about yourself, with honesty. You can do it in a way that you probably can't with anyone else, not with close friends or your wife or people you work with. You might want to see that as an opportunity.'

'The problem I have with all of this' – Alan gestured around the room – 'is that you think you can solve problems just by talking about them. I've always seen myself as a practical person. If there's a problem, I believe in going out and fixing it. Talking about it doesn't get it done.'

Frieda's expression was unchanged but she felt a familiar kind of weariness. This again. So often the first proper session was like a particularly awkward first date. At a first session, people had to claim that they didn't really need help, that they didn't know what they were doing there, that there was no point in just talking about things. Sometimes it took weeks to get beyond that stage. Sometimes you never really got beyond it at all.

'As you said, I'm a doctor,' said Frieda. 'Describe your symptoms to me.'

'They're the same as they were before.'

'Before when?' Frieda leaned forward slightly in her chair.

'When? I don't know exactly. I was young. In my early twenties – it would have been about twenty-one, twenty-two years ago. Why?'

'How did you deal with it then?'

'They went away.' Alan paused, made a strange, anxious grimace. 'Eventually.'

'So for twenty-odd years, you've not felt anything like them, and now they're recurring.'

'Well, yes. But that doesn't mean I need to be here, necessarily. I think my GP just referred me as a way of getting rid of me. My own theory is that doctors basically just want their patients to go away as quickly as possible and stay away. The main way they do it is to give you a pill, but if that doesn't work they send you to another doctor. Of course, what they really want . . .'

Suddenly he stopped. There was a pause.

'Are you all right?' asked Frieda.

Alan slowly twisted his head. 'Can you hear that?'

'What?'

'There's a sort of creaking sound,' he said. 'It's from over there.' He pointed to the far side of the room, the opposite side from the window.

'It's probably just building work,' said Frieda. 'There's a construction project . . .'

She frowned. There really was a creaking noise and it wasn't coming from across the street. It was inside the house. And yet not exactly inside. The noise got louder. The creaking turned into a groaning, and then they could feel it as well as hear it. Then there was what sounded like an explosion in the ceiling and something fell through: plaster and pieces of wood, but mainly it was a man. He landed heavily on the carpet. Chunks of plaster fell on to him. The room was suddenly full of white dust. Frieda just sat there. It was so unexpected that she felt unable to process what was happening. She just stared at it as if a theatrical spectacle was taking place in front of her. And she was waiting to see what would happen next.

Meanwhile Alan had leaped up and run towards the figure slumped on the floor. Could he be dead? Frieda wondered. How could a dead man have fallen through her ceiling? Alan knelt down and touched it, and the figure stirred. Slowly it shifted, pulled itself on to its knees and then stood. He was a man. He was bulky, shaggy-haired, in overalls, but it was difficult to make out anything else about him because he was covered with a film of grey dust. Except that on his face, to the side of one eyebrow, there was a trickle of blood, which ran down over his cheekbone. He looked at Alan and then at Frieda, as if confused.

'What floor is this?' he asked. His accent sounded foreign, Eastern European.

'What floor?' said Frieda. 'The third. Are you all right?'

The man looked up through the hole, then back at Frieda. He patted at his arms and his body, releasing a snowstorm of dust. 'Excuse me a moment,' he said, and walked out of the room.

Frieda and Alan looked at each other. Alan gestured at the chair he'd been sitting in. 'Do you mind?'

'Mind what?'

He dragged the chair under the hole in the ceiling and then stood on it. Frieda looked up at him, then at his feet and his shoes on her chair, and didn't know what to say. Alan's head had disappeared into the hole. She heard a muffled 'Hello' and other words that she couldn't make out. Then she heard another voice that was even more distant. Finally Alan stepped down off the chair.

'Does it look serious?' said Frieda.

Alan pulled a face. 'Lucky I'm not at work.'

'Are you a builder?'

'I work for the housing department,' he said. 'I'd have something to say about that if I was at work.'

'I'll have to get it fixed. Does it look difficult?'

Alan glanced up at the hole, shook his head and sucked air through his teeth in a hiss. 'Rather you than me,' he said. 'Bloody cowboys. If he'd broken his neck, who would have paid for that? These bloody Poles.'

'From the Ukraine,' said a voice from the hole.

'Are you listening?' said Frieda.

'What?' said the voice.

'Did you hurt yourself?'

'It's your ceiling that got hurt,' said Alan.

'I come soon,' said the voice.

Frieda stepped away from the rubble. 'I'm sorry about this,' she said. 'I suppose we'll have to stop here.'

'Did you arrange it?' said Alan. 'Is it a way of breaking the ice?'

'We should make another arrangement. If you're comfortable with that.'

Alan looked up at the hole. 'What's disturbing about that,' he said, 'apart from the shock, is that it shows how close we live to each other. We're like animals in cages on top of each other.'

Frieda raised her eyebrows at him. 'You're talking too much like an analyst. Sometimes someone falling through a hole in the ceiling is just someone falling through a hole in the ceiling. It doesn't mean anything. It's just an accident.' She looked at the rubble and the dust that was now settling on every surface. 'A particularly irritating accident.'

Alan's face turned serious. 'I'm the one who should say sorry,' he said. 'I was being rude to you. That other guy wasn't your fault. My GP wasn't your fault. There are things I'd like to talk to you about. Thoughts. In my head. Maybe you could make them go away.'

'You weren't rude, not really. So I'll see you again on Friday. Assuming I've got this lot cleared up.'

She showed Alan out and then, as she always did, she went to her desk and started to write notes on the session, though it had lasted barely ten minutes. She was interrupted by a knock at the door. A knock, not a ring from the street bell, so she imagined it would be Alan, but it was the man from upstairs, still covered with dust.

'Five minutes,' he said.

'Five minutes *what*?' asked Frieda.

'You stay here,' he said. 'I come back in five minutes.'

Frieda made two phone calls cancelling sessions for later that day. Then, as she sat down to finish her notes, there was another knock on the door. It took her a moment to recognize the man standing there now that he was clean, smelling of soap and dressed in jeans, a T-shirt and a pair of trainers with no socks. His dark brown hair was swept back off his face. He held his hand out. 'My name is Josef Morozov.'

Almost as if she were in a dream, Frieda gave his hand a shake and introduced herself, although for a moment she thought he was going to lift her knuckles to his lips and kiss them.

In his other hand he was holding a packet of chocolate biscuits. 'You like biscuits?'

'No, I don't.'

'We have to talk. Do you have tea?'

'We definitely need to talk.'

'We need tea. I make tea for you.'

Frieda kept almost nothing in the little flat where she saw patients but she did occasionally make herself tea and coffee. So she took him through and watched him while he pottered around her kitchen. With her having to tell him where everything was, it took longer than if she had done it herself. They each took a mug and walked through to the consulting room.

'You could have died,' Frieda said. 'Are you OK?'

He held up his left arm and looked at it as if it belonged to someone else. There was a livid red scar running down the inside. 'I fell from a ladder,' he said, 'and through a window. And once I broke my leg when a . . .' He gestured vaguely. 'It ran on me. With a wall behind me. This was nothing.'

He sipped his tea and looked out of the window at the demolition. 'That is a big job,' he said.

'Shall we talk about the big job in here?'

Josef turned and looked at the rubble on the floor, then up at the hole. 'It is bad,' he said.

'This is where I work,' said Frieda.

'You cannot work here,' said Josef.

'So what am I going to do?' said Frieda. 'By which I mean, what are *you* going to do?'

Josef looked up at the hole again, then gave a melancholy smile. 'I am to blame,' he said. 'But the person who built that floor, he is the one who is really to blame.'

'I'm not so bothered about your floor,' said Frieda. 'What matters to me is my ceiling.'

'It's not my floor. I am doing the work while the people are at their house in the country. This is their town flat. You work every day?'

'Every day. Except weekends.'

He turned to her and put the hand that wasn't holding the mug on his heart, in a gesture that had a certain theatrical flourish. He even gave a slight bow. 'I will fix everything for you.'

'When?'

'It will be better than it was before I fell through the hole.'

'You didn't fall through the hole. You *made* the hole.'

He frowned thoughtfully. 'When do you need to work here?'

'I'd like to work here tomorrow, but I guess that's out of the question.'

Josef looked around. Then he smiled. 'I put a partition here,' he said. 'I work behind it. You have your office. When you're not here, I put new paper up. Paint it. I'll paint it a proper colour.'

'This is a proper colour.'

'You give me a key and the partition will be up tomorrow and you will have your office again. Just a smaller office.'

He held his hand out. Frieda pondered just a moment. She was giving her key to a man she had never met before. But what else was she going to do? Find another builder? What was the worst that could happen? Never ask that question. She opened a drawer, found a spare key and gave it to Josef. 'You're Ukrainian?' she said.

'Not Polish.'

The best ones are the shy ones, with their anxious smiles and their wobbling bottom lips. The ones who miss their mother and who sit on the steps in the cold, damp weather until their teacher comes and makes them stand up, run around. You need them eager to please, obedient. You can mould.

There's a little boy who is sitting on the small wooden seesaw, waiting for someone to climb on to the high other end. But no one

73

comes and he goes on sitting there. At first, he is smiling and hopeful, then bit by bit his smile freezes on his face. He glances around. He sees the other children looking at him and deciding not to join him. He tries to call another boy over but the other boy ignores him.

He's a possibility. You have to know what you're looking for but you have to be careful as well. It doesn't matter how long it takes. Time isn't a problem.

Chapter Ten

'That was interesting,' said Sandy.

They were walking hand in hand through the City towards his flat, just a few hundred yards away. On either side of them, imposing buildings rose up and towered over them, their height almost obscuring the sky. Banks and financial institutions and august law firms with their names above the doors. The smell of money. The streets were clean and deserted. Traffic lights changed from red to green and back, but only the occasional cab passed through them.

They had been to a leaving party for a doctor who worked with Sandy, and whom Frieda had also known for several years. They had arrived separately, but halfway through the evening, Sandy had come up to where Frieda was standing in a group and placed his hand on her back. She had turned towards him and he had bent his head and kissed her on the cheek, too near her mouth and too lingering for it to be a greeting between acquaintances. It was a clear statement, and of course he had meant everyone to notice it. When she had turned back to the people she had been talking to, she saw how interest brightened their glances, though nobody said anything. Now they had left together, aware of all the eyes following them, the speculation they were leaving behind. Frieda and Sandy, Sandy and Frieda – did you know, did you guess?

'Next thing I know you'll be inviting me to meet your boss. Oh, I forgot – you *are* the boss, aren't you?'

'Do you mind?'

'Mind?'

'That people know we're a couple.'

'Is that what we are?' she asked sardonically, though her heart was beating hard.

They had reached the Barbican. He turned and took her by her shoulders. 'Come on, Frieda. Why is it so hard? Say it out loud.'

'Say what?'

'We're an item, a couple. We make love, make plans, talk to each other about what we did in the day. I think about you all the time. I remember you, what you said, how you felt. God, here I am, a forty-something consultant. My hair's going grey and I feel like a teenager. Why is it so difficult for you to say it?'

'I liked it when we were a secret,' Frieda said. 'When nobody knew about us except us.'

'It couldn't stay a secret for ever.'

'I know that.'

'You're like a wild animal. I'm afraid that if I move suddenly, if I make the wrong sort of sound, you'll run away.'

'You should get a Labrador,' said Frieda. 'I had one when I was a child. Every time you left her, she howled. She was as grateful every time you came home as if you'd been away for ten years.'

'I don't want that,' said Sandy. 'I want you.'

She moved closer to him and put her arms under his thick coat and his suit jacket. She could feel the warmth of his body through his thin shirt. His lips were against her hair. 'I want you, too.'

In silence, they entered the building. In the lift, they turned to each other as the doors shut and kissed so fiercely that she could taste the blood on her lip, pulling apart as they reached his floor. Inside the flat, he took off her coat and let it fall to the floor. He unzipped her dress, lifted her hair and undid the clasp on her necklace, letting the thin silver chain coil into the palm of his hand, then placing it on the small table in the entrance hall. Kneeling on the wooden floor, he pulled off one shoe, then the next. He looked up at her and she tried to smile. Being happy scared her.

'I'm not from Poland,' Josef said, yet again, to the only other man in the pub, which was warm and cosy and down-at-heel and which he didn't really want to leave.

'I don't mind. I like Poles. Got nothing against them.'

'I am from the Ukraine. It is very different. In the summer we –'

'I drive buses.'

'Ah.' Josef nodded. 'I like buses here. I like to go on the top floor at the front.'

'Your turn.'

'I am sorry?'

'Another one of these, mate.'

He held out his glass. Josef thought he had bought the last round. He put his hand into the pocket of his jacket, which wasn't going to be thick enough to last him through the winter, and felt the coins there. He wasn't sure he had enough for another round, but he didn't want to be rude to his new friend, who was called Ray and was pink and round.

'I will buy you a beer but perhaps not for me,' he said at last. 'I must go now. Tomorrow I start work for a woman.'

Ray gave a conspiratorial smile that disappeared when he saw Josef's expression.

She loved the feel of the wind on her face. She loved the cool darkness and the way the streets around her were quite empty, only the sound of her footsteps and the rustle of dry leaves disturbing their silence. In the distance, though, she could still hear the rumble of traffic. She walked under the small bridge where, for as long as she had been taking this route, a pair of boots had hung from the parapet, swinging in the wind. At Waterloo Bridge she always paused for a while to gaze at the great buildings massed on either side of the river and listen to the soft, lapping sound of water against the shore. This was where London was on public view. From here, it spread for miles in either direction, dwindling at last into suburbs and then a tamed kind of countryside that Frieda never visited if she could help it. She turned her back to the river. Not far away, her narrow little house was waiting for her, with its dark blue door, the chair by the fire, the bed she had made that morning.

When she arrived home, it was well past three o'clock, but although her body was tired, her brain was teeming with thoughts and images, and she knew that she wouldn't be able to sleep. A colleague of hers who was a sleep expert had told her that it was often helpful to focus on a tranquil image – a lake or a meadow of long grass, she had suggested – and that was what Frieda did now, lying in her bed with the curtains half open so that she could see the moon. She imagined herself inside the drawing that hung in the rented room where she worked, walking through the warm, dusty colours of its landscape. But instead she found herself imagining the picture that Alan Dekker had talked about, of a ship in a gale, with lashing ropes, everything in frantic motion. That must be how it sometimes felt inside his head, she thought. And then, thinking of Alan, she remembered her ceiling exploding and a body falling through in a shower of dust and plaster. She wondered if her room would be ready for her tomorrow, except, of course, that tomorrow was today, and in about three hours it would be time to get up.

When Josef arrived at the flat, Frieda could barely see him at first behind the huge panel of chipboard he was carrying. He leaned it against a wall in the consulting room and looked up at the hole.

'I've got a patient coming in half an hour,' Frieda said.

'This takes ten minutes,' said Josef. 'Fifteen, maybe.'

'Is this to patch the hole up?'

'Before the hole gets better, it must first get worse. I will make it larger, pull the bits away. Afterwards I can make it strong and good.' He gestured at the board. 'This I will use to make a wall here and to give you your room back. I have measured and cut two pieces and it will fit.'

Frieda had so many questions and reservations about this process that she didn't know which to express first. 'How will you get in and out?' she asked lamely.

'Through the hole,' said Josef. 'I put the ladder down and then afterwards I will pull it up.'

He walked out and returned a couple of minutes later with two bags, one of tools and the other with different-sized pieces of wood. With amazing speed he wedged the first board into place and then Frieda heard various bangs coming from the side she couldn't see. She peered round into the tiny end of the room, now half blocked in by the board. 'What's this going to look like when you've finished?' she said.

Josef gave a rap at the board to check its solidity. He seemed satisfied. 'The hole, filled in,' he said. 'Then the boarding goes away. Then one afternoon, the ceiling, papered and painted. And if you want it, the rest of the room painted. Same afternoon.' He looked around. 'Painted a proper colour.'

'This is the proper colour.'

'You choose. Boring colour, if you like. The people upstairs, they pay for it. I mix in with what they're paying.'

'I'm not sure that's right,' said Frieda.

Josef shrugged. 'They make me work somewhere dangerous where you fall through the floor. They can pay for it a little bit.'

'I'm not convinced about this,' said Frieda.

'I get the second board now and then you have your room back. Just a bit smaller for a while.'

'All right.'

Frieda looked at her watch. Soon she would be sitting in this diminished room, hearing Alan's grim dreams and his waking sadness.

Chapter Eleven

'Honestly, Alan, I don't know why you have to be so secretive all of a sudden.'

It was after supper and Carrie had been flicking through the channels with the remote control, but now she turned the television off and turned to him, folding her arms. She'd been snappy and thin-skinned all evening. Alan had been waiting for this conversation.

'I'm not being secretive.'

'You're not telling me anything that goes on in there. I was the one who encouraged you to go and now you're shutting me out.'

'It's not like that.' Alan tried to think of how Frieda had put it earlier that day. 'It's a safe place,' he said. 'Where I can say anything.'

'Aren't you safe here? Can't you say anything to me?'

'It's not the same. She's a stranger.'

'So you can say things to a stranger that you can't say to your own wife?'

'Yes,' said Alan.

'What kind of things? Oh, sorry, I forgot. You can't tell me, can you, because they're secret?' She wasn't used to being sarcastic. Her cheeks were flushed.

'It's nothing bad. They're not secret like that. I'm not telling her I'm having an affair, if that's what you're thinking.'

'If that's what you want.' Carrie's voice was tight and high. She shrugged and turned the television back on.

'Don't be like this.'

'Like what?'

'Hurt. As if I've done something to offend you.'

'I'm not offended,' she said, in the same clipped voice.

He took the remote out of her hand and turned off the television again. 'If you really want to know, what we talked about today was us not managing to have a baby.'

She turned to face him. 'Is that why you're not well?'

'I don't know why,' he said. 'I'm just telling you what we talked about today.'

'It's me who can't have the baby too.'

'I know.'

'I'm the one who's been prodded and poked and who has to wait for my period every month.'

'I know.'

'And it's not as if . . .' She stopped.

'It's not as if it's your fault,' Alan finished for her wearily. '*My* fault. I'm the one with a low sperm count. And I'm the one who's impotent.'

'I shouldn't have said that.'

'It's all right. It's true, after all.'

'I didn't mean it. It's not a question of fault. Don't look like that.'

'Like what?'

'As if you're about to cry.'

'What's so wrong with crying?' Alan asked, surprising himself. 'Why shouldn't I cry? Why shouldn't you?'

'I do, if you want to know. When I'm by myself.'

He picked up her hand and fiddled with the wedding ring on her finger. 'You have secrets from me too.'

'We should have talked about it more. But I keep thinking it will still be all right. Lots of women wait for years. And if it doesn't happen, maybe we can adopt. I'm still quite young.'

'I wanted my own son,' said Alan, softly, almost as if he was speaking to himself. 'That's what I was talking about today. Not having a child, it doesn't just make me sad, it makes me feel wrong, like a botched piece of work. As if I'm unfinished inside – and then all these things rush in to fill the emptiness.' He stopped. 'It sounds stupid.'

'No,' said Carrie, although she wanted to cry out: *What about me? My son, my daughter? I would have been a good mother.* 'Go on.'

'It's not fair. Not fair on you either. I've let you down and I can't put it right. You must wish you'd never met me.'

'No.' Though of course there'd been times when she had thought how much easier it would have been with a different kind of man, confident and with sperm that could swim right up her, like salmon up a river. She winced. The two things seemed to go together, but she knew that wasn't right. It wasn't Alan's fault.

'It all came pouring out of me, things I didn't even know I'd been thinking. She's quite a scary woman, but somehow you can talk to her as well. After a bit, it wasn't even like talking to a person. It was like walking around in a house I'd never been into before, finding things, picking them up and looking at them, letting myself just wander around inside myself. And then I found myself saying this thing . . .' He stopped, passed his hand across his forehead. He was suddenly feeling a bit sick, a bit out of breath.

'What?' asked Carrie. 'What thing?'

'I have this picture in my mind – it sounds daft. It seems so real, as if I'm looking at it or remembering it or something, not just imagining it. Almost as if it's happening to me.'

'*What*'s happening? What picture, Alan?'

'Me and my son together. A little five-year-old, with bright red hair and freckles and a big grin. I can see him plain as day.'

'You see him?'

'And I'm teaching him to play football.' He gestured towards the small back garden that he'd been neglecting recently. 'He's doing really well, controlling the ball, and I feel so proud of him. Proud of myself, too, being a proper dad, doing what dads do with their sons.' His chest was tight, as though he'd run a long distance. 'You're standing at the window looking at us.'

Carrie didn't speak. Tears were running down her cheeks.

'Recently I haven't been able to get the picture out of my mind – sometimes I don't want to, but sometimes I think I'll go mad with it. She said, did I think it was me as a boy that I'm seeing, or the boy inside me or something, and wanting to rescue him in some way? But it's not like that. I'm seeing my son. Our son.'

'Oh, God.'

'The one we're waiting for.'

*

It's always like this. There comes a moment when you just know. It's as simple as that. After all these months of watching, of waiting for the tug on the line and the bait to be taken, of being patient and careful, of wondering if this one is possible or that one, of never giving up or getting downhearted, then suddenly it happens. You just have to be ready for it.

He's small and skinny, maybe young for his age, though it's hard to tell. He hangs back from his classmates at first; his eyes dart around, to see where he'll be wanted. He's wearing jeans that are a bit too big for him and a thick jacket that's almost down to his knees. He comes closer. He has round brown eyes and round copper-coloured freckles. He's wearing a grey woolly hat with a bobble on it, but then he pulls it off and his hair is a flaming red. It's a sign, it's a gift, it's perfect.

So now it's just a question of time. You've got to get it right. There'll never be another as perfect as this.

Chapter Twelve

Josef liked this way of working. The clients were away and would only visit maybe every two weeks. He could live in the flat most of the time. He could eat there, if he wanted. In the past he had worked mainly as part of a team, and that was mainly good too, all the people with their specialities – the plasterer, the carpenter, the electrician – a version of a family that argued and fought and tried to get along with each other. But this was almost a holiday. He could work when he liked, even in the middle of the night, when it was dark outside and as quiet as it ever got. And in the day, sometimes, for example on a day like this, when it was about two in the afternoon and his eyes got heavy, he would put his tools down and lie back. He closed his eyes and thought at first about the problem of the hole and how far it needed widening to clear out the damaged wood and cracked plaster and then, for no reason at all, he started to think of his wife, Vera, and of the boys. He hadn't seen them since the summer. He wondered what they were doing now, and then they faded as if they had walked into a mist, but slowly, so there wasn't a clear moment when he couldn't see them – and then he was asleep, dreaming dreams he wouldn't remember when he woke, because he never remembered his dreams.

At first he thought the voice was part of his dream. It was the voice of a man, and before he could make out the meaning of the words he could feel their sadness, a raw sadness that sounded strange coming from a man. This was followed by a silence and another voice spoke and this one he knew. It was the voice of the woman downstairs, the doctor. Josef raised his hand and felt the roughness of the chipboard on his fingers. He saw the glow of the hole in the ceiling above him and slowly, dully, realized where he was: on the floor in her room. As he heard the two voices – the man's quavering, the woman's clear and calm – he felt a growing sense of alarm. He was listening to a confession, something that nobody else was meant to hear. He looked up at the ladder. If he tried to climb it, he would be heard. Better just to lie where he was and hope it would be over soon.

'My wife was angry with me,' the man said. 'It was as if she was jealous. She wanted me to tell her what I'd told you.'

'And did you?' said Frieda.

'Kind of,' said the man. 'I told her a version of it. But then, as I was telling her, it made me feel that I hadn't really told you properly.'

'What didn't you say?'

There was a long pause. Josef could hear the beat of his heart. He smelt the alcohol on his own breath. How could they not hear him or smell him?

'Can I really say anything here?' said the man. 'I'm asking because I realized when I was talking to Carrie that there's always some kind of limit on what I can say. I mean, I can only say the sort of things to her that husbands are supposed to say to their wives, and when I'm out with a friend, I can only say the sort of things that friends are meant to say to each other.'

'This is the place where you're allowed to say anything. There are no limits.'

'You'll just think this is stupid . . .'

'I don't care whether it's stupid or not.'

'And you won't tell anyone what I say?'

'Why would I do that?'

'You promise?'

'Alan, I'm professionally bound to respect your privacy. Unless you're confessing to a serious crime. Or planning one.'

'I'm confessing to bad feelings.'

'Then tell me what they are.'

Josef thought that what he really ought to do was to put his fingers in his ears. He wasn't meant to hear this. He was meant *not* to hear it. But he didn't. He couldn't stop himself. He wanted to know. What did it matter, really?

'I've been thinking,' said the man. 'I was talking about wanting a child. Wanting a son. So why aren't I just going to have fertility treatment and taking Viagra? It's a medical problem, not something to do with my head.'

'So why aren't you?'

'I had this feeling about my son, about this little boy, this boy who looks like me. It was like a hunger. But these attacks I've been having, where I've been almost collapsing, fainting, making a complete idiot of myself. They're not about that hunger. They're about something else as well.'

'What are they about?'

'Guilt.'

Another silence.

'What kind of guilt?' said Frieda.

'I've been thinking about that,' said the man. 'And I saw it like this. I want this boy. I want him kicking a ball with me. And I'm here wanting him to be with me. But he's not there wanting me to be with him. Does that make sense?'

'Not entirely,' said Frieda. 'Not yet.'

'It's obvious. They don't ask to be born. We want them. I guess it's an instinct. But what's the difference between that and an addiction? You take heroin to stop you wanting heroin. You've got an itch for a child and you get a child to stop that itch.'

'So you think having a child is a selfish act?'

'Of course it is,' said the man. 'It's not as if you consult the child.'

'Are you saying you feel guilty because your desire to have a child is selfish?'

'Yes.' Long pause. 'And also . . .' He stopped. Josef agreed with Frieda – there was something else going on here. 'Also, it's this urgent kind of wanting. Maybe it's what women feel.'

'What do you mean by that?'

His voice was a mutter. Josef had to strain to hear him.

'I've heard of women who don't feel complete until they've had a child. It's like that but even more. I feel – I've always felt – as if there's something missing from me, kind of like a hole in me.'

'A hole in you? Go on.'

'And if I had a child it would plug that hole. Does that sound creepy?'

'No. But I'd like to explore this urgency and hunger more. What would your wife say if you told her that?'

'She'd wonder what kind of man she'd married. I wonder what kind of man she married.'

'Maybe a part of a marriage is keeping some things to ourselves.'

'I had a dream about my son.'

'You make it sound like he exists.'

'He did in the dream. He was standing there, like me that age. Red-haired, little school uniform. But he was far away, on the other side of something huge, like the Grand Canyon. Except it was completely dark and incredibly deep. I was standing on the edge looking across at him. I wanted to go to him but I knew that if I stepped forward I'd fall into the darkness. It's not exactly a happy dream.'

Now Josef thought of his own little sons and he really did feel ashamed. He pushed the joints of his fingers into his mouth and chewed them. He wasn't sure why. Maybe as a punishment or to take his mind off what he was hearing. He didn't exactly stop listening to the words but he stopped translating them. He tried to let them become music that just flowed past him. Finally, he could hear that the session was coming to a close. The voices changed in pitch and became more distant. He heard the door open. This was his chance. As quietly as he could, he got up and started to climb up the ladder, gently, to avoid any creaking. Suddenly he heard banging.

'Is that you?' said a voice. There was no question about it: it was her voice. 'Are you in there?'

For a desperate moment, Josef thought of staying silent and maybe she would go away.

'I know you're there. Don't pretend. Get through that hole and come round here now.'

'I heard nothing,' said Josef. 'It's no problem.'

'Now.'

'How long were you there?' said Frieda, white with anger, when they were face to face.

'I was asleep,' said Josef. 'I was working there, fixing the hole. And I slept.'

'In my room.'

'Behind the wall.'

'Are you completely insane?' said Frieda. 'This is private. It's as private as it's possible to be. What would he think if he found out?'

'I will not tell him.'

'Tell him? Of course you won't tell him. You don't know who he is. But what did you think you were doing?'

'I was asleep and then the voices woke me.'

'I'm so sorry that we disturbed you.'

'I try not to listen. I am sorry. I will not do it again. You will tell me the times to work and I will block the hole.'

Frieda took a deep breath. 'I cannot believe I've held a therapy session with a builder in the same room. But all right, that's fine. Or fairly fine. Just fix the bloody hole.'

'It will only be a day. Or two days. Or a little bit more. The paint is slow to dry now it is cold.'

'Do it as quickly as you can.'

'But there is one thing I don't understand,' said Josef. 'What's that?'

'If a man wants to have a child, then you do something about that. You don't just talk about it. You go out into the world and you try to solve the problem. You see a doctor and you do whatever it is so you have a son.'

'I thought you were asleep,' said Frieda, with a look almost of horror.

'I was sleeping. The noise woke me. I heard some talk. He is a man who needs a son. He made me think of my own sons.'

Frieda's expression of anger slowly collapsed into a smile. She couldn't help herself. 'You want me to discuss my patient with you?' she said.

'I thought that it wasn't good just with words. He needs to change his life. Get a son. If he can.'

'When you were overhearing, did you hear the bit where I said it was completely secret? That nobody would know what he told me?'

'But what is the point of just talking, if he doesn't do anything?'

'You mean like lying asleep instead of repairing the hole you fell through?'

'I will fix it. It's almost done.'

'I don't know why I'm talking to you about this,' said Frieda. 'But I'll say it anyway. I can't sort out Alan's life, get him a son with red hair. The world's a messy, unpredictable place. Maybe, just maybe, if I talk to him, as you put it, I can help him to deal with it a little bit better. It's not much, I know.'

Josef rubbed his eyes. He still didn't look properly awake. 'Can I buy you a glass of vodka to say sorry?' he said.

Frieda looked at her watch. 'It's three in the afternoon,' she said. 'You can make me a cup of tea to say sorry.'

When Alan left Frieda it was already getting dark. The wind had rain in its tail, and shook dead leaves off the trees in small gusts. The sky was a sullen grey. There were puddles glinting blackly on the pavement. He didn't know where he was walking. He blundered along the side roads, past unlit houses. He couldn't go back home, not yet. Not to Carrie's watching eyes, her solicitous anxiety. He had felt a bit better while he was in the warm, light room. The swarming, lurching sensation inside him had calmed down and he'd just been aware of how tired he was, how heavy with exhaustion. He almost could have slept, sitting on the small grey sofa opposite her and saying things he could never say to Carrie because Carrie loved him and he didn't want that to end. He could imagine the expression on his wife's face, her wince of distress, quickly suppressed. But this woman's expression didn't change. There was nothing he could say that would hurt or disgust her. She was like a painting, the way she could be so silent and still. He wasn't used to that. Most women nodded and murmured, encouraging you along but at the same time stopping you going too far, keeping you on the right track. Well, his mother had been like that at least, and Lizzie and Ruth at work. And Carrie, of course.

Now that he'd left, though, he didn't feel so good. The troubling feelings were closing in on him again, or rising up in him. He didn't know where they came from. He wished he could go back to the room, at least until they subsided again – but he didn't think she'd like that at all.

93

He remembered what she had said about fifty minutes exactly. She was stern, he thought, and he wondered what Carrie would make of her. She'd think Frieda was a tough nut. A tough nut to crack.

There was a small, enclosed green on his left, with three winos at one end of it drinking cider out of cans. Alan stumbled inside and sat on the other bench. The drizzle was gathering strength now: he could feel drops of rain on his head and hear them pattering into the damp leaves that lay in heaps on the ground. He closed his eyes. No, he thought. Carrie couldn't understand him. Frieda couldn't, not really. He was alone. That was what was cruellest. Alone and incomplete. At last, he stood up again.

It was as if it was meant to happen. Call it what you want: fate, destiny, something in the stars. The little boy with red hair and freckles was all on his own. His mother was late again. What did she expect to happen? Now he was looking around him. He was looking at the open gate and at the road beyond. Come on. Come on, my little one. Come through the gate. That's it. That's the way. Gently now. Don't look back. Come to me. Come to me. Now you're mine.

His mother had a bright blue raincoat and red hair; she was easy to spot. But today she wasn't at the gates with the other mothers, and most of the children had already left. He didn't want Mrs Clay to make him wait in the class-room, not again. It wasn't allowed but he knew the way home and, anyway, he'd meet her before he got there, run-ning along with her hair coming loose because she was late. He sidled towards the gate. Mrs Clay was looking at him, but then she had to blow her nose; she covered her whole wrinkly face with a big white handkerchief, so he slipped out. Nobody saw him go. There was a pound coin lying in the road in a shallow puddle and, glancing round to make sure it wasn't some kind of joke, he picked it up and rubbed it with the corner of his shirt. If his mother didn't meet him before then, he would buy sweets at the corner shop or a packet of crisps. He looked up the road but still couldn't see her.

Chapter Thirteen

For a long time now, Frieda had learned to organize her life so that it was as serene and dependable as a water-wheel, each section dipping through experience and rising up again. So the familiar days went round and round with a sense of defined purpose: her patients came on their allotted days, she saw Reuben, she met friends, she taught chemistry to Chloë, she sat by her fire and read or drew little sketches with a soft pencil in her attic study. Olivia believed that order was a kind of prison that prevented you experiencing things, and that recklessness and chaos were expressions of freedom, but for Frieda, it was order that allowed you the freedom to think, to let thoughts into the space you had created for them, to find a proper name and shape for the ideas and feelings that were lifted up during the days, like silt and weeds, and by naming them, in some sense lay them to rest. Some things wouldn't rest. They were like muddy clouds in the water, stirring beneath the surface and filling her with unease.

Now there was Sandy. They ate and talked and slept together, and then Frieda went home without staying the night. They were starting, in a way that was complicated, disturbing and exciting, to get entangled with each other, finding out about each other, exploring each other, offering confidences. How far was she going to let him into her life? She tried to imagine it. Did she want to become a couple, wandering around like mountaineers who were tied together?

Last night Sandy had stayed at her house for the first time. Frieda didn't tell him that nobody else had stayed the night there since she'd bought it. They had seen a film, eaten a late meal in a little Italian restaurant in Soho, and then they had gone back to hers. After all, it was so close, it made sense, she had said, as if it was a casual decision not a momentous step. And now it was Sunday morning. Frieda had woken early, while it was still quite dark. For one moment, before she remembered, she had felt a jolt of alarm at seeing the figure beside her. She had eased herself out of bed, showered and then gone downstairs to light the fire and make herself a cup of coffee. It felt odd, dislocating, to have someone else there to start the day with. When would he go home? What if he didn't?

When Sandy came downstairs, Frieda was opening the bills and official correspondence that she always left to the weekend.

'Good morning!'

'Hi.' Her tone was abrupt and Sandy raised his eyebrows at her.

'I can go now,' he said. 'Or you can make me a cup of coffee and I'll go.'

Frieda looked up and smiled grudgingly. 'Sorry. I'll make you coffee. Or –'

'Yes?'

'Usually on Sunday mornings I go to this place round the corner for breakfast and the papers, and then go to the Columbia Road market to buy flowers, or just to look at them. You can come along, if you'd like.'

'Yes, I would.'

Frieda usually had the same breakfast on Sunday – a toasted cinnamon bagel and a cup of tea. Sandy ordered a bowl of porridge and a double espresso from Kerry, who was trying to keep a professional expression. When she caught Frieda's eyes she raised her eyebrows in approval, disregarding Frieda's scowl. But Number 9 was already filling up and neither Kerry nor Marcus had much time for them; only Katya was at a loose end, wandering between tables. Every so often, she stopped by Frieda and Sandy's and put her index finger into the bowl of sugar to suck.

There was always a stack of newspapers by the counter. Frieda collected several of them and put them in a pile between them. She had the sudden alarming sense that they had been transformed over the past few days into a settled couple – one who went to functions together, who spent the night together, who rose on Sunday morning to read the papers in companionable silence. She took a large bite of bagel and then a gulp of her tea. Was it such a bad thing?

This was often the only time during the week that Frieda read the papers from cover to cover, and for the past few weeks she had been so caught up by Sandy that perhaps she had let her world shrink to her work and to him. She said as much to him now. 'Although maybe it doesn't matter, to be cut off from what's happening in the world every so often. It's not as if I can do anything about it. Like not knowing if shares have risen by a point or not matters. Or –' she picked up one of the papers lying open and pointed to a headline '– that someone I don't know has done something terrible to someone else I don't know. Or a celebrity I haven't heard of has broken up with another celebrity I haven't heard of.'

'That's my guilty pleasure,' said Sandy. 'I . . . Hang on, what's up?'

Frieda wasn't paying attention. She was suddenly absorbed in a news story she was reading.

Sandy leaned over and read the headline: 'Little Mattie Still Missing: Mum's Tearful Plea'. 'You must have heard about it. It's only just happened. It was all over the papers yesterday.'

'No,' murmured Frieda.

'Think of what the parents must be going through.'

Frieda looked at the photograph across three columns of a young boy with bright red hair and freckles, a lop-sided grin on his face, and his blue eyes looking sideways towards whoever was behind the camera. 'Friday,' she said.

'He'll probably be dead by now. I feel sorry for the poor bloody teacher who let him go. She's become a hate figure.'

Frieda didn't really hear what he was saying. She was scanning the story about Matthew Faraday who had slipped out of his Islington primary school unnoticed on Friday afternoon and been last seen going towards the sweetshop a hundred yards or so away. She picked up another paper and read the same story again, a bit more colourfully written, with a sidebar by a profiling expert. She picked up each paper in turn – it seemed every angle had been covered. There were pieces about the parents' agony, the police investigation, the primary school, the

99

reactions of the community, the safety of our children today.

'What a strange thing,' Frieda said, as if to herself.

It was raining and there weren't many people in the flower market. Frieda was glad of the rain. She liked the feel of it in her hair and she welcomed the street's emptiness. She and Sandy walked past stalls selling great bunches of flowers and plants. It was only the middle of November but already they were selling things for Christmas – cyclamen, sprigs of holly, hyacinths in ceramic bowls, wreaths for front doors and even bunches of mistletoe. Frieda ignored all of these. She loathed Christmas, and she loathed the run-up to Christmas, the frenzied shoppers, the tat in the shops, the lights that were put up too early in the streets, the Christmas songs that belted out from overheated shops day after day, the catalogues that poured through her door and into her bin, and above all the insistence on the value of family. Frieda did not value her family and they did not value Frieda. A great gulf lay between them, impassable.

The wind was flapping the awnings of the stalls. Frieda stopped to buy a large bunch of bronze chrysanthemums. Alan Dekker had dreamed of a son with red hair. Red-haired Matthew Faraday had vanished. Eerie, but meaningless. She pushed her face into the damp fragrance of the flowers and took a deep breath. End of story.

She couldn't help pondering it, though. And that night – a wild and windy night that clattered bin lids along streets, bent trees into strange shapes, sped clouds in dark masses through the skies – she insisted to Sandy that she needed to spend some time alone, and went for a walk, and found her feet took her to Islington, past the grand houses and civilized squares to the poorer pockets. It didn't take her long to get there, just fifteen minutes or so, and eventually she found herself standing looking at the bank of flowers already stacked up outside the primary school where Matthew had last been seen. Some of the flowers were already dying inside their cellophane wrappers and she caught a sweet whiff of decay.

Whales are not fish. Spiders have eight legs. Butterflies come from caterpillars and frogs come from tadpoles and tadpoles come from the thick dotted jelly Mrs Hyde sometimes has in a jam jar at school. Two and two makes four. Two and two makes four. Two and two makes four. He didn't know what happened next. He couldn't remember. Mummy will come soon. If he squeezed his eyes tight shut and counted to ten, very slowly – one hippopotamus, two hippopotamus – when he opened them again, she would be there.

He closed his eyes very tightly and counted, then opened them. It was still dark. She was cross with him, that was it. It was a lesson. He'd gone outside without her tight warm hand. She said never do that, do you promise, Matthew, and he'd promised. Cross my heart hope to die. He'd eaten the sweets. Never take food from a stranger, Matthew. It was a spell. Magic potions, they can change you into what you're not. Small, like an insect in the corner of the room, and then Mummy wouldn't see him; perhaps she would *step* on him. Or he had a different face, a different body, the body of a scary animal or a monster, but him trapped inside it. She would look at him and not understand that it was him, Matthew, her little muffin, her honey-bunch. But his eyes would be the same, wouldn't they? He would still be looking out of himself with his eyes. Or he would have to call and shout to tell her who he really was, but his mouth was stuck shut and all he could hear when he cried was an echoey humming in his head that was like one of those horns you hear when you're on a ferry-boat at sea, going on holidays with Mummy and Daddy. Lonely in the distance and a shiver of dread goes through you, though you don't know why, and you want to be hugged and safe because the world is wide and deep and full of surprises that make your heart too big inside your body.

He needed a wee. He concentrated on not needing a wee. He was too big to wet himself. People laughed and pointed and held their noses. Warm wet, then cool, then cold and stinging against his thigh and the thin, high smell at the back of his nose. His eyes were wet too, stinging wet. He couldn't wipe them. Mummy. Daddy. I am very sorry I did wrong. If you take me home now, I will be good. I promise.

Or he had been turned into a snake, because his arms weren't arms any more but part of his body, though he could wiggle his fingers, and his feet weren't feet any more but stuck together. Once upon a time, there was a little boy called Matthew who broke a promise and who ate a magic potion and was turned into a snake to punish him. Slithering on the floor. Wood under his cheek. He could feel it and he could smell it. If he wriggled, could he move like a snake? He bunched up his body and straightened it again and his body jerked across the floor. Suddenly his face met something cool and firm, with a curved point at the end. He lifted his head and nudged it but it didn't move. Then he stretched himself and laid his cheek on top of it, to see what it was. Once, in Hide and Seek, he had hidden in his parents' wardrobe. He had curled up in the darkness, giggling and a bit scared, just a tiny stripe of light between the double doors, and waited to be found. He could hear them in the house, looking in stupid places like behind curtains. He had put his head on something like this then. Now his wet cheek felt a coil of string and a knot.

The shoe pulled away and his head fell back on the floor with a thump. The shoe poked him in his side. Too hard. A small bright light went on and he rolled over so he was staring up at it and he couldn't see anything now except the piercing light. It exploded in his eyes and flowered inside his head, and around its throbbing centre the darkness was even darker.

The light went off. The shoe pushed him to one side. There was a sudden rectangle of grey in the blackness, then a click and the grey disappeared.

Chapter Fourteen

Frieda rang the bell on the familiar door. It made no sound and she couldn't tell whether it was broken or whether it was ringing deep within the house. She pushed the button again. Still no sound. She rapped the heavy knocker several times. She stepped back from the door and looked at the windows. There were no lights visible, no movement, no sign of any presence. Could he have gone away? She knocked again, more heavily this time, so that the door shook. She bent down and pushed the letterbox open. She peered through. There were letters on the mat. She was about to leave when she heard something from inside. She knocked again. Now there was definite movement. She heard footsteps approaching, a rattling, the sound of a bolt being pulled and then the door opened.

Reuben narrowed his eyes, as if even the grey of a cloudy November morning was too much for him. He was dressed in a pair of grubby jeans and a partially unbuttoned shirt. It wasn't immediately clear that he recognized Frieda. He seemed puzzled and confused. Frieda could smell alcohol and tobacco and sweat. He had clearly spent at least one night in his clothes.

'What's the time?' he said.

'Quarter past nine,' said Frieda.

'Morning or night?'

'It looks like daytime to me.'

'Ingrid's gone,' said Reuben.

'Where?'

'She's left me. She left and she said she's not coming back. She wouldn't tell me where she was going.'

'I didn't know. Can I come in?'

'Better not.'

Frieda pushed her way past him. She hadn't been to the house for more than a year and it had an abandoned look to it. A window was cracked, a light fitting had come off the ceiling and bare wires were exposed. She looked around and found a phone under a newspaper in the hall. She took a scrap of paper from her pocket and dialled the number on it. After a brief conversation, she rang off.

'Where does the phone live?'

'Anywhere,' said Reuben. 'I can never find it.'

'I'll make you some coffee.'

As Frieda entered Reuben's kitchen, she had to hold her hand over her mouth to stop herself retching at the smell. She looked at the wreckage of dirty plates, pans, glasses, boxes and wrappings of half-finished takeaway meals.

'I wasn't expecting company,' said Reuben. His tone was almost defiant, like that of a child who had smashed up his toys. 'Needs a woman's touch. This is better than upstairs.'

Frieda felt an impulse just to flee the horrible scene and leave him to it. Hadn't Reuben said something like that to her years ago? 'You've got to let them make their own mistakes. All you can do is to follow and make sure they don't scare the horses or get arrested or damage anyone apart from themselves.' She couldn't do it. There was no question of clearing up, but she decided she could make at least some sort of pathway through the squalor. She pushed Reuben into a chair where he sat, rubbing his face and muttering. She put the kettle on. Scattered around the kitchen were various half-full and quarter-full bottles: whisky, Cinzano Bianco, wine, Drambuie. She tipped them all down the sink. She found a bin-bag and filled it with old scraps of food. At least that showed he hadn't only been drinking. She piled crockery in the sink and then, when it was full, around the sink. She opened cupboards and found a jar of instant coffee somewhere high up and forgotten. It hadn't been opened. She used the end of a spoon to tear open the paper covering the top of the jar. She washed up two mugs and made them each a hot black coffee. Reuben looked at it, gave a groan and shook his head. Frieda lifted the mug towards his mouth. He took a couple of sips and gave another groan. 'Burned my tongue.'

Still she held the mug, tipping it into his mouth, encouraging him, until half of it was gone.

'Come to gloat, have you?' Reuben said. 'This is where I've come to. This is where Reuben McGill has ended up. Or are you going to offer condolences? Are you going to say how very, very sorry you are? Or are you going to give me a lecture?'

Frieda lifted her coffee mug, looked at it and put it back on the table. 'I came to ask you for advice,' she said.

'That's a laugh,' said Reuben. 'Look around you. You think I'm in any kind of position to be dispensing advice?'

'Alan Dekker,' said Frieda. 'The patient I took over from you. Remember him?'

'Took over from? You mean the one you had me removed from. The one that involved me getting suspended from my own clinic. That one. The problem is, I don't remember very much about him because my own old student, my protégée, had me booted off the case. So what's the problem? Has he complained about you as well?'

'The problem is, he's got under my skin.'

'Has he now?'

'The last couple of days I've not been sleeping properly.'

'You never did sleep properly.'

'But it was the dreams I've been having. I feel like I've been infected by him. I wondered if you'd felt anything about him. I thought that might have been why it went wrong between you and him.'

Reuben took a gulp of coffee. 'Christ, I hate this stuff,' he said. 'You remember Dr Schoenbaum?'

'He was one of your trainers, wasn't he?'

'That's right. He was analysed by Richard Steiner. And Richard Steiner was analysed by Thomas Bayer and Thomas Bayer was analysed by Sigmund Freud. Schoenbaum was like my hotline to God and he taught me that when you were an analyst you weren't a human being. You were more like a totem pole.'

'A totem pole?'

'You were just there. And if your patient comes in and tells you his wife just died, you don't even offer your condolences. You analyse why he feels the need to tell you that. Schoenbaum was brilliant and he was charismatic and I thought: Fuck that. With my patients I was going to be everything that he wasn't. I was going to hold the

patient's hand, and in our little room I would do everything they did and go everywhere they went and feel
everything they felt.' Reuben leaned across the table
towards Frieda and she could see his eyes close up, yel-
lowy, red-veined in the corners. His breath was sour,
reeking of coffee and alcohol and rubbishy food. 'You
wouldn't believe where I've gone. You wouldn't believe
the shit that flows through the human brain, and I've
walked through it up to my neck. Men have told me things
about children and women have told me things about
their fathers and their uncles, and I don't know why they
didn't just go out of the room and blow their fucking
brains out, and I thought if I went on the journey with
them, if I showed them that they weren't alone, that someone could share it, then maybe they could come back and
make something of their lives. And you know what? After
thirty years of it, I've had it. You know what Ingrid said to
me? She said I was pathetic and that I was drinking too
much and that I had become boring.'

'You did help people,' said Frieda.

'You reckon?' said Reuben. 'They'd probably have done
just as well if they'd taken a few pills or done a bit of exercise or just done nothing. Anyway, I don't know what it
did for them, but it didn't do me any fucking good. Just
look around. This is what it looks like when you let these
people inside your head. So if you came here wanting
some advice, I'll give you some: if a patient starts getting
to you, give them to someone else. You won't help them
and you won't help yourself. There. You can go now.'

'It's not that I've let him get to me, not in the way you
mean. It's just – well, curious. He's curious.'

'What do you mean?'

Frieda told him about her sessions with Alan, and about the startled feeling she had had when she opened the paper and read about Matthew. Reuben didn't interrupt. For a moment, Frieda almost forgot where she was. The years rolled away and she was a student again, articulating her fears to her mentor Reuben. He knew how to listen, when he tried; he leaned slightly forward and his eyes didn't leave her face.

'There,' she said at the end. 'Do you see what I mean?'

'Do you remember that patient you had years ago – what was her name? Melody or something.'

'Melanie, you mean?'

'That's it. She was a classic somatizing patient. Irritable bowel syndrome, spells of dizziness and fainting, you name it.'

'And?'

'Her anxieties and repressions were embodied in her physical symptoms. She couldn't admit them, but her body found a way of expressing them.'

'So you think . . .'

'People are very strange and their minds are stranger. Look at that woman who had an allergy to the twentieth century. What was that about? I'm suggesting that Alan is doing something of the same thing. Panic can be free-floating, you know, attaching itself to whatever comes along.'

'Yes,' said Frieda, slowly. 'But he thought about a red-haired child before Matthew disappeared.'

'Hmm. Well, it was a good theory. In fact, it's still a good theory – it just applies to you instead of your patient.'

'Ingenious.'

'I'm half serious – you're anxious about Alan, you can't get to the bottom of him. So you're attaching his fantasy son to a convenient symbol.'

'A snatched child is hardly a symbol.'

'Why not? Everything is a symbol.'

'Rubbish,' said Frieda, but she laughed. Her mood had lifted. 'What about you?'

'Oh, OK,' said Reuben. 'It's your turn to give advice. Here I am. No woman. No job. I've been drinking gin out of coffee cups. What do you recommend, Doctor? Is it all to do with my mother?'

Frieda looked around. 'I think you should tidy up,' she said.

'You're a behaviourist, are you?' asked Reuben, sarcastically.

'I just don't like mess. You'd feel better.'

Reuben slapped his head so hard that Frieda flinched. 'There's no point in clearing up out here if you're fucked up in *here*,' he said.

'At least you'll be fucked up in a tidy house.'

'You sound like my mother.'

'I liked your mother.'

There was a loud knock at the door.

'Who the fuck can that be?' said Reuben, irritably. He shuffled out of the room. Frieda took her mug of coffee and poured it over the dishes in the sink. Reuben came back into the kitchen. 'There's some guy asking for you,' he said.

He was followed by Josef.

'That was quick,' said Frieda.

'Is he a cleaner?' said Reuben.

'I am a builder,' said Josef. 'You have had a party?'

'What's he doing here?'

'I asked him to come,' said Frieda. 'As a favour. For which you will pay. So be polite. Josef, I wondered if you'd fix about five things here. Like the doorbell and a broken window and there's a light that's come off the wall.'

'The boiler doesn't work properly,' said Reuben.

Josef looked around. 'Your wife is gone?' he said.

'She's not my wife,' said Reuben. 'And yes. As you can see. I did this all by myself.'

'I am so sorry,' said Josef.

'I don't need your sympathy,' said Reuben.

'Yes, you do,' said Frieda. She touched Josef's shoulder lightly with her hand. 'Thank you. And you're right. Talking isn't always enough.'

Josef inclined his head in his characteristic courtly gesture of acknowledgement.

Chapter Fifteen

'Frieda?'

'Sorry.'

'You're miles away. What were you thinking about?'

Frieda hated it when people asked her that. 'Nothing much,' she said. 'The day ahead. Work stuff.' She had slept so badly that her eyes stung. Now she felt brittle and on edge and she didn't want to make conversation with Sandy, who had slept beside her, murmuring things in his dreams she couldn't make out.

'There are things we should talk about.'

'Things?'

'Yes.'

'Is this the how-many-men-have-I-slept-with conversation?'

'No. We can save that for later, when we've got enough time. I want to talk about our plans.'

'What am I doing this summer, you mean? I should warn you that I hate flying. And sunbathing on beaches.'

'Stop it.'

'Sorry. Ignore me. It's seven thirty in the morning and I've been awake most of the night with my brain fizzing. The only plans I can make right now are ones for the next eight hours.'

'Come to mine tonight. I'll cook us something simple and we can talk.'

'That sounds ominous.'

'It's not.'

'I have a patient at seven.'

'Come after that.'

Frieda never took notes during a session; she did that afterwards, then wrote them up on the computer in the evenings or at weekends. But she occasionally made drawings or simple doodles on the pad of paper she kept at hand. It helped her to concentrate her thoughts. She did that now, sitting in the repaired room, newly painted a colour called 'Bone', to Josef's obvious disapproval. She loosely sketched Alan's left hand, which rested, for the moment, on the arm of his chair. Hands were difficult. His had a thick gold band on his wedding finger, chewed skin round his thumbnail, prominent veins. His index finger was longer than his wedding-ring finger; that was supposed to mean something but she couldn't remember what. Today he was more than usually restless, twisting in his seat, sitting forward, then shifting backwards, rubbing the side of his nose. She noticed a rash had broken out on his neck and there was a toothpaste stain on his shirt. He was talking, very fast, about the son he wanted. Words that had been forbidden and jammed inside him for so many years now spilled out. She drew in the knuckle of his little finger and listened very carefully, trying to quell the unease prickling through her, raising goose pimples on her skin.

'Being called Dad,' he was saying now. 'Having him trust me. Never letting him down. He plays football and likes board games. He likes being read to at night, books about dinosaurs and trains.'

'You're making it sound like he exists.'

'Is that a problem?'

'You're missing something so badly that you're making it come true in your mind.'

Alan rubbed his hands all over his tired face, as though he was washing it thoroughly. 'I want to tell someone,' he said. 'I want to be able to speak it out loud. It's like when I fell in love with Carrie. I'd had girlfriends before, of course, but nothing that felt like that. I felt freed from myself.' He looked at Frieda and she stored away the phrase for later. 'Those first few months, I just wanted to say her name out loud to anyone. I'd find ways of getting her into the conversation. "My girlfriend Carrie," I'd say. It made it feel real when I said it to someone else. It's a bit like that now, as if I just have to say it to someone because that eases this pressure inside me a bit. If that makes sense.'

'It does. But I'm not here to make what isn't real seem real, Alan,' said Frieda.

'You said everyone needs to make a story out of their lives.'

'So what do you want to do about this story?'

'Carrie says we can adopt. I don't want to. I don't want to fill out forms and have people decide if I'm fit to be a parent. I want *my* son, not someone else's. Look.' Alan took his wallet out of his jacket pocket. 'I want to show you something.'

He pulled out an old photograph. 'Here. This is what I imagine my son to look like.'

Frieda took it reluctantly. For a moment, she couldn't speak.

'Is this you?' she asked eventually, staring at the slightly chubby little boy in blue shorts standing by a tree, a football under one arm.

'Me when I was about five or six.'

'I see.'

'What do you see?'

'You had very red hair.'

'It started going grey before I was thirty.'

Red hair, glasses, freckles. A shiver of disquiet ran through her and this time she voiced it. 'You look very like the little boy who's gone missing.'

'I know. Of course I know. He's my dream.'

Alan looked at her and tried to smile. A single tear ran down his face, into his smiling mouth.

He mustn't eat anything. He knew that. It was all right to drink water, warm stale water from a bottle, but he mustn't eat. If he ate, he wouldn't be able to go home ever. He would be stuck here. Hard fingers forced open his mouth. Things were pushed inside him and he spat them out. Once some peas went down and he coughed and choked to make them come back again but he could feel them going down. Did a few peas count? He didn't know the rules. He had tried to bite the hand and the hand had hit him and he had cried and the hand had hit him again.

He was a dirty boy. His trousers went stiff with his wee and they smelt bad and yesterday night he had done a poo in the corner. He couldn't help it. His tummy had burned so badly he'd thought he was going to die. He was turning into liquid and fire. Everything was runny inside him. Hot and shivery. Everything hurt and felt wrong. He was clean now, though. Scrubbing brush and scalding water. Pink sore skin. Bristles on his teeth and against his gums. One of his teeth was wobbly. The tooth fairy would come. If he stayed awake, he could see her and tell her to save him. But if he stayed awake, she wouldn't come. He knew that.

And something nasty on his hair. Black and gluey and with a strong smell, like when you walk past men working on the roads with drills that make a heavy thumping sound that gets inside your head. His hair felt strange now. He was turning into someone else. If there was a mirror, he would see someone else in it. Who would he see? Someone with a glaring, wicked face. Soon it would be too late. He didn't know the words to say to turn the spell around again.

Bare boards. Nasty cracking green walls. Blind tied down on the window. One bulb hanging from the ceiling with a frayed cord. A white radiator that burned his skin if he touched it and made groaning sounds in the night, like an animal that was dying on the road. A white plastic potty, cracked. It made him feel ashamed to look at it. Mattress on the floor with dark stains on it. One stain was a dragon and one stain was a country but he didn't know which country. One stain was a face with a beaky nose and he thought it was a witch's face, and one stain was from him. There was a door but it didn't open for him. Even if he had hands to use, and even if it opened, Matthew knew he wouldn't be able to go through it. There were things on the other side that would get him.

Detective Constable Yvette Long looked around the Faradays' living room. There were toys scattered about: a large red plastic bus and several little cars on the rug, reading books and picture books, a monkey glove puppet. On the coffee-table, there was a large pad of lined paper with Matthew's attempts at writing – painstaking, lopsided letters in red felt tip, the Bs and Ds reversed. Andrea Faraday sat opposite her. Her long red hair was tangled and greasy and her face puffy from crying. It seemed to Yvette Long that she'd been crying solidly for days.

'What else can I tell you?' she said. 'There's nothing to say. Nothing. I don't know anything. Do you think I wouldn't tell you? I go over and over everything.'

'Can you think of anything that seems suspicious, any strange person hanging around?'

'No! Nothing. If I hadn't been late – oh, God, if I hadn't been late. Please get him back. My little boy. He still wets his bed at night sometimes.'

'I know how painful this is. We're doing everything we can. In the meantime . . .'

'They won't know anything about him. He's allergic to nuts. What if they give him nuts?'

DC Long tried to keep her face calm and put a hand on Andrea's arm. 'Try to think of anything that might help.'

'He's just a baby, really. He'll be crying out for me and I can't come to him. Do you understand what that feels like? I missed the bus and I was late.'

Jack had taken Frieda's advice. Today he was wearing black trousers, a pale blue shirt, only the top button undone, and a grey woollen jacket whose pockets, Frieda saw, were still sewn up. His shoes were cheap-looking, shiny black brogues; they probably still had the price sticker on the soles. He had even brushed his hair away from his face and shaved, though he'd missed a patch under his jaw. He no longer looked like a dishevelled student but a trainee accountant, or maybe a new recruit to a religious cult. Jack referred to his notebook and talked about his cases. It was a desultory process. Frieda was finding it hard to concentrate. She looked at her watch. They were done. She nodded at Jack, and then she asked: 'Imagine that a patient confesses to a crime. What do you do?'

Jack sat up a bit straighter. He looked suspicious. Was Frieda trying to catch him out in some way? 'What sort of crime? Speeding? Shoplifting?'

'Something really serious. Like murder.'

'Nothing goes beyond the room,' Jack said doubtfully. 'Isn't that what we promise?'

'You're not a priest in a confessional,' said Frieda, with a laugh. 'You're a citizen. If someone confesses to a murder, you call the police.'

Jack's face turned red. He'd failed the test.

'But now then: what if you *suspect* a patient of committing a crime?'

Jack hesitated. He chewed the tip of his thumb.

'I'm not looking for wrong or right answers.'

'How do you suspect them?' he said at last. 'I mean, do you just have a gut feeling? You can't just go to the police on a gut feeling, can you? Gut feelings are often completely wrong.'

'I don't know.' Frieda was talking to herself rather than to him. 'I don't really know what that means.'

'The thing is,' said Jack, 'if I let myself, I could suspect lots of people of being criminals. I saw a man yesterday who said things that were completely gross. I felt poisoned just listening to him. I kept thinking of what you said to me once about the difference between imagining and doing.'

Frieda nodded at him. 'That's right.'

'And you're always telling us that our job is not to deal with the mess in the outside world but the mess in the person's head.' He paused. 'This is one of your patients, isn't it?'

'Not exactly. Or maybe.'

'The easiest thing would be just to ask him.'

Frieda looked at him and smiled. 'Is that what you'd do?'

'Me? No. I'd come to you and do what you told me.'

Frieda walked to the Barbican after her patient left, so she didn't get there until half past eight. It was raining, at first just a slight drizzle but by the time she arrived it had turned into a downpour, so that puddles formed on the pavement and cars driving past sent up shining arcs of water from their wheels.

'Let me get you a towel,' Sandy said, when he saw her. 'And one of my shirts.'

'Thanks.'

'Why didn't you take a cab?'

'I needed to walk.'

He found her a soft white shirt, pulled off her shoes and tights and dried her feet, towelled her hair. She curled up on the sofa and he handed her a glass of wine. Inside the flat it was warm and bright; outside, the night was wild and wet, and the lights of London glimmered and dissolved.

'This is nice,' she said. 'What can I smell?'

'Garlic prawns with rice and a green salad. Is that all right?'

'Better than all right. I'm not really a cook myself.'

'I can live with that.'

'That's good to know.'

They ate sitting at the small table. Sandy lit a candle. He was wearing a dark blue shirt and jeans. He looked at her with an intensity that unnerved her. She was used to her students and her patients being curious about her but this was different.

'Why don't I know anything about your past?'

'Is this the serious talk?'

'Not exactly. But you withhold.'

'Do I?'

'I feel you know far more about me than I know about you.'

'It takes time.'

'I know it does. And we have time, don't we?'

She held his gaze. 'I think so, yes.'

'This has taken me by surprise,' he said.

'That's the way of love.' The word slipped out before she could check herself; it must have been the wine.

Sandy put his hand over hers. He looked suddenly serious. 'There *is* something I've got to say.'

'You're not going to tell me you're married?'

He smiled. 'No,' he said. 'Not that. I've been offered a new job.'

'Oh.' Relief flooded through her. 'I thought you were about to say something terrible. But that's good, isn't it? What job?'

'A full professorship.'

'Sandy, that's fantastic.'

'At Cornell.'

Frieda put her knife and fork neatly together and pushed her plate away from her. She put her elbows on the table. 'Which is in New York.'

'Yes,' said Sandy. 'That one.'

'So you're moving to the States.'

'That's the plan.'

'Oh.' She suddenly felt cold, and very sober. 'When did you say yes?'

'A few weeks ago.'

'So you've known all along.'

He turned his face away from her. He looked both embarrassed and irritated at being embarrassed. 'When I got the job, I hadn't even met you.'

Frieda picked up her glass and took a sip of wine. It tasted sour. It was as if the light had changed and everything looked different.

'Come with me,' he said.

'Like a good woman should.'

'You've got contacts. You can work there just as well as here. We could both begin again, together.'

'I don't want to begin again.'

'I know I should have told you.'

'I let my guard down,' said Frieda. 'I let you into my house, into my life. I told you things I haven't told anyone else. You were planning this all the time.'

'With *you*.'

'You can't make plans for me. You knew something about us that I didn't know.'

'I didn't want to lose you.'

'When are you going?'

'New Year. In a few weeks. I've sold the flat. I've found somewhere in Ithaca.'

'You *have* been busy.' She heard her voice, cool, bitter and controlled. She wasn't sure she liked the sound of it. Really she was feeling hot and weak with distress.

'I didn't know what to do,' he said. 'Please, my beloved Frieda, come with me. Join me.'

'You're asking me to give everything up here and start again in America?'

'Yes.'

'How about if I ask you to give up your professorship there and stay with me here?'

He got up and walked to the window, his back to her. He looked out for a few seconds, then turned round. 'I wouldn't,' he said. 'I can't.'

'So?' said Frieda.

'Marry me.'

'Fuck off.'

'I'm proposing to you, not insulting you.'

'I should just go.'

'You haven't given me an answer.'

'Are you serious?' said Frieda. She felt as if the alcohol had hit her hard.

'Yes.'

'I have to think about it on my own.'

'You mean, you might say yes?'

'I'll tell you tomorrow.'

Chapter Sixteen

When Tanner opened his front door he looked surprised. Detective Chief Inspector Malcolm Karlsson introduced himself.

'My assistant talked to you,' said Karlsson.

Tanner nodded and led him through into a dingy front room. It was cold. Tanner got on his knees and fiddled with an electric bar heater that had been placed in the hearth. As he fussed around making tea and serving it, Karlsson looked around the room and remembered going out with his grandparents when he was a child to see their friends, or vaguely distant relations. Even thirty years later the memory gave off a smell of dullness and duty.

'I'm doing your old job,' said Karlsson, thinking as he said it that it seemed like a rebuke. Tanner didn't look like a detective. He didn't even look like a retired detective. He was wearing an old cardigan and shiny grey trousers and he had shaved himself clumsily, leaving patches of stubble.

Tanner poured tea into two different-sized mugs and handed the large one across. 'I never planned to stay in Kensal Rise,' he said. 'When I took early retirement, we were going to move to the coast. Somewhere away to the east, like Clacton or Frinton. We started to get brochures. Then my wife got ill. It all became a bit too complicated. She's upstairs. You'll probably hear her shout for me.'

'I'm sorry,' said Karlsson.

'It's meant to be the men who get ill straight after retiring. But I'm fine. Just knackered.'

'I spent a few days looking after my mum when she had an operation,' said Karlsson. 'It was harder than being a copper.'

'You don't sound like a copper,' said Tanner.

'What do I sound like?'

'Different. I guess you went to university.'

'I did, yes. Does that stop me being one of the lads?'

'Probably. What did you study?'

'Law.'

'Well, that's a bloody waste of time.'

Karlsson took a sip of his tea. He could see little spots of milk floating around on the surface and there was a slight sour taste.

'I know why you're here,' said Tanner.

'We're looking for a missing kid. We drew up some parameters. Age of child, time of day, type of location, means, opportunity, and a name popped up on our computer. Just one. Joanna Vine. Or is it Jo?'

'Joanna.'

'My one's called Matthew Faraday. The papers call him Mattie. I suppose it fits better into a headline. Little Mattie. But his name is Matthew.'

'She disappeared twenty years ago.'

'Twenty-two.'

'And Joanna was taken in Camberwell. This little boy was in Hackney, right?'

'You've been following the story.'

'You can't avoid it.'

124

'True. Go on, then.'

'Joanna was in summer. This was winter.'

'So you're not convinced?'

Tanner thought for a moment before he replied, and he started to look a little more like the senior detective he had been. When he spoke, he counted points off on his fingers. 'Convinced?' he said. 'Girl, boy. North London, south London. Summer, winter. And then there's a gap of twenty-two years. What's that all about? He snatches a child, waits half a lifetime, then takes another. But you think they're connected. Is there some clue you haven't told the press?'

'No,' said Karlsson. 'You're right. There's no obvious reason at all. I approached it from the other direction. Thousands of children go missing every year. But once you eliminate the teenage runaways, the ones taken by other family members, the accidents, then already we're down to a very small number. How many children are killed by a stranger every year? Four or five?'

'Something like that.'

'Suddenly these two disappearances look like each other. You know how difficult it is to take a child. You need to get the child without a fuss, avoid being seen and then . . . what? Dispose of the body so that it's never found or send them abroad or I don't know what.'

'Have the press got on to this theory of yours?'

'No. And I'm not going to help them.'

'It's not a fact,' said Tanner. 'You can't base the whole inquiry on it. That was our problem. We were sure it was the family. Because that's what the numbers tell you. It's always the family. If the parents are separated it's the father, or an uncle. The way I remember it, he didn't have a proper alibi at first, so we spent too much time on him.'

'Did he have a proper alibi?'

'Proper enough,' he said glumly. 'We thought it was just a matter of making him crack and hoping he hadn't killed his daughter already. Because that's what always happens. Except when it doesn't. But you don't need me to tell you all this. You've read the file.'

'I have. It took me a whole day and there was basically nothing there. I wanted to ask you if there was anything you hadn't put in the file. Suspicions, maybe. Instincts. Guesses.'

Tanner leaned back on the sofa. He was breathing deeply. 'Do you want me to say I'm haunted by the case? That it's why I took early retirement?'

'Is it true?'

'I could deal with the dead bodies. I could even deal with the people walking free that I knew had done it. I could deal with their solicitor standing next to them on the pavement talking about his client being vindicated and grateful to the jury for seeing sense. In the end it was just the paperwork and the targets. In the end I just couldn't be doing with it.'

'Joanna Vine,' said Karlsson, gently. 'What happened with the inquiry?'

'Nothing. Nothing at all. I'll tell you what it was like. I've got this cupboard door in the kitchen and it doesn't have a handle. To open it you have to push your finger-nails into the crack and just get a bit of purchase on it and ease it open. The Joanna Vine inquiry was like going through the motions. We set up an office and we took hundreds of statements and we wrote reports and we gave press conferences and we had meetings about our progress. But there wasn't a single actual piece of evidence. There was nothing you could push your fingernails into and ease away at.'

'So what happened?'

'We needed smaller rooms for the press conferences. We ran out of things to do. Suddenly it was a year later. Nothing else had happened. Nobody had cracked.'

'What did you think?'

'Think? I just told you what I thought.'

'I mean, how did it smell to you? What was your guess?'

Tanner gave a sour laugh. 'I couldn't work it out. After a couple of days, I thought we'd find her in a ditch or a canal or a shallow grave. With these sick bastards it's usually an impulse thing. Then they just try and get rid of the evidence of what they've done. This didn't feel like that, but I didn't know what it did feel like. There was just nothing. How do you analyse nothing? Maybe he – or she – just buried her in the right place. So how's *your* inquiry going?'

'It reminds me of yours. For a few hours we hoped he'd turn up, that he'd got lost or hidden in a cupboard or stayed with a friend. We interviewed the parents. They're not separated. We talked to an aunt. The wife's brother lives nearby. He's unemployed, drinks. We really leaned on him. And now we're waiting.'

'What about CCTV?'

'He's either clever or lucky. The camera at the school turned out on inspection not to be working. It's a closely guarded secret that about a quarter of cameras are either faulty or not switched on. But we know he walked away from school. There are a few cameras on shop fronts and next to a pub just before his home. He didn't show up on these, but I'm told they were poorly angled, so this was inconclusive. But the walk home passes along the side of a park that has no cameras at all.'

'Can't you check number-plates driving in and out of the area?'

'What? In and out of Hackney? This isn't a red-light district at two in the morning. We wouldn't know where to start.'

'Maybe you'll need to wait another twenty-odd years.'

Karlsson stood up. He took a card from his wallet and handed it to Tanner, who looked wryly amused. 'You know what I'm going to say,' said Karlsson. 'But if there's anything, anything at all, just give me a ring.'

'It's not a good feeling, is it?' said Tanner. 'When you need to come and talk to people like me?'

'It was helpful,' said Karlsson. 'I'm almost glad that it was as bad for you as it's been for me.'

They walked together to the door.

'I'm sorry about your wife,' said Karlsson. 'Is she getting better?'

'Worse,' said Tanner. 'It'll take a long time, the doctor says. You need a cab?'

'My driver's outside.'

Karlsson stepped out and then thought of something, something he hadn't meant to say. 'I dream about him,' he said. 'I can't remember the dreams when I wake up but I know they're about him.'

'I did as well,' said Tanner. 'I used to try a couple of drinks before I went to sleep. That helped sometimes.'

'I missed you last night,' Sandy said.

Frieda looked around the kitchen. It already seemed like foreign territory.

'I was just having breakfast. Do you want . . .'

'No, thank you.'

'At least it's not raining any longer. You look lovely. Is that a new jacket?'

'No.'

'I'm gabbling like an idiot. I'm sorry about last night. I'm sorry. You were right to be angry.'

'I'm not angry any more.'

'No,' said Sandy. 'Because you've decided not to come with me. Is that right?'

'I can't leave everything,' she said. 'Even to be with you.'

'But aren't you scared of losing what we have?'

She hadn't meant it to happen, but somehow they were kissing each other, and then he was peeling off her jacket, her shirt, and they were stumbling on to the sofa together, his mouth against hers, her hands on his naked back, pulling him closer for the last time. He called out her name, over and over again, and she knew that she would wake in the night and hear that cry.

Afterwards, she said, 'That was a mistake.'

'Not for me. I don't leave until after Christmas. Let's spend that time together. Try to work things out.'

'No. I don't do long goodbyes.'

'How can you bear to leave, after that?'

''Bye, Sandy.'

After she had gone, he stood by his window and looked down at the square she would come out on to. And after a few minutes there she was, a slim and upright figure making her way swiftly towards the road. She didn't look up.

Chapter Seventeen

'The boss is going to be spitting mad,' said DC Foreman, gloomily.

There were several of them in the operations room, although Karlsson was out and not expected until later. They were thumbing through the morning's papers, where the Matthew fever showed no sign of abating. In one tabloid, there were nine pages given over to him – several photographs of him, interviews with people who knew him or claimed to know him, pieces about psychological profiling, a long feature about Matthew's home life. There were speculations about the state of the Faradays' marriage. Sources 'close to the heart of the operation' had said as much.

'Who the fuck was that, then?'

'They're flying kites. They know it's usually the dad or the step-dad.'

'He was miles away. There's no way he could be a suspect. Why would they print such a thing?'

'Why do you think? Matthew's money. I read somewhere that papers put on tens of thousands in circulation if they have front-page news about him. This could run and run.'

'Blood money.'

'Easy to say. Who here's been offered money yet?'

'What – for leaking information?'

'You will be. Just wait.'

'The boss is not going to be happy.'

'Nor his boss. I know for a fact that the commissioner is taking a very personal interest in the case.'

'Crawford's just a fucker.'

'A fucker who can make life pretty uncomfortable.'

'Karlsson's the real copper. If anyone can solve this case, he can.'

'Then it looks like no one can, doesn't it?'

Twenty-two years: but when Karlsson told Deborah Teale who he was he saw the hope in her eyes, and the fear as well. She put two fingers on her lower lip and leaned against the door jamb as if the earth was shifting under her.

'There really is no news about your daughter,' he said quickly.

'No, of course not,' she said. She gave a small, shaky laugh, pressing a hand against her chest. 'You said that when you called. It's just . . .' And she trailed to a halt because what was there to say, after all? It's just that . . . how do you stop waiting, how do you stop hoping and dreading? Karlsson couldn't stop himself thinking of what it must be like for her, even after all these years. The discovery of a little body in a ditch would be a relief to her. At least she would know, and there would be a grave where she could lay flowers.

'Could I come in?' he asked her, and she nodded and stood back to let him enter.

Everyone's house has a different smell. Tanner's had been musty, faintly rank, as if the windows hadn't been opened for months, an odour that caught in the back of your throat, like old flower water. Deborah Teale's house smelt of Flash and Ajax and polish and, under that, fried food. She led him into the front room, apologizing for mess that wasn't there. All round the room he saw photographs, but none of Joanna.

'I just wanted to ask you some questions.' He eased himself into a chair that was too low for him, trapping him in its softness.

'Questions? What's left to ask?'

Karlsson didn't know the answer to that. He found himself wondering why he was here, revisiting a tragedy that had almost certainly nothing to do with Matthew Faraday. He looked at the woman opposite him, her narrow face and thin shoulders. He had checked her in the file. She must be fifty-three now. Some people – for instance, his former wife's new boyfriend – spread and solidified into a comfortable version of themselves as they got older, but Deborah Teale looked as though the years had pressed down on her, rubbing away her youth and softness.

'I've been looking at the case again.'

'Why?'

'Because we never solved it,' he replied. It wasn't a lie but it wasn't the whole truth either.

'Joanna's dead,' Deborah Teale said. 'Oh, I keep on imagining that she might be out there somewhere, but really I know she's dead, and I'm sure you do too. She probably died the day we lost her. Why do you need to rake over old ground? If you find her body, then come and tell me. You won't find her killer now, will you?'

'I don't know.'

'You probably have to go through unsolved crimes every so often to satisfy some bureaucratic rule or other. But I've said everything there is to say. I've said it over and over again. Until I thought I'd go mad. Do you have any idea of what it feels like to lose a child?'

'No, I don't.'

'That's something,' she said. 'At least you're not telling me you know how I feel.'

'You described Joanna as an anxious little girl.'

'Yes.' Deborah Teale frowned at him.

'And she knew not to trust strangers?'

'Of course.'

'Yet she disappeared without a sound in the middle of the afternoon, on a busy street.'

'Yes. As if she'd been a dream.'

Or as if she trusted the person who took her, thought Karlsson.

'At some point, you have to tell yourself it's over. Do you see? You have to. I saw you looking at the photos when you came in. I know what you were thinking, of course: that there were none of Joanna. You probably thought that was a bit unhealthy.'

'Not at all,' said Karlsson, truthfully. He was a great believer in denial. In his experience, that was how people stayed sane.

'That's Rosie, and that's my husband, George. And my two younger children, Abbie and Lauren. I wept and I prayed and I mourned, and then at last I said goodbye and I moved on and I don't want to go back again. I owe it to my new family. Does that sound callous to you?'

'No.'

'It does to some people.' Her mouth twisted bitterly.

'You mean your ex-husband?'

'Richard thinks I'm a monster.'

'Do you still see him?'

'Is that what this is really about? You still think he did it?'

Karlsson looked at the woman opposite him, her gaunt face and her bright eyes. He liked her. 'I don't think anything, really. Except it hasn't been solved.'

'I gather his place is like a shrine. Saint Joanna amid the whisky bottles. I don't suppose that means anything, though.'

It didn't. In Karlsson's experience, murderers were often sentimental or narcissistic people. He could easily imagine a father murdering his daughter and then weeping over her with tears of drunken, maudlin self-pity.

'Do you ever see him now?'

'Not for years. Unlike poor Rosie. I try to persuade her to keep away from him but she somehow feels responsible for him. She's too kind-hearted for her own good. I wish –' She stopped.

'Yes?'

But she shook her head violently. 'I don't know what I was going to say. I just wish. You know.'

Richard Vine insisted on coming to the police station rather than seeing Karlsson at his flat. He had put on a suit, shiny with age and tight around his waist and chest, and a white shirt done up to the collar, constricting his Adam's apple. Above it his face looked pouchy and his eyes were faintly bloodshot. His hands trembled when he took the mug of coffee. He gulped at it.

'If there are no new clues, what's this about?'

'I'm reviewing the case,' Karlsson replied carefully. He wished that he was interviewing Richard Vine in his own home: you can tell a great deal from someone's surroundings, even when they try to prepare them in advance for visitors. He was probably ashamed to let strangers see it.

'You lot spent the whole investigation trying to get me to confess. Meanwhile the real bastard got away.' He paused, dragged the back of his hand across his mouth. 'Have you been to see her as well, or is it just me?'

Karlsson didn't answer. He felt oppressed by the grief and mess of the lives he was visiting. Why was he talking to this man? On a whim, baseless intuition; out of hopelessness and because he had no real clues. Matthew Faraday and Joanna Vine, two cases separated by twenty-two years and joined together by nothing more than the fact that they were the same age and had vanished without trace in the middle of the day, near a sweet shop.

'She's the one who lost her. She was supposed to be looking after her and she let a nine-year-old kid do it for her. And then she just gave up on her. Packed up her pictures and put them all in a box, moved house, married Mr Respectable, forgot about me and Joanna. *Life has to go on.* That's what she came to me and said. *Life has to go on.* Well, I'm not giving up on our daughter.'

Karlsson listened, his head propped on one hand and his pencil describing useless doodles over his opened notepad. It sounded like he'd said this too often, to whoever at the bar would listen to him.

'Would you describe Joanna as a trusting child?' he asked, just as he'd asked Deborah Teale.

'She was a little princess.'

'But did she trust people?'

'You can't trust anyone in this world. I should have told her that.'

'Would she have trusted a stranger?'

A strange expression came into Richard Vine's face, cautious and speculative. 'I don't know,' he said at last. 'Perhaps. Perhaps not. She was only five, for God's sake. It ruined my life, you know. One day things were going OK and then – well, it was like pulling on one of those bits of knitting that Rosie's always doing when she comes to see me. Everything simply comes undone and in just a few moments nothing's left to show anything was ever there.' He looked at Karlsson and for a second the detective saw in his face the man he had once been. 'That's why I can't forgive her. Things didn't unravel for her like they did for me. She should have suffered more. She didn't pay the right price.'

At the end of the interview, standing to leave, he said, 'If you see Rosie, tell her to come and see me. At least she hasn't deserted her old dad.'

The first punch missed his jaw and landed on his neck. The second was in his stomach. Even as he staggered back, putting his hands in front of his face, Alec Faraday was struck by how silent it all was. He could hear a plane in the sky above him and the traffic on the main road to his right – he thought he could even hear a radio playing in the distance – but the men didn't make a sound, except their breathing was heavy, almost like a grunt every time they landed a punch.

There were five of them. They had hoods up; one was wearing a balaclava. He fell to his knees and then to the ground, trying to ball himself up against their blows, trying to protect his face. He felt a boot hard against his ribs and another on his thigh. Someone hacked him viciously in the groin. Somewhere he heard something crack. His mouth was full of liquid, stuff he was spitting out. Pain was like a river gushing through him. He saw the frosty Tarmac glinting beneath him and then closed his eyes. There was no point in struggling. Didn't they understand that it would be a relief to be dead?

At last someone spoke. 'Fucking nonce.'

'Paedo bastard.'

There was a hawking sound and something wet landed on his neck. There was another blow but now it seemed to be happening to someone else. He heard steps receding.

He had eaten a bit of potato mush with gravy because he couldn't hold it in his mouth any longer, though he had spat out most of it and it was still on the floor, like sick. There was a chicken leg on the floor as well and it was smelling funny now. He had eaten some spaghetti hoops because he was crying and it just went down him and he couldn't help it. The room was full of the smell of rotting food and of his own body. He put his head down and sniffed his skin and it was sour. He licked at it and he didn't like the taste of himself.

But he had found out that if he stood on tiptoe on the

mattress and wiggled his head under the stiff blind, he could manage to get under it and then he could see out of the window. Just the bottom corner. All smeary and then clouded with his breath too. If he put his forehead against the glass, it was so cold it made him ache. He could see sky. Today it was blue and hard and made his eyeballs jump. There was a roof opposite that was white and glittering and it had a pigeon on it that was looking at him. If he strained, he could just see the road. It wasn't like the road where he lived when he was Matthew. Everything was broken. Everything was empty. Everyone had run away because they knew bad things were coming.

'I don't remember. I really can't remember. Don't you see? I don't know what I know myself and what I've been told since and what I made up to comfort myself and what I've dreamed about. Everything is muddled up. It's useless to ask me. I'm no help to you. I'm sorry.'

The woman opposite him was apologetic. Karlsson had seen photographs of Rosie Teale as a young child and now here she was at thirty-one. There is something strange about fast-forwarding to adulthood: her dark hair pulled tightly back from her thin, triangular face, bare of makeup; her dark eyes, which seemed too large for her face; the pale lips, slightly chapped; the bony, ringless hands that lay plaited in her lap. She looked both younger and older than her years and slightly malnourished, Karlsson thought. 'I know. You were nine years old. But I just wonder if there's anything, anything at all, that you've thought about since you were last interviewed by the police. Anything you saw or heard or – I don't know – smelt, sensed.

Anything. She was there and then she wasn't, and in those few seconds there must have been *something*.'

'I know. And sometimes I think . . .' She stopped.

'Yes?'

'I think I do know something, but I don't know I know it – if that doesn't sound stupid.'

'No, not at all.'

'But it's no good. I don't know what it is and the more I try to catch it the more it disappears. It's probably some illusion anyway. I'm trying to find something that was never there in the first place, just because I'm so desperate to find it. Or if it was ever there, it's long gone. My mind feels a bit like one of your crime scenes: at first I refused to visit it at all, I literally couldn't bear to, and then I went over it with muddy boots so many times that there's nothing left.'

'You'll tell me if anything does occur to you?'

'Of course.' Then she said, 'Is this anything to do with the little boy who's gone missing, Matthew Faraday?'

'Why do you ask?'

'Why else would you be here now, after all this time?'

Karlsson suddenly felt he ought to say something. 'You were only nine. No one in their right mind would ever blame you.'

She smiled at him. 'Then I'm not in my right mind.'

Chapter Eighteen

Karlsson was already in a bad mood when Yvette Long came into his office and told him there was a woman to see him. She looked nervously at the expression on her boss's face.

'How's Faraday?'

'Not well. Smashed jaw, broken ribs. You need to make a statement in about half an hour. The press are already waiting.'

'They did it,' Karlsson said. 'They stirred it up. What did they think would happen? I'm sure they're shocked. Any leads on who did it?'

'Nothing.'

'How's the wife?'

'About how you'd expect.'

'Who's with her now?'

'A couple of officers from Victim Support. I'm going back there later.'

'Good.'

'And the commissioner wants to see you once you've made your statement.'

'Not good.'

'Sorry.' For a moment, Yvette Long thought of putting a hand on his shoulder. He looked so tired.

'You know who I've just been talking to?'

'No.'

'Brian Munro.' Yvette Long looked blank. 'He's in charge of the CCTV footage.'

'Has he found anything?'

'He's found cars. Lots and lots of cars. Cars with one person in, cars with more than one person in. Cars with the number of persons undetermined. But, as he says, with nothing to cross-check against it's not even looking for a needle in a haystack. It's like looking for hay in a haystack.'

'You could cross-check it with known offenders. Or people on the sex offenders register.'

'Yes, that thought has occurred to us and Brian just spent a very long time telling me what a long and complicated process that is going to be. And I could make it a bit less long by putting people on it, people who could be knocking on doors and taking statements.'

'About this woman,' said Yvette Long.

'Who is she?'

'She says she wants to talk to you about the investigation.'

'Get someone from the office to have a word with her.'

'She said she wanted to talk to the officer in charge.'

Karlsson frowned. 'Why are you wasting my time with this?'

'She asked for you by name. It sounded as if she knew people.'

'I don't care if she . . .' Karlsson groaned. 'It'll be quicker just to see her. But she hasn't chosen the right day to waste my time. Who is she?'

'I don't know. She's a doctor.'

'A doctor? For God's sake, just bring her in.'

Karlsson kept a large notebook on his desk for writing notes, making lists, doodling. He turned it to a blank page. He picked up a pen and clicked it several times. The door opened and Yvette Long stepped halfway into the office. 'This is Dr Frieda Klein,' she said. 'She ... er ... she wouldn't say what it was about.'

The woman stepped past her and DC Long left the room, closing the door. Karlsson was slightly disconcerted. Normal people behaved oddly with the police. They became nervous or too eager to please. They felt as if they'd done something wrong. This woman was different. She looked around the office with apparent curiosity, and then, when she turned to him, he felt as if she was assessing him. She took off her long coat and tossed it on to a chair by the wall. She pulled another chair forward in front of his desk and sat on it. He had a sudden and very irritating feeling that *he* was the person who had come to see *her*.

'I'm Detective Chief Inspector Malcolm Karlsson,' he said.

'Yes, I know.'

'I understand that you have something you want to tell me personally.'

'That's right.'

Karlsson wrote the name 'Frieda Klein' on his notepad and drew a line under it.

'And it's relevant to the disappearance of Matthew Faraday?'

'It might be.'

'Then you'd better tell me, because we don't have much time.'

For a moment she looked awkward. 'I feel hesitant about saying this,' she said. 'Because I'm pretty sure you'll feel that I'm wasting your time.'

'If you're sure, then you should go away and not waste any more of it.'

For the first time, Frieda Klein looked directly at him with her large, dark eyes. 'I've got to,' she said. 'I've been thinking about it all week. I'll tell you and then I'll leave.'

'So tell me.'

'All right.' She took a deep breath. Karlsson thought for a moment of a little girl on a stage who was about to recite something. A deep breath before taking the big leap.

'I'm a consultant psychoanalyst,' she began. 'Do you know what that is?'

Karlsson smiled. 'I've picked up a bit of education here and there,' he said. 'Despite being a copper.'

'I know,' she said. 'You read law at Oxford. I checked.'

'I hope that makes me worthy of your respect.'

'I've started seeing a new patient. His name is Alan Dekker. He's forty-two years old. He came to see me because he has been suffering from severe and recurrent anxiety attacks.' She paused. 'I think you should talk to him.'

Karlsson wrote the name down. Alan Dekker. 'This is to do with the disappearance?' he asked.

'Yes,' she said.

'Has he confessed?'

'If he'd confessed, I would have dialled 999.'

'So?'

'Alan Dekker's anxiety is based on a fantasy about having a son – or about *not* having a son. This fantasy shows itself in a dream that seems to involve seizing a child in a way that struck me as similar to this boy's disappearance. And before you say that the dream may have been caused by hearing about it, he first had the dream before Matthew Faraday disappeared.'

'Anything else?' said Karlsson.

'I felt that Dekker's desire for a son was a narcissistic fantasy. That is, it was really about himself.'

'I know what "narcissistic" means.'

'But then I happened to see a photograph of my patient as a boy and it was very similar in certain ways – certain striking ways – to Matthew Faraday.'

Karlsson had stopped taking notes. He was just waggling the pen between two of his fingers. Now he pushed his chair back from the desk. 'The problem is that on the one hand we don't have the evidence we would like. Nobody saw Matthew being taken. Maybe he wasn't taken. Maybe he ran away and joined a circus. Maybe he fell down a manhole. On the other hand, we've got more help than we know what to do with. As of this morning, five people have confessed to taking him, none of whom could have done so. Since the TV show about him last week, we've had thirty thousand-odd calls to deal with. He's been spotted in different parts of the UK and in Spain and Greece. People have suspected their husbands, boyfriends, neighbours. His poor bloody father was beaten up last night because the tabloids don't like the look of him. I've been contacted by profilers who've told me that the perpetrator is a loner, who has difficulty in relating to others, or that it's a couple, or that it's a gang trading children on the Internet. I've heard from a medium, who tells me that Matthew is in an enclosed space some-where underground, which is useful, because it saves us looking in Piccadilly Circus. Meanwhile there are journalists writing that it all happened because we didn't have enough bobbies on the beat or cars on the road or functioning CCTV cameras. Or else that it's all the fault of the 1960s.'

'The sixties?' said Frieda.

'That's the explanation I like best, because it's about the only one that doesn't seem to be basically my fault. So you'll excuse me if I'm not automatically grateful for someone you think might be, in some unspecified way, linked to the crime. I'm extremely sorry, Dr Klein, but what you've told me doesn't sound much different from someone saying that their next-door neighbour's been spending a lot of time in his shed lately.'

'You're right,' said Frieda. 'That's what I would have said myself.'

'So why did you come and see me about it?'

'Because once the thought had entered my mind, I had to say something about it.'

Karlsson's expression hardened. 'You mean, to get it on the record?' he said. 'So that if something went wrong it would be my fault instead of yours?'

'Because it was the right thing to do.' Frieda stood up and reached over for her coat. 'I knew it was nothing. I just needed to be sure.'

Karlsson stood up and walked around his desk to lead her out. He felt he'd been too harsh with her. He'd taken the frustrations of a bad morning out on a woman who was just trying to be helpful. Even if uselessly. 'You can see it from my point of view,' he said. 'I can't go around interviewing people based on someone's dream. I know you're the analyst and I'm not, but people have these sorts of dreams all the time and they don't mean anything.'

At this it was her turn to speak sharply. 'I'm not going to take lessons from a detective about what dreams mean. If that's all right.'

'I was just saying –'

'Don't worry,' said Frieda. 'I'm not going to waste your time any more.' She started to pull her coat on. 'This wasn't just some little dream he'd been having for years, the way most anxiety dreams are. He'd had the dream a long time ago when he was a young man and now he'd suddenly had it again.'

Karlsson had been about to say goodbye, about to steer her out of the door, when he stopped. 'What do you mean "again"?' he said.

'You don't want to hear the details,' said Frieda. 'But before it had been a definite desire for a daughter and now it was a son. One of his worries was that there was something sexual about the change.'

'Change?' Frieda looked puzzled by Karlsson's expression. 'You're saying he had the dream before? A long time ago?'

'Does this matter?'

There was a pause.

'I'm just curious,' said Karlsson. 'For my own reasons. How old was he?'

'He was just out of his teens, he told me. Twenty or twenty-one. Well before he met his wife. Then, suddenly, the dreams stopped.'

'Take your coat off,' said Karlsson. 'Sit down. I mean, please. Sit down, please.'

With a slightly wary expression, Frieda laid her coat across the chair where it had been before and sat back down. 'I don't really see . . .' she began.

'Your patient, he's what? Forty-three?'

'Forty-two, I think.'

'So that previous dream would have been twenty-two years ago?'

'Something like that.'

Karlsson leaned back on the front of his desk. 'Let me get this straight. Twenty-two years ago, he has a dream about a little girl. Taking a little girl. Then nothing. And now he has a dream about taking a little boy.'

'That's right.'

Suddenly Karlsson's eyes narrowed in suspicion. 'You're being straight with me, right? You haven't spoken to anyone on the case. You haven't done your own research.'

'What are you talking about?'

'No one's put you up to this?'

'What?'

'I've had journalists coming in pretending to be witnesses, just to see what we've got. If this is some kind of wind-up, you should be aware that you'll face prosecution.'

'I was just putting on my coat and now I'm facing prosecution?'

'You don't know anything apart from the Matthew Faraday disappearance?'

'I don't read the papers that often. I hardly know anything about the Faraday case. Is there some problem?'

Karlsson rubbed his face almost as if he were trying to

148

wake himself up. 'Yes, there is a problem,' he said. 'The problem is that I don't know what to think.' He mumbled something that Frieda couldn't make out. It sounded as if he were arguing with himself, which was exactly what he was doing. 'I think I'm going to talk to that patient of yours.'

Chapter Nineteen

Frieda stepped into her house with a small sigh of relief, letting the shopping bag drop to the floor while she took off her coat and scarf. It was cold and dark outside, frost in the air and the sense of winter closing in, but inside was snug. There was a light on in the living room and the fire was laid ready; she lit it before going into the kitchen with the bag. Reuben always said that there were two types of cook: the artist and the scientist. He was clearly the artist, flamboyant with improvisations, and she was the scientist, exact and a bit fussy, following every recipe to the letter. A level teaspoon had to be level; if a recipe said red wine vinegar then nothing else would do; pastry dough had to be left in the fridge for the full hour. She very rarely cooked. Sandy had been the cook in their relationship and now . . . Well, she didn't want to think about Sandy because that hurt the way a toothache hurt, flaring up suddenly and taking her breath away with its electric sharpness. She just assembled ingredients on her plate and tried not to think of him with his pots and pans and wooden spoons, making meals for one. But today she was following a simple recipe that Chloë had inexplicably emailed her, with urgent instructions to try it, for a curried cauliflower and chickpea salad. She looked doubtfully at it.

She put on her apron, washed her hands, drew down the blinds, and was chopping the onion when her doorbell rang. There was nobody she was expecting and people didn't often turn up at her house unannounced, except young men with dodgy smiles selling dusters, twenty for a fiver. Perhaps it was Sandy. Did she want it to be? She quickly remembered it couldn't be. He had gone on the Eurostar to Paris this morning for a conference. She still knew those kinds of things about him and so she was able to imagine him in the life she had vacated. Soon enough that would change. He would do things she knew nothing about, see people she had never met or heard of, wear clothes she had never seen, read books he wouldn't discuss with her.

The doorbell rang again and she laid down the knife, rinsed her hands under cold water, and went to answer.

'Am I disturbing you?' asked Karlsson.

'Obviously.'

'It's a bit cold out here.'

Frieda stood back and let him walk into her hall. She noticed how he wiped his shoes – rather elegant black ones, with blue laces – on her mat before hanging his black coat, splattered with rain, next to hers.

'You were cooking.'

'Brilliant. I can see why you became a detective.'

'This will only take a minute of your time.'

She led him into her living room, where the fire was still feeble and lacking warmth. She crouched before it and carefully blew its flames before taking a seat opposite Karlsson and folding her hands carefully on her lap. He noticed how straight she sat, and she noticed that one of his front teeth was very slightly chipped. This surprised her: Karlsson seemed otherwise punctilious about his

151

appearance, almost dandyish: his soft charcoal-grey jacket, his white shirt, and a red tie so thin it was like an ironic stripe down his chest.

'Is it about Alan?' she said.

'I thought you would want to know.'

'Have you talked to him?'

She sat up straighter in her chair. Her expression didn't waver, and yet Karlsson had the impression that she was holding back a wince of anticipated distress. She was paler than the last time they had met, and tired as well. He thought she looked unhappy.

'Yes. His wife, too.'

'And?'

'He didn't have anything to do with the disappearance of Matthew Faraday.'

He could sense a release of tension.

'You're sure?'

'Matthew disappeared on Friday, November the thirteenth. I believe Mr Dekker was with you that afternoon?'

Frieda thought for a moment.

'Yes. He would have left at two fifty.'

'And his wife says that she met him shortly after that. They went home together. A neighbour came round just after they got back and stayed for a cup of tea. We checked.'

'So that's that,' Frieda said. She bit her lower lip, holding back the next question.

'They were shocked to be questioned,' he said.

'I imagine.'

'You're probably wondering what I told them.'

'It doesn't matter.'

'I said they were part of a routine inquiry.'

'What does that mean?'

'It's just one of those phrases.'

'I'll tell him myself.'

'I thought you might.' Karlsson stretched his legs out in front of the fire, which was crackling away now. He half wished Frieda would offer him a cup of tea or a glass of wine so that he could stay in this cocoon of dimly lit warmth, but she didn't seem about to do that. 'He's a curious man, isn't he? All jangled up. But nice. I liked his wife.'

Frieda shrugged. She didn't want to talk about him. She had probably done enough damage already. 'I'm sorry I wasted your time,' she said neutrally.

'Don't be sorry.' He raised his eyebrows at her: '"Dreams are often most profound when they seem most crazy."'

'You're quoting *Freud* at me?'

'Even coppers read sometimes.'

'I don't think dreams are profound. Usually I hate it when patients tell me their dreams as if they're some magic fable. But in this case –' She broke off. 'Well, I was wrong. And I'm glad.'

Karlsson stood up and she did too.

'I'll let you get back to your cooking.'

'Can I ask you one thing?'

'What?'

'Is this about Joanna Vine?'

Karlsson looked startled, then wary.

'Don't look so surprised. Twenty-two years ago. That was what made you jump. It took me five minutes online and I'm not even very good on a computer.'

'You're right,' he said. 'It seemed . . . I don't know, odd.'

'And that's the end of it?'

'Seems like it.' He hesitated. 'Can I ask *you* something now?'

'Go ahead.'

'As I'm sure you know, we live in an age where almost everything is contracted out.'

'I was aware of it.'

'You know the kind of thing, fewer staff on the books, even if it costs more in the end. Even we have to contract things out.'

'And what has this got to do with me?'

'I was wondering if you could give me a second opinion. We'd reimburse you, of course.'

'A second opinion on what?'

'Would you consider talking to the sister of Joanna Vine, who was nine when she went missing and who was with her when she vanished?'

Frieda looked speculatively at Karlsson. He seemed slightly embarrassed. 'Why me? You know nothing about me and you must have people of your own who do this kind of thing.'

'That's true, of course. To be honest, it's just a long shot. A whim.'

'A whim!' Frieda laughed. 'That doesn't sound very rational.'

'It's not rational. And you're right, I don't know you, but you made a connection –'

'A false connection, as it turns out.'

'Yes, well, that's as may be.'

'You must be desperate,' said Frieda, not unkindly.

'Most cases are pretty straightforward. You advance by routine investigation and you follow the rulebook. There's blood, there are fingerprints, there is DNA, there are images caught on CCTV, there are witnesses. It's all pretty obvious. But every so often you get a case where the rulebook just doesn't seem to apply. Matthew Faraday's disappeared into thin air, and there's nothing to follow. We're clueless. So now we have to take anything we're given – any rumour, any idea, any possible connection with another crime, however tenuous.'

'I still don't see what I can do that someone else can't.'

'Probably nothing at all. As I said, it's a long shot and I'll most likely get hauled over the coals for wasting public money on duplicating work unnecessarily. But maybe, just maybe, you have insight that others don't. And you're an outsider. Possibly you'll be able to see things we've become blind to because we've looked at them so hard and for so long.'

'This whim of yours . . .'

'Yes?'

'The sister.'

'Her name is Rose Teale. The mother remarried.'

'Did she see anything?'

'She says she didn't. But she just seems paralysed by guilt about it.'

'I don't know,' said Frieda.

'You mean, you don't know if it could be helpful?'

'It depends what you mean by helpful. When I hear that, what I want to do is deal with her guilt, help her move on. Do I think she's got a memory hidden somewhere that someone could find? I don't think memory really works as simply as that. Anyway, it's not my thing.'

'So what is your thing?'

'Helping people with the stuff, the fears and desires and jealousies and sorrows, they have inside them.'

'What about helping to find a lost boy?'

'What I provide for my patients is a safe place.'

Karlsson looked around him. 'This is a nice place,' he said. 'I can see why you wouldn't want to step out of it into the mess of the world.'

'The mess of someone's mind isn't so very safe, you know.'

'Will you think about it?'

'Certainly. But don't expect me to call you.'

At the door, he said, 'Our jobs are very similar.'

'You think so?'

'Symptoms, clues, you know.'

'I don't think it's the same at all.'

When he had gone, Frieda returned to the kitchen. She was just painstakingly separating the cauliflower into florets as instructed by Chloë's recipe when the doorbell rang once more. She paused and listened. It wouldn't be Karlsson again. And it wouldn't be Olivia, because Olivia usually hammered on the knocker as well as ringing, or even called through the letterbox, yoo-hooing imperiously. She lifted the pan of onions off the hob, thinking that she wasn't very hungry anyway; all she wanted was a few crackers with cheese. Or nothing, just a mug of tea and bed. But she knew she wouldn't be able to sleep.

She opened the door a crack, leaving it on a chain.

'Who is it?'

'Is me.'

'Is who?'

'Is me, Josef.'

'Josef?'

'Is cold.'

'Why are you here?'

'Very cold.'

Frieda's first impulse was to tell him to go away, then to slam the door. What was he doing coming around like this? Then she felt something she had felt ever since she was a girl. She imagined someone looking at her, judging her, commenting on her. What would she be saying? 'Look at that Frieda. She rings him up, asks him a favour and he does it straight away, no questions asked. Then he comes to her, cold, lonely, and she just shuts the door against him.' Sometimes Frieda wished the imaginary person would just go away.

'You'd better come in,' she said.

Frieda drew the chain off the bolt and opened the door. Biting wind and darkness gusted into her house and Josef fell in with them.

'How did you know where I live?' she asked suspiciously, before he lifted his face to her. She drew in her breath sharply. 'What's happened to you?'

Josef didn't answer immediately. He crouched down and started trying to untie his laces, which were fused in a complicated sodden knot.

'Josef?'

'I mustn't put dirt in your nice house.'

'That doesn't matter.'

157

'There.' He pulled off one thick boot, whose sole was coming loose. His socks were red and patterned with reindeer. Then he started work on the next. Frieda examined his face. The left cheek was puffy and bruised and there was a gash on his forehead. The next boot was off now; he lined it up neatly with its pair and put them against the wall, then straightened.

'This way,' said Frieda, and led him into her kitchen. 'Sit down.'

'You are cooking?'

'Not you, too.'

'Sorry?'

'I was, kind of.' She ran cold water over a folded hand towel and gave it to him. 'Press this against your cheek, and let me look at your head. I'm going to wash it first. It'll sting.'

As she wiped away the blood, Josef just stared ahead of him. In his eyes she saw something fierce. What was he thinking? He smelt of sweat and whisky but didn't seem altogether drunk.

'What happened?'

'There were some men.'

'Have you been in a fight?'

'They shout at me, they push me. I push back.'

'Push?' said Frieda. 'Josef, you can't do this. One day someone will pull a knife.'

'They called me a fucking Pole.'

'It's not worth it,' said Frieda. 'It's never worth it.'

Josef looked around. 'London,' he said. 'It's not all like your lovely house. Now, we can drink vodka together.'

'I don't have any vodka.'

'Whisky? Beer?'

'I can give you some tea before you go.' She looked at the cut, still oozing blood. 'I'll put a plaster on that. I think you'll get away without having stitches. You might have a small scar.'

'We give help to each other,' he said. 'You are my friend.'

Frieda thought of arguing with that but it felt too complicated.

He knew the cat wasn't really a cat. It was a witch pretending to be a cat. It was grey, not black like they usually are in books, and it had lumps of fur hanging from it, which normal cats didn't have. Its eyes were yellow and they stared at him without blinking. It had a rough tongue and claws that pricked him. Sometimes it pretended to be asleep but then one yellow eye would open and it had been watching him all the time. When Matthew was lying on his mattress, it would climb onto his naked back and dig its claws into his skin, and its greasy grey fur would make him itch. It laughed at him.

When the cat was there, Matthew couldn't look out of the window. It was hard to look out anyway because his legs shook too much and his eyes hurt in the light that came from behind the blind, the light from another world. That was because he was turning into something else. He was turning into Simon. There were red marks on his skin. And spots inside his mouth that stung when he drank water. Half of him was Matthew and the other half was Simon. He had eaten the food that was pushed into his mouth. Cold baked beans and floppy fat chips like worms.

If he pressed his head against the floor just by his mattress, he could hear sounds. Little bangs. Bad voices. Something humming. For a moment it reminded him of before, when he was whole, and his mummy – when she was still his mummy before he let go of her hand – cleaned the house and made things safe for him.

Today, when he looked out of the bottom corner of the window, the world had changed again and it was white and shining and it should have been beautiful but his head hurt too and beauty was only cruel.

Chapter Twenty

The shabby little train was almost empty. It creaked and rattled its way through the hidden parts of London – the backs of terraced houses with their soggy winter gardens, the dark-stained walls of abandoned factories, nettles and rosebay willowherb sprouting from cracks in the brickwork, glimpses of a canal. Frieda saw the hunched figure of a man in a thick coat, holding a fishing rod out over the brown, oily water. Lighted windows flashed past and occasionally Frieda glimpsed a person framed there: a young man watching television, an old woman reading a book. From a bridge, she looked down at a high street, Christmas lights looped round lamp-posts, people moving along the road carrying bags or tugging children, cars spraying water from their wheels. London unwound like a film.

She got out at Leytonstone. It was dusk and everything looked grey and slightly blurred. The orange street-lights shimmered on the wet pavements. Buses swayed past. The road where Alan lived was long and straight, a corridor of late-Victorian terraces lined with stout plane trees that must have been planted at the same time as the houses were built. Alan lived at number 108, at the far end. As she walked, slowing slightly to put off the moment she had to face him, she glanced into the bay windows of other houses, seeing the large downstairs rooms, the views through to the back gardens, lying dormant in winter.

Frieda had steeled herself for this. Even so, there was a tightness in her chest as she pushed open the gate and rang at the dark green door. In the distance, she could hear a jaunty double chime. She was cold and she was tired. She allowed herself to think of her own house, the fire she would light later on, once this was over with. Then she heard footsteps and the door swung open.

'Yes?'

The woman in front of her was short, stockily built. She stood with her legs slightly apart and her feet planted firmly on the ground, as if she was prepared to do battle. Her hair was brown and cut short. She had large and rather beautiful grey eyes, pale smooth skin with a mole just above her mouth, a firm jaw. She wore jeans, a grey flannel shirt rolled up to the elbows, and no makeup. She was looking at Frieda through narrowed eyes. The line of her mouth was grim.

'I'm Frieda. I think Alan's expecting me.'

'He is. Come in.'

'You must be Carrie.'

She stepped into the hall; something pressed against her calf and she looked down. A large cat was winding itself around her leg, a purr rumbling in its throat. She bent down and ran a finger along its thrumming spine.

'Hansel,' said Carrie. 'Gretel's around somewhere.'

It was warm and dark inside, and the air smelt pleasantly woody. Frieda felt as though she had entered a different world from the one suggested by its façade. She had expected the house to be like the others she had walked by, with walls knocked down, french windows built, everything a continuous open space. Instead, she was in a warren of

162

passageways, tiny rooms, tall cupboards and wide shelves crammed with objects. Carrie led her past the front room, but Frieda had time to see a snug enclosure with a wood-burner fitted into the wall, and a glass-windowed cabinet full of birds' eggs, feathers, nests made of moss and twigs and even, standing at one pane of glass, a stuffed kingfisher that looked a bit balding. The room backing on to it – the one that most people would have knocked through – was even smaller, and was dominated by a large desk on which stood several balsawood model planes, the kind Frieda's own brother used to make when he was young. Just the sight of them brought back the smell of glue and varnish, the feel of small adhesive blisters on the fingertips, the memory of those tiny tubs of grey and black paint.

On the wall outside the kitchen there was a group of family photographs in frames – some of Carrie as a small child, squashed with two sisters on a garden bench, standing posing with her parents; others were of Alan. In one, he stood with his parents, a small, blocky figure between two tall and spindly ones, and she tried to look at it more closely as she passed.

'Have a seat,' said Carrie. 'I'll call him.'

Frieda took off her coat and sat down at the small table. The catflap in the back door rattled and another cat slid through, this one black and white and orange, like a pleasing jigsaw. She jumped up on Frieda's lap and settled there, licking one paw delicately.

The kitchen was a room of two halves. To Frieda it felt like a physical demonstration of two different spheres of interest, a precise delineation of Alan's place in the house and Carrie's: the woman who cooks and the man who makes and mends. On one side there were all the things you usually find in a kitchen: oven, microwave, kettle, scales, a food processor, a magnetic strip for the sharp knives, a spice rack, a tower of pots and pans, a bowl of green apples, a small shelf for the recipe books, some of which were old and worn while others looked untouched, an apron hanging on a hook. On the other side, the wall was lined with narrow boxed shelves. Each separate compartment was labelled, in large neat capital letters: 'Nails', 'Tacks', 'Screws 4.2 × 65mm', 'Screws 3.9 × 30mm', 'Chisels', 'Washers', 'Fuses', 'Radiator keys', 'Methylated spirits', 'Sandpaper – rough', 'Sandpaper – fine', 'Drill bits', 'Batteries – AA'. There must have been dozens, hundreds of these compartments; the effect reminded Frieda of a beehive. She imagined all the work that must have gone into it – Alan with his blunt fingers delicately putting these small objects in place, on his round baby-face a look of contentment. The image was so strong that she had to blink it away.

In another situation, she might have said something sardonic, but she was aware of Carrie's eyes fixed on her, of the peculiar dynamic between them. Carrie spoke for her, drily: 'He's building a shed in the garden.'

'I thought *I* was organized,' said Frieda. 'This is on a different scale.'

'The gardening things are all in there.' Carrie nodded towards a narrow door next to the window, presumably meant for a pantry. 'But he hasn't done much gardening recently. I'll look for him. He might be asleep. He's tired all the time.' She hesitated, then said abruptly, 'I don't want him upset.'

Frieda didn't answer. There were too many things she could have said, but nothing that would have prevented Carrie from seeing her as a threat.

Frieda listened to Carrie as she went up the stairs. Her voice, curt when she spoke to Frieda, was tender, like a mother's, when she called her husband. A few moments later, she heard them come down the stairs, Carrie's footsteps light and firm, Alan's slower and heavier, as though he was putting his whole sagging weight onto each step. When he came into the room, rubbing his fists into his eyes, she saw how tired and defeated he looked.

She stood up, dislodging the cat. 'I'm sorry to have disturbed you.'

'I don't know if I was asleep,' he said. He seemed bewildered. Frieda noticed how Carrie put her hand against his back to guide him into the room and took her place behind his chair like a guard. He bent down and picked Gretel up, held her against his broad chest and put his face into her fur.

'I needed to see you,' Frieda said.

'Shall I go?' asked Carrie.

'This isn't a therapy session.'

'I don't know,' said Alan. 'You can stay if you want to.'

Carrie bustled around the kitchen, filling the kettle, opening and closing cupboards.

'You know why I'm here,' said Frieda at last.

As he stroked the cat on his lap, Frieda was reminded of the way he rubbed his hands up and down his trousers when he was in her room, as if he could never keep entirely still. She took a deep breath.

'During our sessions I was struck by resemblances to

165

the case of a boy who has disappeared. He's called Matthew Faraday. So I talked to the police about it.'

Behind her, Carrie clattered angrily with cutlery, then banged her mug down in front of her. Tea slopped over the brim.

'I was wrong. I'm very sorry to have caused you extra distress.'

'Well,' said Alan, slowly, drawing out the word. He didn't seem to have anything to add to it.

'I know that I said to you that in my room you were safe and could say anything,' continued Frieda. Carrie's presence made her self-conscious. Instead of talking to Alan she was reciting the words she had rehearsed in advance, and they sounded stilted and insincere. 'There were these coincidences between your fantasies and what was going on in the outside world and so I felt I had no choice.'

'So you're not really sorry,' said Carrie.

Frieda turned towards her. 'Why do you say that?'

'You think you acted right in the circumstances. You feel justified. In my book, that's not being sorry. You know when people say to you, *I'm sorry if*, because they can't bring themselves to say *I'm sorry that* . . . That's what you're doing. You're apologizing without really apologizing.'

'I don't want to do that,' said Frieda, carefully. She was impressed by Carrie's pugnacity and touched by her fierce protectiveness towards Alan. 'I was wrong. I made a mistake. I brought the police into your life in a way that must have been shocking and very painful to you both.'

'Alan needs help, not being accused of things. Taking that poor little boy! Look at him! Can you imagine him doing such a thing?'

Frieda had no trouble in imagining anybody doing anything.

'I don't blame you,' he said. 'I keep thinking maybe they're right.'

'Who's right?' said Carrie.

'Dr Klein. That detective. Maybe I did grab him.'

'Don't talk like that.'

'Maybe I'm going mad. I feel a bit mad.'

'Tell him he's not,' urged Carrie. There was a wobble in her voice.

'It's like being in a nightmare, all out of control,' said Alan. 'I'm handed from one crappy doctor to another. Finally I meet someone I trust. She makes me say things I didn't even know I was thinking, and then reports me to the police for saying them. Who turn up and want to know what I was doing on the day that little boy went missing. I just wanted to sleep at night. I just wanted peace.'

'Alan,' said Frieda. 'Listen to me now. Many people feel they're going mad.'

'That doesn't mean I'm not.'

'No, it doesn't.'

He smiled suddenly, his face breaking into a grin that made him look suddenly younger. 'Why does it make me feel better not worse when you say that?'

'I wanted to come and tell you what I did and to say sorry. But also I'll quite understand if you don't want to come back to see me. I can refer you to someone else.'

'Not someone else.'

'Do you mean you want to carry on?'

'Will you be able to help me?'

'I don't know.'

Alan sat in silence for a moment. 'I can't think of anything else that wouldn't be worse,' he said.

'Alan!' said Carrie, as if he had betrayed her. Suddenly Frieda felt for the other woman. Patients very often talked to Frieda about their partners and about their family but she wasn't used to meeting them, to getting involved.

She stood up, taking her trench coat from the back of the chair and putting it on. 'You need to talk about it,' she said.

'We don't need to talk about it,' said Alan. 'I'll see you on Tuesday.'

'If you're sure.'

'Yes.'

'Good. I'll let myself out.'

Frieda closed the kitchen door on them and stood on the other side, feeling like a spy. She could hear the rise and fall of their voices. She couldn't make out whether they were arguing. She peered more closely at the photographs of Alan and his parents. He was chubby and solemn and had the same anxious smile, the same look of dismay. One portrait of the parents looked as if it had been taken by a high-street photographer. Probably for an anniversary. They were wearing their best clothes. The colours were almost garish. Frieda smiled and then her smile froze. She looked more closely at the picture. She muttered something to herself, a sort of reminder.

Hansel accompanied her to the door and watched her leave with his golden, unblinking eyes.

'Why the fucking fuck did you leave him?'

'I didn't say I'd left him. I said it was over.'

'Oh, come on, Frieda.' Olivia was striding around her living room, stumbling in her heels, trampling over clothes and objects, a very full glass of red wine in one hand and a cigarette in the other. The wine kept slopping over the rim of the glass and spreading small drops in her wake and the cigarette's ash grew longer until it, too, scattered to the floor, to be ground into the grubby carpet by Olivia's emphatic heel. She was wearing a gold, glittery cardigan, too tight for her and stretched open across her breasts, a pair of blue jogging pants with a stripe down the legs, and summer sandals with stiletto heels. Frieda wondered if she was having a slow, garrulous nervous breakdown. Sometimes it seemed that half the people around her were in states of collapse. 'He wouldn't have left you in a million years,' Olivia was saying. 'So why?'

Frieda didn't really want to talk about Sandy. She certainly didn't want to talk about him to Olivia. It turned out she wouldn't be given a chance to anyway.

'Number one, he's a hunk. God, if you saw some of the men I've been dating recently – I don't know how they have the nerve to pass themselves off as "attractive male". I see them walking through the door and my heart sinks. They want some gorgeous blonde woman but they don't seem to think they need to make an effort themselves. How desperate do they think we are? I'd jump at someone like Sandy.'

'You never actually met him . . .'

'And why not? Where was I? Yes. Number two, he's rich. Well, he must be quite rich – he's a consultant something-or-other, isn't he? Think of his pension. Don't look at me like that. It matters. I can tell you it bloody fucking matters. It's hard being a woman alone, let me tell you, and you've got no safety net, have you, with your bloody family writing you out of their wills? God, I hope you knew that – I haven't just let the cat out of the bag, have I?'

'It's not a great surprise,' said Frieda, wryly. 'But I don't want their money – and anyway I don't think they've got any to leave, have they?'

'Well, that's OK, then. Where was I?'

'Number two,' said Frieda. 'You probably don't want to go any higher than two, do you?'

'Yeah, rich. I'd marry him just for that. Anything to get out of this dump.' She kicked viciously at a wine bottle that was on its side by the sofa and it rolled away, dribbling red from its mouth. 'Number three, I bet he loves you, so that should be three and four and five, because it's a rare thing to be loved.' She stopped abruptly and flung herself into the sofa. Some of the wine left in her glass flew out in a violent daub of crimson onto her lap. 'Number four – or should that be six? – he's nice. Isn't he? Maybe he isn't, because I seem to remember that you have a thing for scary men. OK, OK, I didn't mean that, strike it. Number seven –'

'Stop it. This is demeaning.'

'Demeaning? I'll show you demeaning.' She gestured round the room. Ash swirled in a powdery arc round her. 'Number five or ten or whatever, you're not getting any younger.'

'Olivia. Shut up, do you hear me? You've gone too far and if you go on I'm going to leave. I came round here to teach Chloë some chemistry.'

'Which Chloë hasn't turned up for so you're stuck with me until she arrives, which may be never. You'll soon be too old to have children, you know, though from where I'm sitting maybe that's a lucky escape. Have you thought about that? All right, all right – you can give me that look of yours to freeze the blood, but I've had two, no, three glasses of wine now' – and she took a last dramatic gulp from her glass – 'and you can't intimidate me. I'm insulated. I can say what I please in my own house, and I think you're a bloody fool, Dr Frieda Klein-with-lots-of-letters-after-your-name. There, now I've had three glasses. Maybe it was four. I think it must have been. You should drink more, you know. You might be clever, but you're tremendously stupid as well. Maybe it runs in the Klein blood. What did Freud say? I'll tell you what he said. He said, "What do women want?" And do you know how he answered that?'

'Yes.'

'I'll tell you how. He said, "They want love and work."'

'No. He more or less concluded that they want to be men. He said girls have to come to terms with being failed boys.'

'Wanker. Anyway – where was I?'

'What's that noise?'

Olivia went out of the room, shrieked, and returned glassy-eyed. 'That noise,' she said, 'is Chloë throwing up on the mat in the hall.'

Chapter Twenty-one

As Frieda was paying the cab driver, she saw Josef standing in her doorway.

'What are you doing here?' she said. 'You don't have a standing invitation, you know. You can't just turn up whenever you feel like company.'

As if in explanation, he held up a bottle. 'It is good vodka,' he said. 'Can I come in?'

Frieda unlocked the door. 'How long have you been here?'

'I just waited. I thought maybe you come back.'

'I'm not going to sleep with you. I've had a fucking awful day.'

'No sleeping.' Josef looked reproachful. 'Just a drink.'

'I could do with a drink,' said Frieda.

While Josef lit the fire in the grate, Frieda rummaged in the back of a cupboard and found a packet of crisps. She emptied them into a bowl. She brought it through with two small glasses. The fire was already crackling. As she came into the room, she saw Josef before he knew she was back. He was staring into the flames with a different expression from the smile he'd greeted her with.

'Are you sad, Josef?'

He looked round. 'Far away,' he said.

'Why don't you go home?'

'Next year, maybe.'

Frieda sat down. 'Do we need juice with this?'

'Good on its own,' he said. 'For the taste.'

He unscrewed the top and delicately filled the two glasses to within a couple of millimetres of the rim. He handed one to Frieda. 'Drink the first one all at once,' he said.

'I think I'd like that.'

They both tossed the drink back. Josef gave a slow grin. Frieda picked up the bottle and looked at the label. 'Christ,' she said. 'What is it?'

'Russian,' he said. 'But good.' He refilled their glasses. 'What was bad in your day?'

Frieda took another sip of Josef's vodka. It stung the back of her throat and then it spread hot through her chest. She told Josef about sitting on Olivia's bathroom floor as Chloë knelt with her face over the lavatory, retching and heaving, even when there was nothing left to vomit out. Frieda hadn't spoken much, just leaned across and gently touched her on the back of her neck. Afterwards she had wiped Chloë's face with a cold flannel.

'I didn't know what to say. I just kept thinking what it would be like, when you're sick and you're vomiting, to have some older woman lecture you about drinking sensibly. So I didn't say anything.'

Josef didn't answer. He just looked into his glass of vodka as if there was a faint light in the centre of it and he needed all his concentration to see it. Frieda found it comforting to talk to someone who wasn't trying to be clever or funny or reassuring. So then she told him about her visit to Alan. To her own astonishment, she heard herself telling Josef how she had previously gone to the police about him.

'What do you think?' Frieda asked.

Very slowly, with a care that had now become exaggerated, Josef filled her glass once again. 'What I think,' he said, 'is that you shouldn't think about it. It's better not to think about things too much.'

Frieda sipped at the drink. Was this the third glass? Or the fourth? Could it be the fifth? Or had Josef been topping up the drinks so that it didn't really count as separate drinks but instead one sort of elasticated drink that gradually grew? She was just starting to agree with the idea of not thinking when her phone rang. She was so surprised by what she had been about to say that she let it ring several times.

Josef looked puzzled. 'You don't answer?'

'All right, all right.' Frieda took a deep breath. She didn't feel entirely clear-headed. She picked up the phone. 'Hello.'

'I love you.'

'Who is this?'

'How many women ring you up to say they love you?'

'Chloë?'

'I do love you, although you're so stern and cold.'

'Are you still drunk?'

'Do I have to be drunk to tell you I love you?'

'I tell you what, Chloë, you should go to bed and sleep it off.'

'I'm in bed. I feel dreadful.'

'Stay there. Drink lots of water through the night, even if it makes you feel sicker. I'll call tomorrow.' She put the phone down and pulled an exasperated face at Josef.

'No,' he said. 'It's good. You fix things. You are like me. Two days ago a woman rings me, someone I worked for.

She is screaming. I get to her house. There is water bursting from a pipe like a fountain. There is five centimetres of water in her kitchen. She is still screaming. It's just a simple valve. I turn the valve, I drain the water. That is you. There is an emergency, they phone you, you rush in and rescue them.'

'I wish I was,' said Frieda. 'I'd like to be the person who knew what to do when someone's boiler had broken or their car wasn't working. That's the sort of expertise that really makes things better. You're the person who fixes the leaking pipe. I'm the person who's hired by the company who made the pipe to come along and try to persuade the screaming patient not to sue them.'

'No, no,' said Josef. 'Don't say that. You're being self . . . self . . .'

'Conscious.'

'No.'

'Sabotaging.'

'No,' said Josef, waving his hands around as if he was trying to act out the meaning of the words he couldn't find. 'You are saying, "I am bad", so that I say, "No, you are good, you are very good."'

'Maybe,' said Frieda.

'Don't just agree,' said Josef. 'You should argue.'

'I'm too tired. I've had too many vodkas.'

'I am working with your friend Reuben,' said Josef.

'He's not necessarily my friend.'

'Strange man. But he talks about you. I am learning about you.'

Frieda gave a shudder. 'Reuben knew me best ten years ago. I was different then. How is he?'

'I am making his house better.'

'That's good,' said Frieda. 'That's probably what he needs.'

'Do you want to tell me why it was so urgent to see me?'

Sasha Wells was in her mid-twenties. She was dressed in dark trousers and a jacket that seemed designed to disguise the shape of her body. Even so, and even though her dirty blonde hair was dishevelled, and she kept running her fingers through it, pushing strands out of her eye even when they weren't in her eye, and though she was just a bit too thin, and though the fingers of her left hand were stained from cigarette smoking, and though she wouldn't meet Frieda's gaze except to give an ingratiating half-smile, her beauty was obvious. But her large dark eyes seemed to be apologizing for it. She made Frieda think of an injured animal, but the kind of animal that reacts to being injured not by fighting back but by curling up and retreating. Neither of them spoke for some time. Sasha was fidgeting with her hands. Frieda was tempted to let her have a cigarette. She was clearly desperate for one.

'My friend Barney has a friend called Mick who says you're great. That I can trust you.'

'You can say anything you like,' said Frieda.

'All right,' said Sasha, but so quietly that Frieda had to lean forward to make her out.

'I take it you've already been seeing a therapist.'

'Yes. I was seeing someone called James Rundell. I think he's quite famous.'

'Yes,' said Frieda. 'I've heard of him. How long have you been seeing him for?'

'About six months. Maybe a bit more. I started just after I got my job.' She pushed her hair away from her face, then let it fall forward again. 'I'm a scientist, a geneticist. I like my work, and I have good friends, but I was stuck in a rut and I couldn't seem to get out of it.' She gave a little grimace that only made her more beautiful. 'Bad relationships, you know. I was letting myself get messed around a bit.'

'So why are you here?'

There was a long pause.

'It's difficult,' she said. 'I don't know how to say it.'

Suddenly Frieda felt that she knew what was coming. She thought of that feeling when you stand on the platform of an underground station when a train is coming. Before you hear anything, before you see the light at the front of the train, you feel a breath of warm air on your face, you see a piece of scrap paper flap around. Frieda knew what Sasha was going to say. She did something she couldn't ever remember having done before in a therapy session. She stood up, stepped closer to Sasha and put her hand on the young woman's shoulder.

'It's OK,' she said. Then she sat back down. 'You can say anything here. Anything.'

At the end of the fifty minutes, Frieda arranged a further session with Sasha. She took down a couple of phone numbers and an email address. She sat in silence for a few minutes. Then she made a phone call. Then another, longer, one; then a third. When she had finished, she put on a short leather jacket and walked briskly out and across to Tottenham Court Road. She hailed a taxi and gave an address that she had jotted down on the back of an envelope. The taxi made its way through the streets north of Oxford Street, then along Bayswater Road and south through Hyde Park. Frieda was looking out of the window but she wasn't really paying attention. When the taxi drew to a halt, she realized she hadn't been concentrating and that she had no real idea where she was. It was a part of the city she barely knew. She paid the driver and got out. She was standing outside a small bistro-style restaurant in what was otherwise a largely residential street of white stucco houses. The restaurant had small baskets of flowers hanging from the eaves. In summer people would be eating outside, but it was too cold for that today, even for Londoners.

Frieda stepped inside and was hit by the warmth, the low hum of talk. It was a small place with no more than a dozen tables. A man came over, wearing a striped apron.

'Madame?' he said.

'I'm here to see someone,' she said, looking around the room. What if he wasn't there? What if she didn't recognize him? There he was. She'd seen him at a couple of conferences, and in photographs accompanying an interview in a magazine. He was sitting in the far corner with a woman. They were apparently on their main course and deep in conversation. She walked across the room and stood by the table. He looked round. He was dressed in dark trousers and a beautiful shirt, a black and white pattern that shimmered. He had very short dark hair and was just slightly unshaven.

'Dr Rundell?' Frieda said.

He got up from his chair. 'Yes?' he said.

'My name's Frieda Klein.'

He looked puzzled. 'Frieda Klein. Yes, I've heard of you but . . .'

'I've just been talking to a patient of yours. Sasha Wells.'

He still looked puzzled, but also wary. 'What do you mean?'

Frieda had never hit anyone before. Not really. Not with her fist, not using the full weight of a punch. It caught him right on the jaw and he fell backwards, across his own table, bringing it down on top of him with the food and the wine and the water and the bottles of oil and vinegar. Even Frieda, standing over him, panting, her blood humming in her ears, was startled by the havoc she had caused.

As he stepped through the door of the interview room, Detective Chief Inspector Karlsson tried to force his features into a frown.

'When you get your phone call, it's traditional to use it for your lawyer,' he said. 'Or your mother.'

Frieda glowered up at him. 'You were the only person I could think of,' she said. 'On the spur of the moment.'

'You mean, in the heat of battle,' said Karlsson. 'How's your hand?'

Frieda held up her right hand. It was wrapped in a bandage but some spots of blood had started to show through.

'It's not like in the movies, is it? When you punch someone, they don't just get up. It damages them and it damages you.'

'How is he?' asked Frieda.

'Nothing's broken,' said Karlsson. 'No thanks to you. But he's got one hell of a set of bruises and they're going to look even worse tomorrow and probably even worse the day after.' He leaned over and took hold of Frieda's right hand. She flinched slightly. 'Can you move your fingers?' She nodded. 'I've seen people shatter their knuckles with a punch like that.' He gave her hand a little pat, which made her flinch again, and let it go. 'And have you ever heard the expression about not kicking a man when he's down? I understand that Dr Rundell is a fellow psychoanalyst. Is this how you settle your professional disagreements?'

'If you're here to charge me,' said Frieda, 'just get it over with.'

'This isn't my area,' said Karlsson. 'But I suppose that in normal circumstances you'd be facing a charge of actual bodily harm and criminal damage. I'm assuming – God knows why – that you've got a clean record. So you might get away with a month or so in Holloway.'

'I'm happy to go to trial,' said Frieda.

'Well, sadly, I think you may be denied your day in court. I've just been talking to the arresting officer and apparently Dr Rundell is very insistent on not pressing charges. My colleague is not a happy man. He's not happy at all.'

'What about the restaurant?'

'Indeed,' said Karlsson. 'I've even seen the photographs. You know, in the past when I've encountered crime scenes of this kind, when the victim has refused to press charges, it's usually involved gang intimidation of some kind. Is there something you're not telling us?' His attempt to suppress a smile now failed. 'Drug deal gone wrong?'

'It's a private matter.'

'And even then,' said Karlsson, 'I've never heard of the victim insisting on paying for all the damage himself.' He paused. 'You're not the kind of person I'd expect to be arrested for brawling in public. And now you don't seem to be particularly happy that you've escaped the sort of thing that most people would be afraid of, you know, like being put on trial and convicted and sent to prison, that sort of thing.'

'I'm not bothered,' said Frieda.

'You're a hard one,' he said. Then his expression changed. 'Is there something I should know about this? Something criminal?'

Frieda shook her head.

'What's he been up to, then?' said Karlsson. 'Sleeping with his patients?'

Frieda's expression didn't change.

'I can't condone this,' said Karlsson. 'This isn't Sicily.'

'I don't care whether you condone it or not.'

'You were the one who rang me.'

Frieda's expression softened. 'You're right,' she said. 'I'm sorry. And thank you.'

'I've come to say that you can go and, in fact, to give you a lift back – but look,' he said, a little desperately. 'What would the world be like if everyone settled things like this?'

Frieda stood up. 'What *is* the world like?' she said.

Chapter Twenty-two

On Tuesday afternoon, Frieda said to Alan, 'Tell me about your mother.'

'My mother?' He shrugged. 'She was . . .' He stopped, frowned, look at the palms of his hands as if he could find the answer there. '. . . a nice woman,' he finished lamely. 'She's dead now.'

'I mean, your other mother.'

It was as if she had punched him very hard in the stomach. She even heard the whoosh of surprised pain that escaped him, and he bent forward slightly, his face screwed up. 'What do you mean?' he managed.

'Your birth mother, Alan.'

He made a faint and querulous sound.

'You *were* adopted, weren't you?'

'How did you know?' he whispered.

'Not by magic. I just saw the photograph of them in your house.'

'And?'

'They both have blue eyes. Yours are brown. It's genetically impossible.'

'Oh,' he said.

'When were you going to tell me?'

'I don't know.'

'Never?'

'It's not got anything to do with this.'

'Are you serious?'

'I was adopted. End of story.'

'You are longing to have a child of your own, so acutely that you have vivid fantasies about it, and prolonged attacks of acute anxiety. And you think that the fact that you were adopted isn't relevant?'

Alan shrugged. He lifted his eyes to hers, then dropped them again. Outside, the crane's arm lifted higher in the hard blue sky. Great gobbets of mud dropped from its serrated jaw. 'I don't know,' he muttered.

'You want a son who looks exactly like you. You reject the idea of adopting a child. You want your own – with your genes, your red hair and freckles. As if you want to adopt yourself, rescue yourself and look after yourself.'

'Not that.' Alan looked as though he would like to jam his fingers into his ears.

'Is it such a secret?'

'Carrie knows, of course. And one friend. I told him once after a few drinks. But why should I talk about it to everyone? It's private.'

'Private from your therapist?'

'I didn't think it was important.'

'I don't believe you, Alan.'

'I don't care what you believe. I'm telling you.'

'I think you know it's important. It's so important you can't bring yourself to mention it or even think about it.'

He shook his head slowly from side to side, like a tired old bull being baited.

'Some secrets give a form of freedom,' said Frieda. 'Your own private space. That's good. Everyone has to have those kinds of secrets. But some secrets can be dark and oppressive, like a horrible dank cellar you don't dare go into but you always know is there, full of ugly underground creatures, full of your nightmares. Those are the secrets you need to confront, shine a light on, see what they really are.'

As she spoke, she thought of all the secrets she had been told over the years, all those illicit thoughts, desires, fears that people gave to her for safe keeping. Reuben had felt poisoned by them in the end, but she had always carried them with a sense of privilege, that people allowed her to see their fears, allowed her to be their light.

'I don't know,' said Alan. 'Maybe there are things it's best not to dwell on.'

'Otherwise?'

'Otherwise you'll just get upset when there's nothing to be done anyway.'

'Do you think that perhaps you're here, with me, because there are too many things you haven't dwelled upon and they've built up inside you?'

'I don't know about that. We just never discussed it,' said Alan. 'Somehow I just knew we couldn't go there. She wanted me to think of her as my mother.'

'Did you?'

'She *was* my mother. Mum and Dad, that was all I knew. That other woman, she has nothing to do with me.'

'You didn't know your birth mother?'

'No.'

'No memory at all?'

'Nothing.'

'Do you know who she was?'

'No.'

'You never wanted to know?'

'Even if I did, it would be no use.'

'How do you mean?'

'No one knew.'

'I don't understand. You can always find out, you know, Alan. It's really quite straightforward.'

'That's where you're wrong. She made sure of that.'

'How?'

'She dumped me. In a little park near a housing estate in Hoxton. The newspaper boy found me. It was winter and very cold and I was wrapped up in a towel.' He glared at Frieda. 'Like in a fairy tale. Except that this is real. Why should I care about her?'

'What a way to start your life,' said Frieda.

'I can't remember it, so it doesn't matter. It's just a story.'

'A story about you.'

'I never knew her, she never knew me. She doesn't have a name, a voice, a face. She doesn't know my name either.'

'It's quite hard to go through pregnancy and give birth and then abandon your baby and never be discovered,' said Frieda.

'She managed it.'

'So you were tiny when your parents adopted you. You never knew anything else?'

'Right. Which is why it doesn't have anything to do with what I'm feeling now.'

'Like when you were talking about having your own child, and then about the possibility of adopting.'

'I told you. I don't want to adopt. I want my own child, not someone else's.'

Frieda looked at him steadily. He met her gaze for a few

seconds, then dropped his eyes, like a boy who has been caught out in a lie.

'Our time is up. We'll meet again on Thursday. I want you to think about this.'

They both stood up. He shook his head slowly from side to side again, in that futile, hapless gesture of his, as though he was trying to clear it.

'I don't know if I can do this,' he said. 'I'm not cut out for it.'

'We'll take it one step at a time.'

'Through the darkness,' said Alan, words that caught Frieda off balance so she could only nod at him.

When Frieda returned home, she found a small package on her doormat and at once recognized Sandy's handwriting on the envelope. She stooped and picked it up very carefully, as if it might explode with any sudden movement. But she didn't open it immediately. She took it to the kitchen and made herself a cup of tea first, standing at the window while the kettle boiled, looking past her reflection at the darkness outside and the night sky, which was clear and cold.

Only when she had a mug of tea in her hand and was sitting at the table did she open the package and take out a silver bangle, a small sketchpad with a couple of her drawings in it and a soft-leaded pencil, five hair grips held together by a thin brown hairband. That was all. She shook the envelope, but there was no letter or note. She looked at the paltry objects lying on the table. Was that really all she had left there? How was it possible to leave so little trace?

The phone rang and she picked it up, wishing even as she did so that she had left it to the answering machine.

'Frieda. You've got to help me. I'm at my wit's end here and her stupid fucking father isn't any help either.'

'I'm here, you know,' said Chloë. 'Even if you wish I wasn't.'

Frieda held the receiver slightly away from her ear. 'Hello?' she said. 'Which one of you am I meant to be talking to?'

'You're talking to me,' said Olivia, her voice high and shrill. 'I rang you because I just happen to be at the end of my tether. If *someone*'s rude enough to pick up the other phone and eavesdrop, then that *someone* has only got themselves to blame if they hear things they'd prefer not to hear.'

'Blah blah blah blah,' jeered Chloë. 'She wants to gate me for being drunk. I'm sixteen. I was sick. Get over it. She should gate herself.'

'Chloë, look –'

'I wouldn't talk to a dog the way she talks to me.'

'Nor would I. I like dogs. Dogs don't shout and nag and feel sorry for themselves.'

'Your *brother* just said it was part of growing up,' said Olivia, ending on a sob. She always called David Frieda's brother or Chloë's father when she was more than usually angry with him. 'He should try a bit of growing up himself. It wasn't me who ran off with some young tart with dyed hair.'

'Careful, Olivia,' said Frieda, sharply.

'If you try to gate me, I'll go and stay with him.'

'I'd love that, except why do you think he wants you? He left you, didn't he?'

'You both have to stop this now,' said Frieda.

'He didn't leave me, he left *you*. I don't blame him.'

'I am now going to put the phone down,' said Frieda, very loudly, and she did.

She got up and poured herself a small glass of white wine, then sat down again. She fingered the objects that Sandy had returned, turning them over in her fingers. The phone rang.

'Hello,' came Olivia's small voice.

'Hi.' Frieda waited.

'I'm not coping very well.'

Frieda took a sip of wine and rolled its coolness in her mouth. She thought of her bath, her book, the fire that was laid, the thinking she needed to do. Outside, it was winter and an ill wind blew through the dark streets. 'Do you want me to come round?' she said. 'Because that would be fine.'

Chapter Twenty-three

The following afternoon, Karlsson called a press conference at which the Faradays faced a bank of photographers and journalists to make an appeal for the return of their son that would reawaken public interest.

Karlsson had spent the morning looking through the statements his team had gathered from hundreds of so-called witnesses and the dwindling reports of possible sightings. He stood to one side. He watched the couple as the lights flashed in their faces – faces that had undergone such a change since Matthew had disappeared. Day by day, he'd seen grief carving new lines, stretching the skin, dulling the light in their eyes. Alec Faraday's face was still puffy and bruised from his attack, and he moved stiffly because of his broken rib. They both looked thin and strained, and her voice cracked as she talked of their darling boy, but they managed to get through it all right. They said the usual heart-breaking things. They begged the world at large to help in the search and the person in particular to give them back their beloved boy.

It was useless, of course. These shows were largely designed to put pressure on the parents, to see if they were the guilty ones. But they all knew the Faradays couldn't have done it. Even the papers that had accused him had done a brazen U-turn, turning him into a suffering saint instead. He'd been with a client in the accountant's office where he worked and had dozens of witnesses. She'd been rushing from her job as a medical receptionist to get to the school on time to collect him. And the notion that whoever it was who had grabbed Matthew would suddenly have a change of heart when he heard them speak and saw their ravaged faces was absurd, not least because the child was almost certainly dead and had been for some time. So it was left to the world to respond – and respond it would, and the deluge of misinformation and false hope that had been mercifully drying up would flood them again.

That evening, he stayed late at work. He stared at the photos of the boy, of the place he had disappeared, at the large map in the investigation room, dotted with pins and flags. He read through statements. His brain throbbed and his chest ached.

He stared and the other boy stared back. It was Simon. He put up a hand towards Simon, to see if he was friendly, and Simon put up his hand too, at the same time, but he didn't smile. He was very thin and very white and his bones stuck out on his shoulders and his hips, and his willy looked like a little pink snail. When he took a step towards Simon, Simon took a step towards him. A jerky little step, like a puppet moves, and then like a puppet Simon folded to the floor and Matthew folded to the floor and they were staring at each other. Matthew put one finger to the boy's tiny face, goblin face, hollows for cheeks and holes for eyes and a bandaged mouth, and touched the cold, speckled mirror and watched the tears stain the skin where he pressed.

He felt hands behind him, he felt himself being held. Soft words, breath on him.

'You're going to be our little boy,' the voice said. 'But don't be our bad little boy. We don't like bad little boys.'

When Frieda opened the door to Karlsson, he stood at the threshold as though she was expecting him, and in a way she was. She had known that this was not the end of the case of Matthew Faraday.

'Come in,' she said.

They went into the front room, where a fire was burning and a stack of academic journals lay on the arm of her chair.

'Am I disturbing you?'

'Not really. Have a seat.' He was carrying a leather bag, slung over his shoulder. He laid it on the floor and took his coat off. He sat down. She hesitated, and then said, 'Do you want something to drink? Coffee?'

'Perhaps something a bit stronger.'

'Wine? Whisky?'

'Whisky, I think. It's that kind of night.'

Frieda poured them both a small tumbler of whisky, adding a splash of water, then sat down opposite him. 'How can I help?'

Her manner was softer than usual. It almost brought tears to his eyes.

'It's all I think of. I get up and I think about him and I go to bed and I dream about him. I go to the pub with the guys and we talk about stuff and I hear the words coming out of my mouth. It's amazing how you can go around pretending everything's normal when it's not. I talk to my kids on the phone and ask them about their day and tell them silly, cheerful stuff about mine, and all the time I'm just seeing him. He's dead, you know. Or, at least, I hope he is because if he isn't . . . What's the best that can happen? That we find his body and catch the bastard who did it. That's the best.'

'Is it really as hopeless as that?'

'In ten years' time, in twenty, I'll still be the copper who didn't rescue Matthew Faraday. When I'm retired – like the old detective I visited who was in charge of the Joanna Vine case – I'll sit in my house and think about Matthew and wonder what happened, where he's buried, who did it and where they are now.'

He swirled his whisky round in his tumbler, then took a gulp. 'You probably spend half your time with people who are burdened by guilt, but in my experience, people don't feel nearly enough guilt. They feel shame when they're caught, all right, but no guilt if they're not. All over the world there are people who have done terrible things and they're living perfectly contented lives, with their families and friends.'

He swilled back his whisky and Frieda poured more into his tumbler without asking him. She hadn't touched hers.

'If I feel like this,' he said, 'think of the parents.' He pulled his tie loose impatiently. 'Am I going to be haunted all my life?'

'Have you never had a case like this before?'

'I've had my share of murders and suicides and domestic abuse. It's hard to keep your faith in human nature; maybe that's why I'm divorced and pouring my heart out to a woman I've met just a few times, rather than to my wife. He's only five, the age of my youngest.'

'There's no answer to what you're feeling,' said Frieda. A strange mood enveloped the room where they sat, dreamy and sad.

'I know. I just needed to say it to someone. Sorry.'

'Don't say sorry.'

She didn't say anything else. She looked into her glass and Karlsson looked at her, seeing a new side to her. After a while, he said, 'Tell me about your work.'

'What do you want to know?'

'I don't know. Are you a doctor?'

'Yes. Though you don't have to be. I specialized in psychiatry before training. It's a long process and a strict discipline. I've got lots of letters after my name.'

'OK. And are your patients mostly private? How many do you see a day? What are they like? Why are you doing it? Does it work? That kind of thing.'

Frieda gave a small laugh, then started counting off his questions on her fingers. 'One, I'm a mixture of private and NHS. I get referrals from the Warehouse Clinic, where I trained and worked for years, and from GPs and hospitals, and I also take people who come to me off their own bat, usually because someone they know has recommended me to them. It's important to me not just to take on people who are rich enough to be able to afford therapy; otherwise it would be like treating the disease of the rich. Privately, therapy is quite expensive.'

'How much?'

'I have this rule of thumb. I charge two pounds for every thousand they earn – so if you earn thirty thousand you'd give me sixty pounds for each session. I had one client who told me he'd have to pay me five hundred thousand an hour, in that case. Luckily for him, I have a cut-off point of a hundred pounds. I have been known to take people for almost nothing, though my colleagues frown on that. Anyway, I'd say that about seventy per cent of my patients are NHS referrals, maybe a bit less.

'OK. Number two, I usually see my patients three times a week, and I usually have seven patients – in other words, about twenty sessions a week in all. I know therapists who have eight sessions each day – that's forty in a week. As one patient leaves, the next arrives. It makes them wealthy, but I couldn't do that. Nor would I want to.'

'Why not?'

'I need to absorb things, think about each person I see, make proper process notes. I don't need more money than what I get now. I need time. What was next?'

'What are they like?'

'I don't know how to answer that. They don't have much in common with each other.'

'Except they're in a mess.'

'Most of us are in a mess at some time in our lives, wretched beyond bearing or dysfunctional beyond tolerating or simply stuck.' She fixed him with her piercing glance. 'Don't you think?'

'I don't know.' Karlsson frowned, uncomfortable. 'Do you ever turn people away?'

'If I think they don't need therapy, or if I think they'd be better off with someone else. I only take on people I think I can help.'

'And what made you become a therapist?' This was

what he really wanted to know but had little expectation of her answering. They had sat companionably together and talked, and yet he did not understand her much better or have more sense of her vulnerabilities or doubts. She kept herself to herself, he thought. The self-possession that had struck him so forcefully at their first meeting rarely wavered.

'That's enough questions for one night. What about you?'

'What about me?'

'Why did you join the police force?'

Karlsson shrugged, then stared into his whisky. 'Fuck knows. Recently, I've been asking myself why I didn't become a lawyer, the way I was meant to, earning serious money and sleeping properly at night.'

'What's the answer?'

'There isn't an answer. I work too hard, get paid too little, am drowning in paperwork, only get noticed when things go wrong, get pissed on by the press and by my own boss, and the public distrust me. And now that I'm heading up the Murder Investigation Team, I get to meet lots of killers and wife-beaters and perverts and drug dealers. What can I say? It just seemed like a good idea at the time.'

'You like it, then.'

'Like it? It's what I do, and I think I do it pretty well, most of the time. Though you wouldn't guess it from this case.'

He seemed to remember something and reached into his bag. He took out two cardboard files. 'These are statements made by Rosalind Teale. She's the sister of Joanna Vine. The first statements were made just after the disappearance and then we interviewed her again the other day.'

'Is there something significant about them?'

'I know you're resistant, but I'd like you to have a look at them.'

'What for?'

'I'd be interested in anything you had to say.'

'Now?'

'That would be good.'

Karlsson refilled his glass and didn't add water. He stood up and walked around the room as if he was at a gallery. Frieda didn't like being watched while she was reading. And she didn't like the idea of him looking at her possessions and using them to try and learn something about her. But the quickest way to get him to stop was to read the statements. She opened the older one and began, making herself read slowly, word by word.

'Have you read all these books?' Karlsson asked.

'Shut up,' said Frieda, in a mumble, without even looking up from the file. As she moved on to the second, more recent, file, she was aware of Karlsson, out of her eyeline. Finally she closed it. She didn't speak, although she knew that Karlsson was waiting.

'So?' he said. 'If she was your patient, what would you ask her?'

'If she was my patient, I wouldn't ask her anything. I would try to stop her feeling guilty about her sister. Apart from that, I think she should be left alone.'

'She's the only possible witness,' said Karlsson.

'And she didn't see anything. And it's more than twenty years ago. And every time you talk to her you damage her all over again.'

Karlsson came over and sat back down so that he was

facing Frieda. He contemplated his whisky glass. 'This is good stuff,' he said. 'Where did you get it?'

'Someone gave it to me.'

'Tell me something else about the statements,' said Karlsson. 'You're clever. Don't you see this as a challenge?'

'Don't think you can taunt me,' said Frieda.

'I'm not taunting you. I'm at a stage where I'd be grateful for any input. I'm interested in anyone who knows about things I don't know about.'

Frieda paused for a moment. 'Have you thought about the possibility that Joanna might have been taken by a woman rather than a man?'

Karlsson put his glass down very gently on the low table by his chair. 'Why do you say that?'

'The disappearance was quick,' said Frieda. 'Rosie Vine only lost sight of her sister for a minute or so. It doesn't seem as if there was any fuss, any noise. This wasn't someone being snatched on a quiet lane and thrown into the back of a van. This was a street that people walked along, with shops on it. I could imagine a little girl walking off with a woman. Taking her hand.' Frieda imagined the scene, the little girl walking away, trustingly. Then she tried not to imagine it.

'That's very interesting,' said Karlsson.

'Don't patronize me,' said Frieda. 'It's not very interesting. It's obvious and you must have considered it from the beginning.'

'The idea had occurred to us,' he said. 'It's a possibility. You've got to admit, though, you're interested.'

'Why are you asking me this?' said Frieda. 'What are you trying to get me to say?'

'I'd like you to talk to Rose Teale. Maybe you can get to her in a way we can't.'

'But what's there to get at?' She picked up the file and flicked through it.

'Isn't it frustrating?' said Karlsson. 'When I read the statement, I have this fantasy that I could get in a time machine and be there just for a minute, just for five seconds, and then I could find out what really happened.' He gave a sour smile. 'That's not the way grown-up policemen are supposed to talk.'

Frieda looked at the statement again: the little girl talking about her younger sister. She felt she was being asked to go on a journey and after she had said yes it would be too late to turn back. Was there any point to this? Was there anything she could contribute? Well, maybe. And if she could, she must.

'All right,' she said.

'Really?' said Karlsson. 'That's great.'

'What I'd need,' said Frieda, 'are those police artists who are used for creating likenesses. Have you got that?'

Karlsson smiled and shook his head. 'No,' he said. 'We've got something much better.'

Chapter Twenty-four

Tom Garret was visibly excited to meet someone who knew what he was talking about when he described the neurological aspects of facial recognition.

'The old idea of the photofit was based on this primitive notion that we see faces as a collection of bits – blue eyes, a large nose, bushy eyebrows, a sharp chin – and when we put them together we have a face we recognize. But that's not how we really see faces and that's why photofit reconstructions look ridiculous.'

'Not exactly ridiculous,' said Karlsson.

'Comical. And almost useless. As you know' – and now he turned firmly towards Frieda – 'the *fusiform gyrus* area of the brain is specifically associated with facial recognition and if it's damaged the patient is unable to recognize any faces at all, even of close relatives. We've harnessed that idea in creating this program based on holistic facial recognition.'

'Excellent.'

Frieda leaned more closely towards Garret's monitor.

Garret continued talking about evolutionary facial composite systems and genetic algorithms until Karlsson coughed and reminded them that Rosalind Teale was sitting outside. 'Is it all right if we stay here?' he said.

'That's fine,' said Frieda. 'But please leave everything to me.'

Frieda had read the file and seen photographs but she was still shocked by Rose Teale's appearance. She looked like someone who had suffered a traumatic episode the previous day, not more than twenty years in the past. Had this woman not received any help? Had she not been attended to? Rose glanced around her, at Garret, who was tapping at a keyboard and didn't look at her; at Karlsson, who was leaning on the wall with his arms folded. When Frieda stepped forward and introduced herself, she didn't ask questions, just let herself be led across the room and placed in a chair. Frieda sat opposite her. Karlsson had said that it might make Rose feel better to be useful. Looking at the passive, defeated woman in front of her, Frieda doubted that.

'I've done everything,' she said. 'I've tried to remember. I've gone over and over it. There's nothing left.'

'I know,' said Frieda. 'You've done everything you possibly could.'

'So why am I here?'

'There are ways of accessing things in your mind that you don't know are there. It's nothing magical. More like opening an old filing cabinet that you'd forgotten about. I'm not going to ask you any questions,' said Frieda, 'and none of us expects anything of you. I just want you to bear with me for a moment. Can you do that?'

'What do you mean?'

'I'd like us to try something. I don't want you to think about it. Just do as I say.' Frieda now let her voice become softer. 'I know that you're probably feeling tense, coming into a police station and talking to people you don't know, but I'd like you to sit comfortably and relax as if someone was going to read you a story. I want you to close your eyes.'

Rose looked distrustful. Her eyes flickered towards Karlsson. He remained impassive. 'All right.' She closed her eyes.

'I want you to think back to that day,' said Frieda. 'I want you to go back there and imagine yourself leaving school, walking along the pavements, crossing the road, looking at shops, people, cars. Don't say anything. Just imagine yourself doing it.'

Frieda looked at the young woman's face, the fine lines at the corners of her eyes, the flickering eyelids. She waited for a minute. Two minutes. She leaned forward and spoke even more quietly, almost in a whisper. 'Don't say anything, Rose. Don't try and remember anything. I want you to do something for me. Just imagine a woman. Young or middle-aged. You decide.' Frieda saw Rose's features flicker in puzzlement. 'Just do it,' she continued. 'Don't worry about it. Don't even think about it. Just think of a woman. Any woman, whoever comes into your head. Maybe she's standing on the edge of the pavement, by the kerb. She's just got out of a car and she's looking around. Put her in the scene with you. Look at her. Can you do that?'

'All right.'

'Have you done it?'

'Yes.'

'Wait,' said Frieda. 'Wait and look at her. Look at the woman who came into your head. Remember what she looks like.'

A minute passed. Frieda saw that Karlsson was frowning at her. She ignored him. 'All right,' she said. 'You can open your eyes now.'

Rose blinked, like someone who had just woken and was dazzled by the light.

'I want you to go over and sit with Tom and he's going to show you something.'

Tom Garret stood up and gestured Rose into the chair he'd been sitting in. As she sat down, he made a questioning face at Frieda as if to ask, Is this for real?

'Go on,' said Frieda.

He gave a shrug. On the screen was a grid showing eighteen female faces.

'None of them look like her,' said Rose.

'They're random,' said Tom. 'They're not meant to look like her. What I want you to do is to click on the six that feel most like her. You should do it quickly without thinking too hard. Don't worry. There's no right or wrong answer. It's not a test.'

'What's the point of this?'

'It's just an exercise,' Frieda told her. 'I want to see what happens.'

Rose gave a sigh, like someone giving in reluctantly. She put her hand on the mouse and moved the cursor around.

'None of them are like her,' she repeated.

'Choose the ones that are closest,' said Tom. 'Or the ones that are least unlike.'

'All right.' She clicked the cursor on one face, the narrowest, then on another, then another, until six were highlighted. 'Is that it?'

'Now click "done",' said Tom.

She did so and the screen refilled with eighteen new faces.

'What are these?' Rose asked.

'These are generated from the six you chose,' said Tom. 'Now choose six more.'

She went through the process again, then again and again, over and over. Occasionally she stopped and closed her eyes before continuing. Looking over her shoulder, Frieda could see a change gradually occurring. A crowd of strangers was gradually evolving into a family group whose resemblance grew stronger and stronger. The face became thinner, the cheekbones more prominent, the almond shape of the eyes more pronounced. After twelve generations, the faces didn't just look like a family but siblings, and after two more generations they were almost identical.

'Choose one,' said Tom.

'They're almost the same.' Rose hesitated. The cursor wavered around the screen before landing on one of the faces. 'That's it.'

'That's the face you saw?' said Frieda.

'I didn't *see* it. It's the face I made up in my imagination.'

Now Karlsson came over and looked at the image. 'What about the hair?' he asked.

'I didn't see the hair. The face I made up was wearing a scarf.'

'I can do a scarf.' Tom clicked on a drop-down menu and the face appeared eighteen times with different kinds of scarf. Rose pointed at one.

'Is that it?' said Frieda.

'A bit,' said Rose. 'It's quite like it, I think.'

'That's good, Rose,' said Frieda. 'You've done really well. Thank you very much.'

'What do you mean I've done well?'

'I know it was hard for you, going back there. That took courage.'

'I haven't been back there. I didn't remember anything. I just pictured a face and then you tried to re-create it. It's clever but I don't see how it helps you.'

'We'll see. Could you wait outside for a moment?'

Karlsson waited until Rose was safely outside the room and the door was closed. 'What was that about?'

'Don't you trust your own facial-recognition system?'

'I don't mean the facial-recognition system. I brought you in here because I thought you might be able to hypnotize her or something. Wave a needle in front of her eyes. I thought you could do some of your psychological stuff and dredge up hidden memories. Instead you got her to make up a face.'

'I did some research work a few years ago,' said Frieda. 'I was working with people who had areas of blindness in their visual field. What we did was show them a collection of dots that were in the area of their visual field that wasn't functioning. They couldn't see them, but we asked them to take a guess at the number. In most cases, they would guess right. The input was bypassing their conscious mind but was still being processed. There was no point in going over Rose's conscious memories. She's spent her life going over and over them. By now they've been hopelessly contaminated even if she did see something. I thought this might be a way of bypassing all that.'

Karlsson looked across at Tom Garret. 'What do you think? This is all bullshit, right?'

'You're talking about blindsight, right?' Tom asked Frieda.

'That's right,' said Frieda.

'Bullshit,' Karlsson repeated. He was clearly very angry.

'I haven't heard about it applying to memory,' Tom said.

'I thought it was worth a try.'

Karlsson sat in the chair and looked at the screen, at the middle-aged woman in a scarf staring back at him. 'Did you really?' His tone was thick with sarcasm. 'This is just playing stupid fucking games. Blindsight!'

'Can we print it out?' Frieda asked Tom, pointedly ignoring Karlsson, but he took the sheet of paper as it came out of the printer and waved it in her face.

'This is so much rubbish. Rose probably just made it up. To be helpful. She's the helpful kind. She doesn't want to disappoint us.'

'Right,' said Frieda. 'That's the most likely.'

'And if she didn't make it up, if you really did tap into some memory of the day, this might just be the face of a woman who was out doing her shopping.'

'That's right.'

'And if, and it's about the biggest fucking if I've ever come across, this woman was involved, then what we have is a picture of someone from twenty-two years ago with no suspects to compare it with, no witnesses to ask.'

'You could show the picture to other people who were around at the time, to see if they remember anything.'

'And? If they did – which they won't – what use will

that be? Can you bring them in here and put them in a trance and get them to imagine an address?'

'That's up to you,' said Frieda. 'You're the detective.'

'This is what I think.' Karlsson balled up the printout and flung it towards the metal bin, but missed.

'That's clear, at least,' said Frieda.

'You're just wasting my time.'

'No. *You're* wasting *mine*, Detective Chief Inspector Karlsson. And wasting it rudely.'

'You can leave now. Some of us have got real work to do.'

'Gladly,' said Frieda. She stooped and picked up the screwed-up paper.

'What do you want that for?'

'A souvenir, maybe.'

Rose was outside, sitting on a chair with her hands in her lap, staring into the distance.

'We're done,' said Frieda. 'And we're very grateful to you.'

'I don't think I helped much.'

'Who knows? It was worth a try. Are you in a hurry?'

'I don't know.'

'Ten minutes.' Frieda took her by the forearm and steered her out of the station. 'There's a café down the road.'

She got a pot of tea for two and a muffin in case Rose was hungry, but it lay untouched between them.

'Have you ever had counselling?'

'Me? Why? Do you think I need it? Is it that obvious?'

'I think anyone would need it who had gone through

206

what you went through. Did you never have any help after your sister disappeared?'

Rose shook her head. 'I talked to a policewoman a bit, when it happened. She was nice.'

'But nothing else?'

'No.'

'You were nine years old. Your sister disappeared from under your nose. You were supposed to be looking after her – at least, that's what you thought. In my view, a nine-year-old can't be responsible for someone. She never came back and you've felt guilty ever since. You think it was your fault.'

'It was,' Rose said, in a whisper. 'Everyone thought so.'

'I very much doubt that – but what matters now is that's what you thought. What you think now. You're like someone whose psyche has developed around the central overwhelming fact of your loss. But it's not too late, you know. You can forgive yourself.'

Rose looked at her and shook her head slowly from side to side, tears gathering in her eyes.

'Yes, you can. But you need help to do it. I can make sure don't have to pay for it. It would take time. Your sister is dead and you need to say goodbye to her and build your own life now.'

'She haunts me,' whispered Rose.

'Does she?'

'It's as if I'm never without her. She's like a little ghost beside me. Always the same age. We're all getting older, and she's there, a tiny girl. She was such a worried little thing. So many things scared her – the seaside, spiders, loud noises, cows, the dark, fireworks, going in lifts, crossing the road. The only time she didn't look anxious was when she was asleep – she used to sleep with her cheek resting against her hands, which she pressed together, as if she was praying. She probably *was* praying when she fell asleep actually – she was probably begging God to keep the monsters away from her.'

She gave a small laugh and then a wince.

'It's all right to laugh about her, and it's all right to remember the ways in which she wasn't perfect.'

'My father's made her into a saint, you know. Or an angel.'

'Hard for you.'

'And my mother doesn't mention her.'

'Then it's time for you to find someone else to talk to about her.'

'Could I come and talk to you?'

Frieda hesitated. 'I'm not sure that's a good idea. I've been involved with your case from the point of view of the police. It would blur the boundaries. But I can recommend someone who I know is good.'

'Thank you.'

'So it's a deal?'

'All right.'

Chapter Twenty-five

In eight days' time, it would be the shortest day of the year. The clinic would close until the beginning of the next year. Patients had to put their troubles on hold. And when they returned, Reuben would probably be there to meet them, if she told Paz he was fit to resume his duties. So here she was on a Sunday afternoon, walking towards his house, ostensibly to return some of the folders he'd left in his room, but he wouldn't be fooled by that for very long. This was Reuben, after all, with his cool, appraising eye and his mocking smile.

Before she could lift her hand to knock, the door flew open and Josef charged through it, in his arms a pile of jagged planks. He swept past her on his way to the over-flowing skip that, she now saw, stood on the road. He hurled his burden into it and returned, rubbing his dusty palms together.

'What are you doing here? It's Sunday.'

'Sunday, Monday, who knows the day?'

'I do. So does Reuben. I hope.'

'Come in. He is on the kitchen floor.'

Frieda stepped in through the front door, not knowing what to expect after her last visit. She couldn't restrain a gasp. It was obvious that Josef had been working here for some time. It wasn't just that the stench of a life abandoned had gone, and in its place was an astringent smell of turpentine and paint, or that bottles, cans and crusted plates had been cleared away and curtains opened. The hall was painted. The kitchen was in the process of being dismantled – cupboards had been ripped out and a new frame to a door into the garden was in place. Outside, on the narrow strip of lawn, the remains of a bonfire smoked. And sure enough, there was Reuben, lying on the floor, halfway under a new porcelain sink.

Frieda was so surprised that for a moment she simply stood and stared at him, with his lovely linen shirt riding up over his stomach and his head quite out of sight.

'Is that really you in there?' she said at last.

The feet in their purple socks twitched and the body wriggled forward. Reuben's face slid out of the sink unit and into view. 'It's not as bad as it looks,' he said.

'You've been caught in the act. DIY? And on a Sunday afternoon. You'll be washing your car next.'

He sat up, pulled down his shirt. 'Not really DIY. Not as such. You know me: left to my own devices, I can't even be bothered to replace a light bulb. I'm just helping Josef out.'

'I should think so. Getting him to work on a weekend. Are you paying him double?'

'I'm not paying him at all.'

'Reuben?'

'Reuben is my landlord,' said Josef. 'He gives me a roof and in return . . .'

'He fixes it,' supplied Reuben, getting to his feet, staggering slightly. Both men laughed, glancing at Frieda to see her reaction. It was a joke they'd obviously rehearsed.

'You've moved in?'

Josef pointed towards the fridge, and Frieda saw a dog-eared photograph attached to it with a magnet: a dark-haired woman seated on a chair, with two small boys formally posed on either side of her. 'My wife, my sons.'

Frieda looked back at Josef. He put a hand over his heart and waited.

'You are a lucky man,' she said.

He took a pack of cigarettes out of his shirt pocket and handed one to Reuben, taking one himself. Reuben produced his lighter and lit them both. Frieda felt irritated. There was something about the two of them, some furtive triumph and naughtiness, as if they were two small boys and she was the bossy grown-up.

'Tea, Frieda?' asked Reuben.

'Yes, please. Though you could at least offer me some of that vodka you've hidden under the sink.'

The two men looked at each other.

'You're here to spy on me,' Reuben said. 'See if I'm fit for duty.'

'Are you?'

'It's the death of the father,' said Reuben. 'What you've always wanted.'

'What I want is for the father to come back to work when he's ready, and not before.'

'It's Sunday. I can drink on a Sunday and still go to work on a Monday. I can drink on a Monday and still go to work on a Monday for that matter. You're not my handler.'

'I make tea,' said Josef, uneasily.

'I don't want tea,' said Reuben. 'English people always think tea makes everything better.'

'I am not English,' said Josef.

'I didn't particularly want to come here,' said Frieda.

'Then why come? Because you were told to? You were *sent*? What? By the eager young Paz? That doesn't sound much like the Frieda Klein I know. The Frieda Klein who does what she pleases.' He dropped his cigarette on to the floor and ground it out with his heel. Josef stooped and picked it up, carrying it carefully in his palm to the rubbish bin where he deposited it.

'How you run your own life is up to you, Reuben. You can drink vodka all day long and trash your house, that's fine. But you're a doctor. Your job is to cure. Some of the people who come to the clinic are very vulnerable, very frail, and they put their trust in us. You're not coming back to work until you can be trusted not to abuse your power. And I don't care how angry you feel with me.'

'I feel angry all right.'

'You feel self-pity. Ingrid's left you and you think you've been treated badly by your colleagues. But Ingrid left because you've been serially unfaithful for years, and your colleagues have responded in the only possible way to your behaviour at the clinic. That's why you're angry. Because you know you're in the wrong.'

Reuben opened his mouth to reply, then suddenly stopped. He groaned, lit another cigarette and sat down at the kitchen table. 'You don't leave a man a place to hide, do you, Frieda?'

'Do you want a place to hide?'

'Of course I do. Doesn't everyone?' He pushed his hands through his hair, which had grown past his shoulders during his enforced leave, so that he looked even more like a poet after a rough night. 'No one likes to feel shamed.'

Frieda sat down opposite him. 'Talking of which,' she said, 'I've done some things that I want to tell you about.'

He smiled at her ruefully. 'Is this your *quid pro quo* to make me feel better? Swapping shame?'

'I want to talk something through,' said Frieda. 'If that's all right.'

'It's all right,' said Reuben. 'It's just completely unexpected.'

On the following Tuesday, Alan told Frieda a story. He didn't speak in his normal way, correcting himself and going backwards and forwards in time, remembering things that he'd left out. He talked fluently, with few pauses, and there was a shape and coherence to his narrative. Frieda thought he must have practised it several times, going over and over it in his head before coming to her, removing all the uncertainties and contradictions.

'Yesterday morning,' he said, once he'd crossed and re-crossed his legs, rubbed his hands up his trouser legs, coughed several times in preparation. 'Yesterday morning I had to go and check on a planning application. Although I'm on leave, I still drop in occasionally to sort things out in the department. There are certain things only I know about. It was over in Hackney, a converted office block near the Eastway. You know the area?'

'It's not really my part of London,' said Frieda.

'Things are a bit chaotic there with all the Olympic construction. It's like a new city being jerry-built on top of the wreckage of an old one. And they can't push the completion date back, so they're just throwing more and more people at it. Anyway, after I'd finished there, I went for a walk. It was cold, but I felt like some fresh air, just to get my head clear. To be honest, going in to work at the moment makes me feel a bit rattled.

'I walked along the canal, then turned off it and walked into Victoria Park. It felt like an escape, going somewhere different. There were quite a few people in the park, but no one was hanging about. Everyone seemed to be in a hurry: heads down, walking quickly, everyone with somewhere to go to except me, or that was how it seemed to me. I wasn't really watching them, though. I sat on a bench for a bit, next to the bowling green. I was thinking about the last few weeks and wondering what lay ahead of me. I was quite tired. I'm always tired nowadays. Things were a bit blurred. I could see some of the cranes over towards Stratford and the Lee Valley Park. I got up and walked along between the ponds. There's a bandstand there and a fountain. Everything looked abandoned and shut down for winter. I came out the other side, crossed the road and started looking into the windows of the shops. I looked at an antiques place – well, antiques is probably a bit of a grand word for it. Odds and ends mostly. I used to buy a lot of old furniture. I thought I had an eye for it. It pisses Carrie off. She wants me to get rid of the stuff I've got, not get anything new. But still, I like to look, see what prices people are asking. Anyway, there were some funny old places there. There was a hardware shop with mops and buckets and a strange clothes shop that sold the sort of stuff that old women wear, cardigans and tweed coats. You're wondering why I'm telling you this, aren't you?'

Frieda didn't respond. 'I was standing outside another bric-à-brac shop, full of stuff you couldn't imagine anyone buying or selling. I remember, I was staring at a stuffed owl that was perched on a sort of fake tree branch and I was half wondering whether Carrie would allow another dead bird into the house.

'Just at that moment, a woman came walking towards me. I wasn't paying attention to her at first. She was walking through my field of vision, if you understand what I mean. She was wearing a bright orange jacket and a very short tight skirt and these high-heeled boots.'

Alan fidgeted and looked down. He went on speaking but no longer met Frieda's eyes.

'Suddenly, I realized she was talking to me. She said, "Oh, you!" and she pushed herself close against me.' Alan faltered and then continued. 'She put her arms round me and she kissed me. She – It was a proper kiss. With her tongue. You know when you're in a dream and strange things happen to you and you just accept them and go along with it? It was like that. I didn't push her away. I felt as if I was in a film or something, that it wasn't really happening to me but to someone else.' He swallowed hard. 'There was blood on my lip. Then, after a bit, she pulled back. She said, "Call me. It's been a while. Haven't you been missing me?" And then she was gone. I couldn't move. I just stood there and watched her walking away in her orange jacket.'

There was a silence.

'Is there anything else?' asked Frieda.

'Isn't that enough?' said Alan. 'A woman I don't know coming up and kissing me? You want more than that?'

'I mean, what did you do?'

'I wanted to follow her. I didn't want it to end. But I went on standing there and then she was gone and I was back in myself, if you see what I mean, dull old Alan who nothing really happens to.'

'What did this woman look like?' asked Frieda. 'Or did you only see her jacket and skirt and boots?'

'She had long hair, sort of blonde-red. Jangly ear-rings.' Alan touched the lobes of his own ears. He coughed and turned red. 'Big breasts. And she smelt of cigarettes and something else.' He wrinkled his nose. 'Like yeast or something.'

'And her face?'

'I don't know.'

'You didn't see her face?'

He looked bewildered. 'I don't remember it. I think she was –' he coughed '– you know, nice-looking. It all happened so suddenly. And my eyes were shut a lot of the time.'

'So, you have an erotic, arousing experience with an unknown, almost faceless woman, in the street.'

'Yes,' said Alan. 'But I'm not like that.'

'Did this really happen?'

'Sometimes I think it didn't – that I just went to sleep on the bench in the park and dreamed it.'

'Did you enjoy it?'

Alan thought for a moment and almost gave a grin. He seemed to catch himself at it. 'I felt excited, if that's what you mean. Yes. If it happened, that's bad, and if I made it up, that's bad as well. In a different way.' He grimaced. 'What would Carrie say?'

'You haven't told her?'

'No! No, of course not. How can I tell her that, although we haven't had sex in months now, I let some attractive woman with big breasts kiss me but I don't know if it really happened or if I just wanted it to?'

'What do you make of it?' asked Frieda.

'I've told you before, I've always thought of myself as invisible. People don't really notice me, and if they do, it's because they've got me mixed up with someone else. When this happened, I think a little bit of me was tempted to go off with this woman, be the person she mistook me for. It sounded as if he was having more fun than I was.'

'So what do you want me to say?'

'After it happened, I was totally confused and then I thought, That's the sort of thing Dr Klein wants me to tell her. Mostly I think what I've told you has been quite boring, but I thought this was weird and a bit creepy and it would be just the sort of thing I should tell you.'

Frieda couldn't stop herself smiling at that. 'You think I'm interested in weird and creepy things?'

He let his head drop into his hands. Through his fingers, he said, 'Everything used to be so simple. Now nothing's simple. I don't even know who I am any more, or what's real and what's in my mind.'

Chapter Twenty-six

'So what do you think?' said Frieda.

Jack pulled a face. 'It's a classic fantasy,' he said.

They were sitting in Number 9, their habitual meeting place now for Jack's mentoring sessions, which had become less formal and more frequent. Jack was nursing his second cappuccino. He liked it here: Kerry fussed over him, a mixture of motherly and flirtatious; Marcus sometimes came out of the kitchen and insisted that he try his latest creation (today a marmalade Bakewell tart that Jack ate, though he didn't really like almonds or marmalade) and Katya sometimes came and sat on Frieda's lap. Jack thought Katya liked Frieda the way cats like people who don't fuss over them. Frieda would ignore her or, sometimes, simply lift her off and deposit her on the floor.

'In what way?'

'For men, anyway. A sexually provocative woman approaches, pulls you out of your boring everyday life into a weird, more exciting existence.'

'So what does this woman represent?'

'It might be you,' said Jack, and took a hasty gulp of his coffee.

'Me?' said Frieda. 'Large-breasted, orange jacket, tight short skirt and blonde-red hair?'

Jack went red and looked around the café to see if anybody had overheard. 'It's a sexualized version of you,' he said. 'It's a classic example of transference. You're the woman who is stepping into his ordinary life. He can talk to you in ways that he can't talk to his own partner. But he still needs to disguise it by expressing it in terms of this exaggeratedly sexual female figure.'

'Interesting,' said Frieda. 'A bit like a textbook, but interesting. Any other theory?'

Jack thought for a moment. 'I'm interested in this story he keeps telling of his anonymity, that he keeps feeling he's being mistaken for other people. This may be an example of solipsism syndrome. You know, it's the dissociative mental state where people feel that they're the only person who is real and everybody else is an actor or has been replaced by a robot or something like that.'

'In which case he would need an MRI scan.'

'It's just a theory,' said Jack. 'I wouldn't recommend that unless there were other symptoms of cognitive impairment.'

'Any other possibilities?'

'I was taught to listen to the patient. I suppose there is a possibility that a woman simply mistook him for someone else and that the whole thing doesn't mean much at all.'

'Could you imagine going up to a girl and actually kissing her by mistake?'

Jack thought of mentioning a couple of examples where it would be all too easy and then thought better of it. 'He must have looked pretty similar to the person she thought he was,' he said. 'If it really happened. But if I've learned anything from you it's that what we're here to do is to deal with what's inside the patient's head. In a way, the truth of what happened isn't relevant. What we need to concentrate on is the meaning that Alan gave to the event and what he meant by telling you about it.'

Frieda gave a frown. It felt strange to hear her own words being parroted back at her like that. They sounded both dogmatic and unconvincing. 'No,' she said. 'There's a huge difference between someone who is mistaken for other people, for whatever reason, and someone who believes that he is mistaken for other people. Don't you think it would be interesting if we could find out whether that encounter really happened?'

'It might be *interesting*,' said Jack, 'but it's just totally impractical. You'd have to wander round Victoria Park on the off-chance of seeing someone who was in the neighbourhood two days ago – and whom you wouldn't recognize anyway because you don't know what she looks like.'

'I was hoping you might have a go,' said Frieda.

'Oh,' said Jack.

Jack was tempted to say several things: that it had nothing to do with his training and that it was unprofessional of her to ask him; that the chances of finding this woman were zero, and that even if he found her it wouldn't be worth the trouble. He even wondered if there might be some rule about checking up on patients without their permission. But he didn't say any of those things. Really, he was quite pleased that Frieda had asked him. In a curious way he was even more pleased that she had asked him to do something out of the ordinary. If it had been some straightforward extra work, that would have been a chore. But this was just slightly inappropriate and there was a certain kind of intimacy about that. Or was he kidding himself?

'All right,' he said.

'Good.'

'Frieda!'

The voice came from behind him, and before he saw whose it was, he noticed how Frieda's face darkened.

'What are you doing here?'

Jack twisted round and saw a woman with long legs, dirty blonde hair and a face that looked very young and unformed under its dramatic makeup.

'I've come for my lesson. You said we should meet here for a change.' She glanced at Jack and he felt himself blush.

'You're early.'

'You should be pleased.' She sat down at their table and pulled off her gloves. Her fingernails were bitten and painted dark purple. 'It's so cold out there. I need something to warm me up. Aren't you going to introduce us?'

'Jack's just going,' said Frieda, shortly.

'I'm Chloë Klein.' She held out a hand and he took it. 'Her niece.'

'Jack Dargan,' he said.

'How do you two know each other, then?'

'Never mind that,' said Frieda, hastily. 'Chemistry.' She nodded at Jack. 'Thanks for your help.'

It was a clear dismissal. He got to his feet.

'Nice meeting you,' said Chloë. She seemed very pleased with herself.

Jack emerged from Hackney Wick station and looked at his street map. He made his way over to the junction where the Grand Union Canal branched off to the east from the river Lea. He was wearing a sweatshirt, a sweater, a cagoule, cycling gloves and a woolly hat with earmuffs but he was still shivering with the cold. The surface of the canal was gritty with a slush that hadn't quite hardened into ice. He walked along the towpath until he saw the gates to the park on his right. He looked at the notes he had taken from Frieda. He could see the playground ahead. There was an icy wind that stung his cheeks so he couldn't tell whether they were cold or hot. Nevertheless, he could see buggies and muffled, bundled-up little figures in the playground. There were even two track-suited figures on the tennis court. Jack stopped and pressed his face against the wire. They were two grizzled old men, hitting the ball back and forwards hard and low. Jack was impressed. One of them charged the net and the other lobbed him. The player chased back. The ball landed just inside the line.

'Out!' the player shouted loudly. 'Bad luck!'

Jack felt his fingers freezing inside his gloves. As he walked away from the court, he took his right hand out of the glove and pushed it inside his shirt against his chest to try to bring some feeling back into his fingers. He turned left on to the main path. On his right he could see the bowling green and then, as he walked along, the band-stand and the fountain. He looked around. There was almost no one. Dotted about were people with their dogs. Far away to one side there was a group of teenagers, josh-ing, pushing each other. This wasn't the weather for anyone with anywhere sensible to go. He thought of Alan Dekker walking here to clear his mind, if he really had been here at all. In fact, now that Jack was here, he was starting to believe that Alan must have been telling some version of the truth. The details about the canal, the playground and the bandstand were too precise. Why bother with that if it was all a dream? As he walked, Jack felt as if he was clearing his mind as well, in the fierce northerly wind. He'd been feeling discontented with the whole idea of therapy. Was it really so important to talk about things? Was talking about things just another way of getting tangled up with your patient, when what you really should be doing was making them better? Maybe that was another reason why he had agreed to do this for Frieda. It felt good to be going out in the world and seeing if Alan had been telling the truth or not. But, then, what were the chances of finding anything out?

Jack came out of the southern corner of the park, crossed the road and walked along the row of shops. They were just the way Alan had described them. When he got to the hardware shop, he actually stepped inside. It was the sort of place that he hadn't thought existed any more and it seemed to contain virtually everything he ought to have got for the house he shared, but had never quite got around to buying: washing-up bowls, step-ladders, screwdrivers, torches. He should come back here with his friend's car and load up. A few more steps took him to the second-hand shop with the stuffed owl in the window. It was scruffy and losing feathers, and it seemed to be staring back at him with its large doll's eyes. Jack tried to imagine shooting an owl and stuffing it. It had no price tag. It probably wasn't for sale.

He looked around. This was where Alan had met the woman. If he'd met her. He had said that the street had been empty and that he had suddenly seen her coming towards him. Could she live somewhere here? Jack stepped back and looked above the shops. There did indeed seem to be flats above them and there were entrances along the road between the shop fronts, some of which were boarded up, with 'For Sale' signs above them. But he couldn't just start ringing doorbells at random and seeing if a large-breasted woman answered. The next shop along was a launderette with a cracked window. Alan hadn't mentioned that she was carrying washing, but he hadn't said that she was empty-handed either. Jack stepped inside, inhaling the warm steam gratefully. There was a woman right at the back folding some washing. When she saw Jack she stepped towards him. She was black-haired with a mole above her lip.

'You here for a service wash?' she said.

'Someone I know may have been in here a couple of days ago,' said Jack. 'A woman dressed in a bright orange jacket.'

'Never seen her.'

Jack thought he should say something, decided not to and then changed his mind. 'I'm a doctor, by the way. You might want to get that mole looked at.'

'What?'

Jack touched his own face just above his mouth. 'It might need checking.'

'Mind your own fucking business,' said the woman.

'Yes, right, sorry,' said Jack, and eased out of the shop.

Next door was a café, a real old-style greasy spoon. He stepped inside. It was empty except for a toothless old man in the corner, sucking noisily at his tea. He looked at Jack with his watery eyes. Jack looked at his phone: twenty past one. He sat at a table and a woman in a blue nylon apron came over; she was wearing slippers that shuffled along the not-very-clean floor. Jack looked up at the blackboard and ordered fried eggs, bacon, sausage, grilled tomato and chips and a cup of tea.

'Anything else?' said the woman.

'There's a woman, dresses in a bright orange jacket, blonde hair, lots of jewellery, does she come in here?'

'What you want?' said the woman, in a strong accent. She was looking at him suspiciously.

'I wondered if she came in here.'

'You say you meet her here?'

'Meet her?'

'Not here.'

There were several more exchanges of questions at the end of which Jack didn't know whether the waitress knew the woman or even whether she had understood his questions at all. The food arrived and Jack felt strangely happy. It felt like the sort of meal that he could only eat alone, in an unfamiliar place, among strangers. He was just dipping his chips into the remains of the egg yolk and planning what to do next, when he saw her. Or, rather, he saw a woman in a bright orange jacket over tight black leggings, wearing high heels, her hair long and blonde, walking past the window. For a moment, he sat transfixed. Was it a hallucination, or had he really just seen her? And if so, what to do? He couldn't let her go. This was real life. He had to approach her. But what could he possibly say? He jumped up, spilling tea over the greasy remains of his meal, and scrabbled in his pocket for change. He threw far too many coins down on the table. Several spun off and fell to the floor. He raced out of the door, ignoring the calls of the waitress. She was still visible, her jacket a vivid flare among the greys and browns of the other people on the street.

He ran towards her, feeling immediately out of breath. For someone in high heels, she walked surprisingly fast. Her hips rolled. As he got nearer he saw that her feet were bare and swollen in the sandals, which looked a size too small. He drew level and put a hand on her forearm. 'Excuse me,' he said.

When the woman turned her head, he felt a tremor of shock running through him. He'd been expecting someone young and beautiful, sexy at least – that was what Alan's story had implied. But this woman wasn't young. Her breasts sagged. Her face was lined and creviced, and under the thickly applied makeup, the skin was pasty. He saw a rash of red spots on her forehead. Her eyes, circled with dark liner and fringed with heavily mascaraed lashes, were flecked with red. She looked bleary and ill and wretched. He saw her draw her features into an approximation of a smile. 'What can I do for you, darling?'

'Sorry to disturb you. I just wanted to ask you something.'

'I'm Heidi.'

'Well – Heidi – I – it's difficult to explain but –'

'You're a shy one, aren't you? Thirty quid for a blow-job.'

'I wanted to talk to you.'

'Talk?' He could feel her indifferent glance and his face flamed. 'We can talk, if that's what you want. It'll still cost you thirty quid.'

'It's just about –'

'Thirty quid.'

'I'm not sure if I've got that much on me.'

'Stopped me on a whim, did you? There's a cash machine up the road.' She pointed. 'And then you can come and see me if you still want to talk. I live at forty-one B. Top bell.'

'But I don't think you understand.'

She shrugged. 'Thirty quid and then I'll understand as much as you want.'

Jack watched her as she crossed the road. For a moment he thought of simply going home, as fast as he could. He felt obscurely ashamed of himself. But he couldn't go, now that he'd found her. He went to the cash machine and took out forty pounds, then made his way to 41B. It was above a shop that had once been a halal butcher's, according to the sign, but was now closed down. There was graffiti all over its metal shutters. Jack took a deep breath. He felt that everyone who passed must be looking at him, grinning to themselves, as he pressed the top bell. Heidi buzzed him up.

She was wearing a low-cut, lime green top. Alan had said she smelt of yeast, but now she had clearly sprayed herself with perfume. She had applied fresh lipstick and brushed her hair.

'Come in, then.'

Jack stepped over the threshold into a small sitting room that was dimly lit and oppressively hot. Thin purple curtains were pulled across the window. On the wall opposite, above the large low sofa, was a reproduction of the *Mona Lisa*. There were china ornaments on every spare surface.

'I should tell you at once that I'm not what you think.' His voice came out too loudly. 'I'm a doctor.'

'That's all right.'

'I want to ask you something.'

Her smile disappeared. Her eyes were watchful and suspicious. 'You're not a punter?'

'No.'

'A doctor? I'm clean, if that's what you're thinking.'

Jack felt slightly desperate. 'You know this man,' he said. 'With grey hair, stocky.'

Heidi let herself down on to the sofa. Jack saw how tired she was. She picked up a bottle of sweet Dubonnet that was at her feet and filled a small glass to the brim, tipped it down her throat in one swallow that made her throat work. A small thick dribble worked its way down her chin. Then she took a cigarette from the packet on the table, put it in her mouth, lit it and inhaled hungrily. The smoke hung in the heavy air.

'You kissed him the other day.'

'You don't say.'

Jack was forcing himself to speak. An acute physical discomfort was making him squirm in his seat. He saw himself the way that this woman, Heidi, must be seeing him: prurient, puritanical, smutty, an awkward young man who had not grown out of his adolescent anxieties about women in spite of his age and his profession. He could feel the sweat on his brows. His clothes itched on him.

'I mean, you came up to him in the street and kissed him. Just near the café and the shop with the owl in the window.'

'Is this your idea of a sick joke?'

'No.'

'Who's set you up to it?'

'No, honestly, you've got me wrong – but my friend, he was surprised, and I just wanted to find out if –'

'Dirty dog.'

'Sorry?'

'Your friend. Strange company you keep, I must say. At least he pays, though. He likes paying. It gives him the right to treat us as dirty as he wants.'

'Alan?'

'What's that?'

'He's called Alan.'

'No, he isn't.'

'What's his name with you?'

Heidi poured herself another brimming glass of Dubonnet and drank it down.

'Please,' he said.

He took the money from his back pocket, removed a ten-pound note, and passed the rest over.

'Dean Reeve. And if you tell him I told you, I'll make you sorry. I swear.'

'I won't tell. Do you happen to know where he lives?'

'I've been there once, when his wife was away.'

Jack rummaged in his pocket and found a pen and an old receipt. He handed them across and she wrote on the back of it and returned them.

'What's he done?'

'I'm not sure,' said Jack.

As he left he handed over the last ten-pound note. He wanted to apologize, though he didn't know what·for.

Jack sat opposite a man with a bald head and a waxed moustache who was reading a magazine about guns.

When he had told Frieda he had actually found Alan's mystery woman, she had insisted on meeting him at his place. Jack had feebly protested: he didn't want her to see where he lived, particularly not in the state it had been in when he'd left this morning. He worried about which of his housemates would be there and what they might say. To make matters worse, the train back got delayed in a tunnel – passenger under a train, the announcement said. He was fumbling with his key in the lock when he saw her coming up the road. It was getting dark and she was wrapped up against the cold, but he would have recognized her anywhere, just from the way she walked, swift and upright. She was so purposeful, he thought, and a wave of exultation passed through him, because he had been successful and had something to give her.

She reached him as he was pushing open the door. The hall was full of junk mail and shoes; there was a bicycle leaning against the wall that they had to squeeze past. Loud music was coming from upstairs.

'It might be a bit messy,' he said.

'That's all right.'

'I don't know if there's any milk.'

'I don't need milk.'

'The boiler's not completely working.'

'I'm wearing warm clothes.'

'It's warm in the kitchen.' But when he saw it, he backed out of it rapidly. 'I think the living room might be more comfortable,' he said. 'I'll plug in the radiator.'

'It's fine, Jack,' said Frieda. 'I just want to hear exactly what happened.'

'It was unbelievable,' said Jack.

The living room was nearly as bad as the kitchen. He saw it through Frieda's eyes: the sofa was a horrible leather affair that someone's parents had given them when they moved in; it had a wide rip along one arm that was disgorging white fluff. The walls were painted a vile green; there were bottles and mugs and plates and strange items of clothing everywhere. Some dead flowers stood on the windowsill. His squash bag was open in front of them, a dirty shirt and a balled pair of socks on the top of it. The anatomically correct skeleton he had had since his first term at university stood in the centre of the room hung with flashing Christmas lights, several hats piled up on its skull and some lacy knickers hanging off its long fingers. He swept the magazines off the table and covered them with a coat that was lying on the sofa. If he was in a session with Frieda, he could have told her about the chaos he lived in and how it made him feel slightly out of control of his own life as well. If it was him who read those magazines (which it wasn't, though he had glanced surreptitiously at them every so often), he could have told her about that as well. He could have explained that he felt he was living in a limbo state, between his old university life and the world of adulthood, which always seemed to belong to other people and not to him. He could describe the mess of his soul. He just didn't want her to see it for herself.

'Have a seat. Sorry, let me move that.' He took the laptop and the ketchup bottle from the chair. 'It's just temporary,' he said. 'Some of my housemates are a bit disorganized.'

'I've been a student,' Frieda said.

'We're not students, though,' said Jack. 'I'm a doctor,

kind of. Greta's an accountant, though you wouldn't believe it.'

'You found her.'

'Yes,' said Jack, brightening. 'Can you believe it? I'd just about given up, and then suddenly there she was. It was a bit disturbing, though. It doesn't make sense, really – and she was both the woman Alan told you about and . . . well, she wasn't. Not really.'

'From the beginning,' Frieda commanded.

Under her concentrated gaze, Jack told her everything that had happened. He repeated the conversation with the woman word for word, as near as he could manage. At the end, there was a silence.

'Well?' he said.

The door opened and a face peered in. It saw Frieda and leered expressively, then withdrew. Jack flushed to the roots of his hair.

'Dirty dog?'

'That's what she called Alan, except she said his name was Dean.'

'Everything Alan said was true.' Frieda seemed to be talking to herself. 'All the things we thought might be inside his head were in the outside world all the time. He wasn't making it up. But the woman – the one he said he'd never seen before – knew him.'

'Knew this Dean Reeve,' corrected Jack. 'At least, that's what she said.'

'Why would she lie?'

'I don't think she was lying.'

'She described everything the way he did, except she says it happened to someone else.'

'Yes.'

'Is he lying to us? If he is, what's it about?'

'She wasn't the glamorous woman I'd been expecting,' said Jack. He felt awkward talking about Heidi, but he wanted to tell Frieda how he'd felt, standing in the hot, sickly-sweet room, trying not to think about all the men who had trudged up the narrow stairs. He remembered her red-flecked eyes and felt slightly sick, as though it was his fault.

'I've had colleagues who look after sex workers,' said Frieda. She was looking at him as though she could see his thoughts. 'Mainly they're addicted, abused and poor. There's not much that's glamorous about it.'

'So Alan goes to prostitutes under the name of Dean. And then he can't bring himself to actually confess it straight out, but has to wrap it up in this strange story of his, which takes away his responsibility for it and makes her less damaged. Is that what you think?'

'There's one way to find out.'

'We could go there together.'

'I think it would be better if it was just me,' said Frieda. 'You did really well, Jack. I appreciate it and I'm very grateful to you. Thank you.'

He mumbled something incomprehensible. She couldn't tell whether he was pleased by her praise or disappointed at being left behind.

Chapter Twenty-seven

Alan's meeting with Heidi had happened near Victoria Park. The address that Jack had got was for Brewery Road in Poplar, several miles further east. Frieda took the overland train there. She stared out from the platform at the river Lea, grubby and grey, as it twisted its way in the last few curves before it spilled itself into the Thames. She turned away from it and walked past the bus station and under the huge road junction. She could feel the rumble of lorries over her. The underpass led in one direction to a superstore. She looked down at her map and turned to the right, into the residential area on the other side. This had been in the heart of the old East End, which had been flattened during the Blitz by bombs intended for the docks. Every couple of hundred yards, a few surviving houses stood defiantly among the flats and tower blocks that had been built on top of the bomb sites. These new estates were already stained and faded and crumbling. Some had bikes and flowerpots on their narrow balconies, and curtains at their windows. Others were boarded up. In one courtyard, a gang of teenagers huddled round a bonfire made of broken-up furniture.

Frieda walked slowly, trying to get a feel for the area, which had never been more than a name to her. It was a part of the city that had been forgotten and betrayed.

Even the way it had been built on felt like a kind of rejection. She passed a defunct petrol station, with pits in the forecourt where pumps had once stood, and the remains of a red-brick building standing jaggedly behind. Then a row of shops, only two of which were still open – a barber's and a shop selling fishing tackle. A wasteland where nettles grew on the cracked concrete. She passed a series of roads that had been named after western counties – Devon, Somerset, Cornwall – and another after poets: Milton, Cowper, Wordsworth.

At last she reached a stretch of buildings that had escaped the bombs. Frieda looked through the railings of a primary school. In the playground boys were kicking a football. To one side, a group of little girls in headscarves were giggling. She passed a factory that was closed down. A sign on the front announced redevelopment as office spaces and apartments. Then there was a pub with grimy windows and a row of houses. Every single door and window was blocked up with sheet metal, bolted to the walls. Frieda looked at her map again. She crossed the street and turned right into Brewery Road. It curved to the right so that she couldn't see where it led, but a sign at the turning had marked it as a cul-de-sac. At the corner there were some more shops, all closed down and abandoned. Frieda read the old signs. There had been a cab firm, an electronics shop, a newsagent. There were multiple estate agent boards on the front. Leases for sale. Then there were the houses. Many were abandoned, others divided up into flats, but one of them had scaffolding on the façade. Someone had taken the plunge. After all, it was only a few minutes from the Isle of Dogs. In ten years, they would all have been renovated and there would be a restaurant and a gastropub in the road.

He pushed his face against the glass. Skeletons of snow fell in the lost world. Her hair was black and he couldn't see her face. He knew she wasn't real. There weren't people like that any more. Small and clean like a dancer on a music box who turns and turns if you wind the key. Once there was a woman with long red hair who called him honey-bunch. When he had been Matthew, before he lost her hand.

If she looked up, would she see his face? But it wasn't his face any more. It was Simon's face and Simon belonged to someone else.

The dancer disappeared. He heard the bell ringing.

She reached number seventeen, the address on her piece of paper. It had, in its own way, been done up. The front door was painted a dark glossy green. A Georgian-style architrave had been built over it. The window frames on the front of the house were all gleaming new aluminium. The little garden wall had fragments of broken glass cemented along the top, like a warning. What was she going to say? What, really, was she trying to find out? Frieda felt that if she started to think about it, she would just stop and leave. So she didn't think. She pressed the doorbell and heard the chime inside. She waited and pressed the bell and listened.

Nothing, she said to herself, but immediately it was clear that there was something. She heard a sound inside, which turned into footsteps. The door swung inwards. A woman was standing there, blocking the entrance. She was large and pale and fat, and her fatness was emphasized by the black T-shirt that was too small for her and by the black leggings that reached only halfway down her calves. She had a tattoo, like a purple braid, around her upper left arm and another – a bird, a canary perhaps, Frieda thought – on her forearm. Her blonde hair had dark roots and she had blue makeup around her pouchy eyes, lipstick that was so purple it was almost black, like a bruise. She was smoking a cigarette and she tapped the ash on the doorstep, so that Frieda had to step to one side to avoid it. It made Frieda think of being a girl and going to the fair, the dangerous rickety fair that she remembered from when she was very little and that probably wouldn't be allowed nowadays. The eight-year-old Frieda had handed her fifty pence to women like her, sitting in glass booths at the entrance to the haunted house or the dodgems.

'What do you want?'

'I'm sorry to disturb you,' she said. 'Does Dean Reeve live here?'

'Why?'

'I just wanted to have a quick word.'

'He's not here,' said the woman, not moving.

'But he lives here?'

'Who wants to know?'

'I just want a word with him,' said Frieda. 'It's to do with a friend of a friend. It's not a big deal.'

'Is this about a job?' said the woman. 'Has something gone wrong?'

'Not at all,' said Frieda, trying to sound reassuring. 'I just want a quick word. It'll only take a minute. Do you know when he'll be back?'

'He just popped out,' said the woman.

'Could I wait for him?'

'I don't let strangers in my house.'

'Just a couple of minutes, please,' said Frieda, firmly, and stepped up to the woman, almost touching her. She was more than ever aware of her bulk and her hostility. Behind her, the house was dark and smelt with an odd sweetness she couldn't quite identify.

'What do you want with Dean?' The woman sounded angry and also frightened. Her voice rose slightly.

'I'm a doctor,' said Frieda, and with that she was into the warmth of the narrow hallway. It was painted a dark red, so that it felt even narrower than it was.

'What sort of doctor?'

'Nothing to worry about,' said Frieda, crisply. 'Just routine. It won't take a moment.' She tried to make herself sound more confident than she felt. The woman pushed the front door and it shut with a click.

She looked around and gave a start. On a small ledge above a doorway to the left, there was a small stuffed bird, some sort of hawk, with its wings outstretched.

'Dean got it from a shop round the corner. Got it cheap. You can't give them away now. Gives me the creeps.'

Frieda stepped through the door into the front room. It was dominated by a large-screen television, amplifiers and speakers, joined with a complicated array of wires. DVDs were piled on the floor. The front curtains were closed. The only furniture was a sofa facing the room and, on the far wall, an enormous chest of miniature drawers.

'That's unusual,' said Frieda.

The woman stubbed out her cigarette on the mantelpiece and lit another one. Her nails were painted but Frieda could see the yellow around the tips. Her finger had swollen around the large gold wedding ring on her fourth finger.

'He got it from the reclamation place. It's from one of those old clothes shops. Those drawers were for little things, like socks or balls of wool. Dean uses it for his tools and bits and pieces, you know, fuses, screws, rulers. Stuff for his models.'

Frieda smiled. The woman seemed happy enough to have someone to talk to, although there were beads of sweat on her large forehead and her eyes were darting around nervously, as though she expected someone to step into the room at any minute.

'What does he make?'

'He makes these boats. Real proper miniatures. He takes them over to the ponds and gives them a runaround.'

Frieda looked about as if she were searching for something. She had an odd feeling she couldn't quite place. As if she had been here before, like a dream that receded the more she tried to capture it. A thin tortoiseshell cat stepped delicately into the room and wound itself around her ankles, and as she bent down to stroke it, another one entered. It was large and a matted grey with giant fur balls hanging off its coat. She stepped back. She didn't want to touch it. She saw two more cats entwined in the corner of the sofa. That was the smell: cat litter and cat shit and air freshener.

'How many cats have you got?'

The woman shrugged.

'They come and go.'

He lay on the floor with his ear to the wood and listened to the voices. The one he knew, and the other one. Soft, clear, a stream running through him. It would take away the dirt. He was a dirty boy. Wash his mouth out. He had no idea. Didn't deserve. Should be ashamed. Filthy.

'My name's Frieda.' She spoke slowly, feeling as though she had stepped into a looking-glass world. 'Frieda Klein.' Then, when the woman didn't answer, she said, 'Who are you?'

'Terry,' said the woman. She ground her cigarette into an overflowing ashtray, and then took another, holding out the packet to Frieda as well. Frieda had given up smoking years earlier. Ever since, she had felt allergic to it. She hated the smell of it in the air, in people's clothes. But it would give her an excuse to stay. There was always something companionable about smoking together. She remembered it from teenage parties: it gave you something to do with your hands, something to fiddle with when you couldn't think of what to say. You still saw it, people standing in doorways on the street. Soon that would be banned as well. Where would they go then? She nodded, took the cigarette and leaned forward as Terry flicked the cheap plastic lighter. Frieda had a drag and felt the now unfamiliar rush. She exhaled and almost felt dizzy with it.

'Does Dean live here all the time?'

'Course.' In the painted, swollen flesh of her face, Terry's eyes narrowed. 'What do you mean?'

'And he works here?'

'He goes out.'

'What does he do?'

The woman looked at her. She chewed her lower lip and tapped the ash into the ashtray. 'Are you checking up on him?'

Frieda made herself smile. 'I'm just a doctor.' She looked around. 'I guess he's some kind of builder. Is that right?'

'He does a bit of that,' said Terry. 'Why do you want to know?'

'I just met someone who knows him.' She heard how feeble her words sounded. 'I wanted to ask him a question. Get some information. I'll go in a minute, if he's not back.'

'I've got things to do,' said the woman. 'I think you'd better go now.'

'I'll go in a minute.' Frieda gestured with the cigarette. 'When I've finished this. Do you work?'

'Get out of my house.'

And then she heard the sound of the front door. She heard a voice from outside the room.

'In here,' called Terry.

A shape appeared in the door. Frieda saw a flash of leather jacket, jeans, work boots and then, as he stepped into the light, it was unmistakable. The clothes were different, except for the brightly checked shirt, but there was absolutely no doubt.

'Alan,' she said. 'Alan. What's going on?'

'What?'

'It's me . . .' said Frieda, and then she stopped. She realized how very, very stupid she had been. Her mind became a fog. She didn't know what to say. She made a desperate effort to pull herself together. 'You're Dean Reeve.'

The man looked between the two women.

'Who are you?' His voice was quiet, uninflected. 'What are you doing here?'

'I think there's been a mix-up,' said Frieda. 'I met someone who knows you.'

She thought of the woman in the orange jacket and thought of Terry. Dean's wife. She looked at his expressionless face, his dark brown eyes. She tried another smile but the man's expression changed.

'How did you get in here? What are you up to?'

'I let her in,' said Terry. 'She said she wanted to talk to you.'

The man stepped towards Frieda and raised his hand towards her, not as if he was going to hit her but as if he was going to touch her to see if she was really there. She took a step back.

'I'm sorry. I think there's been a mistake. Mistaken identity.' She paused. 'Has that happened to you before?'

The man looked at her as though he could see inside her. It felt as if he were touching her, as if she could feel his hands on her skin.

He knew he had to warn her. They would catch her and turn her into something else as well. She wouldn't be a dancer any more. They would tie her feet up. They would block her mouth.

He tried to shout but only made his humming that was

trapped inside his mouth and at the back of his throat. He stood up, swaying and with the nasty taste in his mouth that never went away, and jumped up and down, up and down, until there was red in his eyes and his head swam and the walls leaned in towards him and he fell on the floor again. He banged his head against the wood. She would hear him. She must.

'Who are you?'

The voice was the same as well. A bit more sure of itself, but the same.

'Sorry,' said Frieda. 'My mistake.' She held up the cigarette. 'Thanks for this. I'll let myself out, shall I? Sorry to mess you around.' She turned and, as casually as she could, walked out of the room and tried to open the front door. At first she couldn't work out which handle to pull but then she found the right one, opened the door and stepped outside. She tossed the cigarette down and walked slowly at first and then, when she turned the corner, broke into a run and ran all the way to the station, even though her chest was hurting and she could hardly breathe and the bile was rising in her throat. She felt as though she was running through a thick mist that obscured all the familiar signposts and made the world uncanny, unreal.

He saw her go. Slow, then faster, then she danced. She had escaped and she would never come back because he had saved her.

The door behind him opened.

'You've been a very naughty little boy, haven't you?'

*

When she was safely on the train, she wished, for the first time in her life, that she had a mobile phone. She looked around. There was a young woman a few seats down who looked harmless enough so she stood up and walked over to her.

'Excuse me.' She tried to sound matter-of-fact, as if this was an ordinary request. 'Could I please borrow your mobile?'

The woman pulled her earplugs out of her ears.

'What?'

'Could I borrow your mobile, please?'

'No, you fucking can't.'

Frieda pulled her wallet out of her bag. 'I'll pay you,' she said. 'A fiver?'

'Ten.'

'OK. Ten.'

She handed it over and took the woman's mobile, which was very small and thin. It took her several minutes to grasp how to make a single call. Her hands were still shaking.

'Hello. Hello. Please put me through to Detective Inspector Karlsson.'

'Who shall I say is calling?'

'Dr Klein. Frieda.'

'Will you hold on a moment?'

Frieda waited. She gazed out of the window at the scarred buildings flowing past.

'Dr Klein?'

'Yes.'

'I'm afraid he's busy at the moment.'

Frieda remembered their last meeting; his anger with

her. 'It's urgent,' she said. 'There's something he needs to know.'

'I'm sorry.'

'I mean, *now*. I need to talk to him now.'

'Do you want to talk to someone else?'

'No!'

'Can I take a message for you?'

'Yes. Tell him to ring me at once. I'm on a mobile. Oh, but I don't know the number.'

'It's on my display,' said the voice at the other end.

'I'll be waiting.'

She sat with the phone in her hand, waiting for it to ring. The train stopped and a group of scruffy, spotty teenagers crowded into the carriage, all boys with jeans pulled down below their concave buttocks, except for one scrawny girl who, under her clumsy makeup, looked about thirteen. As Frieda watched, one of the boys held a can of white cider to her lips and tried to make her drink it. She shook her head, but he persisted, and after a few seconds, she opened her mouth and let him pour some in. The liquid dribbled down her small chin. She was wearing an unzipped fur-lined parka and under that, Frieda saw, just a halter-neck top over her flat breasts and sharp collarbone. She must be freezing, the poor pinched-looking brat. For a moment, Frieda considered going over and hitting the sniggering youths with her umbrella, then thought better of it. She'd done enough for one day.

The train juddered to a halt outside the next station. Snow was falling again, improbably large occasional flakes spinning past her window. Frieda squinted: was that a heron on the bank, tall and still and elegant among the brambles? She stared at the mobile, willing it to ring, and when it didn't she phoned again, heard the same voice at the other end, once more asked for Karlsson, and was once more told – in a voice stiff with politeness – that he was still not available to take her call.

'Who was she?'

His voice was calm, but still she shrank away from him.

'I don't know. She just rang on the doorbell.'

Dean took her chin gently in his hand and tipped her face so that she was gazing straight into his eyes. 'What did she want?'

'I just answered the door. She pushed in. I didn't know how to stop her. She said she was a doctor.'

'Did she tell you her name?'

'No. Yes. Something a bit different.' She licked her purple lips. 'Frieda and then a short name. I dunno . . .'

'You'd better tell me.'

'Klein. That's it. Frieda Klein.'

He let go of her chin. 'Dr Frieda Klein. And she called me Alan . . .' He smiled at his wife and tapped her lightly on the shoulder. 'Wait for me. Don't go anywhere.'

The train made a sudden lurch forward, then stopped again with a hissing of brakes. Frieda watched the girl drink more cider. One of the boys put his hand up her skirt and she giggled. Her eyes were glassy. The train jerked into motion. Frieda got her little address book out of her bag and flicked through the pages until she came to the name she wanted. She thought about asking the young woman for her mobile again, but decided against it.

At last the train creaked into a station, through the slow-falling snow. Frieda got out and went at once to the phone box at the entrance. It didn't take coins. She had to push in her credit card before dialling.

'Dick?' she said. 'It's me, Frieda. Frieda Klein.'

'Dick' was Richard Carey, a professor of neurology at Birmingham University. She had been on a panel with him at a conference four years before. He'd asked her out and she'd made an excuse but they'd stayed in touch in a vague kind of way. He was just the kind of person she needed. Well connected, knew everyone.

'Frieda?' he said. 'Where have you been hiding?'

'I need a name,' Frieda said.

Chapter Twenty-eight

Frieda had cancelled all her patients that morning but she was back in time for her afternoon sessions, including the one with Alan. As she walked to her office, she felt the smell of Dean Reeve's house was still clinging to her: cigarette ash and cat shit. The day was closing in already. It was only three days from the shortest day of the year. The snow of the morning had turned to a sleety rain that melted in muddy rivulets on the road. Her feet were damp inside her boots and her skin felt raw. She longed for her house, her chair by the fire.

Alan was the last of her patients. She had been dreading seeing him, with a feeling that almost amounted to a physical repugnance, and had to steel herself when he eventually walked through the door, his face red from the cold and water speckling his duffel coat. She clenched her hands into fists under the long sleeves of her jersey, and made herself greet him calmly and take her seat opposite him. His face looked no different from the last time she had seen him, and no different from the man she had met a few hours earlier. It was hard for her not to gape at him. Should she tell him what she knew? But how could she? What would she say? I've been investigating your life, without your knowledge or consent, checking up on the truth of what you tell me in confidence within these four walls, and I have found you have an identical twin. Or did he already know? Was that what he was hiding from her and from his wife? Was there some strange conspiracy going on?

'What will I do if I can't cope over Christmas?'

He spoke to her. She strained to hear the words and to reply to them intelligibly. Through his frail voice she heard the tone of Dean Reeve, stronger, almost mocking. When she had met Dean she had seen Alan and now with Alan she saw Dean. At last he was going, standing up and struggling his bulky body into the duffel coat, buttoning up the toggles with painstaking care. He was thanking her. Saying he didn't know how he would have got through this without her. She shook his hand formally. Now he was gone and she sank back into her chair and pressed her fingers against her temples.

Dean stood on the opposite side of the road, smoking another cigarette. He had been there for nearly one hour and still she hadn't appeared. When she came, he would follow her, see where that led, but the light in her room was still on and every so often he could see shapes in the window. He looked at each person who went into the building and came out. Some of them were hooded against the rain and he couldn't make them out. It was cold, nasty weather, but he didn't much mind that. He wasn't one of those whingers who couldn't get their feet wet, who opened an umbrella at the first hint of rain or stood in the doorways of shops and offices to wait for it to pass.

Across the road, the door opened once more and a figure came out. He himself came out. As he looked around, his face was quite clear. Unmistakable. Dean became very still. He stood like that until the figure was almost out of sight. A smile crossed his face and he lifted a hand towards the man who was him, as if he could draw him back.

Well, well, well. Ma, you sly old fox.

Frieda sat motionless for ten minutes, her eyes closed, trying to clear the sludge of her thoughts. Then, abruptly, she rose to her feet, pulled on her coat, turned off the lights, double locked the door and left.

She headed straight for Reuben's house. She had no doubt that he would be there. He and Josef seemed to have settled into a routine of drinking beer and vodka and watching quiz shows on TV. Reuben would shout out the answers and, if he was right, Josef would marvel at him and toast him with a shot.

As it happened, Reuben was alone, cooking himself an omelette, and there was no sign of Josef, although his ancient white van was parked outside, the front wheel up on the pavement.

'He's upstairs,' said Reuben.

'Is he alone?'

Reuben gave a challenging smile, as if he was daring Frieda to say something disapproving. She looked at the photograph of Josef's wife and sons, still stuck with a magnet on the fridge door. With their formal pose, old-fashioned clothes and dark eyes, they belonged to another world. 'It was you I wanted to talk to. I need your advice.'

'Strange how you need it now when I'm not exactly in the best state to give it.'

'Something's happened.'

Reuben ate his omelette out of the frying-pan while

Frieda talked. Every so often he shook Tabasco sauce over it, or lifted his glass to take a sip of water. Halfway through the story, he stopped eating, however, laying down his fork and quietly pushing the pan away from him. He heard her out in absolute silence, though in the brief pauses Frieda thought she could hear a bed creaking upstairs.

'So,' she said, when she had finished. 'What do you think?'

Reuben stood up. He went to the newly installed french windows and gazed out at the sodden, neglected garden. It was dark; only the bent shapes of bushes and bare trees could be clearly seen and, beyond that, the lit windows of someone else's kitchen. The creaking seemed to have stopped. He turned round.

'You've crossed a line,' he said, grinning. He seemed unreasonably cheerful.

'I've crossed several.'

'I think you should, one, go to the police and don't take no for an answer.' He was counting them off on his fingers. 'Two, tell Alan everything you know about him. Three, see this Cambridge expert. In no particular order, but as quickly as you can.'

'Yes.'

'Oh – and four, see your own supervisor. Have you still got one?'

'She's lying dormant.'

'Maybe it's time to wake her up. And don't be so tortured about it. It doesn't suit you.'

Frieda stood up. 'I was going to see if Josef would drive me to Cambridge. This probably isn't a good time to ask him.'

'I think they've finished.' Reuben went to the bottom of the stairs and yelled, 'Josef! Have you got a minute?'

A muffled shout came from upstairs and shortly afterwards Josef came down the stairs, his feet bare. When he caught sight of Frieda he looked uneasy.

Frieda walked back through Regent's Park, her hands deep in her coat pockets. The cold northerly wind felt good, as if it was drowning her thoughts. After she had crossed Euston Road, she stopped at a shop and bought a bag of pasta, a jar of sauce, a bag of salad and a bottle of red wine. Back at her front door, she was fumbling for her key when she felt a touch on her shoulder that made her jump.

'Alan,' she said. 'What the hell are you doing here?'

'I'm sorry. I needed to talk to you. I couldn't wait.'

Frieda looked helplessly around. She felt like a wild animal that had been tracked back to its lair. 'You know the rules,' she said. 'We have to stick to them.'

'I know, I know, but . . .'

The tone was pleading. His duffel coat was wrongly buttoned and his hair was dishevelled; his face looked blotchy from the cold. Frieda had her key in her hand and it was hovering near the lock. She had many rules, but the absolute one, the inviolable one, was that she never let a patient into her house. It was always the patient's fantasy, to get into her life, to discover what she was really like, to get a hold on her, to do to her what she was doing to them, to find out her secrets. But so many rules had been broken. She put the key in the lock and turned it.

'Five minutes,' she said.

*

He held his hand in front of him. Fingers turned to twigs. No one would want to eat him now. Dirty bare feet; they weren't feet any more. They were roots creeping into the earth and soon he wouldn't be able to move at all.

But they tore him up and they wrapped him round and he could feel his twigs snapping and his roots were stuffed into a sack and his mouth was stoppered up with soil and he was crammed into new darkness. They were taking him to market. This little pig went to market. Who would give a gold coin for him? He was gripped and picked up and he sank down further to the bottom of the sack and the voices grunted and said rude words and the witch shouted that Simon Said, Simon Said but Simon didn't say anything because his mouth was shut and his voice was all gone now.

Bump, bump, bump. Then he was lying on something hard and there was a bang above him. The darkness was even darker and there was a new smell, oily and deep. He heard a loud cough, a splutter, a hum, which felt like the noise the witch-cat made when it dug its paws in and out of his sore skin, but louder. His body was bouncing up and down. His head was banging up and down on the hard surface.

Then he was still again. There was a click and he felt hard fingers pincer him through the sack, locking on to his shoulder, his soft thigh. He knew his body was falling apart because he could feel pain running through him like a river, into every crack of him. He didn't know the word for 'why?' and he couldn't remember the word for 'please'. Nothing left. No Matthew left. Bumped along the ground. Cold. So cold. Cold like fire. There was something rattling and heaving and the voice grunted again and then suddenly he was being pulled from the sack.

Two faces in the gloom. Mouths opening and shutting. Simon Said no but he couldn't speak. They were pushing him into a hole. Was it an oven, even though his fingers were twigs, were icicles, too sharp to eat? But it couldn't be an oven because there was no heat, only a throbbing cold darkness. Mouth unravelled and he opened it but nothing came out. Only breath.

'Make a sound and you'll be cut into little pieces and fed to the birds,' said the voice of the master. 'Do you hear?'

Did he hear? He heard nothing now, except the sound of stone being dragged over earth and then it was black night and cold night and silent night and lost night and only his heart still spoke, like a drum under his stretched skin. I-am, I-am, I-am.

Chapter Twenty-nine

'I saw Alan yesterday,' said Frieda.

It was almost the first time she had spoken. When Josef had picked her up in his van, he had talked about Reuben and about work and about his family. When Frieda at last spoke, it was almost as if she were speaking to herself.

'He is your patient, no?'

'He came to my house. He found out where I lived and came to my house. I told him that if he was in trouble, he could get in touch any time. But he was meant to phone me, not knock on my door. It felt like a violation. If things had been normal, I would have sent him away. I would probably have stopped seeing him, referred him to someone else.'

Josef didn't reply. He was steering his van across several lanes. 'We take the motorway here, right?'

'That's right.' Frieda moved her hands up in an involuntary gesture of self-protection as Josef swung his van into a gap between two lorries.

'It's OK,' said Josef.

Frieda looked around. They were already at the beginning of a kind of countryside, frosty fields and lonely trees.

'A violation,' said Josef. 'Like when I came to your house.'

'That's different,' said Frieda. 'You're not my patient. I'm a mystery to them. They fantasize about me and quite often they fall in love with me. It's not just me. It's part of the job but you have to be careful.'

Josef looked across at her. 'Do you fall in love also?'

'No,' said Frieda. 'You know everything about them, all their fantasies, their secret fears, their lies. You can't fall in love with someone if you know everything about them. I don't tell patients about my life and I don't let them anywhere near my house.'

'So what did you do?'

'I broke my rule,' said Frieda. 'I let him into my house, just for a few minutes. For once, I had to admit that he had a right to be curious.'

'You tell him everything?'

'I can't tell him everything. I don't understand things myself. That's why we're driving out here.'

'So what you tell him?'

Frieda looked out of the window. Funny to live in a farm ten minutes out of London. She'd always thought that if she lived out of London it would be somewhere far away, somewhere that would take hours, days to get there. An abandoned lighthouse, that would be good. Perhaps not even abandoned. Could analysts retrain as lighthouse keepers? Were there still lighthouse keepers?

'It was difficult,' said Frieda. 'I tried to make it as painless as possible for him. Maybe I was making it painless for *me*. But how painless can you be when you tell someone that you've found a brother he knew nothing about?' She couldn't tell how much Josef understood.

'He was angry with you?'

'He didn't really react so much as go all still,' said Frieda. 'People are often shocked into a kind of strange calmness when you tell them really big things, things that change their whole life. I said there was more that I'd be able to tell him soon, but that the police might become involved again – although of course I don't know about that. I don't know if this has anything to do with the little boy or if everything has just got tangled up in my imagination. Anyway, I said I was sorry about that if it did happen, but that this time it was nothing at all to do with him. That's a lot to deal with in one go.'

'What did he say?'

'I tried to get him to say something, but he didn't want to talk. He put his head in his hands for a while. I think he might have been crying, but I'm not sure. He probably needs to go away and think about things, let them settle.'

'He will meet his twin?'

'I don't know,' said Frieda. 'I keep thinking about it. I have this feeling that it won't happen. Anyway, I think the issue for Alan is the guilt that he feels but doesn't understand. It was when I told him I was going back to the police that he looked most shattered. It's hard for him to face any more of that. It was better he heard it from me. I thought he might get angry with me but he seemed in a state of shock. He just left. I felt I'd let him down. My real job is to help my patient.'

'You find the truth,' said Josef, confidently.

'There's nothing in my job description about finding the truth,' said Frieda. 'It's about helping my patient to cope.'

Frieda looked down at the route instructions she had printed out. It was all very simple. After another half-hour on the M11 they turned off and drove to a small village a few miles from Cambridge.

'It must be here,' she said.

Josef turned into a short gravel drive that led to a large Georgian house. The drive was lined with gleaming cars, so it was difficult for the van to squeeze through. 'They look expensive,' he said.

'Try not to scrape them,' said Frieda. She stepped out of the van and felt her feet sink into the gravel. 'Do you want to come in? I could say you were my assistant.'

'I listen to the radio,' said Josef. 'It makes my English better.'

'This is great of you,' she said. 'I'll pay you.'

'You will pay me by cooking a meal,' he said. 'An English Christmas meal.'

'I think it would be better if I paid you, probably,' she said.

'Go in,' he said. 'Why are you waiting?'

Frieda turned and waded through the gravel to the front door. There was an elaborate Christmas garland on it. She pressed the bell but couldn't hear anything, so she rapped on the door with the large brass knocker. The house shook with it. The door was opened by a woman wearing a long, elaborate dress. She had a welcoming smile on her face that faded as soon as she saw Frieda.

'Oh, it's you,' she said.

'Is Professor Boundy here?' said Frieda.

'I'll get him,' said the woman. 'He's with our lunch guests.' She paused for a moment. 'I suppose you'd better come in.'

Frieda stepped into the large hallway. She could hear

a murmur of voices. The woman walked across the hall, her heels echoing on the wooden floor. She opened a door and Frieda glimpsed a group of people, men in suits, women in smart dresses. She looked around the large hall – on one side an ornate staircase curved upwards. In a niche in the wall there was a bonsai tree. She heard footsteps and turned to see a man coming towards her. He had grey hair swept back from his face and rimless spectacles. He was wearing a dark suit with a brightly patterned tie.

'We're about to sit down to lunch,' he said. 'Was there any reason we couldn't have talked on the phone?'

'Five minutes,' said Frieda. 'That's all we need.'

He looked ostentatiously at his watch. Frieda found it almost amusing to be treated so rudely.

'You'd better come into my study,' he said.

He led her across the hallway to a room at the far end. It was lined with bookshelves except for a wall of french windows giving out on to a large lawn. A path led away from the house and culminated in a gazebo with a stone seat. He sat down behind a wooden desk. 'Dick Lacey spoke very highly of you,' he said. 'He said you needed to see me urgently and that it wouldn't wait. Even though it's Christmas and I'm with my family. So I agreed to see you.' He unfastened his watch and laid it on the desk. 'Briefly.'

He gestured at an armchair but Frieda ignored him. She walked towards the window and looked out, considering how to begin. She turned round. 'I've just had a strange experience,' she said. 'A patient of mine has certain family issues. One factor is that he was adopted. He was abandoned as a baby and knows nothing whatever about his birth family. He's never made any attempt to find them. I don't think he'd know even how to begin going about it.'

She paused for a moment.

'Look,' said Professor Boundy. 'If this is about tracing relatives . . .'

Frieda interrupted him: 'Certain things happened and I got the address of someone I thought might be connected to him. This isn't the sort of thing that I do but I visited the house, unannounced.' Suddenly Frieda felt almost embarrassed. 'I find this bit difficult to explain. When I went inside the house, it was like being in a dream. I should say that I've been to Alan's house. Alan's my patient. When I went into this other house, I had this feeling: "I've been here before." They weren't identical, but there was something about one that reminded you of the other.'

She looked at Professor Boundy. Would he think she was insane? Would he laugh?

'In what way?' he said.

'Some of it was just a feeling,' said Frieda. 'Both houses felt closed-up. Alan's house was cosy, full of small rooms. The other house was like that but even more so, almost claustrophobic. It seemed to be shutting the light out. But there were other, odder, things in common. Both of them keep things in neat little drawers with labels on the front. There were even the strangest things in common. For example, I was startled to find that both of them had a stuffed bird on display. Alan had a poor little stuffed kingfisher and Dean had a stuffed hawk. It was uncanny. I didn't know what to make of it.'

She looked at Professor Boundy. He was now leaning back in his chair, his arms crossed, staring at the ceiling. Was he just waiting for her to finish?

'It was more than that,' said Frieda. 'It was like a dream. When I stepped into Dean Reeve's house, it was like somewhere I'd been before, like going back somewhere you lived as a small child. You know you've been there but you don't know why. It was a feeling both houses had, a hot, closed-in feeling. Anyway, I was there with his partner, or wife, and then he – Dean – arrived. For a moment I thought it was Alan and that he was leading a double life. Then I realized that Alan wasn't just abandoned as a baby. He had a twin he didn't know about.'

'Abandoned *because* he had a twin,' said Professor Boundy.

'What?'

There was a knock and the door opened. It was the woman who had let Frieda in. 'We're just sitting down, dear,' she said. 'Shall I tell them you're about to arrive?'

'No,' said Professor Boundy, without looking round at her. 'Start without me.'

'We can wait.'

'Go away.'

The woman – evidently Boundy's wife – looked at Frieda with an expression of suspicion. She turned and left without a word.

'And close the door,' said Boundy, in a loud voice. The door to the study closed gently.

'I'm sorry about that,' he said. 'Can I get you something? We've got some champagne open.' Frieda shook her head. 'What I was about to explain is that mothers would have twins that they were unable to deal with, so they would put up one for adoption. Or sometimes just abandon one.' Boundy looked up at the ceiling again, then fixed Frieda with a gaze that was almost fierce. 'So why did you drive all the way up to Cambridge to see me?'

'Because of what I told you. I've been thinking about what it was that I saw when I went into the house. It felt a bit like magic, and I don't believe in magic. I talked to Dick Lacey and I checked up on you and I learned that you're specifically interested in twins who have been reared separately. Of course I know that's a subject of considerable interest for the debate about nature and nurture. I've read papers about it. But what I encountered seemed beyond the range of science and reason. It felt more like an elaborate charade, some kind of mind trick being played on me. So I needed to talk to an expert.'

Boundy leaned back once more. 'I'm certainly an expert,' he said. 'This is the issue: I'm interested in the role genetic factors play in the development of personality. Researchers have always been interested in twins, but the problem is that they generally share the same environment as well as the same genes. What we'd really like to do is to take two identical children, bring them up in different environments and see what the effect is. Unfortunately, we're not allowed to do that. But sometimes, just sometimes, people do it for us by separating their twins at birth. These identical twins are perfect for us. Their genetic makeup is identical, so any variation must be environmental. So we've been looking for these twins, and when we found them, we looked in great detail at their life histories. We gave them personality tests, medical examinations.'

'And what did you find?'

Boundy got up, walked to the bookshelf and took out a book. 'I wrote this,' he said. 'Well, co-wrote it. The ideas are mine. You should read it.'

'But in the meantime,' said Frieda.

Boundy laid the book on his desk almost reverently, then half sat on the desk edge. 'Just over twenty years ago, I gave the first paper on our findings at a conference in Chicago. It was based on an assessment of twenty-six pairs of identical twins reared separately. Do you know what the response of my fellow professionals was?'

'No.'

'It was a rhetorical question. The response was divided between those who accused me of incompetence and those who accused me of dishonesty.'

'What do you mean?' asked Frieda.

'To take one example, one twin lived in Bristol and the other in Wolverhampton. When they were reunited in their late thirties, they discovered that they had both married women called Jane, divorced them and married women called Claire. They both owned miniature railways as a hobby, they both cut out savings coupons from the back of cereal packets, they both had moustaches and sideburns. Then there was a pair of female twins. One lived in Edinburgh, the other in Nottingham. One was a doctor's receptionist, the other a dentist's receptionist. Both liked to dress in black, both were asthmatic, both were so afraid of lifts that they took the stairs even in tall buildings. And so on and so on. When we examined non-identical twins, the effect disappeared almost completely.'

'So why the accusations?'

'Other psychologists just didn't believe me. What was it that Hume said about miracles? Anything – fraud, human error, whatever – is more likely, so that's what you should assume and that's what people did assume. People stood up after my talk and said that I must have been mistaken, that the twins must really have known about each other. Or that the researchers went looking for resemblances and cherry-picked the evidence, the argument being that any two lives will probably have something odd in common.'

'I think I would have been dubious,' said Frieda.

'You think I wasn't?' said Boundy. 'We checked everything. The twins were interviewed by different researchers, we checked the subjects' backgrounds, everything. We tried to knock it down, but the findings were robust.'

'If it's robust,' said Frieda, 'then what the hell's it about? You're not talking about some kind of ESP, because if so . . .'

Boundy laughed. 'Of course not. But you're a therapist. You think that we're just rational beings, that we can talk about our problems and . . .'

'That's not exactly –'

Boundy continued as if he hadn't heard her. 'People talk about our brains being like computers. If that's true – which it isn't – then the computer comes into the world with a lot of its software pre-installed. You know, like a female turtle that spends its whole life at sea. It doesn't learn how to come ashore, lay its eggs and bury them by watching its mother. Certain neurons just start to fire in ways we don't understand and it just knows what to do. What my twin studies showed is that a lot of what look like responses to the environment, decisions made using free will, are just the working out of patterns that the subject was born with.' Boundy spread his hands like a magician who had just performed a particularly clever trick. 'So there we are. Problem solved. You don't have to worry about going mad.'

'No,' said Frieda, not looking at all as if she was relieved by what she'd heard.

'The problem is that these separated twins are getting rarer. Social workers are less likely to separate them, adoption agencies keep them together. It's good for the twins, of course. Not so good for people like me.' He frowned. 'But you haven't answered my question. Why was it so urgent?'

When Frieda answered, it was almost as if her mind was elsewhere. 'You've been very helpful,' she said. 'But there's something I've got to do.'

'I might be able to help you. Do you want to find out more about the family of your patient?'

'Probably,' said Frieda.

'It's just that my team have got a great deal of expertise in finding out about the hidden histories of families. Discreetly. We've built up some useful informal contacts over the years. They're good at finding out things about people's families that they don't know themselves. In the way that you seem to have stumbled across, but a bit more systematically.'

'That might be useful,' said Frieda.

'If there's anything I can do to help . . .' said Dr Boundy. His tone had now become warmer, and almost casual. 'It might make up for my rudeness when you arrived. I'm sorry about that, but you walked into the middle of one of those ghastly occasions when we invite the neighbours in. You know the sort of thing. It's the worst time of year.'

'I understand.'

'Obviously they won't be able to get on to it until after the holiday. As you know, Britain is now closed for business for the next ten days or so. But if you give me the names of these two brothers, their addresses perhaps, any other details you know of, maybe we could make some checks when we're all back.'

'What kind of checks?' said Frieda.

'Family-tree stuff,' said Dr Boundy. 'And if they've had any dealings with the social services, any criminal records, credit problems. It would be for your eyes only. We're very tactful.' He picked his book up from his desk and handed it to Frieda. 'You can read this and see how careful we are.'

'All right,' said Frieda, and she wrote down the two names and addresses.

'Probably nothing will come of it,' said Dr Boundy. 'I can't promise anything.'

'Don't worry.'

He took the book back from her. 'Let me sign it for you,' he said. 'At least it'll stop you going off and selling it.' He wrote in it and then handed it back to her.

She looked at the inscription. 'Thank you,' she said.

'Can I offer you some lunch?'

She shook her head. 'You've been a great help. But I'm in a hurry.'

'I quite understand,' he said. 'Let me show you out.'

He walked her to the front door, talking as he did so of colleagues they might have in common, of conferences they might both have attended. He held his hand out to shake hers, then seemed to think of something. 'They're interesting,' he said, 'these separated twins. I did a paper once about twins where one of them had died in the womb. They seemed to know, even if they didn't know, if you know what I mean. It's as if they were in mourning for something they didn't know existed and were forever trying to recover it.'

'What's the effect of that on a life?' asked Frieda. 'Feeling incomplete like that. What do you do with it?'

'I don't know,' said Boundy. 'It feels important, though.' Now he shook her hand. 'I hope we'll meet again soon,' he said.

He stood and watched as she climbed into the van and as it trundled down the drive, narrowly missing a parked Mercedes that belonged to the Master of Professor Boundy's college. After he closed the front door, he still didn't join the guests. He stood in thought for a few moments, then walked back to his study and shut the door. He picked up the phone and dialled.

'Kathy? It's Seth. What are you doing? . . . Well, stop and come over here and I'll tell you about it when you get here . . . I know it's Christmas, but Christmas happens every year and this is once in a lifetime.' He looked at his watch. 'Half an hour? . . . Fine. I'll be here.'

Boundy put the phone down and smiled, listening to the hum of conversation and chink of glasses in the room beyond.

Chapter Thirty

Frieda got back into the van and Josef turned off the radio. He looked at her expectantly.

'Let's get out of here,' she said. 'And give me your mobile. I've got a call to make.'

But there was no signal for a few miles. When at last a single bar appeared on the mobile screen, she ordered Josef to stop.

'I smoke,' he said, and climbed out of the van.

Frieda called the police station. 'I need to speak to Detective Inspector Karlsson. I know he won't be there on a Saturday and I know you won't give me his home number, but I'll give you this mobile number and you can tell him he has got to phone me at once. Tell him that if he doesn't call me within the next ten minutes I am going to ring up the newspapers and give them the information about Matthew Faraday that he is refusing to listen to. Tell him those exact words.' The woman at the other end started to speak but Frieda cut her off. 'Ten minutes,' she said.

She watched Josef. He looked very peaceful, sitting by the side of the road under a tree that was leafless and bent out of shape after decades of wind blowing across this flat landscape. The sky was white and the ploughed field looked like a frozen brown sea.

The mobile rang.

'Frieda here.'

'What the fuck are you on about?'

'We need to meet at once. Where are you?'

'At home. It's the day I have with my children. I can't leave.'

'Where do you live?' She wrote down the address he gave her on a scrap of paper. 'I'll be right there.'

She opened her door and called Josef over. 'Home?' he asked, as he climbed back into the van.

'Can you take me one more place first?'

Karlsson lived just off Highbury Corner in a Victorian semi-detached house that had been divided into several flats. As Frieda went up the steps to the raised front door, she could see through the window just beneath her into the lower ground flat that was his. As she looked, he crossed her field of vision carrying a tiny girl, her arms and legs wrapped around him like a koala bear.

That was how he came to the door. He hadn't shaved and was wearing jeans and a thick blue cardigan. The girl had yellow curls and chubby bare legs. She was sobbing, her wet cheek pressed against his chest. She opened one gleaming blue eye to peer at Frieda and closed it again.

'Where have you been?'

'Football traffic.'

'This isn't a good time.'

'I wouldn't be here at all if you hadn't ignored my calls.'

The large living room was strewn with toys and children's clothes. A boy sat on the sofa watching cartoons on the television and posting popcorn into his mouth. Very carefully, Karlsson unwound his daughter's arms and legs and placed her beside her brother. Her wails grew louder.

'Just for a few minutes,' he said. 'Then I'll take you both swimming, I promise. Give her some popcorn, Mikey.'

Without taking his eyes off the screen, the boy held out the tub and she took a fistful and pushed it into her mouth. Fragments stuck to her chin. Frieda and Karlsson stood at the other end of the room, at the large window from where she could see Josef in the van. Karlsson was slightly behind her, as if he was shielding his children from her.

'Well?'

Frieda went through the events of the past days, and as she did so, Karlsson's posture stiffened and the expression on his face changed from irritated impatience to fierce concentration. When she had finished, he didn't speak for a moment. Then he picked up his mobile.

'I'll have to get someone to look after the children. Their mother lives in Brighton.'

'I could do it,' said Frieda.

'You're coming with me.'

'How about Josef?'

'Josef?'

Frieda pointed to the van.

'What?' said Karlsson. 'Are you insane?'

'He's a friend,' Frieda said. 'He's been looking after a colleague of mine. He's actually a builder.'

Karlsson looked doubtful. 'You can vouch for him?'

'He's my friend.'

She went out to Josef.

'Home?' he said once more to her. 'I am cold and also now hungry.'

'I need you to look after a couple of little children for me,' she said.

He didn't seem at all surprised. He nodded docilely and climbed out of the van. She couldn't tell if he had understood her.

'They might be upset. Just – I don't know – give them sweets or something. A friend will take over.'

'I am father,' he said.

'I'll be back as soon as I possibly can.'

Josef wiped his boots very thoroughly on the doormat. Karlsson appeared, already in his coat and carrying a bag. 'Let me introduce you to the kids,' he said. 'Their mother will be here in about an hour and a half. Thanks for helping out. Mikey, Bella, this man is going to take care of you until Mummy comes. Be good for him.'

Josef stood in front of the two children who stared up at him. Bella's mouth opened: she was about to howl.

'I am Josef,' he said, and made his slight, formal bow.

Chapter Thirty-one

There was a ring at the door. Dean Reeve didn't even turn his head. He was expecting it. He stood, and ran up the stairs to Terry, who was painting the little room in clumsy white strokes. She had almost done: just a few square feet were left unpainted. He stroked her hair. 'All right?' he said.

'Course.'

'You'd better be.'

'I said I am.' The bell rang again. 'Aren't you going to answer it?'

'They're not going away. You get that finished. Quickly now.'

He walked down the stairs and opened the door. It wasn't who he was expecting. Standing on his doorstep was a young woman. She wore rimless spectacles and her brown hair was tied up with just a few strands spilling over her forehead. She was dressed in a black suede jacket with blue jeans and leather boots that almost reached her knees. She was carrying a leather briefcase. She smiled. 'Are you Dean Reeve?' she said.

'Who are you?'

'I'm sorry just to barge in on you. My name is Kathy Ripon and I'm here to make you an offer. I work for a university and we're doing research into people we choose virtually at random. All I want to do is to give you a questionnaire and go through it with you. It's a simple personality test. It would just take half an hour of your time, a bit more maybe. I'd do it with you. And then we would, of course, recompense you for your time. My employers will pay you a hundred pounds.' She smiled. 'All for filling out a simple form. Which I'll help you with.'

'I haven't got the time for this.' And he started to shut the door.

'Please! It won't take long. We'll make it worth your while.'

He stared at her, his eyes narrowing. 'I said no.'

'How about a hundred and fifty?'

'What's this about?' he said. 'Really. Why me?'

'It's quite random.'

'Then why so eager? Go and knock next door.'

'There's no catch,' she said, although she was becoming slightly flustered. 'Your name won't be used in any of the research. We're just doing an investigation into personality types.' She reached into the pocket of her coat and pulled out a wallet. She took out a card and held it out to him. It had a photograph of her on it. 'You see?' she said. 'That's the institute where I work. You can phone my boss, if you want. Or look at our website.'

'I'll ask you again, why me?'

She smiled again, a little falteringly this time. The money was usually enough, and she didn't understand what the problem was. 'Your name came up on our database. We look for all sorts of people to use in our study and yours was one of the names. It's a hundred pounds for half an hour of your time. It'll be no trouble.'

Dean thought for a moment. He looked at the woman's nervous face, then over her shoulder, up and down the empty street. 'Come in, then.'

'Thank you.'

For one moment, she felt a tremor of disquiet running through her, but then shrugged it off and stepped inside.

'I don't think you're telling me the whole truth,' he said, and the door shut behind them with a small, firm click.

Dark, so dark. Very quiet. The drip of water. Dry swollen tongue tasted the iron wetness. Then the rustle of tiny feet. Are there long yellow teeth waiting to chop me up into little bits for the birds? He mustn't speak, mustn't say a word. Body burning with cold but mustn't speak.

Scraping sound. Grunting sound. Lighter darkness to scrape his soft eyes. Soft voice of Master. Mustn't speak. Not a sound shall escape. Mustn't even breathe.

Scraping sound and darker darkness.

Oh, no. Oh, no. It wasn't him making this sound. Like a wild animal panting. Like a wild animal screaming next to him. Over and over and over. Something scrabbling at him, shaking him, shouting, screaming and screaming, cracked high madness of screaming, his ears were going to burst. He mustn't speak. It was a test and he couldn't fail because if he failed it was over.

Still it went on. It was outside him and it was inside him, a shriek swelling and echoing, and he couldn't escape. Fingers over ears, body in a ball, head on stone, sharp knees on sharp stones, grit in eyes, burning skin, don't make a sound. Once upon a time there was a little boy.

It didn't go the way Frieda thought it was going to. They didn't jump in the car and head straight to the house. Instead, an hour later, Frieda found herself sitting in

Karlsson's office giving a statement to a uniformed officer while Karlsson stood to one side, frowning. At first, Frieda could scarcely control herself.

'Why are we sitting here?' she said. 'Don't you think the situation is just a bit urgent?'

'The quicker we get your statement, the quicker we can get a warrant and the quicker we can act.'

'We don't have time for this.'

'You're the one who's holding us up.'

Frieda had to take a deep breath, just so she could speak calmly.

'All right,' she said. 'So what do you want me to say?'

'Keep it simple,' said Karlsson. 'All we want is for the judge to grant the warrant. So don't go into detail about your patient's dreams or fantasies or whatever they were. In fact, don't even mention them.'

'You mean, don't tell the truth?'

'Just tell the part of the truth that's helpful to the process.' He looked at Yvette Long. 'Ready?' She smiled at him and clicked her pen. Frieda thought: She's in love with her boss. Karlsson paused for a moment. 'You want to say, "During therapy with my patient Alan Dekker, he made certain statements that implicated his brother Dean Reeve in the abduction of blah blah blah."'

'Why don't you just dictate it yourself?'

'If we go into too much detail, the judge may start asking difficult questions. If we find the boy, it doesn't matter if it was the man in the moon who told you about it. We just need the warrant.'

Frieda gave a brief statement while Karlsson nodded and made occasional comments.

'That'll do,' he said finally.

'I'll sign anything,' said Frieda. 'Just as long as you do something.'

Yvette handed her the form. She signed it, and the copy underneath.

'What do I do now?' said Frieda.

'Go home, whatever you want.'

'What are you going to do?'

'Our job. We'll wait for the warrant, which should be delivered in an hour or two.'

'Can't I help?'

'This isn't a spectator sport.'

'That's not fair,' said Frieda. 'I told you about it.'

'If you want to come on police operations, you'll need to join the force.' He paused. 'Sorry. I don't meant to be . . . Look, I'll let you know what happens as soon as I can. That's all I can do.'

Back in her house, Frieda felt like a child who had been dragged out of the cinema five minutes before the film ended. At first she walked up and down her living room. All the action was happening somewhere else. What could she possibly do? She rang Josef's mobile and got no reply. She called Reuben and he told her that Josef wasn't back. She ran herself a hot bath and lay in it with her head mostly under the water, trying not to think and failing. She got out and put on some jeans and an old shirt. Clearly there were things she needed to do. She needed to make some sort of plans for Christmas. She'd been resisting it for weeks but she had to do something. She had appointments with patients to rearrange. It seemed impossible even to consider any of this now.

She made herself coffee, a whole pot, and steadily drank her way through it. She felt suddenly as if she were the subject of a psychological experiment designed to demonstrate how lack of control and autonomy resulted in intense, almost paralytic, symptoms of anxiety. It was almost six o'clock, and thoroughly dark, when there was a ring at the door. It was Karlsson.

'Is it good news?'

Karlsson brushed past her. 'You mean was he there? No, he wasn't.' He picked up Frieda's half-finished cup of coffee and took a sip. 'It's cold,' he said.

'I can make you some.'

'Don't bother.'

'I should have been there,' said Frieda.

'Why?' asked Karlsson, sarcastically. 'So you could have looked in a cupboard we missed?'

'I'd like to have seen Dean Reeve's demeanour.'

'His demeanour was confident, if that's what you mean. The demeanour of someone with nothing to hide.'

'And I've seen the house before. I could see if they'd done anything to it since I was there.'

'Unfortunately the warrant doesn't allow us to bring tourists.'

'Wait,' said Frieda.

She poured the last from the cafetière into a new mug and heated it in the microwave. She handed it to Karlsson. 'You want anything with it?' she said. 'Or in it?'

He shook his head and took a sip of coffee.

'So that's that,' said Frieda.

'That photofit you did the other day. That reconstruction of the woman's face.'

277

'What about it?'

'Have you got it?'

'Yes.'

There was a pause.

'I don't just mean, "Have you got it?" I mean, can you get it and show it to me?'

Frieda went out of the room and came back carrying the printout. She smoothed it out on the table. 'It got a bit scrunched up,' she said.

Karlsson leaned over and looked at it.

'While the officers were turning the house upside down and then turning it the right side up again, I wandered into their bedroom. I saw this on the wall.' From his side pocket he took a small framed photograph. He laid it down on the table next to the printout. 'Remind you of anything?'

Chapter Thirty-two

'It's the same woman,' said Frieda.

'Similar.' Karlsson rubbed his face violently with his fist.

'It must be.'

'You think so, do you?'

'Of course.'

He looked grimly at her.

'This is the woman Rose remembered,' Frieda said.

'Rose didn't remember. She was led by multiple choice through a succession of images that were narrowed down to this. That is not the same as remembering.'

'It's her. Of course it is. Can you think of any other explanation?'

'It doesn't need a fucking explanation. Through a series of suggestions, a damaged young woman came up with a face she might have seen twenty-two years ago or she might have imagined or made up, which happens to look a bit like the photograph of a woman in the house of someone who is a sort of half-suspect for a different crime. How do you think that would go down in court?'

Frieda didn't reply.

'And in the meantime, there is no sign of Matthew. When I say no sign, I mean nothing. Not a thread or a fibre. And there was one room they had just finished painting. The paint was still wet. If he'd been kept in there, any trace of him would have been covered. You know what I think? I think he died long ago and I'm being led by the nose into a world of shadows and hopes. If it were the kid's parents, it would be understandable. But you've bought into it.'

Frieda stared at the photograph so intently that it almost hurt her head. 'It's an old family picture,' she said.

'Probably.'

'Look.' Frieda put her hand across the picture, covering the hair.

'What?'

'Don't you see the likeness? Dean Reeve. And Alan as well. It must be his mother. *Their* mother.' Frieda started murmuring to herself, as a way of thinking.

'Am I meant to understand what you're saying?' Karlsson asked.

'Remember what I said about a woman? Joanna wouldn't have walked off with a man like Dean Reeve. But she might have done with her. Don't you think?'

'Sorry,' said Karlsson. 'My mind was on other things, like conducting an investigation, interviews, evidence, little things. There are rules. They have to find clues, evidence.'

Frieda ignored him. She stared hard at the photograph, as if it could yield up its secrets to her. 'Is she still alive? She wouldn't be that old.'

'We'll find out,' he said. 'It's something to follow up.'

Frieda suddenly remembered. 'Are your children OK?'

'They're back with their mother, if that's what you mean.'

'Were things all right with Josef?'

'He made them pancakes and drew patterns on their legs with indelible ink.'

'Good. In the meantime, are you keeping a watch on Dean?'

'For what it's worth,' Karlsson's tone was grim. 'Even if you're right, he knows we're on to him. So.'

'You mean he won't lead you to Matthew because he'll assume you're watching him?'

'That's right.'

'But if they've stowed Matthew somewhere, they need to feed him, give him water.'

He gave a shrug. His face was sombre. 'It's probably not him,' he said. 'If it was him, he probably killed him straight away. If he didn't kill him straight away, he probably killed him after you knocked at the door. And if he didn't . . . well, all he has to do is sit and wait.'

Karlsson bent over Rose where she sat, examining the photograph. Her kitchen was small and cold and there was a brown stain on the ceiling. The wall heater was rumbling and a tap was dripping.

'Well?' he asked at last.

Rose looked up at him. He was struck by how very pale and delicate her skin was, with small blue veins visible under the surface.

'I don't know,' she said.

'But you think it may be her?' He wanted to take her by her thin shoulders and shake her.

'I don't know,' she repeated. 'I don't remember.'

'It rings no bells.'

She shook her head hopelessly. 'I was just a little girl,' she said. 'It's all gone.'

Karlsson straightened up. His back was aching and his neck felt stiff and sore. 'Of course,' he said. 'What was I expecting anyway?'

'I'm sorry. But you don't want me to say something that misleads you, do you?'

'Why not?' They were both startled by his sudden harsh laugh. 'Everybody else is.'

Frieda sat at her chess table and played through one of the games from her book of classic matches, Beliavsky versus Nunn in 1985. The felted pieces moved up the board. The fire flickered in the grate. The clock ticked away the minutes. The pawns fell and the queens advanced. She thought about Dean and Alan, with their dark brown eyes. She thought about Matthew and held his freckled, merry face in her mind. She thought about Joanna, with her gap-toothed, anxious smile. She tried not to hear their thin high voices screaming out in anguish for their mothers to come and rescue them. Her brain felt as though it was falling between the cracks on the board. Something: there must be something she had missed, some tiny, hidden key that could slide into the unyielding mystery and lever it open. No matter what horrors it revealed, anything would be better than this state of unknowing. She let herself remember how Matthew's parents had looked at the press conference – their terror-struck faces. What would it be like to be them, lying in bed night after night and imagining their son crying for them? What had it been like for Joanna's parents, month by month, year by year, never knowing and never having a grave on which they could lay their flowers?

At midnight, her phone rang.

'Were you asleep?' asked Karlsson.

'Yes,' said Frieda, lifting a bishop off the board and holding it in a clenched fist, waiting.

'I'm going to visit Mrs Reeve. She's in an old people's home in Beckton. Will you come with me?'

'She's alive, then. Yes, of course I'll come.'

'Good. I'll send a car for you first thing tomorrow.'

Once, when she was a student, Frieda had gone to Beckton to see the gasworks that looked like a colossal ruin standing in the desert. She still had the photographs she had taken. All of that was gone now; only a grassed-over slag heap showed where it had once been. Everything old and strange seemed to have been demolished, and in its place were lines of eighties houses, apartment blocks, shopping malls and light industrial units.

River View Nursing Home – its name was misleading – was a large modern building in raw orange brick, all on one floor and built around a courtyard with a small balding lawn in the middle, no trees or shrubs. There were metal grids over metal-framed windows. Frieda thought it looked like an army barracks. There were wheelchairs, zimmer frames, walking-sticks, a big jug of plastic flowers in the overheated entrance hall, and a smell of pine air freshener with something like porridge being cooked. She could hear a radio playing but otherwise it was very quiet. Their footsteps echoed. Perhaps most of the residents were still in bed. In the living room, there were only two people – one, a tiny sliver of a man whose bald head shone and whose round glasses caught the light; the other, a large woman dressed in what looked like a voluminous orange cape, with her neck in a brace and her feet in oversized fluffy slippers. Jigsaws were laid out on tables, waiting.

'Mrs Reeve's this way.' The woman led them down a corridor. She had metal-grey hair, twisted into tight, even curls. Her buttocks rolled as she walked and she had strongly muscled calves and forearms, lips that turned down even when she smiled. Her name was Daisy, but she didn't look like a Daisy.

'I warn you,' she said, before she pushed open the door that had a small spy-hole on the outside, 'she's not going to tell you much.' She gave her turned-down smile.

They stepped into a small square room. The air was muggy and smelt of disinfectant. There were bars over the window. Frieda was struck by the bareness. Was that what a life boiled down to? A narrow bed, a picture of the Bridge of Sighs on the wall, a single bookshelf holding a leather-bound Bible, a china dog, a vase with no flowers in it, and a large silver-framed photograph of the son she had chosen to keep. In an armchair by the wardrobe there was a stocky figure in a flannel dressing-gown and thick brown support tights.

June Reeve was short, her feet barely reaching the floor, and she had the same faded grey hair that Alan and Dean had. When she turned her head towards them, Frieda couldn't at first see the likeness to her picture. Her face had spread. Its shape seemed to have disappeared and all that was left were features in flesh – a sharp chin, a small dry mouth, brown eyes that were her sons' eyes but looked cloudy. It was impossible to tell how old she was. Seventy? A hundred? Her hands and her hair seemed young; her aimless gaze and her voice much older.

'Visitors for you,' Daisy said loudly.

'What's she done to her hands?' asked Karlsson.

'She chews at her fingers until they bleed, so we put mitten bandages on her.'

'Hello, Mrs Reeve,' said Frieda.

June Reeve didn't reply, although she gave a curious jerk with her shoulders. They advanced further into the room, which was barely large enough to contain the four of them.

'I'll leave you, then,' said Daisy.

'Mrs Reeve?' said Karlsson. He was grimacing and stretching his mouth, as if clear enunciation would carry the sense to her. 'My name is Malcolm Karlsson. This is Frieda.'

June Reeve's head swivelled. She fixed her milky gaze on Frieda.

'You're Dean's mother,' said Frieda, kneeling on the floor beside her. 'Dean? Do you remember Dean?'

'Who's asking?' Her voice was slurred and hoarse, as if her vocal cords were damaged. 'I don't like busybodies.'

Frieda looked into her face and tried to read a story from the wrinkles and folds. Had that face been there twenty-two years earlier?

June Reeve rubbed her mittened hands against each other. 'I like my tea strong, with lots of sugar.'

'This is hopeless,' said Karlsson.

Frieda leaned in close to the old woman's sour smell. 'Tell me about Joanna,' said Frieda.

'Never you mind that.'

'Joanna. The little child.'

June Reeve didn't reply.

'Did you take her?' Karlsson's tone was harsh. 'You and your son. Tell us about it.'

'That's not going to help,' said Frieda. She said gently, 'It was outside the sweetshop, wasn't it?'

'Why am I here?' asked the old woman. 'I want to go home.'

'Did you give her sweets?'

'Lemon sherbet,' she said. 'Jelly babies.'

'Is that what you gave her?'

'Who's asking?'

'Then you put her in a car,' said Frieda. 'With Dean.'

'Have you been a naughty girl?' Something like a lewd grin appeared on her face. 'Have you? Wetting yourself like that. Biting. *Naughty.*'

'Was Joanna naughty?' asked Frieda. 'June, tell us about Joanna.'

'I want my tea.'

'Did she bite Dean?' Pause. 'Did he kill her?'

'My tea. Three sugars.' Her face puckered as if she would cry.

'Where did you take Joanna? Where is she buried?'

'Why am I here?'

'Did he kill her at once, or did he hide her somewhere?'

'I wrapped him in a towel,' she said belligerently. 'Somebody would have found him and taken him. Who are you to judge?'

'She's talking about Alan,' Frieda said quietly to Karlsson. 'He was found bundled up in a little park on a housing estate.'

'Who are you, anyway? I didn't ask you in here. People should mind their own business. Butter wouldn't melt.'

'Where's the body?'

'I want my tea, I want my tea.' She raised her voice until it cracked. 'Tea!'

'Your son, Dean.'

'No.'

'Dean hid Joanna somewhere.'

'I'm not telling you anything. He'll look after me. Muckrakers. Nosy-parkers. Bloody stuck-up ponces.'

'She's upset.' Daisy had appeared in the door. 'You won't get any more out of her now.'

'No.' Frieda got to her feet. 'We'll leave her in peace.'

They left the room and walked back up the corridor.

'Has she ever said anything about a girl called Joanna?' Karlsson asked.

'She keeps herself to herself,' Daisy said. 'Spends most of her time in her room. She doesn't really talk much at all, except to complain.' She grimaced. 'She's pretty good at that.'

'Have you ever thought she seemed guilty about anything?'

'Her? She just feels angry. Put-upon.'

'What about?'

'You heard a bit of it. People interfering.'

As they made their way out, Karlsson didn't speak.

'Well?' said Frieda.

'Well what?' said Karlsson bitterly. 'I've got a woman

trying to reconstruct a face after twenty-two years of not remembering it. I've got an identical twin with disturbing dreams and fantasies, and now I've got a woman with Alzheimer's talking about lemon sherbet.'

'There were things in what she said. Fragments.'

Karlsson pushed the front door open with too much force so that it gave a bang.

'Fragments. Oh, yes. Bits of nonsense, shadows of memories, strange coincidences, odd feelings, half-baked intuitions. That's what this whole fucking case boils down to. I could ruin my career over this, like Joanna's detective twenty-two years ago.'

They stepped into the cold and stopped.

'Morning,' said Dean Reeve. He was freshly shaved and his hair had been combed away from his face. He was smiling amiably at them. It felt like a challenge.

Frieda couldn't speak. Karlsson nodded curtly.

'How's my ma today?' He held up a grease-spotted brown-paper bag. 'I'm bringing her a doughnut. She likes her doughnut on Sunday. Her appetite is the one thing she hasn't lost.'

'Goodbye,' said Karlsson, in a hoarse voice.

'I'm sure we'll see each other again,' said Dean, politely. 'One way or another.'

And as he passed them, he gave Frieda a wink.

Chapter Thirty-three

Just after ten, Frieda was sitting alone in her consulting room. She looked at her watch. Alan was late. Was that a surprise? After what he had learned about himself and about her own deceptive behaviour, did she really expect him to come back at all? He had been neglected by one therapist and deceived by a second. What would he do now? Perhaps he would just give up on therapy. It would be a logical conclusion. Or he could make a complaint. Again. This time the results might be bad. Frieda thought about this but found it hard to take seriously; that could all unfold later. Meanwhile, she felt she was in the wrong place. She had been awake for what felt like the whole night, hour after hour. Normally, she would have got up and got dressed and left the house and walked through the empty streets, but she just lay there and went over in her mind what Karlsson had said. He was right. She had exposed dreams and fragments of memories, or images that felt like memories, likenesses. Because that was what she did, that was her currency: the things that happened inside people's heads, the things that made people happy or unhappy or afraid, the connections that they made for themselves between separate events that could lead them through chaos and fear.

Now there was something else. Somewhere out there was Matthew. Or Matthew's body. Perhaps, probably, he had been killed within an hour of being taken. That was what the statistics told you. What if he was alive, though? Frieda made herself think of it as if she was forcing herself to stare at the sun, however much it hurt. What must it have been like for that other detective, Tanner? Did he reach a point of hoping he would find a dead body? Just so that he would know. There was a ring at the door and Frieda buzzed Alan up.

When she opened the door, he walked in quite casually and sat down in his usual chair. Frieda sat opposite him.

'I'm sorry,' he said. 'The tube just stopped in a tunnel for twenty minutes. There was nothing I could do.'

Alan fidgeted in his chair. He rubbed his eyes and pushed his fingers through his hair. He didn't speak. Frieda was used to this. More than that, she felt it was important not to break silences, not to fill them with her own chatter, however frustrating it might feel. The silence itself could be a form of communication. At times she had sat with a patient for ten or twenty minutes before they spoke for the first time. She even remembered a problem from when she was training: if a patient fell asleep, should she wake them up? No, insisted her supervisor. Being asleep was itself a statement. She had never quite managed to accept that. If it was a form of communication, it was expensive and unproductive. She had felt that a gentle nudge wasn't really a violation of the therapeutic relationship. As the silence continued, she started to think that some kind of a nudge might be necessary this time.

'When someone doesn't want to talk,' she said, 'sometimes it's because there's too much to talk about. It's hard to know where to begin.'

'I just felt tired,' said Alan. 'I've been having trouble sleeping, and I've been working again, on and off, which I have found hard.'

There was another pause. Frieda felt baffled. Was he playing games with her? Was his silence a sort of punishment? She also felt frustrated: this was a time to be exploring his new sense of who he was, not shying away from it.

'Is that really the reason?' she said. 'Are we going to pretend it never happened?'

'What?'

'I know you're going to be affected by what you've learned,' she said. 'It must be like turning your world upside down.'

'It's not as bad as that,' he said, looking puzzled. 'But how did you know? Has Carrie rung you? Has she been going behind my back?'

'Carrie?' she said. 'I think we're at cross-purposes here. What's going on?'

'I'm having these memory losses. I thought that was what you were on about.'

'What do you mean, memory losses?'

'I sent Carrie some flowers, arranged for them to be delivered, and then I didn't remember doing it. What does that mean? I should do stuff like that more often. But why don't I remember? This is what going mad is like, isn't it?'

Frieda paused. She couldn't make any sense of this. It was as if Alan were talking in a language she didn't quite understand. Worse, she had a feeling that something, somewhere, was wrong. Then a thought occurred to her and it was like a blow. She had to compose herself so that she could speak without her voice trembling.

'Alan,' she said, hearing her voice from far off. 'Do you remember coming to my house on Friday night?'

He looked alarmed.

'Me? No. No – I would have known.'

'You're saying you didn't come to my house?'

'I don't even know where you live. How could I have come? What's this about? I couldn't have forgotten that. I was home all evening. We watched a film, we got a take-away.'

'Excuse me a moment,' Frieda said, as calmly as she could manage. 'I've got to . . .' She walked out of the room and into the little bathroom. She leaned over the sink. She thought she might be sick. She took a few slow, deep breaths. She turned on the cold tap and felt the water on her fingertips. A few more breaths. She switched the tap off. She walked back into the consulting room.

Alan looked up at her, concerned. 'Are you all right?' he said.

She sat down. 'You're not going mad, Alan. But I just need to be sure. Since our last session here, you've made no attempt to contact me – you know, to talk about things?'

'Is this some kind of game you're playing? Because if it is, you've no right.'

'Please.'

'All right,' said Alan. 'No. I haven't made any attempt to contact you. The sessions are draining enough.'

'We've got to stop here. I'm sorry. I'd like you to wait outside for a few minutes and then we'll talk again.'

Alan stood up. 'What's going on? What the hell are you talking about?'

'I need to make a call. It's urgent.'

She almost hustled Alan out of the door, then ran to the phone and called Karlsson on his mobile. She knew it was going to be bad, and as she explained what had happened it felt worse and worse.

'How could this happen?' said Karlsson. 'Are you blind?'

'I know, I know. They're identical, really identical. And he must have seen his brother. He was dressed like him. Or enough like him.'

'But why did he do it? What was the point?'

Frieda took a deep breath and told him.

'Jesus,' he said. 'What did you say to him?'

'I told him what I thought he needed to know. I mean what Alan needed to know.'

'In other words, you told him everything.'

'Pretty much,' said Frieda. She heard a sound from the other end of the line. 'What was that?'

'That was me kicking my desk. So you told him what you suspected about him. How could you do that? Don't you look at your patients?' There was the sound of another kick. 'So he knew we were coming?'

'He must have been prepared. Also, I think he gave flowers to Alan's wife. Someone did. I think it must have been him.'

'What for?'

'I guess he's trying to show who's in control.'

'We know that already. Him. We'll need to bring him in anyway. And that wife or partner of his. For what it's worth.'

'He's playing with us.'

'We'll see about that.'

Chapter Thirty-four

Seth Boundy called Kathy Ripon's mobile. He listened as it went to voicemail. He left another message, although it only said what his previous messages had: call me at once. He checked his emails again, to make sure that she hadn't contacted him in the few minutes since he'd last checked. He went through his junk mail just in case her message had ended up there. He was irritated. He couldn't think properly about anything else. What was she playing at?

His wife knocked at the door of the study and came in before he could tell her he was busy. 'It's lunch,' she said.

'I'm not hungry.'

'I thought you were going shopping. You haven't done any of the things you said you were going to. Are you expecting me to buy something for your sister?'

'I'll do it later.'

'We're only three days from Christmas. You're on holiday.'

Boundy gave his wife a look that made her back off and close the door. This time he rang Kathy's landline. It rang and rang and nobody picked up. He tried to remember: she lived in Cambridge, of course, but where did she go during holidays? Where did her parents live? He vaguely remembered her talking to him about her background, but he hadn't paid proper attention. Yet there was something snagging at his memory. What was it? Something about cheese. That cheese-rolling competition in her home town.

He Googled cheese-rolling and immediately came up with dozens of entries on the cheese-rolling competition that took place on Cooper's Hill in Gloucester every year.

Seth dialled Directory Enquiries and asked for the number of Ripon, he didn't know the first name, in Gloucester. It turned out there was only one. He dialled. A woman answered. Yes, it was Kathy's mother. No, she wasn't there. She was coming home for Christmas but she hadn't arrived yet. No, she didn't know where her daughter was. Seth Boundy put the phone down. What had started as irritation had turned into puzzlement and now was turning into anxiety. That woman, Dr Klein, why had she needed to contact him so urgently? Why couldn't it have waited? He had been so excited about the idea of this fresh, undiscovered pair of twins that he'd hardly thought about it. What had he done? For a few minutes he sat in his chair, frowning heavily. Then he picked up his mobile once more.

The high thin sound had gone long ago; he didn't know how long. There weren't any days any more; everything was endless night. But it had only been with him for the time his mother used to take to read a story to him at bedtime, when he used to be Matthew. *Red Riding Hood*, but she was gobbled up by the wolf. *Hansel and Gretel*, but they lost their way in the woods and their father never came to find them. There had been panting, snuffling, shrieking, roaring, like a rusty machine that has gone wrong and is chopping itself up. Then quickly the horrible sounds had gone and left him quiet again. Just rustling in the corner and drip of water and scamper of heart and foul smell of himself. His body had run out of him. He was lying in the remains of himself. But he was alone. He had kept his promise. He hadn't made a sound.

Frieda paced up and down her room, aware of Alan sitting outside. She didn't want to talk to him until Karlsson arrived. She'd got enough wrong already. The phone rang and she snatched it up.

'Frieda?'

'Chloë! I can't speak now. I'll ring you later, OK?'

'No, no, no! Wait. My dad's going to Fiji at Christmas.'

'I'm busy.'

'Don't you fucking care? What am I going to do? He was supposed to take me somewhere, not his bimbo girlfriend. I'm going to be shut up in our squalid rat hole all Christmas with my mother.'

'Chloë, we can talk about this later!'

'I've got a razor here, you know. I'm sitting in my bedroom with a razor.'

'I'm not going to be blackmailed!'

'You're my *aunt*. You're supposed to love me. I've not got anyone else to love me. He doesn't. And my mother – she's just a head-case. I'll go mad. I will.'

'I'll come round this evening. We can discuss it then.'

'But can we come to yours at Christmas?'

'Mine?'

'Yes.'

'My house is tiny, I can't cook, I won't have a tree. And I hate Christmas.'

'Please, Frieda. You can't just let me rot here.'

'OK, OK.' Anything to get her off the phone. 'Now I'm going.'

Frieda was impressed by Karlsson. He seemed able to do several things simultaneously: speaking urgently on his phone to someone back at the police station, issuing orders in a clear, clipped voice, steering her and a bewildered Alan out of the building and towards his car. Karlsson held the door open. 'I'd like you and Dr Klein to come with me. We'll explain on the way.'

'Have I done something?' Alan said.

Frieda put a hand on his shoulder. Karlsson sat in the front seat of the car. She heard fragments of his barked orders: 'Keep them separate,' he said. And then: 'I want them to go through every fucking inch of that house.'

Meanwhile Frieda talked to Alan as clearly and calmly as she could manage. As she did so, she had the strange feeling that she had told the same story to the same face and she couldn't help comparing the two. How had she not noticed the difference? Their expressions were similar but with Alan everything seemed to come as a blow. Halfway through, he whispered, 'I've got a mother. And a twin brother. How long have you known?'

'Not long. Just a few days.'

He took a long, shuddering breath. 'My mother . . .'

'She doesn't remember anything really, Alan. She's not well.'

He looked down at his hands. 'Is he very like me?'

'Yes.'

'I mean, is he *like* me?'

Frieda understood. 'In some ways,' she said. 'It's complicated.'

Alan looked up at her with a sharpness she had only seen glimpses of previously. 'This isn't about me, is it?' he said. 'Not really. You're using me to get at him.'

For a moment Frieda felt ashamed but she was almost pleased at the same time. He wasn't just whimpering and collapsing under the news. He was fighting back. He was angry with her. 'That's not what it's really about. I'm here for you. But there's . . .' She gestured around her. '. . . all this.'

'You reckon he was acting out what I wanted?'

'It may be that you have some feelings in common,' Frieda replied.

'So I'm like him?'

'Who knows?' Karlsson said from the front, making Alan jump. 'But we'd like a statement. We'd be grateful for your co-operation.'

'All right.'

As they approached the police station, they saw a group of men and women gathered on the pavement, some with cameras.

'What are they doing here?' Frieda asked.

'They're just camped out,' said Karlsson. 'Like gulls round a rubbish dump. We'll drive round the back.'

'Is he in there?' asked Alan, suddenly.

'You won't have to see him.'

Alan pressed his face against the glass, like a small boy peering in at a world he didn't understand.

Chapter Thirty-five

Frieda sat with Alan in a small bare room. She could hear phones ringing. Someone brought them some tea, tepid and very milky, and went away again. There was a clock on the wall and the minute hand turned slowly, taking them through the afternoon. Outside it was glitteringly cold; inside it was warm, stale, oppressive. They didn't really talk. It was the wrong place. Alan kept taking his mobile out of his pocket and looking at it. At one point, he fell asleep. Frieda stood up and looked out of the small window. She saw a Portakabin and a skip. It was getting dark.

The door opened and Karlsson stood there. 'Come with me.' She saw at once that he was seething with anger. His face twitched with it.

'What's wrong?'

'This way.'

They went through an open-plan room that was heaving with activity, phones ringing, chatter. A meeting was going on at one end. They stopped outside a door.

'There's someone you should see,' Karlsson said. 'I'll be back in a minute.'

He opened the door for her. Frieda was about to ask something and then stopped. The sight of Seth Boundy was so unexpected that for a moment she couldn't remember who he was. He looked different as well. His hair was standing up in small peaks and his tie was pulled loose.

His forehead was shiny with sweat. He stood up when he saw her, but sat down again at once.

'Sorry, I don't understand,' said Frieda. 'What are you doing here?'

'I was simply being a responsible citizen,' he said, in a murmur. 'I simply expressed a concern, and I was whisked off to London. It's really –'

'Concern. What concern?'

'One of my research students appears to have gone missing. It's probably nothing. She's a grown woman.'

Frieda took a seat opposite Boundy. She put her elbows on the table between them and gazed at him. His eyes shifted nervously from her face to the window and back again. When she spoke it was in a quieter, harder tone. 'But why here? Why are you in London?'

'I –' He halted and pushed his fingers back into his hair. His glasses were crooked on his nose. 'You see, it was such an opportunity. You're not a scientist. These subjects are getting rarer and rarer.'

'It was the addresses,' Frieda said. He licked his lips and looked at her uneasily. 'You sent someone to the addresses I gave you.'

'It was just to make initial contact. Routine stuff.'

'And you've not heard from her?'

'She's not picking up the phone,' said Boundy.

'Why didn't you tell me?'

'It was just routine.'

'Who is this student?'

'Katherine Ripon. She's very capable.'

'And you sent her there on her own?'

'She's a psychologist. It was just a brief interview.'

'Do you realize what you've done?' said Frieda. 'Don't you know who this man is?'

'I didn't,' said Boundy. 'I just thought you were trying to keep them to yourself. You didn't tell me anything about him.'

Frieda was about to shout at or slap him and then she stopped herself. Perhaps it was her fault as much as his. Shouldn't she have realized what he might do? Wasn't she meant to be good at reading people? 'You really haven't heard from her?'

Boundy didn't seem to be listening.

'She will be all right, won't she?' He spoke half to himself. 'It's not my fault. She will turn up. People don't just vanish.'

Karlsson took a moment to get himself under control. He didn't want to lose his temper or let his fear show. Anger should be a weapon to be used discriminately, not a weakness and a loss of control. Everything else was for later. He walked into the room, shutting the door carefully behind him, and sat down opposite Dean Reeve, observing him in silence for a few moments. He was so like the man who had just been sitting in his car that at first the similarities obscured any difference. They were both slightly on the short side, strong and stocky, with round faces; both had grey hair that had a cow-lick in the centre and still showed the faint coppery tint of the red it had once been – the red of Matthew Faraday and of the boy of Alan's fantasies. They both had arresting brown eyes and skin that was marked with ancient freckles. They were both wearing checked shirts – although Alan's was blue and green, he remembered, whereas Dean's was more colourful. And they bit their nails, they had a habit of rubbing their hands against their thighs and of crossing and recrossing their legs. It was quite uncanny, like a strange and troubling dream where nothing is single, where everything resembles something else. Even the way he bit his lower lip was the same. But when Dean, folding his arms on the table and leaning forward, opened his mouth, he no longer reminded Karlsson of his twin brother, although the two of them had the same slightly muffled voice, blurred round the edges.

'Hello again,' he said.

Karlsson was holding a folder and placed it in front of him. He flapped it open, removed a photograph and placed it in front of Reeve, rotating it so that it was the right way up for him. 'Look at it,' he said.

He examined Reeve's face for a response, a shimmer of recognition in the eyes. He saw nothing at all.

'Is this him?' asked Reeve. 'I mean the boy you're looking for.'

'Don't you read the papers?'

'No, I don't.'

'Or watch TV?'

'I watch the football. Terry watches the cooking programmes.'

'And what about this? Do you recognize this girl?'

Karlsson placed the long-ago photograph of Joanna in front of Reeve, who looked at it for a few seconds, then shrugged.

'Is that a no?'

'Who is she?'

302

'You don't know?'

'If I knew, why would I ask you?'

Reeve didn't look at Karlsson but he didn't seem to be avoiding his gaze either. Some people, when you get them into an interview, just crack immediately. Others show signs of stress: they sweat, they stumble over their words, they babble. Karlsson quickly saw that Reeve wasn't one of them. If anything he looked indifferent, or perhaps slightly amused.

'Haven't you got anything to say?' said Karlsson.

'You haven't asked me a question.'

'Have you seen him?'

'You asked me that when you came to my house before. I told you then. And I still haven't seen him.'

'Have you any knowledge of his whereabouts?'

'No.'

'Where were you on the afternoon of Friday, November the thirteenth at around four o'clock?'

'You've done this before. You're just asking me the same question. And I'm going to give you the same answer. I don't know. It's a long time ago. I was probably at work, or on my way back from work. Or maybe I was already at home, ready for the weekend.'

'Where were you working then?'

Reeve shrugged. 'Dunno. I do a bit here, a bit there. I'm my own boss. That's how I like it. No one can muck you around then.'

'Perhaps you could try a bit harder to remember.'

'Maybe I was working for myself that day. Terry's always on at me to do up the house. Women, eh!'

'Were you?'

'Perhaps. Perhaps not.'

'Mr Reeve. We are going to be interviewing all your neighbours, anyone who might have seen you that day. Perhaps you could be a little more exact.'

He scratched his head with mock solemnity. 'There aren't many neighbours,' he said. 'And we keep ourselves to ourselves.'

Karlsson sat back in his chair and folded his arms. 'There's a woman called Katherine Ripon. She's twenty-five years old. She was last seen three days ago when setting out from Cambridge to visit two addresses. One of them was yours.'

'Who is she?'

'She's a scientist. She wanted to talk to you for some kind of research project and now she's disappeared.'

'What did she want to talk to me about?'

'Have you seen her?'

'No.'

'We're talking to your wife as well.'

'She can say no as well as I can.'

'And our warrant to search your house is still active.'

'You've already searched it.'

'We're searching it again.'

Reeve gave a faint smile. 'I know that feeling. It's a nasty one, isn't it? When you've lost something and you get so desperate you start looking in the places you've already looked.'

'And we will be going through all the CCTV footage. If she was in your area, we will find out.'

'Good for you,' said Reeve.

'So if there is anything you need to tell us, best to do it now.'

'I've got nothing to tell you.'

'If you tell us where he is,' said Karlsson, 'we can come to an agreement. We can make it all go away. And if he's dead, you can at least put an end to this, put the parents out of their misery.'

Reeve took a tissue from his pocket and loudly blew his nose. 'Have you got a bin?' he said.

'Not in here,' said Karlsson.

Reeve placed the scrunched-up tissue on the table.

'We know that you impersonated your twin brother,' said Karlsson. 'Why did you do that?'

'Did I? I just sent some flowers.' That faint smile crossed his face again. 'She probably doesn't get enough flowers. Women like them.'

'I can keep you here,' said Karlsson.

Reeve looked thoughtful. 'I suppose I could get angry now. I could say that I wanted a lawyer.'

'If you want a lawyer, we can arrange one for you.'

'You know what I really want?'

'What?'

'I'd like a cup of tea. With milk and two sugars. And maybe a biscuit. I'm not fussy. I like all of them: custard creams, ginger nuts, garibaldis.'

'This isn't a café.'

'But if you keep me here, you need to feed me. The fact is, you've searched my house and found nothing. You've brought me in here and asked me if I've seen this child and that woman and I've said no and that's all there is to it. But if you want me to sit here then I'll sit here. And if you want me to sit here all tonight and all tomorrow, I'll do that as well and I'll still be saying no. It doesn't bother me. I'm a patient man. I go fishing. Do you go fishing?'

'No.'

'I go up the reservoirs. I put a mealworm on the hook, throw it in and just sit there. Sometimes I'll sit there for the whole day and the float won't have moved and it's still a good day. So I'm happy to sit here and drink your tea and eat your biscuits, if that's what you want, but it's not going to help you find that boy.'

Karlsson looked over Reeve's head at the clock on the wall. He watched the second hand moving around the face. Suddenly he felt nauseous and had to swallow hard.

'I'll get you your coffee,' he said.

'Tea,' said Reeve.

Karlsson left the room and a uniformed officer stepped past him to take his place in the interview room. He walked quickly, almost at a trot, out into the yard at the back. It had been a car park but they were doing building work, adding an extension. He sucked in the cold dark air in gulps as if he was drinking it. He looked at his watch: it was six o'clock. He felt as if the time was scratching at him. A face was watching him from a lighted window and for a moment he thought it was the face of the man he had just been interviewing, then realized it was that of his twin brother, Alan. His head spun uselessly. He went back inside and told an officer to fetch the tea for Reeve, then went down to the basement interview room where Terry had been taken. When he entered, she was in the middle of an altercation with the female police officer. The officer turned round. 'She wants to smoke.'

'Sorry,' said Karlsson. 'It's health and safety.'

'Can I go out and have one?' she said.

'In a minute. When we've had a chat.'

He sat down and looked across at her. She was dressed in jeans and a shiny electric green bomber jacket. Between the bottom of her jacket and the top of her jeans there was a roll of white skin. Karlsson glimpsed the edge of a tattoo. Something Oriental. He forced himself to give an affable smile. 'How long have you two been together?' he asked.

'What's this about?' she said.

'Background information.'

She was squeezing her hands together, massaging her fingers. She really was desperate for a cigarette. 'Always, if you're so interested. Just ask what you've got to ask.'

Karlsson showed her the photograph and she looked at it as though it was some meaningless squiggle. He showed her the photograph of Joanna Vine and she barely bothered to glance at it. He told her about the disappearance of Katherine Ripon, but she just shook her head.

'I haven't seen any of them,' she said.

He asked her about her movements on 13 November and she shook her head.

'I dunno.' There was something sluggish and impenetrable about her. Karlsson felt his chest tighten with an angry impatience. He wanted to shake her into a reaction.

'Why were you painting your upstairs room when we came to your house?'

'It needed painting.'

'Every minute that passes,' he said, 'this gets more serious. But it's not too late. If you start co-operating, I'll do everything I can for you. I can help you and I can help Dean, but you've got to give me something.'

'I haven't seen them.'

'If it was your husband and you want to protect him, the best way of doing that is to come clean.'

'I haven't seen them.'

He couldn't get her to say anything else.

Karlsson found Frieda sitting in the cafeteria. At first he thought she was writing something, but when he got closer he saw she was drawing. She had made a sketch on the paper napkin of the half-full tumbler of water on the table in front of her.

'That's good.'

She glanced up and he saw how tired she was, and how pale, almost translucent, her flesh was. He looked away, feeling full of a sense of defeat.

'Do you see your children at Christmas?' she asked.

'Christmas Eve for an hour or so and then Boxing Day.'

'That must be hard.'

He shrugged, not trusting himself to speak.

'I don't have children,' Frieda continued, as if she were talking to herself. 'Perhaps that's because I don't want to be vulnerable to all that pain. I can bear it in patients, but in one's own children, I don't know.'

'I shouldn't have been angry. It wasn't really your fault.'

'No, you were right. I should never have given him those addresses.' She waited a beat. 'No progress with the Reeves, then?'

'DC Long is in with Dean Reeve now, going over the same ground. She's usually good at getting people to talk. But I'm not hopeful.'

He picked up the tumbler that Frieda had been drawing

and drank from it, wiping his mouth on his sleeve. 'There are some people,' he continued, 'who can stand the pressure. As soon as I walked into the interview room and sat down opposite him, I felt it. He's just not bothered.'

'Do you mean he feels safe?'

'It seems like that. He knows we can't touch him. The question is: why?'

Frieda waited. Karlsson picked up the tumbler and examined it, then set it down again. 'The boy's dead,' he said. 'Or if he's not, he will be soon. We're not going to find him. Oh, don't misunderstand me. We're not giving up. We're doing everything we can. It's Christmas, they should be with their kids, but everyone's working all out. We're going through the Reeve house again with a fine-tooth comb. We're knocking on the doors we've already knocked on. We'll find out every job Dean Reeve has worked on in the last year and go there to see if that leads us anywhere. We'll use all the manpower we've got to search the area, with sniffer dogs. But you've seen the area yourself, all those boarded-up houses, old warehouses, those condemned flats. There are thousands and he could be in any one of them – or somewhere completely different. Except we should probably just be looking for a patch of ground that's been recently disturbed, or a body floating in the river.'

'But you think it's him.'

'I can smell it,' Karlsson said savagely. 'I know it's him, and he knows I know. That's why he's enjoying it.'

'He knows he's safe from you. How? Why?'

'Because he's got rid of the evidence.'

'What about his wife? Is she saying anything?'

'Her?' He shook his head in frustration. 'She's worse, if that's possible. She just sits there and looks at you as if what you've said makes no sense at all and repeats the same phrase over and over again. He's the dominant one, that's for sure, but there's no way she doesn't know something. My guess is that she did to Matthew what Dean Reeve's mother did to Joanna: lured him into a car. But it's just that, a guess. I've got not a scrap of evidence.'

'Nothing?'

'Well.' He looked grim. 'We've got our big new clue, of course. Kathy Ripon. She was going to see him and she disappeared. We're talking to the parents, her friends, anyone who might have seen her, mounting a full-scale search, pulling all the CCTV footage – then we'll see if we can place her in the area. The way the media goes on about CCTV, you'd think it's on every street corner and nothing goes unseen, but don't you believe it. Anyway, I sometimes think that days' and weeks' worth of footage to go through can hold up an investigation, rather than help it.' He looked at his watch, grimaced. 'Still, if she went to London that day, as Professor Boundy says, she's bound to be on camera at either King's Cross or Liverpool Street and maybe we can track her from there. There's a window between her leaving Cambridge after he rang her, and the time when we put the Reeve house under investigation later that day.'

'What about Alan?'

'DC Wells is in with him now, taking his statement. His was the other address Kathy Ripon was going to visit, of course.'

'I'll wait for him, I think. See him home.'

'Thank you. Come back after.'

'I don't work for you, you know.'

'Would you please come back after?' But he spoilt it by adding, 'Is that better for you?'

'Not much. But I'll come back because I would like to help.'

'I know the feeling,' Karlsson said bitterly. 'Well, if nothing else works, you can hear about their dreams.'

Chapter Thirty-six

When Frieda offered to take Alan home, he didn't reply. He just stared at her.

'Alan? Have you called Carrie?'

'No.'

'You can call her on the way.'

'I'm not going until I've seen him.'

'You mean Dean.'

'My brother. My twin. My other self. I have to see him.'

'That's impossible.'

'I won't go until I've seen him.'

'The police are interviewing him at the moment.'

'I spent the first forty years of my life not knowing anything about my family, not even having a name, and now I find out that I've got a mother who's still alive, and a twin brother and he's a few feet from me. How do you think that feels? You're supposed to be good at knowing things like that. Tell me!'

Frieda sat down and leaned towards him. 'What do you want from it?'

'I don't know. I can't just go away, knowing I've been so close.'

'I'm sorry,' Frieda said. 'It's not possible. Not now.'

'All right.' Alan stood up and started pushing his arms into his duffel coat. 'Then we'll go to her.'

'Her?'

'My mother. The one who kept my brother but dumped me.'

'Is that why you want to see him? To find out why she chose him over you?'

'There must have been something, mustn't there?'

'You were just two babies. And she won't remember you.'

'I've got to see her.'

'It's late.'

'I don't care if it's the middle of the night. Do you want to tell me where she is or do I have to find out for myself? Somehow. Maybe your detective friend would tell me.'

Frieda smiled and stood up too. 'I'll tell you,' she said. 'If this is how you want it. But ring Carrie and tell her when you'll be home, tell her you're OK. The taxi's on me.'

'Are you coming?'

'If you want me to.'

Karlsson sat in front of Dean Reeve. Every question he asked came back short and fast – a ball thrown at a dead bat, over and over again, with the same sickening little smile on his face. He was watching Karlsson. He knew that Karlsson was angry and he knew that he was feeling increasingly helpless.

He was the same with Yvette Long – except with her his eyes would slide from her face to her body, and to her rage she found herself blushing.

'He's playing with us!' she fumed to her boss.

'Don't let him get to you. If you do that, you're letting him win.'

'He's already won.'

*

313

'Are you sure you're ready for this?' Frieda asked.

Alan stood beside her. He looked frightened and there were already tears in his eyes. 'Will you come in with me?'

'If that's what you want.'

'Yes. Please. I can't –' He gulped.

'OK, then.'

Frieda took him by the hand, as if he were a small child. She led him down the corridor towards the little room where his mother sat. His feet dragged and his fingers were cold in hers. She smiled reassuringly at him, then knocked at the door and opened it. Alan walked in. She could hear his laboured breathing. For a moment he stood quite still, staring at the old woman sitting stooped in her chair. Then he stumbled across to her and sank to his knees beside her.

'Mother? Mum?'

Frieda had to turn away from the expression of horror and abject supplication on his face.

'Have you been a naughty boy again?'

'It's not him. It's me. The other one.'

'You were always naughty.'

'You gave me away.'

'I *never*. I *never* gave you away. Cut my tongue out before I give you away. Who's been saying that to you?'

'You left me. Why did you leave me?'

'Our little secret, eh?'

Frieda, sitting on the bed, watched Mrs Reeve intently. Surely she was talking about what she and her son had done, all those years ago.

'Why me?'

'You're a naughty boy. What's to be done with you, eh?'

'I'm Alan. I'm not Dean. I'm your other son. Your lost son.'

'Have you got a doughnut for me?'

'You have to tell me why you did it. I have to know. Then I'll leave you in peace.'

'I like my doughnuts.'

'You wrapped me in a thin towel and left me out in the street. I could have died. Didn't you care?'

'I want to go home now.'

'What was wrong with me?'

Mrs Reeve patted his head gently. 'Naughty naughty, Dean. Never mind.'

'What kind of mother are you?'

'I'm *your* mother, dearie.'

'He's in trouble, you know, your precious Dean. He's done something very bad. Wicked.'

'I don't know anything.'

'He's with the police.'

'I don't know anything.'

'Look at me – at *me*. I'm not him.'

'I don't know anything.' She started to rock back and forward on her chair, her eyes fixed on Frieda, crooning the words as if they were a lullaby. 'I don't know anything. I don't know anything. I don't know anything.'

'Mum,' said Alan. He took her hand cautiously, screwing up his face, and tried out the word: 'Mummy?'

'Naughty. Very naughty.'

'You never even cared, did you? You never gave me a thought. What kind of person are you?'

Frieda stood and took Alan's arm. 'Come on,' she said. 'This is enough. You need to go home, where you belong.'

'Yes,' he said. She saw his face was streaked with tears. 'You're right. She's just a nasty old woman. She's not my mother. I don't even hate her. She's nothing to me, nothing at all.'

They sat in the cab in silence. Alan gazed at his hands and Frieda gazed out at the night. Snow was falling once again, this time settling on the pavements and the roofs and the branches of the plane trees. It would be a white Christmas, she thought, the first in many years. She remembered as a child tobogganing down the hill near her grandmother's house with her brother. Stinging cheeks and snowflakes in her eyelashes and her open, shouting mouth, the world a white and rushing blur. How long since she had been tobogganing, or built a snowman or hurled a snowball? How long, for that matter, since she had seen her brother or sister? Her parents? Her whole childhood world had disappeared, and in its place she had constructed a world of adult responsibilities, of other people's pain and need, of order and compartments, well-guarded boundaries.

'It's here, on the left,' Alan was saying to the driver, who brought his cab to a stop. He got out. He didn't close the door but Frieda didn't follow.

'Won't you come in?' he said. 'I don't know how to say this to her.'

'To Carrie?'

'I want you to help her understand.'

'But, Alan . . .'

'You don't understand what it feels like, what I've found out today, what's been happening to me. It won't come out right. She's going to be shocked.'

316

'Why do you think that me being there will help?'

'You'll make it – I don't know – professional or something. You can tell her what you told me and it'll feel more, you know, safe or something.'

'Are you coming or going?' the driver asked.

Frieda hesitated. She looked at Alan's anxious face, the flakes falling through the lamplight on the street and settling in his grey hair; she thought of Karlsson waiting at the station, snarling with frustration. 'You don't need me. You need her. Tell her what you know and tell her what you feel. Give her the chance to understand. Then come and see me tomorrow, at eleven o'clock. We'll talk about it then.' She turned to the cab driver. 'Could you take me back to the station, please?'

Chapter Thirty-seven

Frieda had expected the noise to be gone and the station to be dark and deserted, but it wasn't like that. As she entered, she was assaulted by the clatter, the din of metal chairs being pulled back, doors opening and closing, phones ringing, people shouting in the distance in anger or fear, feet clipping along the corridor. Frieda thought that perhaps a police station was at its busiest round Christmas, when drunk people were drunker, lonely people lonelier, the sad and the mad pushed beyond their endurance, and all the pain and nastiness of life rose to the surface. Someone might always fall through the door with a knife in their chest or a needle hanging off their arm, or a woman with a bruised face might lurch towards the desk saying he hadn't meant to hurt her.

'Any luck?' she asked Karlsson, as he came to the front desk to meet her, although she didn't really need to ask.

'Time's running out,' he said. 'Then I'll have to release them. They'll have won. No Matthew Faraday, no Kathy Ripon.'

'What do you want from me?'

'I've no idea. You could talk to them. Isn't that what you do?'

'I'm not a witch. I don't have any magic.'

'Pity.'

'I'll talk to them. Is it official?'

'Official?'

'Will you be there? Will it be taped?'

'How do you want to play it?'

'I want to see them alone.'

Dean Reeve didn't look tired. He looked fresher than Frieda had ever seen him, as if he was feeding off the situation, unassailable. Frieda, pulling her chair up at the table, thought he was enjoying himself. He smiled at her.

'So, they've sent you to talk to me. That's nice. A pretty woman.'

'Not talk,' said Frieda. 'To listen.'

'What are you going to listen to? This?'

He started to tap his forefinger on the table top, the amiable half-smile still on his face.

'So you're a twin,' said Frieda.

Tap tap-tap tap.

'An identical twin at that. How do you feel about that?'

Tap tap-tap tap.

'You didn't know, did you?'

Tap tap-tap tap.

'Your mother never told you. How does it feel to know that you're not unique? To know that there's someone out there who looks like you, talks like you, thinks like you? All this time you thought there was only one of you.' He smiled at her and she persisted: 'You're like a clone. And you never knew anything about it. She kept you in ignorance all this time. Doesn't that make you feel betrayed? Or stupid, perhaps.'

He tapped his stubby finger on the table, eyes fixed on her. The smile on his face didn't change but Frieda could feel his anger on her skin and the room was ugly with it.

'Your plans have all gone wrong. Everyone knows what you've done. How does that feel, to have something you planned in secret suddenly out in the open? Wasn't he going to be your son? Wasn't that the plan?'

The tapping grew louder. Frieda felt it inside her brain, an insidious beat.

'If you're like Matthew's father, how can you place him in danger? Your job is to protect him. If you tell me where he is, you're saving him and you're saving yourself. And you're staying in control.'

Frieda knew he wasn't going to say anything. He was only going to smile softly at her and tap his finger on the table. He wouldn't break down; he would outlast any of them who came and sat opposite him like this, outstare them, hold on to his silence, and every time he did, it was another small victory that strengthened him. She stood up and left, feeling his jeering smile on her back as she went.

Terry was different. She was asleep when Frieda came into the room, her head against her folded hands and a snore whistling from her. Her mouth was open and she was dribbling slightly. Even when she woke up, staring blearily at Frieda for a moment as if she didn't know who she was, she remained slumped in her chair. At times she put her head back on the table, as if she would go to sleep again. Her makeup was smeared. There was lipstick on her teeth. Her hair was greasy. Frieda felt neither fear nor strong anger from her, simply a baleful resentment that she was being made to sit in this bare, uncomfortable room, hour after hour. She wanted to go back to her overheated house and her cats. She wanted a cigarette. She was cold. She was hungry, and the food they'd given her was crap. She was tired – and she looked tired: her face was puffy and her eyes seemed sore. Every so often she wrapped her arms around her big sad body for comfort, hugging herself.

'How long have you and Dean known each other?' asked Frieda.

Terry shrugged.

'When did you marry?'

'Ages ago.'

'How did you meet?'

'Years ago. When we were kids. Can I have my fag now?'

'Do you work, Terry?'

'What are you? You're not a copper, are you? You don't look like one.'

'I told you before, I'm a kind of doctor.'

'There's nothing wrong with me. Except I'm here.'

'Do you feel that you have to do what Dean tells you?'

'I need that fag.'

'You don't need to do what Dean tells you.'

'Yeah, right.' She gave an exaggerated yawn. 'Have you done?'

'You can tell us about Matthew. You can tell us about Joanna and Kathy. That would be a brave thing to do.'

'I don't know what you're on about. You think you know things about my life, but you don't. People like you know nothing about people like us.'

Chapter Thirty-eight

There was an email from Sandy on her computer. He had written it at one o'clock in the morning and in it he said he had tried not to get in touch with her but in the end had found it impossible. He was missing her so much that it hurt. He could not believe that he would never see her again, or hold her in his arms. Could they meet? He was leaving for America in a few days' time, but he would like to see her before that. He had to. Please, he wrote: *please, Frieda, please.*

Frieda sat for several minutes, staring at the message. Then she pressed the delete button. She stood up and poured herself a glass of wine, which she drank, standing by the fireplace, which was full of cold grey ash. It was half past two in the morning, the worst time to be awake and full of urgent desires. She returned to the computer and retrieved the message from Trash. For the past few days, Sandy had seemed long ago and far away. While he had been consumed by thoughts of her, she had been thinking of a stolen boy. Yet now, with this email, the sense of longing rushed back, a flood of sadness. If he was here now, she could talk to him about what she was feeling. He would understand as no one else could. He would listen carefully, without speaking, and to him she could confess failure, doubt, guilt. She could be silent and still he would know.

She wrote: 'Sandy, come round as soon as you get this. It doesn't matter what time.' She imagined how it would feel to open the door and see his face. Then she blinked and shook her head. Once again, she pressed the delete button, saw her message wiped away, turned off her computer and went downstairs to her bedroom.

Three in the morning was a dangerous time to think things over. As Frieda lay in her bed and stared at the ceiling there was clarity to her thoughts, a lack of distraction, but there was also a chill to them, as if she were at the bottom of the sea. She thought of Dean Reeve. And Terry. How could she get inside their heads? Wasn't that supposed to be what she was good at? Frieda had spent most of her adult life sitting in rooms when people talked and talked and talked. Sometimes they told truths they had never spoken aloud before, never even admitted to themselves. People lied or were self-justifying or self-pitying. They were angry or sad or defeated. But just so long as they had talked, Frieda had been able to use their own words and make of them a story that could create some kind of sense of their lives or maybe just a refuge in which they could survive. These were all people who sought her out or were sent to her. What did you do with people who wouldn't talk, who didn't know how to? How did you get at them?

In recent years, she had been to seminars where they had discussed torture. Why was it now? Why was it that people were suddenly so eager to discuss it? So tempted by it? Was it something in the air? Dean Reeve. She had seen his face, seen his slow smile. He wouldn't say anything, whatever you did to him. He would see being tortured as a kind of triumph. You were destroying your own humanity, everything you valued, all for nothing. But Terry. If you – no, Frieda thought, not you, me, Frieda Klein. If I were alone in a room with Terry Reeve. For one hour. Frieda pictured to herself the medical instruments, the scalpels, the clamps. A couple of wires, an electric terminal. A hook in the ceiling. A chain or a rope. A tub of water. A towel. Frieda had medical training. She knew what would cause real, deep pain. She knew how to create the feeling of imminent death. An hour alone with Terry Reeve and no questions asked. Think of it as a mathematical formula. The piece of information, X, is in Terry Reeve's head. If you could conduct the procedure to transfer X out of her head, then Kathy Ripon would be found and brought back to her family, and would have the life she deserved. To do it would be wrong, as wrong as wrong could be. But if she, Frieda, were in the dark somewhere, bound with wire, masking tape over her mouth, what would she think if someone else was sitting in an interview room with Terry Reeve, having qualms, saying to themselves that there are some things we don't do, having the luxury of being good while she, Frieda, or Kathy was still out there in the dark somewhere? Except that maybe Terry Reeve really knew nothing, or almost nothing. So you would be torturing to find an X that wasn't really there, and you'd think, Maybe we haven't tortured enough.

Even so, it was easy to do the right thing to save someone, but would she be willing to do the wrong thing? These were the sort of stupid thoughts that buzzed around the brain at three o'clock in the morning when the blood sugar was low. She knew from her training and from her experience that it was a time that produced negative, destructive thinking. That was why she used to get up in the middle of the night. Going for a walk, reading a crappy book, having a bath, a drink – anything was better than lying in bed tormenting yourself with bleak thoughts. But this time she didn't get up. She made herself stay and worry away at the problem. It was in Dean Reeve's mind. In all probability. And she couldn't get it. What could she do? And then Frieda had a thought. She knew about that kind of thought as well, the brilliant idea you have in the middle of the night, and then you wake in the morning and you remember your great idea and somehow it's congealed, and in the harsh light of morning it's exposed as stupid and trite and ridiculous.

It was only just light when she left her house and headed north across Euston Road and along by the park. When she rang the bell on Reuben's front door it was just after eight. Josef opened the door and Frieda was hit by the smell of coffee and frying bacon.

'Aren't you at work?' she said.

'This is my work,' said Josef. 'And I am staying on site. Come.'

Frieda followed him through to the kitchen. Reuben was sitting at the table, a half-finished breakfast of scrambled eggs, bacon and fried bread in front of him. He put down the newspaper and looked at Frieda with an expression of concern. 'Are you all right?'

'Just tired,' she said.

She felt self-conscious under the gaze of the two men. She pushed her fingers through her hair, as if she thought there might be something trapped in it she couldn't see.

'You look not well,' said Josef. 'Sit.'

She sat down at the table. 'I'm fine,' she said. 'I haven't had proper time to sleep.'

'You want breakfast?' said Reuben.

'No, I'm not hungry,' said Frieda. 'I'll just have a bit of yours.' She took a piece of fried bread from Reuben's plate and chewed it. Josef put a plate in front of her and, over the next few minutes, filled it with egg, bacon and toast. Frieda glanced across at Reuben. Perhaps the reason she looked ill was that he looked so much better.

'You make a nice couple,' she said.

Reuben gulped some coffee. He took a cigarette from the packet lying on the table and lit it. 'I'll tell you that living with Josef is a bloody sight better than living with Ingrid,' he said. 'And don't tell me that that's not a proper way of dealing with my problems.'

'All right, I won't.'

'I've been thinking, I might ask Paz out.'

'Oh no you don't.'

'No?'

'No. Anyway, Paz would say no, if you were stupid enough to put her in the position to do so.'

Josef sat down at the table. He shook a cigarette out from Reuben's packet. Frieda couldn't stop herself smiling at the easy intimacy in the way they interacted with each other. Reuben tossed his lighter over and Josef caught it and lit his own cigarette.

'I'm not here to talk about *your* problems,' she said.

'What's up?' said Reuben.

Frieda picked up a piece of bacon and bit into it. When had she last eaten? She looked at Josef. 'Reuben was my

326

therapist for a while,' she said. 'When you're training you have to be analysed yourself and I used to see Reuben three times a week, sometimes four, and talk about my life. Reuben knows all my secrets. Or, at least, the ones I chose to share with him. That's why it was difficult for him when I tried to step in and help him. It was like a father being told what to do by his delinquent daughter.'

'Delinquent?' said Josef.

'Naughty,' said Frieda. 'Badly behaved. Uppity. Uncontrollable.'

Reuben didn't reply, but he didn't look angry either. The room was almost foggy with the smoke. Reuben and an East European builder: Frieda couldn't remember when she had last been in a room as smoke-filled as this one.

'When you stop therapy,' she continued, 'it's like leaving home. It takes time to start seeing your parents as ordinary people.'

'Are you seeing anyone now?' said Reuben.

'No. I should be.'

'This is a boyfriend,' said Josef.

'No,' said Frieda. 'When therapists ask if you're seeing someone, they mean a therapist. Boyfriends and girlfriends, husbands and wives come and go. Your therapist is the really important relationship.'

'You sound angry, Frieda,' said Reuben.

She shook her head. 'I want to ask you a question,' she said. 'I want to ask you one question and then I'll go away.'

'Then ask it,' he said. 'Do you want to go somewhere private?'

'I'm fine here,' said Frieda. She looked down at her

327

plate. It was almost empty. 'More than anyone else, you're the person who taught me that my job is to sort out what's going on in my patient's head.'

'That is undeniably your job.'

'You can't change your patient's life. You just have to change the patient's attitude to that life.'

'I hope my teaching was a bit more nuanced than that,' said Reuben.

'But what about using a patient as a means of helping someone else?' said Frieda.

'Which sounds like a strange thing to do.'

'But is it wrong?'

There was a delay while Reuben stubbed his cigarette out in a saucer and lit another. 'I know this isn't a session,' he said, 'but, as you know, when a patient asks you a question, what you normally do is try to suggest that the patient already knows the answer and is afraid of it and is trying to pass the responsibility on to the therapist. So, was it worth walking all the way over to Primrose Hill to hear what you knew I was going to say?'

'I still needed to hear it said out loud,' said Frieda. 'And I got a good breakfast.'

Frieda heard the door open and she looked around. A young woman, a very young woman, came in. She was barefoot and wearing only a man's dressing-gown many sizes too big for her. She had messy blonde hair and looked as if she had just woken up. She sat down at the table. Reuben caught Frieda's eye and gave the tiniest of nods towards Josef. The woman held out her hand towards Frieda. 'I am Sofia,' she said, in an accent Frieda couldn't quite place.

Chapter Thirty-nine

'So, just the usual thing?' said Alan. 'You want me to talk.'

'No,' said Frieda. 'I want to talk about something particular today. I want to talk about secrets.'

'There are plenty of those. It turns out that most of the secrets in my life were secrets I didn't even know about.'

'I don't mean those sorts of secrets. I mean the secrets you *do* know about.'

'What kind of secrets?'

'Well, for example, what about the secrets you keep from Carrie?'

'I don't know what you mean.'

'Everyone needs secrets,' said Frieda. 'Even in the closest relationship. You need your own space. A locked room, a desk, maybe just a drawer.'

'You mean a bottom drawer where I keep my porn?'

'It could be,' said Frieda. 'Do you have a bottom drawer where you keep your porn?'

'No,' said Alan. 'I was saying that because it's a cliché.'

'Clichés exist because there's something true about them. If you had a few porn magazines in a drawer somewhere, that wouldn't be a crime.'

'I don't have porn magazines in a drawer or in a box or buried in the garden. I don't know what you're trying to get me to say. I'm sorry to disappoint you but I don't have secrets from Carrie. In fact, I've told Carrie that she's completely free to look in any of my drawers, open my mail, go through my wallet. I've got nothing to hide from her.'

'Let's not call it a secret, then,' said Frieda. 'I'm thinking of another world you can go into. Let's call it a hobby. Lots of men have hobbies and they have a space where they go and do this hobby. It's an escape, a refuge. They go to their sheds and build model aeroplanes or Tower Bridge out of matchsticks.'

'You make it sound stupid.'

'I'm trying to make it sound harmless. I'm trying to find out where your private space is. Do you have a shed?'

'I don't know what you're trying to get at but Carrie and me together do happen to own a shed. I built it myself and I've only just finished it. It's where we keep a few tools and some stuff in boxes. It's locked with a key that hangs by the door out to the yard and we both have access to it.'

'Perhaps I'm giving the wrong impression of what I'm talking about, Alan. What I'm interested in is where you go to create your own space. I'm not trying to catch you out. I just want you to answer the question: have you ever, in your life, had somewhere separate from where you lived where you went in order to pursue some hobby or other, or just to be by yourself, a place nobody else knew about or could find you?'

'Yes,' said Alan. 'When I was a teenager, this friend of mine, Craig, had a lock-up where he kept a car and a motorbike and I used to go there and work on his bike with him. Satisfied?'

'That's exactly what I meant,' said Frieda. 'Did it feel like an escape?'

'Well, you can't exactly work on your motorbike in your front room, can you?'

Frieda took a deep breath, trying to ignore Alan's hostility. 'Anywhere else?'

Alan thought for a moment. 'When I was nineteen, twenty, I used to fiddle around with engines. A friend of a friend had a workshop in one of those places under the arches down in Vauxhall. I worked for him one summer.'

'Excellent,' said Frieda. 'Under the arches. A lock-up garage. Anywhere else you used to go away from home?'

'When I was a kid, I used to go to a youth club. It was in a sort of hut on the edge of a housing estate. We played table tennis. I was never much good at it.'

Frieda thought for a moment. She knew that this was all too straightforward, too superficial, and she was getting nowhere. A few weeks ago, Alan hadn't known he was a twin. Now he did. The source had been contaminated, as Seth Boundy would have said. He was self-conscious; he was performing for her. Perhaps he needed coaxing.

'I want you to imagine something,' she said. 'We've been talking about these refuges away from the home. Somewhere you can get away to. I want you to imagine something. Imagine that you did have a secret. That you had something to hide and you couldn't hide it in your home. Where would you hide it? Don't think of it with your mind. Think of it with your heart. What's your gut feeling?'

There was a long pause. Alan closed his eyes. Then opened them and stared at Frieda with a hunted expression. 'I know what you're asking. This isn't about me, is it?'

'What do you mean?'

'You're playing a game with me. You're using me to find out about him.'

Frieda was silent.

'You're asking me questions not to help me, not to sort out my problems, but because you think it might give you some hint about where to look for that kid. Something you can go to the police with.'

'You're right,' Frieda said finally. 'It was probably a wrong thing to do. No, it was definitely a wrong thing to do. But I thought that if what you said could give any help at all, then it was something we had to try.'

'We?' said Alan. 'What do you mean "we"? I thought I was coming here for help with my problems. I thought when you were asking me questions it was to cure me. You know me. I'd do anything to get that kid back. You can do any of your experiments on me, that's fine. Little kid like that. But you should have told me. You should have fucking told me.'

'I couldn't,' said Frieda. 'If I'd told you, it wouldn't have worked – not that it did work, of course. It was an idea born of desperation. I needed to know what you would come up with spontaneously.'

'You were using me,' said Alan.

'Yes, I was using you.'

'So the police can start looking in lock-up garages and under railway arches.'

'Yes.'

'Which is probably where they're already looking.'

'I guess so,' said Frieda.

There was another pause.

'I think we're done,' said Alan.

'We'll arrange another session,' said Frieda. 'A proper one.'

'I'll need to think about that.'

They stood up, rather awkwardly, like two people who find themselves leaving a party at the same time.

'I've got some last-minute Christmas shopping to get done,' said Alan, 'so it won't be completely wasted. I can walk down to Oxford Street from here, can't I?'

'It's about ten minutes away.'

'That's fine.'

They walked to the door and Frieda opened it to let Alan through. He started to leave, then turned round. 'I've found my family,' he said. 'But it's not much of a reunion.'

'What did you want from it?'

Alan gave a half-smile. 'Always the therapist. I've been thinking. What I really wanted is what you sometimes see in films or read in books where people go to the grave of their parents and grandparents and they sit there and talk to them or just think. Of course, my mother's still alive. It'll probably be easier to talk to her when she's dead. Then I can pretend she was something she wasn't – someone who'd listen to me and who'd understand me; somebody I could pour out my heart to. That's what I'd like. To lie by the grave and talk to my ancestors. Of course, in films it's usually some picturesque graveyard on the side of a mountain or somewhere.'

'We all want some kind of family.' Frieda knew that she was the last person to say it.

'Sounds like something you got out of a cracker,' said Alan. 'I suppose it's the right time of year.'

Chapter Forty

'I'm making the pudding,' said Chloë. She sounded unusually animated. 'Not Christmas pudding. I hate that, and anyway, it's got about a gazillion calories a mouthful. And I would have had to make it weeks ago, which was when I thought I was going to my dad's, before he found himself something better to do. I could buy one, I suppose, but that would be cheating. You have to cook your own Christmas dinner, don't you, not just put something in the microwave for a few minutes?'

'Do you?' Frieda walked with the phone to stand in front of the large map of London that was pinned to the wall. She squinted in the poor light.

'So I'm making this pudding I found online, with raspberries and strawberries and cranberries and white chocolate.'

Frieda put her finger on the area she was examining and traced a route.

'What are you cooking?' Chloë continued. 'I hope it's not turkey. Turkey doesn't taste of anything. Mum said you definitely wouldn't cook turkey.'

'It's not exactly definite.' Frieda was going up the stairs now, to her bedroom.

'Don't tell me you haven't thought about it. Just don't. Please don't. Tomorrow is Christmas Eve. I don't care about presents or stuff; I don't care what we eat, actually. But I don't want you not to even think about it at all, as if it doesn't matter to you one way or the other. I couldn't bear that. Literally. This is Christmas, Frieda. Remember. All my friends are having great family reunions or going to Mauritius with their dads or something. I'm coming to yours. You have to make an effort so that it's special.'

'I know,' said Frieda, forcing herself to respond. She pulled a thick sweater from her drawer and threw it on the bed, followed by a pair of gloves. 'I will. I am. I promise.' The thought of Christmas made her feel a bit sick: a lost boy and a missing young woman, Dean and Terry Reeve free, and she was supposed to eat and drink and laugh, put a paper crown on her head.

'Is it just us three, or have you invited other people? That's fine by me. In fact, I'd like it. It's a pity Jack can't come.'

'What?'

'Jack. You know.'

'You don't know Jack.'

'I do.'

'You only met him once for about thirty seconds.'

'Before you hustled him out of my sight. Yeah. But we're Facebook buddies now.'

'You are, are you?'

'Yeah. We're going to meet when he gets back. Is that a problem?'

Was it a problem? Of course it was a problem. Her trainee and her niece. But it was a problem for later, not now. 'How old are you?' she asked.

'You know how old I am. Sixteen. Old enough.'

Frieda bit her lip. She didn't want to ask, Old enough for what?

'We could play charades,' said Chloë, cheerfully. 'What time shall we arrive?'

'What do you think?'

'How about early afternoon? That's what other families do. They open their presents and mooch around a bit and then they have a blow-out meal in the afternoon or early evening. We could do that.'

'Right.'

She pulled off her slippers; holding the phone between chin and hunched shoulder, she pulled off her skirt and tights.

'We're bringing the champagne. Mum said. That's her contribution. What about crackers?'

Frieda thought of Alan's parting remark and gave herself a mental shake. 'I'll bring the crackers,' she said firmly. 'And it won't be turkey.'

'So what –'

'It's a surprise.'

Before she left the house she called Reuben. Josef answered. Loud music was playing in the background. 'Will you and Reuben come and have Christmas dinner at my house?' she asked, without preamble.

'Already we are.'

'Sorry?'

'We agreed. You cook me an English Christmas. Turkey and plum pudding.'

'I was thinking about something a bit different. Like me not cooking it. What do you do in Ukraine for Christmas?'

'It is my honour to prepare for my friends. Twelve foods.'

'Twelve? No, Josef. One is fine.'

'Twelve foods is mandatory in my home.'

'But that's too much.'

'Never too much.'

'If you're sure,' said Frieda, doubtfully. 'I just thought something simple. Meatballs. Isn't that Ukrainian?'

'No meat. Never meat on the day. Fish is good.'

'Maybe you can get Reuben to help. Another thing: what are you doing right now?'

'I must shop for my meal.'

'I'll pay for the ingredients. It's the least I can do. But before that, Josef, do you want to go on a walk with me?'

'Outside is wet and cold.'

'Not as cold as in the Ukraine, surely. I could do with another pair of eyes.'

'Where are we walking together?'

'I'll see you outside the tube station. Reuben can tell you how to get there.'

Frieda pulled the collar of her coat up to protect her face from the wind.

'Your shoes are wet,' she said to Josef.

'And the feet,' he said. He was wearing a thin jacket that she thought belonged to Reuben, no gloves, and a bright red scarf that he'd wrapped several times round his neck and lower face so his voice was muffled. His hair, damp from the sleet, was flat against his skull.

'Thank you for coming,' she said, and he made his curious little bow, side-stepping a puddle.

'And why is it?' he said.

'A walk around London. It's what I do. It's a way of

thinking. Normally I do it on my own but this time I wanted someone with me. Not just anyone. I thought you could help me. The police have been knocking on doors, looking for Matthew and Kathy, or the bodies of Matthew and Kathy. I needed to come here, just for the smell of it, really.'

She thought of Alan's words. Boarded-up buildings, abandoned workshops under arches, lock-ups, tunnels. That kind of thing. Put yourself in this man's shoes. Think how he'd feel, panicking, casting around for a hiding place. A place where no one will look; a place where if someone cries out for help, they won't be heard. She looked helplessly around at the flats and houses, a few of which were lit up and festooned with Christmas decorations, at the shops with their doors wide open, belting heat into the winter streets, the clogged roads, the shoppers milling past clutching bags full of presents and food. 'Behind thick walls, under our feet. I don't know. We'll start together, then separate. I've got a kind of route planned.'

Josef nodded.

'A couple of hours and then you can go and buy your food.'

Frieda opened up her *A–Z* and found the right page. She pointed at a spot. 'We're here,' she said. She moved her finger half an inch across. 'I think he was kept here. Dean had to move the boy quickly. So I'm going to say that he would take him somewhere not more than half a mile. Maybe a mile.'

'Why?' said Josef.

'What do you mean?'

'Why one mile? Why not five mile? Why not ten mile?'

'Reeve had to think quickly. He had to think of a hiding place nearby. Somewhere he knew.'

'He take him to a friend?'

Frieda shook her head. 'I don't think so,' she said. 'I think you could take an object to a friend, but not a child. I don't believe he'd have that kind of friend. I think he'd put Matthew somewhere. Somewhere he knew he could get back to. But then he was being watched and he couldn't go there.'

Josef crossed his arms as if protecting himself against the cold. 'Many guesses,' he said. 'Maybe he took the boy. Maybe the boy is alive. Maybe he hide him near the house.'

'They aren't guesses,' said Frieda.

'A mile,' said Josef. He put his finger on the map on the spot where Dean Reeve lived. He moved it out. 'A mile?' he said, again, then traced a circle around the spot. 'Six miles square. More, I think.'

'I brought you here to help me,' said Frieda. 'Not to tell me what I already know. If it were you, what would you do?'

'If I steal, I steal equipment. A drill, a sander, sell it for a few pounds. I don't steal a little child.'

'But if you did.'

Josef made a helpless gesture. 'I don't know,' he said. 'A cupboard or a box or a locked room. A place with no people.'

'There are lots of places with no people around here,' said Frieda. 'So? Shall we go for a walk?'

'Which way?'

'We don't know where he is and we don't know where to look, so it doesn't matter. I thought of going in a spiral outwards from his house.'

'Spiral?' said Josef.

Frieda gestured a spiral with her finger. 'Like water running into a hole,' she said. She pointed along the street. 'This way.' They started to walk along the edge of a housing estate named after John Ruskin. She looked up at the terraces. More than half of the flats had metal grilles across the doors and windows to seal them. Any of those would be a possible hiding place. At the end of the housing estate there was a gasworks, with rusted chains across the front gate. An old sign on the railings announced that the site was patrolled by dogs. It seemed unlikely. They were now heading north, and at the end of the road they turned right and east alongside a lorry depot and then a scrap-metal yard.

'It's like Kiev,' Josef said. 'Kiev was like this so I come to London.' He stopped outside yet another row of closed-down shops. The two of them looked up at the old painted signs on the brick façades: Evans & Johnsons Stationers, J. Jones Stores, the Black Bull. 'Everybody gone,' he said.

'A hundred years ago this was a whole city,' said Frieda. 'Down there were the biggest docks in the world. Boats were queuing all the way down to the sea to unload. There were tens of thousands of men working there, and their wives and children. In the war it was bombed and burned. Now it's like Pompeii, except that people are still trying to live here. It would probably have been better if they'd turned it back into fields and forests and marshes.'

A police car drove past and both Frieda and Josef watched it until it turned the corner.

'They looking too?' said Josef.

'I guess so,' said Frieda. 'I don't really know how they do things.'

As they walked on, Frieda glanced at her map to make sure of the way. One of the things she liked about Josef was that he didn't talk when it wasn't necessary. He didn't feel a need to be clever or to pretend to understand things he didn't. And when he did say something, he really meant it. They were just passing an empty warehouse when Frieda realized that Josef had stopped and she had walked on without noticing. She walked back to him.

'Have you seen something?'

'Why are we doing this?'

'I told you.'

He took the map from her and looked at it. 'Where are we?' he asked.

She prodded at the page. He moved his finger on the map, retracing their progress.

'This is nothing,' he said. 'We pass empty houses, empty buildings, empty church. We don't go in. Course we don't go in. We can't look in every hole, in every room, on the roof, in the rooms under the houses. We're not looking. Not looking really. We are walking and you tell me about the bombs in the war. Why are you doing this? To feel better?'

'No,' said Frieda. 'To feel worse, probably. I just hoped that if we came here, walked around the streets, we would find something.'

'The police are looking. They can go into houses, ask questions. That is the job for the police. We being here, we are just . . .' Josef searched for the word and waved his hands helplessly.

'Making a gesture,' said Frieda. 'Doing something rather than nothing.'

'A gesture for what?'

'But we have to do something. We can't just sit at home.'

'Something for what?' said Josef. 'If the boy Matthew is lying in the street we fall over him maybe. But if he is dead or he's locked in a room? Nothing.'

'You were the one who said it to me, you remember?' said Frieda. 'I believed in sitting in a room and talking. You said I should go out and fix people's problems. It didn't really work out, did it?'

'I did not . . .' He paused, searching for the words once more. 'Just going out is not fixing the problem. I don't just stand in a house to fix the house. I build the wall and put in the pipes and the wires. Just walking in the street is not finding the boy.'

'The police aren't finding the boy either,' said Frieda. 'Or the woman.'

'If you're looking for a fish,' said Josef, 'you look where the fish are. You don't just walk in the fields.'

'Is that some Ukrainian proverb?'

'No, it is my idea. But you cannot just walk in the streets. Why do you bring me here to do this? We are like a tourist here.'

Frieda squinted down at the map. She closed it. It had already got damp in the bitter sleet and the pages were ruffled. 'All right,' she said.

Breath. Heart. Tongue on stone. Little wheezy sound in chest. Lights in his eyes. Head of fireworks, red and blue and orange. Rockets. Sparks. Flames. They had lit the fire at last. So cold and then so hot. Ice to furnace. Must pull his clothes off, must escape this wild heat. Body melting. Nothing would be left. Just ash. Ash and a bit of bone and nobody would know this had once been Matthew with brown eyes and red hair, a teddy with velvet paws.

Chapter Forty-one

On the Underground back, jostled by the evening rush-hour, they didn't speak at all. As Frieda opened the front door of her house, she heard the phone ringing. She picked it up. It was Karlsson.

'I don't have your mobile number,' he said.

'I don't have a mobile,' Frieda said.

'I guess you're not the kind of doctor people need in an emergency.'

'What's happening?'

'That's what I'm ringing about. I just wanted to let you know that, as of an hour and a half ago, Reeve and partner are back on the street.'

'You ran out of time?'

'We could have kept them a bit more, if we really wanted. But isn't it better if they're out there? He might make a mistake. He might lead us somewhere.'

Frieda thought for a moment. 'I wish I believed that,' she said. 'It didn't feel like that when I met him. He seemed like a man who had made up his mind.'

'If he slips up, we'll get him.'

'He's sure that you're following him,' said Frieda. 'I think he's probably enjoying it now. We've given him power. He knows what we're going through. I don't think there's anything we could do to him, anything we could give him that would be as much fun for him as that.'

'It's all right for you,' said Karlsson. 'You've got your work. You can get on with it.'

'That's right,' said Frieda. 'It's fine for me.'

After she had put the phone down Frieda sat for a time, staring at nothing. Then she went upstairs and stared out of her bedroom window at the snow-specked roofs. It was a clear cold night. She ran a bath and lay in it for nearly an hour. Then she got dressed and went to her garret study, where she sat at her drawing board. How long had it been since she had sat here like this, with time for herself? She couldn't remember. She picked up her soft pencil and held it between her thumb and forefinger, but didn't draw anything. All she could think of was Matthew, out there somewhere in the fierce cold, perhaps alive and terrified, but probably long dead; of Kathy Ripon, who'd knocked at the wrong door; of Dean and Terry walking away from the police station, free.

Finally she put her pencil down on the blank paper and went downstairs. She laid the fire in the living room and put a match to it, waited until flames were licking at the coal. Then she went to the kitchen again. She found a half-full carton of potato salad in the fridge and ate it with a spoon, just standing at the window. Then she took a tumbler from the sink, rinsed it out and poured some whisky into it. She sipped at it very slowly. She wanted time to pass; she wanted this night to be over. The phone rang and she picked it up.

'You probably didn't think you were going to hear from me for a bit?'

'Karlsson?'

'Of course it is.'

'Well, you're on the phone. I can't see you.'

'Has Reeve tried to contact you?' he said.

'Not since you last rang.'

'He's done it before.'

'What's up?'

'We've lost them.'

'Them?'

'Reeve. And Terry.'

'I thought you were following them.'

'I don't need to justify myself to you.'

'I don't care about you justifying yourself. I just wondered how it could happen.'

'Oh, you know – Underground, crowds and a bit of incompetent fucking police work. Maybe they meant to get away, maybe they didn't. I don't know. And I don't know what they're going to do.'

Frieda looked at her watch. It was past midnight. 'They won't go home. Will they?'

'They could do. Why not? They're not charged with anything. And it's the middle of the night. Where else would they go?'

Frieda forced herself to think. 'It could be a good thing,' she said. 'They might feel free now. That could be good.'

'I don't know,' said Karlsson. 'I don't know enough to even guess. I'm not so sure it matters. Where could they have put them? If they're tied up in a cupboard in an abandoned flat somewhere, how long can they survive without water? If they aren't already . . . well, you know. Anyway, he might contact you. Stranger things have happened. Be prepared.'

After she had put the phone down, Frieda poured herself another inch of whisky and tipped it straight down her throat, feeling it sting and startle her. She went into the living room, but the fire had gone out and the room felt chilly and cheerless. She knew she needed to rest, but the thought of lying in her bed, wide-eyed, her brain hissing with images, appalled her. For a while she lay on her sofa with a rug pulled over her, but sleep eluded her and in its place was a dry, frantic wakefulness. At last she rose and went to the kitchen. She stepped outside into her small yard. The cold made her gasp and brought tears to her eyes but she relished it. It woke her up, scoured her of bleary tiredness, cleared her head and sharpened her thoughts. She stood, coatless and without gloves, until her face was stiff and she could bear it no longer, then returned inside.

She walked to the London map by the front door. The light wasn't good enough to make out all the details, the little street names. She ripped it away from the wall and laid it out on the table in the living room. She switched the ceiling light on. Even that wasn't quite enough. She fetched the reading light from next to her bed, took it to the living room and placed it on top of the map. She got a pencil and made a cross on the street where Dean Reeve lived. She had a sudden vertiginous sense that she was looking down on London from a plane half a mile high on a perfectly clear day. She could see the big landmarks, the curves of the Thames, the Millennium Dome, City Airport, Victoria Park, the Lea Valley. She looked closer, at the streets she had walked with Josef. She saw the cross-hatched areas representing the housing estates, the factories.

She thought of Alan and how she'd failed with him. She had failed both as a therapist and as an investigator. Alan and Dean had the same brains, thought the same thoughts, dreamed the same dreams, the way that two different birds would build identical nests. But the only way into that was through the unconscious, and when she had last talked to Alan, it had been like asking someone to describe the skill of riding a bicycle. Not only had he been unable to express the skill in words but she had damaged the skill. If you start trying to think about how you ride a bicycle while you're riding a bicycle, you're likely to fall off. Alan had found her out and turned on her. Maybe that was a sign of some strength. It could have been a sign that the therapy was working, even that it had run its course, because Frieda felt that the bond between them had been broken and couldn't be restored. He could never give himself up to her again, the way a patient had to. She remembered that last session. It was ironic that the best bit of the session, the only real intimacy they achieved, was after the session was over, as they were leaving, when he no longer saw her as a therapist. What was it he'd said about feeling safe? She tried to remember his words. About his mother. About his family.

A thought struck her. Was it possible? It was the moment when he had given up trying to think of hiding places. Could he have . . . ?

Frieda ran her finger in a spiral around and outwards from Dean Reeve's house and then her finger stopped. She grabbed her coat and scarf and ran from the house, out of the mews and across the square. It was still dark and these smaller streets were deserted; she could hear her own footsteps echoing behind her. It was only when she got to Euston Road, among the traffic of London that never ceases, that she was able to flag down a taxi. As it sped away she went over and over it in her mind. Should she have called the police? What would she have had to say? She thought of Karlsson and his team, knocking on doors, taking statements. Divers had been searching the river. What they wanted was something tangible, a piece of cloth, a mere fibre, a fingerprint, and all she'd been able to offer were memories, fantasies, dreams that sometimes seemed to coincide. But was she just seeing patterns the way children saw shapes in clouds? There had been so many dead ends. Was this just another?

'Where do you want me to drop you?' said the cabbie. She was a woman. That was unusual.

'Is there a main entrance?'

'There's only one that's open,' said the cabbie. 'There's a back one but it's locked up.'

'The front one, then.'

'I'm not sure if it'll be open yet. It's sunrise to sunset.'

'The sun's rising now. Look.'

It was just before eight o'clock, and Christmas Eve.

A few minutes later, the cab pulled up. Frieda paid and got out. She looked at the ornate Victorian sign: 'Chesney Hall Cemetery'. Alan had said that he had the fantasy of visiting a family grave where he would like to lie on the grass and talk to his ancestors. Poor Alan. He didn't have a family grave that he could visit, or not one that he knew of. But did Dean Reeve? The large gates of the cemetery were shut but beside them was a small open entrance for pedestrians. Frieda walked inside and looked around.

It was vast, the size of a town. There were rows and rows of tombstones in avenues. There were statues, broken pillars, crosses. Dotted here and there were mausoleums. One area to the left looked grown over, the graves almost disappearing under foliage. Her breath steamed in the cold.

Ahead, down the main avenue, Frieda saw a simple wooden hut. She saw that the door was open and a light was visible through the window. Did cemeteries keep registers? She started to walk down and as she did so, she glanced at the graves on either side. One caught her eye. The family tomb of the Brainbridge family. Emily, Nicholas, Thomas and William Brainbridge had all died in the 1860s before they had reached ten years of age. Their mother, Edith, had died in 1883. How had she managed it, growing old alone with her dead children dwindling into the past? Perhaps she had had other children to look after, children who had grown up and moved away and were now buried somewhere else.

Something, a rustle perhaps, made Frieda turn round. Through the railings, she could see a figure, indistinct at first, as it moved along, and then it appeared in the entrance and she recognized it. Her. Their eyes met: Frieda looked at Terry Reeve and Terry Reeve looked at Frieda. There was something in her gaze, an intensity that Frieda had never seen before. Frieda took a step forward but Terry turned and moved away; she disappeared out of sight. Frieda ran back the way she had come but by the time she had got out of the cemetery there was no sign of Terry. She looked around desperately. She ran back down the avenue and reached the hut. An old woman was sitting behind an improvised desk. There was a Thermos flask in front of her and a notice saying 'Friends of Chesney Hall Cemetery'. Probably she had a loved-one lying out there somewhere, a husband or child. Perhaps this was where she felt at home, among family. Frieda took out her purse and rummaged through it.

'Have you got a phone?' she said.

'Well, I'm not –' the woman began.

Frieda found the card she was looking for. 'I need to make a call,' she said. 'It's to the police.'

After she had gabbled out her message to Karlsson, Frieda turned back to the old woman.

'I need to find a family grave. Can I do that?'

'We have plans of the cemetery,' the woman answered. 'Almost all of the graves are listed on it. What's the name?'

'Reeve. R-E-E-V-E.'

The woman stood up and moved over to a filing cabinet in the corner. She unlocked it and brought out a thick ledger, filled out by hand in black ink that was faded, and started leafing through it with slow deliberation, licking her forefinger from time to time.

'We have three Reeves listed,' she said at last. 'Theobald Reeve, who died in 1927, his wife Ellen Reeve, 1936, and a Sarah Reeve, 1953.'

'Where are they buried?'

The woman rustled in a drawer and brought out a printed map of the cemetery.

'Here,' she said, placing her finger on the point. 'They're all buried close to each other. If you go up the central path and take the third path on your –'

But Frieda was gone, snatching the piece of paper from her hand and running. The old woman watched her, and then she took her place once more at her desk, unscrewing the lid of her Thermos flask, waiting for the bereaved to come and pay their respects. Christmas was always a busy time.

Frieda tore up the central path and took the path on the right that was narrow but well-worn. On either side were gravestones, some quite new, made of white marble with clear black words etched into them. Others were older, grown over with lichen and ivy, or had tipped backwards. It was hard to make out the names of some of the dead who lay there and Frieda had to run her fingers over the ridges of the letters to make them out. The Philpotts, the Bells, the Farmers, the Thackerays; those who had died old and those who hadn't made it out of their teens; those who still had flowers placed there and those long forgotten.

She moved as quickly as she could among the gravestones, stooping at each one and standing up again, squinting in the dim light. The Lovatts, the Gorans, the Booths. Her eyes burned with tiredness and her chest ached with hope. A blackbird looked at her from a bare thorn bush and in the distance she heard the rumble of cars. Fairley, Fairbrother, Walker, Hayle. And then she stopped and heard the blood pounding in her ears. Reeve. Here was a Reeve – a small, crumbling headstone, tipped slightly to one side. She had found it.

But then, with a crushing sense of failure, she understood that she had found nothing at all. For how could a child be hidden here, among these puny graves that stretched all round her? With a lurch of horror she looked closer at them for freshly turned earth where a body could have been buried, but they were thickly overgrown with weeds. Nobody could be hidden here. She sank to her knees beside Theobald Reeve's inscription, feeling sick with a sense of defeat. Matthew wasn't here after all. It had just been a delusion, a last spasm of hope.

She didn't know how long she knelt like that in the bitter cold, knowing that she had lost. But at last she raised her eyes and started to scramble to her feet, and as she did so she saw it – a high stone mausoleum, almost out of sight behind a tangle of brambles and nettles. She ran towards it, feeling the thorns tear at her. Her feet sank into the slushy mud and the wind whipped her hair round her face so that she could barely see. But she could see enough to know that someone had been there recently. There was a path of sorts where the nettles and brambles had been flattened. She reached the entrance and saw that it was blocked with a heavy stone doorway, but from the ruts in the mud it was obvious that someone had pulled it aside not long ago.

'Matthew,' she shouted, at the blank, mouldering stone. 'Wait! Hold on! We're here. Wait.'

Then she started tearing at the stone with her bare fingers, trying to get a purchase, trying to hear some sound that would tell her he was there, and that he lived.

The stone door gave slightly. A chink appeared. She strained at it. From over the hill she heard cars and she saw headlights. Then there were voices and there were people and they were running towards her. She saw Karlsson. She saw the expression on his face and she wondered if she looked like that as well.

And then they were upon her – an army of officers who could pull the stone back, who could shine their torches into the dank blackness, who could crawl inside.

Frieda stood back. A terrible calm descended on her. She waited.

He couldn't hear his heart any more. That was all right. It had hurt too much when it was beating hard. The Tin Man was wrong. And he couldn't make his breath go in and out properly. It caught in small shudders and didn't fill him up. The fire was gone, and the ice was gone too, and even the hard ground wasn't hard now, because his body was just a feather trembling on its surface and soon it would be lifted up and float away.

Oh, no. Please. No. He didn't want the tearing sounds and he didn't want the white light shredding his eyes. He didn't want the staring faces and the clawing hands and the gabble of voices and the jolting movements. He was too tired for more of the story; he had thought the story was over at last.

Then he saw the dancer, the woman with snowflakes in her hair. She wasn't shouting or running like the others. She stood quite still on the other side of the world with gravestones all round her and she gazed at him and her face was better than smiling. He had saved her and now she had saved him. She bent over him and her lips touched his cheek. The evil spell was broken.

Chapter Forty-two

Frieda stood near the bed, watching. The little figure was still curled in the position they had found him. Then he had been in a state of semi-undress – for in his delirium of death, the boy had ripped off the clothes he had been wearing, the checked shirt a replica of the shirts both twins favoured – and had lain in near-nakedness on the cold earth of the mausoleum. Now he was on a warm-water mattress. He was covered with layers of light cloth and there were monitors attached to his heart. His face, which in the photographs she had seen of him was round and ruddy and full of merriment, was so white it was almost green. His freckles stood out like rusted pennies. The lips were bloodless. One cheek was bruised and puffy. His hands were bandaged for he had ripped his fingers tearing at the stone walls. His hair had been crudely dyed black, with a stripe of red showing at the parting. Only the monitors showed he wasn't dead.

Detective Constable Munster sat in the corner of the room. He was a young man with dark hair and dark eyes and he'd been on the team looking for Matthew since the first day. He was nearly as pale as the boy, and still, as though he were carved in stone. He was waiting for the boy to return to consciousness. Matthew's eyes fluttered and closed again. His lashes were long and red; his eyelids were translucent. Karlsson had asked Frieda to stay as well, until the child psychiatrist arrived. Even so, she felt in the way, excluded from the process, the rapid footsteps, the rattle of trolleys, doctors and nurses murmuring to each other. Worse, she understood the jargon that was being used, the intravenous warm saline, the danger of hypovolaemic shock. They were trying to raise his core temperature and she was just a bystander.

The door opened once again and the parents were ushered in. They had the pale, drawn, gaunt faces of people who have spent days waiting for bad news. Now they had hope, which was a new kind of agony. The woman knelt beside his bed, pushing the tubes aside and taking hold of her son's bandaged hand, pressing her face into his body. Two nurses had to pull her back. The man looked flushed and angrily confused; his eyes darted around the room, taking in all the equipment, the flurry of activity.

'What's wrong with him?'

The doctor was looking at the chart. He took his glasses off to rub his eyes. 'We're doing all we can but he's extremely dehydrated and has severe hypothermia. He's dangerously cold.'

Mrs Faraday gave a sob. 'My little boy. My beautiful son.' She raised his hand to her lips and kissed it, and then fell to stroking his arm and neck, saying over and over again that everything would be all right now, that he was safe.

'But he'll be all right?' said Mr Faraday. 'He will be all right.' As if by insisting, it would become true.

'We're rehydrating him,' said the doctor. 'And we're going to do a cardiopulmonary bypass. It means we attach him to a machine, pump his blood out, warm it up, pump it back in.'

'And then when you do that, he'll be all right?'

'You should wait outside,' said the doctor. 'We'll let you know if there's any change.'

Frieda stepped forward and took Mrs Faraday's hand. She seemed in a daze and allowed herself to be led out. Her husband followed. They were shown into a small, windowless waiting room, just four chairs and a table on which stood a vase of plastic flowers. Mrs Faraday looked at Frieda as if she had just noticed her.

'Are you a doctor?' she said.

'Yes,' said Frieda. 'I've been working with the police. I was waiting for you to arrive.' She sat beside them as Mrs Faraday talked and talked. Her husband didn't speak. Frieda saw how his nails were dirty, his eyes red-rimmed. Frieda hardly spoke but once Mrs Faraday turned and looked her in the eyes and asked if she had children. Frieda said she didn't.

'Then you can't understand.'

'No.'

And then Mr Faraday spoke. His voice was gravelly, as if his throat was sore. 'How long was he in that place?'

'Not long.'

Too long: Kathy Ripon had called at Dean's house on Saturday afternoon. Now it was Christmas Eve. Frieda thought of the last few days. Rain, sleet, snow. There would have been water running down the walls. He would have been able to lick it like an animal. She thought of him again, that first sight, his emaciated, bruised body, the eyes open but unseeing, his mouth drawn back in fear.

That was the worst. At first he hadn't realized he was being rescued. He thought they were coming back for him. And there was something else to think about. Where was Kathy? Did she have a damp wall somewhere?

'What he must have gone through,' said Mr Faraday. He leaned towards Frieda. 'Had he been – was he – you know?'

Frieda shook her head. 'It's been a terrible, terrible thing,' she said. 'But I think he thought of him as his child.'

'Bastard,' said Mr Faraday. 'Have they caught the one who did it?'

'I don't know,' said Frieda.

'He deserves to be buried alive, like my son was.'

A junior doctor came into the waiting room. She was young and very beautiful, with skin like a peach and blonde hair tied back in a tight ponytail; her face glowed. And Frieda knew it was going to be good news.

They knelt on either side of the bed, under the brutal lights and among the hanging tubes. They held his bandaged hands and said his name and crooned nonsense words, as if he was a newborn baby. Poppet and sweetheart and muffin and Mattie-boy and pigeon. His eyes were still shut but his face had lost that deathly tinge, its clayey whiteness. The rigidity of his limbs had softened. Mrs Faraday was sobbing and talking at the same time. Her words of love came out in gulps. He was bleary and barely responsive, as if he had been woken in the middle of the night out of a deep sleep.

'Matthew, Matthew,' murmured Mrs Faraday, almost nuzzling him. He said something and she leaned in even closer. 'What's that?' He said it again. She looked round, puzzled.

'He said "Simon". What does that mean?'

'It's their name for him,' said Frieda. 'I think they gave him a new name.'

'What?' Mrs Faraday started to cry.

DC Munster drew Mr Faraday aside, then leaned over the bed and started to talk to Matthew. He held a photograph of Kathy Ripon in front of the boy's face. His eyes weren't able to focus properly.

'It's not fair,' said Mrs Faraday. 'He's terribly ill. He can't do this. It's bad for him.'

A nurse said that the child psychiatrist was on her way but she'd phoned to say she was stuck in traffic. Frieda heard DC Munster trying to explain that they'd got their son back but other parents were still missing their daughter and Mr Faraday said something angry in response and Mrs Faraday was crying harder than ever.

Frieda pressed her fingers to her temples. She tried to shut out the noise so she could think. Matthew had been snatched from his parents, hidden away, punished, starved, told that his mother was no longer his mother and his father no longer his father, told that he wasn't himself but someone else – a boy called Simon – and then shut away, left to die, naked and alone. Now he lay blinking in an over-lit room, with strange faces looming at him out of his waking nightmare, shouting words he didn't understand. He was a little boy, hardly more than a toddler still. But he had survived. When nobody could save him he had saved himself. What stories had he told himself as he lay in the dark?

She moved to the other side of the bed, across from Mrs Faraday.

'May I?' Frieda said.

Mrs Faraday looked at her numbly but she didn't resist. Frieda moved her face close to Matthew's, so she could talk in a whisper. 'It's all right,' she said. 'You're home. You've been rescued.' She saw a slight flicker of his eyes. 'You're safe. You've escaped from the witch's house.'

He made a sound but she couldn't decipher it.

'Who was there with you?' she said. 'Who was with you in the witch's house?'

Matthew's eyes suddenly clicked open, like a doll's.

'Busybody,' he said. 'Poky-nose.'

Frieda felt as if Dean was in the room, as if Matthew was a ventriloquist's dummy and he was speaking.

'Where is she?' she asked. 'Where did they put her? The busybody?'

'Took away,' he said, in his husk of a voice. 'In the dark.'

Then he started sobbing, twisting his body back and forward. Mrs Faraday gathered up her son and held him, twitching and retching, against her breast.

'That's all right,' said Frieda.

'What's that mean?' asked Munster.

'It doesn't sound good. Not at all.'

Frieda walked out through the waiting room into a corridor. She looked around. An orderly was pushing an old woman in a wheelchair. 'Is there anywhere I can get some water?' Frieda asked.

'There's a McDonald's down by the main entrance,' the orderly said.

She had only just started walking down the long corridor when there was a shout from behind her. It was Munster. He ran towards her. 'I just got a call,' he said. 'The boss wants to see you.'

'What for?'

'They found the woman.'

'Kathy?' Relief tore through her, making her feel dizzy.

'No. The wife,' said Munster. 'Terry Reeve. There's a car for you downstairs.'

Chapter Forty-three

Yvette Long looked at Karlsson and frowned.

'What's wrong?'

'Your tie,' she said. 'It's not straight.' She leaned forward and adjusted it.

'You need to look your best for the cameras,' she said. 'You're a hero. And Commissioner Crawford's going to be there. His assistant just phoned. He's very pleased with you. The press conference is going to be a big one. They've got an overflow hall.'

His mobile vibrated on the table. His ex-wife had left several messages asking him when the hell he was going to collect his children, each one angrier than the one before.

'We've got the little boy back,' said Karlsson. 'That's all they really care about. Where's Terry Reeve?'

'She's just arrived. They've put her downstairs.'

'Has she said anything about Kathy Ripon?'

'I don't know.'

'I want two officers with her every second.'

He picked up his phone and wrote a text message:

Sorry. Call soon

pressed 'Send'. Perhaps she would hear the news and understand, but he knew it didn't work like that: there were other people's children, and then there were your own.

An officer put her head round the door and said that Dr Klein had arrived. Karlsson told the officer to send her straight in. When Frieda came in, he was startled by the fierce gleam in her eyes and recognized in it his own elated weariness, which made the idea of sleep impossible.

'How is he?' he said.

'He's alive,' said Frieda. 'He's with his parents.'

'I mean, will he recover?'

'How do I know?' said Frieda. 'Young children are surprisingly resilient. That's what the textbooks say.'

'And you did it. You found him.'

'I found one, and I gave one away,' said Frieda. 'Forgive me if I don't dance with joy. You've got Terry Reeve.'

'She's downstairs.'

'I passed the mob on the way in,' said Frieda. 'I half expected them to be carrying pitchforks and flaming torches.'

'It's understandable,' said Karlsson.

'They should be back looking after their own children,' said Frieda. 'Where did you find her?'

'At her home.'

'Her home?' said Frieda.

'We were watching it, of course,' said Karlsson. 'And she came home and we arrested her. Simple as that, no brilliant detective work involved.' He gave a grimace.

'Why would she go home?' Frieda was asking herself rather than Karlsson. 'I thought they'd have a plan.'

'They did have a plan,' said Karlsson. 'You stymied it when you saw her at the cemetery. She called him. We know that. We've got her phone. She phoned him. He got away.'

'So why didn't she?' said Frieda. 'And why did she go to the cemetery?'

'You can ask her yourself,' said Karlsson. 'I want you to come in with me.'

'I feel I ought to know already,' said Frieda. 'What is it that lawyers say? You should never ask a question if you don't already know the answer.'

'We need to ask a question that we don't know the answer to,' said Karlsson. 'Where's Kathy Ripon?'

Frieda sat on the corner of Karlsson's desk. 'I've got a bad feeling about that,' she said.

'You had a bad feeling about Matthew,' said Karlsson.

'This is different. They wanted a son. They saw him as a child. Even when they got rid of him, they didn't kill him. They hid him away, like a child being left in the woods in a fairy story.'

'They didn't leave him in the woods. They buried him alive.'

'Kathy Ripon is different. She wasn't part of the plan. She was just an obstacle. But why did Terry go to the cemetery? And then why did she go home?'

'Maybe she wanted to see if he was dead,' said Karlsson. 'Or finish him off. And maybe she wanted to collect something from home before escaping. She may have been checking ahead for her husband. To see if the coast was clear.' Karlsson saw that Frieda's hands were trembling. 'Can I get you something?'

'Just some water,' said Frieda.

Karlsson sat and watched while Frieda drank a polystyrene cup of water and then they both drank cups of black coffee. They didn't speak.

'Are you ready?' he said finally.

Terry Reeve was sitting in the interview room staring in front of her. Karlsson sat opposite her. Frieda stood behind him, leaning against the wall next to the door. It felt surprisingly cool against her back.

'Where's Katherine Ripon?' said Karlsson.

'I haven't seen her,' said Terry.

Karlsson slowly unstrapped his wristwatch and laid it on the table between them. 'I want to make the situation clear to you,' he said. 'I don't know if you have some idea in your head that you're going to face some little charge like reckless endangerment and get a nice little sentence, out in a couple of years for good behaviour. I'm afraid it's not going to be like that. This is a soundproofed room, but if we took you out into the corridor, you'd be able to hear a crowd of people shouting and they're shouting about you. There's one thing we don't like in Britain, and that's people who harm children or animals. And there's another thing, and Dr Klein here would probably consider it sexist, but they particularly hate women who do it. You will get a life sentence and if you think it'll be all pottery classes and readers' groups, then think again. Prison's not like that for people who've done things to children.'

Karlsson paused for a moment. Terry was still staring in front of her.

'But if you tell us where she is,' he continued, 'things could be very different.'

Still she didn't speak.

'Your husband's gone,' said Karlsson. 'We'll get him soon. In the meantime, you're going to take the full force of this. I can give you a way out. But it won't be on offer for very long. If you don't help us, people will get very angry indeed.'

'You can't turn me against him,' said Terry. 'We did everything together.'

'That's what he's relying on,' said Karlsson. 'He gets away. Or tries to get away. And you're left here facing the music.'

'He can rely on me,' said Terry. 'He's always been able to rely on me. I can be strong for him.'

'What are you doing this for?' said Karlsson, almost plaintively. 'It's all over. There's no point.'

She just gave a shrug. Karlsson glanced round at Frieda with a look of defeat. He took his watch and slipped it into his jacket pocket, then stood up and walked over to her. 'What's in it for her? What's she got left to lose?'

'Him, maybe,' Frieda said softly. 'Can I talk to her?'

'Be my guest.'

Frieda walked across and sat down in the chair Karlsson had left. She stared across at Terry and Terry returned her gaze, setting her jaw as if she were challenging her.

'You saved Matthew's life,' said Frieda. 'It sounds funny to say it and I don't think you'll get much credit for it from the mob outside, but it's true.'

Terry looked wary. 'You're just trying to grease up to me. You want to get me to talk.'

'I'm just telling the truth. When I saw you at the cemetery, I knew that Matthew was there. If it had taken any longer to find him, he would have died.'

'So?' said Terry.

'He didn't die. That's something good that's come out

366

of this, isn't it? Is that why you went back? Were you going to see if he was still alive?'

Terry looked contemptuous. 'I've got nothing to say to you.'

'It must have preyed on your mind,' said Frieda. 'In a way, it would have been easier if you'd killed him. But those days you were under observation, when you were in here, you must have had this image of a little boy lying in the dark. So you went back. That was done out of a kind of . . . I'm not sure what the right word is. Care, maybe. And then you saw me and you saw that I saw you. You ran away and you rang Dean. You were caring for him as well. You were looking after him. Did he look after you?'

'You're not going to turn me against him.'

'I'm not trying to.'

'You fucking liar.'

'Matthew's going to be all right,' said Frieda. 'I've just come from the hospital. I think that may be a relief to you.'

'I don't care.'

'I think you do. But now we need to know about Kathy.'

Terry gave her habitual shrug.

'And Joanna – what happened to Joanna, Terry? Where is she buried?'

'Ask Dean.'

'Very well.'

'Where's my tea and fag, then?'

'I want to ask you one last thing: why did you go home?'

'I dunno,' said Terry. 'Why not?'

Frieda thought for a moment. 'I think I know.'

'Yeah?'

'You went to the cemetery and you saw me and you knew we'd find the boy and you phoned Dean and you knew you'd done what you could for him. Then what? Were you really going to run away? Really? What would that mean? Could you have gone on the run? Hidden for ever? Taken a new identity? If it were me, I think I would have thought about it the same way you did. The idea of it would be too tiring. I'd done what I could. I'd want to go home, even if I could only be there for a minute. I'd just want to go home.'

Terry breathed deeply. She felt in the pocket of her jeans and took out a crumpled old tissue and blew her nose loudly. Then she tossed the tissue on to the floor and stared back at Frieda. 'You won't get me to say anything against him,' she said. 'I've got nothing to say.'

'I know.' Frieda stood up, then knelt down and picked up the soggy tissue. 'You needn't add littering to your other problems.'

'Oh, fuck off,' said Terry.

Frieda and Karlsson left the room. Karlsson sent two female officers in to watch Terry. He was starting to say something when another detective came around the corner. He was panting and could hardly get his words out. 'Alan Dekker just called. He's talked to Dean Reeve. He met him.'

'Bloody hell.' Karlsson turned to Frieda. 'You want to come? Hold his hand?'

Frieda thought for a moment. 'No. I've got something to do.'

Karlsson couldn't stop himself smiling. 'Is this not interesting enough for you?'

'There's something I've got to do.'

'Is this Christmas shopping or is it something I should know about?'

'I don't know,' said Frieda.

Karlsson waited but Frieda didn't say any more.

'Fuck it, then.' Karlsson left.

Frieda sat down, and drummed her fingers on a table. Then she got up and walked out into the operations room. At the end there was a clink of glasses, laughter. It felt like the case was completed and celebrations had begun. She rummaged in her pocket for a notebook and flicked through it. She walked over to a desk, picked up a phone and dialled.

'Is that Sasha? . . . It's Frieda . . . Yes, I'm so glad I've caught you. I need a favour, a really big one. Can we meet? . . . I mean now. I can come straight over to wherever you are . . . Great. 'Bye.'

She slammed the receiver down. On the other side of the room, a young detective looked round and wondered what that doctor woman was doing, running across the office.

Chapter Forty-four

Karlsson knocked at the door and it opened almost before his hand dropped back to his side. A small, strong-looking woman stood before him, wearing old jeans and an orange jumper with the sleeves pushed up to the elbows. Her face, bare of makeup, looked tired and anxious.

'Carrie Dekker? I'm Detective Chief Inspector Malcolm Karlsson. And this is Detective Constable Yvette Long. I think you and your husband are expecting us.'

'Alan's in the kitchen.' She hesitated. 'He's quite upset.'

'We just need to ask some questions.'

'Can I stay?'

'If you like.'

Karlsson followed her into the kitchen.

'Alan,' she said softly. 'They're here, Alan.'

He was a crumpled, distraught figure. He was still wearing his shabby duffel coat and sat slumped at the kitchen table. When he lifted his face, Karlsson saw that he looked as if he had been crying for hours, days even.

'This is urgent,' said Karlsson. 'You need to tell us what happened.'

'I told him he shouldn't go,' said Carrie. 'I told him. I said he was putting himself in danger.'

'I wasn't in any danger. I told you. We met in a crowded place. It was only for a few minutes.' He gulped. 'It was like looking in a mirror. I should have told you. I know

I should. A few weeks ago, I had no idea he even existed. I had to see him. I'm sorry.'

He was visibly trembling and there were tears in his eyes again. Carrie sat beside him and took one of his hands between her own. She kissed his knuckles and he leaned his big, heavy head towards her. 'It's all right, my darling,' she said.

Karlsson saw how she protected him, motherly and tender. 'What time did he call you?'

'What time was it, Carrie? About nine, maybe a bit before. I heard they found the little boy.'

'It was partly down to you.'

'I'm just glad I could do something.'

'When he called you, what did he say?'

'He said we had to meet. That he didn't have long and it was our only chance. He told me he wanted to give me something.'

'And you agreed?'

'Yes.' It came out in a mumble. 'I had a feeling that if I didn't, then I would never see him. That it was my only chance and if I passed up on it I would regret it for the rest of my life. Does that sound stupid?'

'Do you have the number he called on?'

'It was a mobile,' said Carrie. 'After Alan left, I did a 1471 and wrote it down.' She passed over a scrap of paper, which Karlsson gave to DC Long.

'Where did you arrange to meet?'

'On the high street. He was already there, he said. By the old Woolworths. It's closed and boarded up now. He said he'd look out for me. Then I told Carrie.'

'You had to, didn't you? I heard you talking on the

phone anyway. I was going to go with him. I wanted to but he said his brother might not talk to him if I was there. So I let him go but not until he'd promised to phone me every five minutes. I had to know he was safe.'

'What time did you meet him?'

'I walked slowly. I felt sick all the way there. About ten minutes.'

'Was he there?'

'He came up behind me. Took me by surprise.'

'What was he wearing? Do you remember?'

'An old leather jacket. Jeans. A woollen hat, kind of greeny-brown colour, I think, which covered his hair.'

'Go on.'

'He called me bro. He said, "Well, bro, it's nice to make your acquaintance." Like it was a joke.'

'What else?'

'Then Carrie rang me on my mobile and I told her it was all OK and I was safe. I said I'd be back as soon as I could. After, he said – sorry, love – he said, "Are you a bit hen-pecked, bro? You don't want a nagging wife, you know. They're the worst, trust me." He said he wanted to have a look at me. And he wanted to give me something.'

'What?'

'Hang on.'

Karlsson watched Alan retrieve a canvas holdall from under the table. It was obviously heavy and it clinked. He put it on the surface between them.

'He wanted me to have his special tools,' he said. 'I haven't looked at them yet.'

He started pulling at the zip with thick fingers.

'Don't touch them,' said Carrie, sharply. 'Don't go touching anything that belonged to him.'

'It was a gift.'

'He's wicked. We don't want that in the house.'

'I'll take them,' said Karlsson. 'Did he say anything else?'

'Not really. He said something stupid. To remember there were worse things than being dead.'

'What does that mean?'

'I don't know.'

'What was his manner? Was he agitated?'

'I was in a state, but he was calm. He didn't seem in a hurry. It was like he knew where he was going.'

'Anything else?'

'No. He patted me on the shoulder, said it was nice to meet me, and then he just left.'

'Which way did he go?'

'I don't know. I saw him turn off the high street. It leads to the bus depot and that waste bit of ground where they're building the superstore.'

'He didn't tell you where he was going?'

'No.'

'You're not protecting him?'

'I wouldn't do that. He's a bad man. There was something about him.' This with sudden venom.

'After you saw him leave, you went home?'

'I rang Carrie to say I was OK and he'd left. I felt strange but it was like a relief as well. Like something had gone out of my life, like I was free of him.'

'You didn't go anywhere or speak to anyone after you saw him go?'

'No. Nobody.'

'And there's nothing else you can think of?'

'That's everything. I'm sorry. I know I've done wrong.'

Karlsson stood up. 'DC Long is going to stay here for the time being, and I'll send another officer over as well. Just do what they say.'

'Will he come back?' Carrie's hands flew to her mouth.

'It's just a precaution.'

'You think we're in danger.'

'He's a dangerous man. This might not be over yet. I wish you'd called us.'

'Sorry. I just – I had to see him. Just the once.'

Karlsson ordered a redeployment around the area where Reeve had met his brother. He didn't feel hopeful, though. It was early afternoon and the paltry day was already fading back into darkness. In houses and flats, Christmas lights glowed in the windows and garlands hung from knockers. There were gaudy trees in shops and the streets were bright with neon bells, reindeers and characters from children's cartoons. A small group of men and women were singing carols outside Tesco Direct and rattling buckets. Once again, spits of snow drifted in the bitter air. It would be a white Christmas of a kind, thought Karlsson, but for him Christmas was an unreal thing. Dimly, he imagined his children in their house far from here: the tree with the presents stacked underneath, the smell of mince pies, their hectic cheeks, family life continuing but without him in it. Matthew had been rescued and was safe, a fact beyond everyone's wildest hopes. The papers would herald him as the best Christmas present his parents would ever have. A miracle. In truth, it felt like a miracle to Karlsson. He had long ago given Matthew up as dead. He knew he was tired, but he didn't feel it. He felt stingingly awake, more clear-headed than he had felt in days.

Frieda was still at the police station when he returned. She was sitting in an empty interview room, quite straight-backed, with her hair newly brushed, drinking from a mug. He smelt peppermint. She looked up expectantly.

'They're still looking. He's out there somewhere. Where can he go?'

'Is Alan all right?'

'Very shocked. Who wouldn't be? He's gone through a traumatic experience and it isn't over yet. His wife's a strong woman.'

'He's lucky to have her.'

'By the look of him, he'll be in touch with you soon.'

'Perhaps, though I might be the last person in the world he wants to see. I'd like to see him. Apart from anything else, he'll soon have the most hated face in the country.'

'I know. And that lot out there . . .' He nodded towards the front of the station, where a crowd was still gathered. 'They're not the most forgiving lot in the world.'

Karlsson left the room and before Frieda even had time to start thinking about what she should do, whether it was time to go home and try to sleep, he burst back in. 'They've found him,' he said.

'Where?'

'In an old dock off the side of the canal just along from where he met Dekker. Under a bridge. He was hanging from it.'

Chapter Forty-five

The car couldn't get Karlsson all the way to the canal. He stopped at a bridge that intersected it. An officer was waiting for him and led him down the steps to the towpath.

'Who found the body?' Karlsson asked.

'Some old man walking his dog,' said the officer. 'He didn't have a mobile and he couldn't find a phone box, so he walked all the way home and he's got a bad leg. It took an hour for someone to get there. If he'd had a mobile, maybe the paramedics could have done something.'

Ahead, Karlsson could see people on the towpath, kids mostly, trying to get a view. He and the officer stepped under the police tape and turned off the main towpath along the small inlet, a watery cul-de-sac. Once it had been a wharf for barges to tie up next to a factory. Now it was abandoned and desolate with bushes growing out of the cracked walls. Several officers were clustered ahead but there was no sense of urgency. One of them said something that Karlsson couldn't hear and the others laughed. Further along the path Karlsson could see one of his team, Melanie Hackett, talking to an officer. He called her over.

'They cut him down,' she said. She gestured at a green tarpaulin on the ground. 'You want a look?'

Karlsson nodded. She pulled the sheet back. He was prepared but he still flinched. The eyes stared upwards at nothing, the pupils enlarged; the swollen tongue protruded between the teeth. Hackett pulled the sheet back further. The rope was gone but the ligature mark along the neck leading behind the ear was clear to see.

'He never even got changed,' she said. 'He's wearing the same clothes he wore in the station.'

'He never went home,' said Karlsson.

Karlsson pulled a face. There was a distinct smell of shit. Hackett saw his expression and pulled the sheet back across.

'It's what happens when you hang yourself,' she said. 'If people knew that, it might put them off doing it.'

Karlsson looked around. There were some windows in the old factory but they had all been blocked up long ago.

'Is the area overlooked from anywhere?'

'No,' said Hackett. 'This bit of the canal's quiet enough and nobody comes up here.'

'I guess that's why he came here.'

'He knew the game was over,' said Hackett.

'Why do you say that?'

'There was a letter in his pocket.'

'What kind of letter?'

'We've got it over in the box with the rest of the stuff we found in his pockets.' She walked over to a small blue crate and pulled out a transparent folder. 'He had a mobile phone, packet of cigarettes, lighter, a pen and this. It was in an envelope with nothing written on the front.'

She handed him the folder. Karlsson could read the note without opening the folder. He moved along the path out of the bridge's shade. It was a small page torn out of a ring-backed notebook. He recognized the large looping handwriting from the signature he'd seen at the bottom of Reeve's witness statement. It was short and easy to read:

I know what's in store. I don't want any of that. Tell Terry sorry. Sorry to leave you, doll. She knows she was always the one for me. She wasn't part of any of this. She won't stand up for herself. Tell her I did my best. Time to go.

Dean Reeve

Karlsson looked over at Melanie Hackett. 'He's left her to it,' he said.

'So what do we do?' she asked.

'Lean on her as hard as we can. She's all we've got.'

Karlsson rang Frieda at home. He told her about the body, about the note.

'Somehow I never imagined him sitting in a court-room.'

'I don't know what that means,' said Karlsson. 'Anyway, I said I'd keep you informed. So, you're informed.'

'And I'll keep you informed,' said Frieda.

'What does that mean?'

'I'm not sure,' said Frieda. 'If anything happens, I'll get back to you.'

After Frieda put down the phone, she sat entirely still. On the table in front of her was a white earthenware coffee cup. The light through the window hit it so that one side was in shadow, a shadow that was almost blue. She had a pad of paper and a piece of charcoal and she was trying to capture it before the light moved, the shape of the cup changed and the image was lost. She looked at the cup and looked down at the page. It was wrong. The shadow on her drawing was like a shadow was meant to look; it wasn't the shadow she was actually looking at. She ripped the page out and tore it in half and then in half again. She was wondering whether she could bear to start again when the phone rang. It was Sasha Wells.

'Merry Christmas,' she said. 'I've got news for you.'

They arranged to meet in Number 9, which was just around the corner from where Sasha worked. As Frieda came into the coffee shop she looked at the tinsel and stars and little globes that had been hung around the room. Kerry greeted her and pointed at the window display. 'You like our Santa Claus?'

'I'd like to see him nailed to a cross,' Frieda said.

Kerry looked shocked and disapproving. 'It's for the children,' she said. 'And Katya did it.'

Frieda ordered the strongest black coffee they could manufacture. When Sasha came in, Frieda thought how different she looked from the shaking, tremulous young woman she'd met a few weeks earlier. Of course, that didn't necessarily mean she was better, but she was wearing a suit, her hair was tied back, and she was dressed to face the world. When she caught sight of Frieda, her face broke into a wide smile. Frieda got up, introduced her to Kerry and ordered a herbal tea and a muffin for her. They sat down at the table together. Sasha's smile turned to a look of concern.

'When did you last sleep?' she asked.

'I've been working,' Frieda said. 'Well?'

Sasha took a bite of the muffin and a gulp of tea almost simultaneously. 'I'm starving,' she mumbled, with her mouth full, and then swallowed. 'Well, I want to say first how grateful you should be to me. I'm in genetics but I don't do testing. However, I know someone who knows someone and furthermore I dragged them out of a Christmas party and got them to do it in about thirty seconds. So basically we've done the test.'

'What was the result?'

'You've got to say, "Thank you."'

'I'm very grateful, Sasha.'

'Admittedly, I do owe you massively for punching that creep and risking going to prison but even so. You're welcome. And at the risk of being extremely tiresome, I need to preface everything by saying that this is completely unofficial, between ourselves.'

'Absolutely.'

'And I'm also going to say that I'm torn between wondering why you want to know about this piece of tissue paper and suspecting that it's better if I know as little as possible.'

'I promise you that it's essential,' said Frieda. 'And it's secret.'

'And of course you're a doctor, blah blah blah, and you know that there are legal issues here, issues of privacy, and that if part of any legal proceedings, this is entirely off the record.'

'Don't worry. That's not a problem.'

'What I mean is that it's great to hear from you, and I'd been hoping we'd meet for a drink and a chat, but I really hope I'm not suddenly going to be asked to testify somewhere.'

'No. I promise.'

'So why did you want the mitochondrial DNA test?'

'Isn't that obvious?'

'I suppose so, in a way, but it's very unusual.'

There was a pause. Frieda felt her voice tremble. 'So what was the result?'

Sasha's expression was suddenly serious.

'It was positive.'

'Ah.' Frieda let her breath out in a long sigh.

'So. That's that,' said Sasha, watching her closely.

'What does that mean? What does it really mean? DNA tests are a balance of probability, aren't they?'

Sasha's expression relaxed. 'Not in this case. You're a medical doctor, aren't you? You've studied biology. The mitochondrial DNA is passed unchanged through females. It matches or it doesn't. In this case, it does.'

'So I can be certain.'

'I'm not sure I want to know, but where do these samples come from?'

'You're right, you don't want to know. Thank you – thank you so much for your help.'

'I didn't help you.'

'But you did.'

'That was me being like a spy,' said Sasha. 'I mean, I've not kept the samples or the documentation. I've told you the result. That's all.'

'Of course,' said Frieda. 'I promised that from the beginning. I just needed to know.'

Sasha drank the last of her tea. 'So what are you doing for Christmas?'

'It just got a bit more complicated.'

'That's what I thought.'

Chapter Forty-six

'Don't you have anything better to do on Christmas Eve?' Karlsson was standing at the door of the interview room. He was tired, his eyes felt gritty and his throat sore, as if he was coming down with something. It was eight o'clock. At last, the police station was almost deserted, half its rooms in darkness.

'Not just at the moment,' said Frieda.

'This had better be good. I was on the point of going home.'

In truth, he didn't really want to go home to his empty flat on the night before Christmas. He let himself think of his kids, hectic with excitement, putting a mince pie out for Santa without him.

'Has she said anything?'

'Not really. Nothing about Kathy.'

Frieda went into the interview room. A young police officer was sitting on a chair in the corner, rubbing her eyes surreptitiously. Terry was slumped in her chair, her face blotchy and tired under her harsh blonde hair. She looked at Frieda with indifference.

'I've nothing to say to you. He's dead. You lot did that. And you've got the boy. What more do you want? I've identified the body. Isn't that enough for you? Just leave me in peace.'

'I'm not here to talk about Dean.'

'I told him.' Jerking her head towards Karlsson, who stood by the door with his arms folded. 'I'm not saying nothing. Like his letter said, I've done nothing wrong.'

'You must be glad Matthew is alive,' said Frieda, looking at Terry's ragged nails, her tired white flesh.

Terry shrugged.

'It must have felt distressing to you, knowing that he was trapped underground and not being able to help.'

Terry yawned widely. Her teeth were nicotine-stained. Behind her, Frieda heard Karlsson stir with impatience.

'Does it help you to know that, in a way, you saved him by going back there?'

'Come on, Frieda,' said Karlsson, stepping forward and speaking in a stifled whisper. 'We've been over this. If she can't help us with Kathy, what's the point?'

Frieda ignored him. She leaned over the table and stared into Terry's brown, dulled eyes. 'A tiny child, snatched from his home and hidden away. Matthew would have become Simon and forgotten his first mother, his first father, all the days before the day he was snatched out of one life and put into another. Poor thing. Poor child. What does someone become, after such a terrifying wrench? How does one deal with one's self, when one's self has been so lost and so changed? Perhaps it's a bit like being buried alive for the rest of one's time here. Is there really nothing you want to say to me, Terry? Dean is dead. There's nothing left for him to do. You have only yourself now, the self you have had to bury. No? You have nothing to say? All right.'

Frieda stood up. She gazed down at Terry for a few seconds. 'I wanted to prepare you. Your sister is outside to see you.'

For a moment, there was a tingling silence in the little room. She could feel everyone's eyes on her.

'What the fuck?' Karlsson said.

'Terry?' Frieda said softly.

'What are you talking about?'

'I'll call her, shall I?'

Frieda's eyes were still fixed on Terry, but Terry's face hadn't changed. She just stared at Frieda, impassive. Frieda opened the door and walked swiftly down the deserted corridor to the waiting room. 'You can come in now, Rose.'

'This is not a bloody West End show. You are not in charge here.'

Karlsson was shouting, walking up and down the room and bellowing. His face was white with rage.

'What do you mean, suddenly announcing it, like a conjuror pulling a rabbit out of a hat?'

'I didn't want a police officer to tell her. I wanted to break it gently.'

'You did, did you?'

'Why are you so angry?'

'Jesus, where do I begin?' Karlsson suddenly stopped his tramping up and down the room and folded into a chair. He rubbed his face violently. 'How did you know?'

'I didn't really know,' said Frieda. 'I just kept thinking about her going home, about what home meant for her. And that they didn't kill Matthew. Even Dean. He didn't kill him. And then I saw her when she was sleeping.'

'Sleeping?'

'I came into the interview room when she had fallen

asleep. She had laid her face on her folded hands. Rose once told me how Joanna went to sleep just like that, her hands as if in prayer and her face on top of them. There are some things you can't erase – a certain smile, perhaps; a little gesture; the way you fall asleep. So I had to know, I had to test it. I got her DNA in the tissue and I got Rose's.'

'She looked so much older. The few records we have of her say she's older, nearer Dean's age. She can't be in her twenties still.'

'She's been poor. Poor and abused all her life.'

'You're going to tell me she's a victim.'

'She is a victim.'

'She's also a perpetrator. She helped Dean snatch Matthew, remember.'

'I know.'

'He would have died. She would have helped murder him. And where's Kathy Ripon? She's not saying.'

'I don't think she knows.'

'Oh, don't you? On what evidence? You feel it, is that it?'

'I suppose so. And it would make a kind of sense. It was a way of becoming a mother.'

'She was under my nose all that time,' Karlsson said.

'It's a triumph,' said Frieda. 'You're already a hero for finding one lost child. Now you've found two. Matthew and Joanna.'

'She's not a lost child.'

'Oh yes she is. And she's the one I really feel sorry for.'

Karlsson flinched as if he was suffering from a blinding headache. 'It was you,' he said. 'You were the one who found them both.'

Frieda stepped forward and put her hand on Karlsson's cheek. He closed his eyes for a moment. 'You know what I want?'

'What?' said Karlsson, softly. 'Recognition, love, like the rest of us.'

'No,' said Frieda. 'I'd like to sleep. I'd like to go home and sleep for about a thousand years and then get back to my patients. I don't want to go into a press conference and explain how I used a patient to find a murderer. I've got things I need to think about and I need to do it in private. I want to crawl back into my burrow. You've found Matthew. You can do a DNA test – a legal one – and show that Terry is Joanna. And Dean Reeve is dead.' There was a silence. Then she added, 'But if you're thinking of charging Joanna with murder, making her the scapegoat now that Dean has killed himself, I'll think again.'

'What are you saying?'

'Or even of complicity.'

'She's guilty and you know it.'

'I know that the crowd out there is howling for her blood – and that, being a woman, she'll be treated even worse than if she were a man. And I also know that she was abducted when she could barely talk; that she was psychologically abused and brainwashed, that she cannot therefore be held responsible for her actions, and that if you think of putting her on trial for what she did as the victim of a crime against her that continued for more than two decades, you'll see me in court as an expert witness for the defence.'

'Don't you think she's responsible for what she did?'

386

'Just try me,' Frieda said.

Karlsson looked at his watch. 'Well, it's Christmas Day.'

'So it is.' Frieda stood up.

'I'll get someone to drive you home.'

'I'd rather walk.'

'It's the middle of the night and it's miles.'

'That's OK.'

'And it's freezing out there.'

'That's OK too.'

It was more than OK: it was good. Frieda wanted to be alone in the dark and the ice of the city she loved; she wanted to walk until her body and mind were exhausted. Her snug house felt like a distant goal, a place she had to achieve through enormous physical effort.

When she had led Rose in to see her sister, she had held on to the young woman's arm and felt the violent trembling that seized her entire body. Rose had stood just inside the doorway and stared with frightening, frightened intensity at the figure who sat before her.

Twenty-two years previously her skinny, dark-haired, gap-toothed little sister had dawdled behind her on the way home and suddenly disappeared, swallowed up by cracks in the pavement. She had haunted Rose. Her thin pale face, her pleading, lisping child's voice, calling her name, had entered her dreams. She had tried to imagine her as she would be at each stage of her life thereafter – at ten, as an adolescent, as a young adult. Computer-generated images of her face had told her what Joanna would have become. She had looked for her on streets, glimpsed her in crowds, known she was dead and never let her go.

How many times had Rose imagined this reunion? How they would gasp, take faltering steps towards each other, stare into each other's eyes, clasp each other close; the words that would spill out, the love and comfort. And now here was an overweight, middle-aged woman with bottle blonde hair and a look of apathetic indifference, even contempt, on her face, as if she was a stranger.

Frieda could see Rose's disbelief, then a sudden terrified recognition that this actually was Joanna. What was it? Perhaps the eyes, the shape of the chin, a turn of the head.

'Jo-Jo?' she said, in a trembling voice.

But Terry – Joanna – didn't react.

'Joanna, is it you? It's me.'

'I don't know what you're on about.'

'I'm Rose. Rosie,' she said, on a sob. 'Do you know me?' She sounded as though she didn't know herself.

'My name's Terry.'

Rose was quivering with distress. She turned to Frieda briefly, then back again. 'You're my sister. Your name's Joanna. You were taken away when you were little. Don't you remember? We looked and looked. You must remember. But now you're back.'

Joanna looked at Frieda. 'Have I got to listen to this?'

'There's time,' Frieda said, to both Rose and Joanna. Neither seemed to hear her.

Frieda walked past the small park, still and white in the moonlight. Past the church squeezed into the fork of two roads, with its huddled gravestones. Under the plane trees, knobbled and bare. Under the strings of Christmas lights, shining on the empty roads. Smashed phone boxes. A rubbish bin that had been turned on its side, leaking its viscous mess onto the pristine scattering of snow. Rusty railings. Boarded doors. Parked cars all in a row. Empty office blocks, all the computers and phones at rest for the holidays. The shops with their graffitied metal shutters. The houses with their blind windows behind which people slept, snored, muttered, dreamed.

A firework exploded on the horizon and fell through the sky in a flower of colour. A police car passed her, a lorry with its driver high up in his cab, a drunk man veering and tacking up the road, his eyes fixed blindly on some distant point. Matthew was alive. Joanna was alive. Kathy Ripon was missing still and must be dead. Dean Reeve was dead. It was half past four on Christmas morning and Frieda hadn't bought her Christmas tree. Chloë was going to be cross.

Chapter Forty-seven

'I bought this for you weeks ago,' said Matthew's mother. She laid a large red fire engine, in its box, by Matthew's bed. 'It's the one you saw in the shop, ages ago. Do you remember? You cried when I said you couldn't have it, but I went back later and got it.'

'I don't think he can really see it,' said Matthew's father, mildly.

'I knew you'd come home. I wanted to be ready for you.'

The little boy opened his eyes and stared. She couldn't tell if he could see her, or was looking through her, at something else.

'It's Christmas. Father Christmas came. We'll see what he brought you in a bit. I told you he wouldn't forget. He always knows where the children are. He knew you were here in hospital. He came specially.'

The voice came, reedy and thin: 'But have I been a good boy?'

'Have you? Oh. None better.'

Matthew closed his eyes. They sat on either side of him and held his bandaged hands.

Richard Vine and Rose sat together in his small room that smelt stale and was too warm. They were eating brunch and opening their presents to each other – a dressing-gown for him, and for her a bottle of perfume, the same perfume he gave her every Christmas, and she had never had the heart to tell him she didn't like it and never used it. Later, she would go to her mother and step-father for Christmas dinner – turkey and all the trimmings, though she had been a vegetarian from the age of thirteen, and so would make do with the trimmings. This had been the arrangement ever since her father had left them and Joanna had disappeared.

She kissed her father on his unshaven cheek, smelling the tobacco, the sweet stench of alcohol, the sweat, trying not to draw back. She knew that after she left him today he would sit in front of his TV and drink himself into a stupor. And as for her mother, who'd so resolutely got on with her life without Joanna, refusing to wait in miserable suspension for the daughter she knew was dead, what would she say, what would she do? Rose was very aware that on the other side of this drab family ritual lay the roar of press attention, frantic curiosity and a world wrenched out of its normal order.

'Thanks,' she said. She dabbed some of the perfume on her wrists. 'That's lovely, Dad.'

All around her were the photos of Joanna. He had never put them away or culled them. Some were faded now, and others slipping in their clip-frames. Rose looked at them, although they were so familiar to her – the wide, anxious smile and dark fringe, the bony knees. The nervous, needy little girl who'd so lodged and grown in her father's memory, preventing him from ever leading a normal life again. She opened her mouth to speak, though she didn't know the words.

'Dad,' she said. 'There's something I need to tell you, before you hear it from someone else. You need to prepare yourself.' She took a deep breath, put her hand on his.

Tanner poured whisky into two tumblers. Karlsson saw that his hands shook, and were liver-spotted, the hands of an old man. 'I wanted to tell you myself,' he said. 'Before it gets in the papers.'

Tanner handed him one of the glasses.

'Merry Christmas,' said Karlsson.

Tanner shook his head. 'We're not having much of a Christmas this year,' he said. 'My wife used to do all that. We'll sit up in the bedroom and watch the TV.' He lifted the glass. 'To a result.'

They clinked glasses and both took a gulp.

'Half a result,' said Karlsson. 'One woman is still missing. She'll never come home.'

'I'm sorry.'

'The press won't care, though. She's only an adult. I already know what the headlines are going to be. "The Best Christmas Present of All". There's going to be a press conference. I'd like you to be there.'

'It's your moment,' said Tanner. 'You deserve it. You got two missing children back alive. That's more than most coppers achieve in a lifetime. How the hell did you manage it?'

'It's a bit difficult to explain.' Karlsson paused for a moment as if he still had to get it ordered in his mind. 'I met this psychiatrist who was seeing Reeve's brother. His twin brother. She learned about the inside of this guy's head, about his dreams, and somehow this tipped her off. In some way.'

Tanner narrowed his eyes, as if he thought his leg was being pulled. 'His dreams,' he said. 'And you're going to say all of this at the press conference?'

Karlsson took a sip of his whisky and held it for a moment in his mouth so that it stung his gums and his tongue. Then he swallowed it. 'My boss wasn't particularly receptive to that aspect of the inquiry,' he said. 'I believe that at the press conference we'll be stressing the effectiveness of my team, the co-operation of other services, the response from the public and from the media, and the lessons it gives us all about staying vigilant. You know. The usual.'

'And the psychiatrist. What does she have to say about that?'

Karlsson gave a slow smile. 'She's a bit of a handful,' he said. 'She's not someone who takes no for an answer. But she doesn't want the attention.'

'You mean the credit.'

'If you like.'

Tanner gestured towards the whisky bottle.

'I'd better go,' Karlsson said.

'One thing,' said Tanner. 'Why didn't she run away?'

'From what?' said Karlsson. 'She didn't know anything else. It was her home. I've got a feeling it still is, in a way. We're all meant to be happy about it, but I'm not sure we've really got her back.'

In the doorway, Tanner started to say something that sounded like 'thank you' when he was stopped by a thumping from upstairs. 'She has a stick,' he said. 'Like those bells you call a butler with.'

Karlsson pulled the door closed behind him.

'This we call *holubsti* in my country,' said Josef. 'The country of Ukraine. And this is pickled fish, which you should catch in the ice but I got from my shop in absence of time.' He cast a reproachful look at Frieda. 'I have here some *pyrogies*, some with potato, some with sauerkraut and some with prune.'

'This is amazing.' Olivia was looking hung-over and dazed. She was wearing a purple silk dress that shone in the candlelight, giving her a voluptuous look, like a film star of the fifties. Beside her sat Paz, who was wearing a very short pink dress and bows in her hair that on anyone else would have looked absurd but only made her seem more luscious than ever.

'My friend and landlord Reuben make you this *pampushky*.'

Reuben lifted up his glass of vodka and took an unsteady bow.

'And above all we have the *kutya*, which is wheat and honey and poppy seeds and nuts. This is essential. With it we may say, "Joy, Earth, Joy."' He paused. 'Joy, Earth, Joy,' he repeated.

'Joy, Earth, Joy,' said Chloë, loud and clear. Her face was shining. She moved a bit closer to Josef, who beamed at her approvingly. She giggled and smirked, and Frieda glanced at Olivia, but Olivia was paying no attention to her daughter's smitten behaviour. She was prodding her fork into the dumplings and pastries that were heaped on plates all around the table.

'How long did this all take, for goodness' sake?'

'Many hours without stoppage. Because Frieda is my friend.'

'Your friend Frieda didn't buy a tree. Or crackers,' said Chloë.

'Frieda is here, you know, and Frieda was busy,' said Frieda. She felt heavy with tiredness, and was regarding the scene as if from a distance. She wondered what Kathy Ripon's parents were doing right now. This Christmas marked their new life, without their daughter. The first of many barren days.

'I can tell you a joke, never mind crackers,' said Reuben, leering at Paz, who ignored him. 'Real Madrid, one. Surreal Madrid, fish. No? Oh, well.'

'We make toasts,' said Josef, who seemed to have taken on the role of host in Frieda's house.

'Fuck all errant husbands,' said Olivia, tossing her vodka into her mouth and over her face.

'Don't be too hard on errant husbands,' said Reuben. 'They're just men, weak and foolish men.'

'To wander far from home,' said Josef.

'Is that a toast?' asked Paz. 'I shall drink to that.' Which she did, with energy.

'Poor Josef,' said Chloë, kindly.

'This is delicious, Josef. Should I be eating the sweet and savoury together like this?' asked Olivia.

'You're quiet,' said Reuben to Frieda.

'Yes. Talking feels too hard.'

'Has it occurred to you that everyone here is missing someone?'

'I suppose you're right.'

'What a collection of left-behinds and misfits we are.'

Frieda looked round the table at the candlelit scene. Paz, sweet and sultry in her ridiculous ribbons; Josef, with his wild hair and sad dark eyes; Chloë, with her flushed cheeks and scarred arms; Olivia, a drunk and sultry mess, spilling her words; and Reuben, of course, ironic about his own downfall, a dandy tonight in his beautiful embroidered waistcoat. Everyone was talking over each other; no one was listening.

'We could do worse,' she said, lifting her glass.

It was the nearest she could get to making a toast or welcoming them into her home.

He rolled off her and Carrie lay back in the dark, panting. She felt the dampness between her legs oozing out on to the sheet. She shifted away from it slightly. She felt his weight beside her. She waited for a moment. She had to say something but she had to wait a minute or two. Just so long as he didn't fall asleep. She counted to fifty before she spoke.

'That was wonderful,' she said.

'It was, wasn't it?'

'The best Christmas ever. It's been so long, Alan, since we've made love like this. There were times I thought we never would again. But now!' She gave a blurred giggle, like a pigeon cooing. 'It's been wonderful.'

'I'm making up for lost time.'

He laid his hand on her naked thigh. She turned and

smiled dreamily at him, running her hands down his spine. 'There's something I have to say.'

'Go on.'

'Don't take this the wrong way. I know what you've been through. I know how horrible it's been, how unsettling in so many different ways. I've tried to support you as much as I possibly could, and I've never, not for one minute, stopped loving you – though sometimes I wanted to shake you and scream at you. But it's over now, and we're going to get our life back, Alan, do you hear me? We both deserve that. We've earned our happiness. We're going to think about adopting, because I know I want a child, and you'd be a wonderful father. I know what you said before about needing to have your own child, but maybe that's changed, after everything you've been through. What matters is that we'll love the child and they'll love us.'

She paused, stroked his thick grey hair. 'And also, at some point you're going to have to start seeing people again. We haven't seen friends for ages. I can't remember when anyone last came here. I understand you want to be alone for a few days, now the nightmare's over, but it can't go on for ever. You'll have to go back to work properly. You have to go back out into the world. I mean, if it's necessary I suppose you could see Dr Klein again.' She paused. 'Alan. Alan? Are you asleep?'

Dean Reeve mumbled something he hoped would sound as if he had been half asleep and hadn't heard her. And if she suspected he was pretending to be asleep as a way of avoiding an awkward conversation, well, that was just as good. He couldn't have expected to keep this up for more than a few days anyway. Even as it was, it had worked out far better than he had ever hoped: not for a second had she doubted him. And she'd been so eager. Quite a passionate creature, to his surprise. But it was just a little holiday for him. He would leave and no one would ever know why. Call it what you will – a mid-life crisis, the trauma of events, a parting of the ways, a wake-up call – what mattered was that he was free and he could start again. He turned, as if in sleep, or as if in half-sleep or in faked sleep, and put his arm over her, feeling her breast, damp with sweat. He thought about poor Terry. Oh, well, he'd had the best of her. And she'd be all right, probably, if she said the things people wanted to hear. And then there was that other girl, the one they hadn't found, the one they would never find now, under the London streets, nothing to say, and even if she could speak from the grave, it couldn't touch him. Nothing could touch him. Even that Frieda Klein, whose slender fingers he had once felt against his and whose cool dark eyes had looked right inside him, had no power over him now. He was remade and could go where he wanted, be whom he liked. Few on this earth are given such permission and granted such liberty. He smiled into Carrie's soft shoulder, smiled into the velvet night, and felt himself slowly sink into a dream about darkness and warmth and safety.

Chapter Forty-eight

On the day before New Year's Eve, an icy, windless day with frost on the car windows and the rooftops, Frieda woke even earlier than usual. She lay in the darkness for a long time before rising, dressing, going downstairs to make herself a pot of tea, which she drank standing by the back door, looking out onto her small patio where everything stood in frosted stillness. In four days' time, she would return to work. A new year: she did not want to make any resolutions. She did not want to give up anything else.

For many days now, as the newspapers and television channels had celebrated Matthew Faraday's return, she had been consumed by the thought of Kathy Ripon, the one they had not been able to save, the one for whom she was responsible. Night after night, she had dreamed of her, and waking she held the picture of the young woman in her head. She had had a nice face, shrewd and self-mocking. She had been sent unwittingly to her fate, over the threshold of Dean Reeve's house, sucked in by that black hole. What had it been like for her? What had it been like when she realized that it was all over and that nobody would come to save her? The thought of it made Frieda nauseous but she made herself think of it, over and over again, as if by doing so she could take some of Kathy Ripon's pain and fear away. Two lost children had been found, but you can't trade lives. They are too dear for that. Frieda knew she would never forgive herself, and she knew too that the story wouldn't be over until Kathy's body was found and her parents were allowed to lay her to rest and start on the process of their great mourning. And that if it hadn't been found yet, it probably never would be found.

At last, turning from her station by the window, she made up her mind and then she acted swiftly, pulling on her long warm coat and her gloves, leaving the house briskly, taking the Underground to Paddington and then boarding the train. It was almost empty, just a few people with suitcases. She didn't want to think too hard about what she was about to do. In truth, she didn't really know what she was about to do.

Heathrow Terminal Three was crowded. It always is. In the middle of the night, on Christmas Day, in February when days are greyest and in June when they are fresh and green, in times of plenty and of recession, in times of grief and celebration, people are always travelling somewhere. Queues wound back from check-in desks: families with too many bags, little children with feverish cheeks sitting disconsolately on giant suitcases, single people looking cool and unencumbered. A tiny black woman pushed a cleaning machine slowly across the floor, her eyes fixed on her task as if she did not notice the heaving crowds, the cross men with big stomachs straining their shirts.

Frieda examined the Departures board. The flight left in two and a half hours. Check-in hadn't yet opened, although already a queue was forming. She went to the kiosk selling coffee and pastries and bought herself a carton of porridge, thick and creamy, then sat herself on a soft bench from where she had a good view.

Sandy was late. She had never travelled with him, but she guessed he was the kind of person who always turned up at the last minute, unflustered. For someone who was leaving the country for an indeterminate length of time, he didn't have much luggage – or maybe he had arranged for all of his things to be shipped over; all of his beautiful clothes and his medical tomes, his heavy-based pans and his tennis and squash rackets, the pictures that used to hang on his walls. He walked up to the check-in desk with two modest bags, and his laptop slung over his shoulder. He was wearing black jeans and a jacket she couldn't remember having seen before. Perhaps he had bought it especially for this trip. His face was unshaven, thinner than when they had last met. He looked tired and pre-occupied and, seeing this, her heart stirred. She half stood, but then sat down again, watching him as he handed over his passport. She saw him speak, nod courteously, place his bags on the belt that carried them away.

She had imagined this moment and played it over in her mind. How she would put a hand on his shoulder and he would turn. How, seeing her there, his face would light up with gladness and relief. They wouldn't smile; some feelings are too great for smiling. Yet when he left the desk, she still didn't move. He stood for a moment, as if he didn't know where he was going, then straightened his shoulders, settled his face into an expression of purpose and moved swiftly towards Departures – long strides as if he was suddenly in a hurry to be gone from there. Now she could only see his back. Now he was disappearing into the throng of passengers who were pressing themselves through the departure doors into the cavernous overlit hall beyond. Frieda knew that if she didn't move, he would be gone from her – gone into his new world without her. It would be over.

She stood up. A curious feeling was gathering in her chest, one of a grave sadness and fixed resolution. She understood that she belonged here – in this cold, windy, crowded, moderate country; in this teeming, dirty, noisy, throbbing city; in the little mews house on a hidden cobbled street that she had made into her refuge; in this only place where she almost belonged. She turned and made her way, going home.

Acknowledgements

This is the first book of a series, and the start of a new journey for us. We would like to thank Michael Morris, Dr Julian Stern and Dr Cleo Van Velsen for their generous help and advice. They shouldn't necessarily be held responsible for our interpretation of that help and advice.

Tom Weldon and Mari Evans have been a source of support and loyalty for more years than any of us probably likes to remember; to them and the dynamic team at Penguin, we owe a huge debt of gratitude.

We're constantly grateful for the unstinting care and support of our agents, Sarah Ballard and Simon Trewin, also of St John Donald and everyone at United Agents. Sam Edenborough and Nicki Kennedy of ILA have protected and looked after us throughout our years of writing together.

Grateful thanks to our copyeditor, Hazel Orme, for keeping such a sympathetic, attentive and careful eye on us, not just in this book, but over so many years and publications.

THE THRILLING SEQUEL TO *BLUE MONDAY*

As the days get longer, the cases get darker . . .

Psychotherapist Frieda Klein thought she was done
with the police. But once more DCI Karlsson
is knocking at her door.

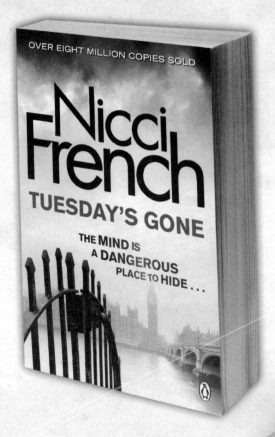

OVER EIGHT MILLION COPIES SOLD

Nicci French

TUESDAY'S GONE

THE MIND IS
A DANGEROUS
PLACE TO HIDE . . .

Read an extract now . . .

Chapter One

Maggie Brennan half walked, half ran along Deptford Church Street. She was talking on the phone and reading a file and looking for an address in the *A–Z*. It was the second day of the week and she was already two days behind schedule. This didn't include the case load she had inherited from a colleague who was now on permanent sick leave.

'No,' said Maggie into the phone. She looked at her watch. 'I'll try to get to the meeting before you finish.'

She put the phone into her pocket. She was thinking of the case she'd just come from. A three-year-old with bruises. Suspicious bruises, the doctor in casualty had said. Maggie had talked to the mother, looked at the child, checked out the flat where they lived. It was horrible; damp, cold, but not obviously dangerous. The mother said she didn't have a boyfriend, and Maggie had checked the bathroom and there was no razor. The mother had insisted that the child had fallen down the stairs. That's what people said when they hit their children, but even so, three-year-olds really did fall down stairs. She'd spent only ten minutes there but ten hours wouldn't have made much difference. If she removed the child, the prosecution would probably fail and she would be disciplined. If she didn't remove the child and he was found dead, there would be an inquiry and she would be fired and maybe prosecuted. So she'd signed off on it. No immediate cause for concern. Probably nothing much would happen.

She looked more closely at the *A–Z*. Her hands were cold because she'd forgotten her gloves; her feet were wet in their cheap boots. She'd been to this hostel before, but she could never remember where it was. Howard Street was a little dead end, tucked away somewhere towards the river. She had to put her reading glasses on and move her finger around on the map before she found it. Yes, that was it, just a couple of minutes away. She turned off the main street and found herself unexpectedly next to a churchyard. She leaned on the wall and looked at the file on the woman she was going to see. There wasn't much there at all. Michelle Doyce. Born 1959. A hospital discharge paper, copied to the social services department. A placement form, a request for an evaluation. Maggie flicked through the forms: no next of kin. It wasn't even clear why she had been in hospital, although from the name of it, she could see that it was something psychological. She could guess the results of the evaluation in advance: just sheer general hopelessness, a pathetic middle-aged woman who needed somewhere to stay and someone to drop in just to keep her from wandering the streets. Maggie looked at her watch. There wasn't time for a full evaluation today. She could manage a basic check-up to make sure that Michelle was not in imminent danger, that she was feeding herself – the basic checklist.

She closed the file and walked away from the church along the side of a housing estate. Some of the flats were sealed up with metal sheets bolted on the doors and windows, but most of them were occupied. From the second level, a teenage boy emerged from a doorway and walked along the balcony, his hands stuffed in the pockets of his bulky jacket. Maggie looked around. It was probably all right. It was a Tuesday morning, and the dangerous people were mostly still in bed. She turned the corner and checked the address she'd written in her notebook. Room 1, 3 Howard Street. Yes, she remembered it now. It was a strange house that looked as if it had been built out of the same materials as the housing estate and had then decayed at the same rate. This hostel wasn't really a proper hostel at all. It was a house rented cheaply from a private land-lord. People could be put there while the services made their mind up what to do with them. Usually they just moved on or were forgotten about. There were some places Maggie only visited with a chaperone, but she hadn't heard anything particular about this one. These people were mainly a danger to themselves.

She looked up at the house. On the second floor there was a broken window blocked up with brown cardboard. There was a tiny paved front garden and an alley that went along the left side of the house. Beside the front door a bin bag had burst, but it had only added to the rubbish that was strewn everywhere. Maggie wrote a one-word note in her notebook. There were five buzzers next to the front door. They didn't have labels next to them but she pressed the bottom one and then pressed it again. She couldn't tell whether it was working. She was wonder-ing whether to knock on the door with her fist or look through the window when she heard a voice behind her. Looking round, she saw a man right behind her. He was gaunt with wiry ginger hair tied back in a ponytail, and piercings right across his face. She stepped to one side when she saw the man's dog, a small breed that was technically illegal, though it was the third one she'd seen since she'd left Deptford Station.

'No, he's a good one,' the man said. 'Aren't you, Buzz?'

'Do you live here?' Maggie asked.

The man looked suspicious. One of his cheeks was quivering. Maggie took a laminated card from her pocket and showed it to the man.

'I'm from the social services,' she said. 'I'm here to see Michelle Doyce.'

'The one downstairs?' the man said. 'Haven't seen her.' He leaned past Maggie and unlocked the front door. 'You coming in?'

'Yes, please.'

The man just shrugged.

'Go on, Buzz,' he said. Maggie heard the clatter of the dog's paws inside and up the stairs and the man disappeared after him. As soon as Maggie stepped inside, she was hit by a smell of damp and rubbish and fried food and dog shit and other smells she couldn't place. It almost made her eyes water. She closed the front door behind her. This must once have been the hallway of a family house. Now it was piled with pallets, tins of paints, a couple of gaping bin bags, an old bike with no tyres. The stairs were directly ahead. To the left, what would have been a door to the front room was blocked up. She walked along, by the side of the stairs to a door further along. She rapped on it hard and listened. She heard something inside, then nothing. She knocked again, several times, and waited. There was a rattling sound and then the door opened inwards. Maggie held out her laminated card once more.

'Michelle Doyce?' she said.

'Yes,' said the woman.

It was difficult for Maggie to define even to herself exactly what was strange about her. She was clean and her hair was brushed, but perhaps almost too brushed, like a small child who had wet her hair and then combed it so that it lay flat over the head, thin enough to show the pale scalp beneath. Her face was smooth and pink, with a dusting of fuzzy hair. Her bright red lipstick extended just a little bit too far off her lips. She wore a baggy, faded, flowery dress. Maggie identified herself and held out the card.

'I just wanted to check up on you, Michelle,' she said. 'See how you are? Are you all right? All right in yourself?'

The woman nodded.

'Can I come in?' said Maggie. 'Can I check everything's OK?'

She stepped inside and took her notebook out. As far as she could tell from a glance, Michelle seemed to be keeping herself clean. She looked as if she was eating. She was responsive. Still, something felt odd. She peered around in the little shabby anteroom of the flat. The contrast with the hallway of the house was impressive. Shoes were arranged in a row, a coat hung from a hook. There was a bucket with a mop leaning in the corner.

'How long have you been here, Michelle?'

The woman frowned.

'Here?' she said. 'A few days.'

The discharge form had said the fifth of January and today was the first day of February. Still, that sort of vagueness wasn't really surprising. As the two women stood there, Maggie became aware of a sound she couldn't quite place. It might be the hum of traffic, or a vacuum cleaner on the floor above, or a plane. It depended how far away it was. There was a smell also, like food that had been left out too long. She looked up; the electricity was working. She should check whether Michelle had a fridge. But by the look of her, she'd be all right for the time being.

'Can I have a look round, Michelle?' she said. 'Make sure everything's all right?'

'You want to meet him?' said Michelle.

Maggie was puzzled. There hadn't been anything on the form.

'Have you got a friend?' she said. 'I'd be happy to meet him.'

Michelle stepped forward and opened the door to what would have been the house's back room, away from the street. Maggie followed her and immediately felt something on her face. At first she thought it was dust. She thought of an underground train coming, blowing the warm grit into her face. At the same time the sound got louder and she realized that it wasn't dust but flies, a thick cloud of flies blowing against her face.

For a few moments she was confused by the man sitting on the sofa. Her perceptions had slowed and become skewed, as if she were deep underwater or in a dream. Crazily, she wondered if he were wearing some sort of diving suit: a blue, marbled, slightly ruptured and torn diving suit and she wondered why his eyes were yellow and cloudy. And then she started to fumble for her phone and she dropped it and suddenly she couldn't make her fingers work, she couldn't get them to pick the phone up off the grimy carpet, as she saw that it wasn't any kind of suit but his naked, swollen, rupturing flesh and that he was dead. Long dead.

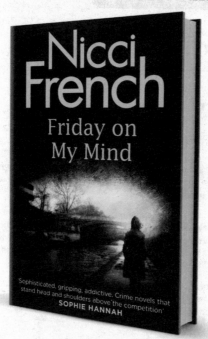

Nicci French

Friday on My Mind

'Sophisticated, gripping, addictive. Crime novels that stand head and shoulders above the competition'
SOPHIE HANNAH

When a bloated corpse is found floating in the River Thames the police can at least be sure that identifying the victim will be straightforward. Around the dead man's wrist is a hospital band. On it are the words Dr F. Klein . . .

But psychotherapist Frieda Klein is very much alive. And, after evidence linking her to the murder is discovered, she becomes the prime suspect.

Unable to convince the police of her innocence, Frieda is forced to make a bold decision in order to piece together the terrible truth before it's too late either for her or for those she loves.

Rich in intrigue, intensity and atmosphere, *Friday on My Mind* is classic Nicci French – a dark, gripping and sophisticated masterclass in psychological suspense in which nothing is quite what it seems . . .

NICCI FRENCH

COMPLICIT

Who is more deadly? An Enemy? A friend? Or a Lover?

Bonnie Graham is in her friend's flat. She is alone, except for the dead body lying in a pool of blood. What happened? What will she do? And is any or all of it her fault?

Bonnie is a music teacher who has spent a long, hot summer in London rehearsing with a band. It was supposed to be fun, but the tricky knots of the band's friendships began to unravel with each passing day.

What was meant to be a summer of happiness, music and love turns deadly as lovers betray, passions turn homicidal and friendship itself becomes a crime.

Someone in the band must be a killer. Is it Bonnie?
And if not – who is it?

'Reels in readers from the start' *Independent*

'Razor-sharp twists and turns' *Daily Express*

'A gripping crime mystery, an accomplished thriller' *Woman* read more   Ⓟ

NICCI FRENCH

WHAT TO DO WHEN SOMEONE DIES

Ellie Faulkner's world has been destroyed. Her husband Greg died in a car crash – and he wasn't alone. In the passenger seat was the body of Milena Livingstone – a woman Ellie's never heard of.

But Ellie refuses to leap to the obvious conclusion, despite the whispers and suspicions of those around her. Maybe it's the grief, but Ellie has to find out who this woman was – and prove Greg wasn't having an affair.

And soon she is chillingly certain their deaths were no accident. Are Ellie's accusations of murder her way of avoiding the truth about her marriage? Or does an even more sinister discovery await her?

'Relentlessly enjoyable and gripping from the first page to the last' *Evening Standard*

'Brilliant. A fast-paced intricately detailed thriller with unexpected twists and turns' *She*

'You'll be totally gripped until a very unexpected twist knocks you for six' *Cosmopolitan*

NICCI FRENCH

UNTIL IT'S OVER

DEAD. UNLUCKY.

London cycle courier Astrid Bell is bad luck – for other people. First, Astrid's neighbour Peggy Farrell accidentally knocks her off her bike – and not long after is found bludgeoned to death in an alley. Then, a few days later, Astrid is asked to pick up a package – only to find the client slashed to pieces in the hallway.

For the police, it's more than coincidence. For Astrid and her six housemates, it's the beginning of a nightmare: suspicious glances, bitter accusations, fallings out and a growing fear that the worst is yet to come.

Because if it's true that bad luck comes in threes, who will be next to die?

'Reads like lightning' *Observer*

'Another nail-biting thriller' *Daily Express*

NICCI FRENCH

LOSING YOU

Nina Landry has given up city life for the isolated community of
Sandling Island, lying off the bleak east coast of England. At night the
wind howls. Sometimes they are cut off by the incoming tide. For Nina
though it is home. It is safe.

But when Nina's teenage daughter Charlie fails to return from a
sleepover on the day they're due to go on holiday, the island becomes a
different place altogether. A place of secrets and suspicions. Where no
one – friends, neighbours or the police – believes Nina's instinctive fear
that her daughter is in terrible danger. Alone, she undergoes a frantic
search for Charlie. And as day turns to night, she begins to doubt not
just whether they'll leave the island for their holiday – but whether they
will ever leave it again.

'You live through every nail-biting minute' *Guardian*

NICCI FRENCH

CATCH ME WHEN I FALL

You're a whirlwind. You're a success.

You're living life on the edge.

But who'll catch you when you fall?

Holly Krauss is a city girl burning the candle at both ends. Despite a comfortable home life, a tough job and friends who admire her, she secretly enjoys taking reckless, dangerous walks on the wild side.

But Holly can't keep those worlds separate forever. Soon enough her secret life bleeds into her safe one and everything spirals out of control. She's making mistakes at home and at work, owes money to the wrong people – and now it seems that someone's stalking her. Could it just be paranoia or is she in very real danger?

And who can you trust when you can no longer trust yourself?

'Highly persuasive … dextrous and edgy' *Independent*

'Terrific storytelling, I read the book in one sitting' *Herald*

NICCI FRENCH

SECRET SMILE

You have an affair.
You finish it.
You think it's over.
You're dead wrong . . .

Miranda Cotton thinks she's put boyfriend Brendan out of her life
for good. But two weeks later, he's intimately involved with her
sister. Soon what began as an embarrassment becomes threatening
– then even more terrifying than a girl's worst nightmare. Because
this time Brendan will stop at nothing to be part of Miranda's life
– even if it means taking it from her …

'Creepy, genuinely gripping' *Heat*

'A must read' *Cosmopolitan*

'Nicci French at the top of her game' *Woman & Home*

NICCI FRENCH

LAND OF THE LIVING

You wake in the dark, gagged and bound.
He says he will kill you – just like all the rest.

Abbie Devereaux is being held against her will. She doesn't know
where she is or how she got there. She's so terrified she can barely
remember her own name – and she's sure of just one thing: that she
will survive this nightmare. But even if she does make it back to the
land of the living, Abbie knows that he'll still be out there, looking
for her.

And next time, there may be no escape.

'Shocking, uncomfortable, exhilarating' *Independent on Sunday*

'Dark, gripping' *Heat*

NICCI FRENCH

THE RED ROOM

The man who almost killed you has been accused of murder.
And you hold the key to his future ...

After psychologist Kit Quinn is brutally attacked by a prisoner, she is
determined to get straight back to work. When the police want her help
in linking the man who attacked her to a series of murders, she refuses
to simply accept the obvious. But the closer her investigation takes her
to the truth behind the savage crimes, the nearer Kit gets to the dark
heart of her own terror.

'Gripping, chilling, moving' *Observer*

'Absorbing, highly addictive' *Evening Standard*

'French is excellent at building up suspense and elegantly exploiting all
our worst fears' *Daily Mail*

He just wanted a decent book to read ...

Not too much to ask, is it? It was in 1935 when Allen Lane, Managing Director of Bodley Head Publishers, stood on a platform at Exeter railway station looking for something good to read on his journey back to London. His choice was limited to popular magazines and poor-quality paperbacks – the same choice faced every day by the vast majority of readers, few of whom could afford hardbacks. Lane's disappointment and subsequent anger at the range of books generally available led him to found a company – and change the world.

'We believed in the existence in this country of a vast reading public for intelligent books at a low price, and staked everything on it'
Sir Allen Lane, 1902–1970, founder of Penguin Books

The quality paperback had arrived – and not just in bookshops. Lane was adamant that his Penguins should appear in chain stores and tobacconists, and should cost no more than a packet of cigarettes.

Reading habits (and cigarette prices) have changed since 1935, but Penguin still believes in publishing the best books for everybody to enjoy. We still believe that good design costs no more than bad design, and we still believe that quality books published passionately and responsibly make the world a better place.

So wherever you see the little bird – whether it's on a piece of prize-winning literary fiction or a celebrity autobiography, political tour de force or historical masterpiece, a serial-killer thriller, reference book, world classic or a piece of pure escapism – you can bet that it represents the very best that the genre has to offer.

Whatever you like to read – trust Penguin.